MASK OF THE WIZARD

Cover illustration © 2016 by Steve Argyle (www.steveargyle.com)
Cover & interior design by Kristy G. Stewart
Map by Maxime Plasse

This is a work of fiction. All characters and events portrayed in
this novel are either products of the author's imagination or are
used fictitiously.

www.vincentriddle.com

ISBN: 978-0-9863083-4-5

Village Dell Books™

MASK
OF THE
WIZARD

VINCENT RIDDLE

VILLAGE DELL
BOOKS

FOR KATIE

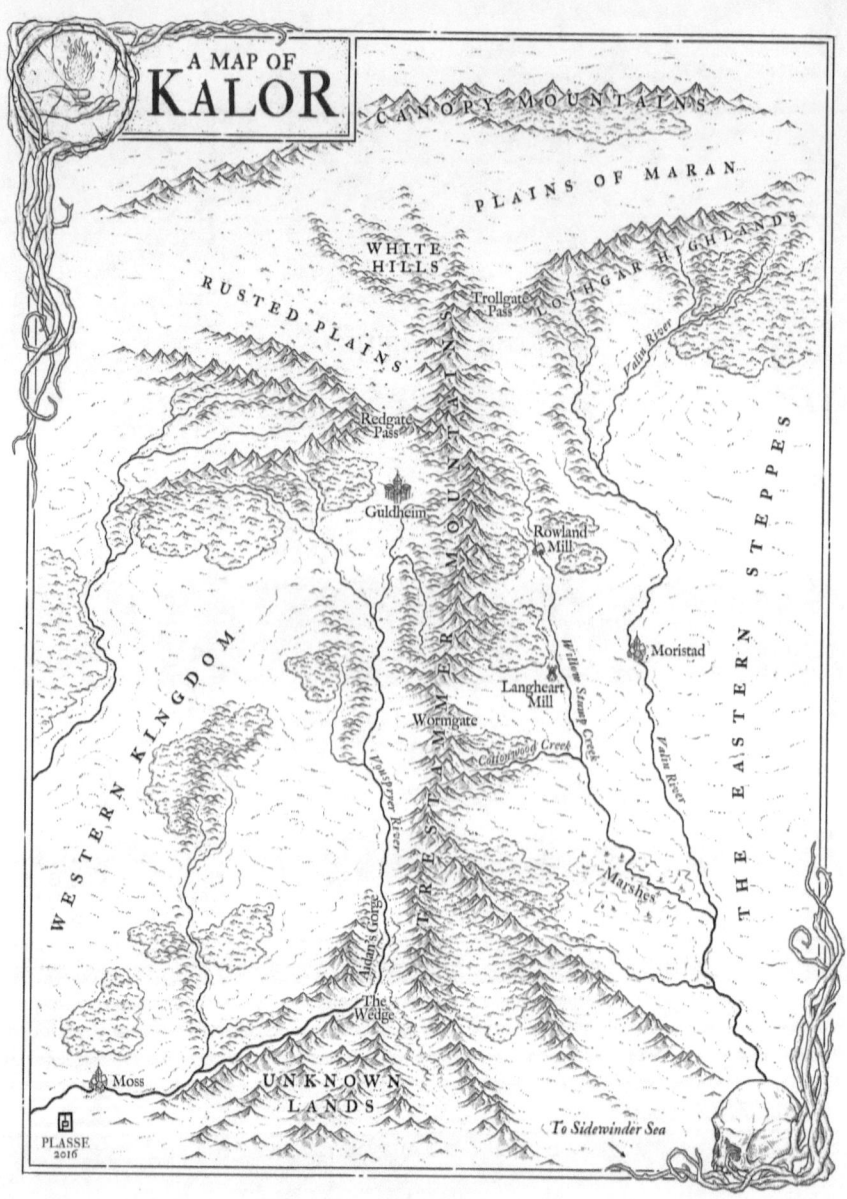

The Creators shaped two worlds.

First came Earth: a hard and unforgiving land where only the cunning ones survived. Humans lived there as they saw fit, for good or ill.

Next came Kalor, where magic ruled. All creatures able to wield this awesome power almost destroyed their world. Therefore, moments before the Creators vanished, they chose bands of humans from ancient Earth, plucked them suddenly out of their daily lives, and placed them on Kalor to provide a balance.

But humanity's survival was never guaranteed.

ONE

Hector sat upon the hot dirt and wondered why his last bite of fish tasted worse than his first.

Nobody liked fish, least of all Hector. It had a nasty aftertaste that stuck on the tongue like moldy cheese, which meant he ate it only when he had to. Old tales spoke of a time when all wild animals were as delicious as honey cakes, but such tales must have come from Earth, because every bite he'd ever swallowed seemed to come back up with every burp.

Yet food was scarce and he craved more. Even though fish tasted vile, a large perch would easily fill his belly, unlike the four minnows he'd netted from a nearby spring earlier in the day. Come to think of it, even one of the skinny rodents roaming these wastelands would be a feast, if he could catch one. Anything to ease his hunger pains.

The Plains of Maran were bleak and uninviting. Stunted, yellow grass hung onto life and the sparsely scattered trees were knotted and dry, stripped of leaves, or blackened by some ancient inferno. As Hector nursed his bandaged leg,

3

he watched the sun dip below the horizon. Soon it would get cold.

His pack mule grew restless. Hector watched it gnaw hungrily on the trunk of the half-dead tree to which it was tied, wondering if the poor thing had lost its mind. In the morning, he would put the scrawny beast out of its misery and cook it for breakfast. Yes, that would make a fine meal.

Then from the north, the beat of hoofs sounded across the hardened land. A single rider.

He took up the handle of his axe and using it for support hauled himself onto his good leg. Although injured, Hector had a lot of fight left in him, and any intruder would find that he was a tough opponent.

He peered into the fading light, tightening his grip on the axe's handle.

Over the top of a rise a cloaked rider appeared, riding at full gallop, whipping his steed frantically, stealing nervous glances behind him. Travel-worn gear, including a broadsword and shield, bounced in rhythm to the horse's furious gait.

Hector relaxed. The rider was his younger brother, Achilles, named after a hero from the same tales that spoke of tasty wild meats. He rode into camp and pulled up hard on the reins.

Hector limped over to hold the steed's harness. "Did you find it? Tell me you found it."

"Aye, I snatched up the best part of the treasure." The scabs on his brother's face indicated he had run into trouble. "But I disturbed something that was keeping watch."

"An ancient guardian?"

"Worse than that. Now hurry. We haven't much time before they catch us."

"They who?"

"The whole host of a demon lord!"

"You don't mean . . . ?"

"I stirred up a hornet's nest, brother." Achilles offered a hand. "Now let me help you up."

The horse was skittish, forcing Hector to let go of the harness. Steading himself, he hefted his axe with both hands and faced the path Achilles had ridden down. "Go on without me. I'll hold the enemy off as long as I can."

"This is no time for heroics, Hector. You'll be dead before you see them coming."

"I'll wager I can give you ten, maybe fifteen, minutes."

"Ha! Not against a skinwalker."

"A what?"

"You heard me," said Achilles. "And that's not the half of it. Hurry!"

Hector had heard from nearby highland folk of a terrible spirit that once walked the dying plains, seeking to take possession of a man in his sleep. He hadn't believed such talk, but Achilles's frightened eyes made him think again.

He dropped his axe and hobbled over to his brother. "Well, why didn't you tell me that in the first place?" He took the other man's hand. "Help me up! Maybe we'll make it to the pass before midnight."

TWO ☉

An icy fog crept down the steep mountain slopes of Trollgate Pass, its gray tendrils moving across the stone like slithering snakes. Granite mountains towered over both sides of the pass, shading a mile-long gorge closed off at the southern end by a manmade wall. Sentries here patrolled the wide rampart in pairs, clad in woolen surcoats and muskrat hats, after the fashion of the highland clans. Each was armed with a longbow of yew slung across his shoulder and a sword strapped to his hip.

Barely a week at this post and Collin was already regretting his bold decision to volunteer as a sentry at the pass. Wouldn't his fighting skills be more useful patrolling eastern trade routes? If it weren't for his clan's faith in him, he might have believed he'd been sent here under false promises. More than once he had wanted to say something about how the contest that had tested him had selected a champion to waste his time here, but he didn't think the grizzled warrior paired with him would take too kindly to complaints. Old

Bremer was a hard man who wasn't shy about reminding him of the "stupidity of youth."

Collin halted beside a brazier to warm his hands over hot coals. He glanced into the fog, attempting to conceal his dread, hoping to shake the feeling that an enemy lay just beyond his sight. Something was different about tonight, something unnatural about the fog and the still night air. Would Bremer laugh at him if he voiced his fears?

The old warrior's head was completely bald, yet he never wore a helmet or hat to ward off the chill. His nose was straight as an arrow and seemingly as long, which was probably why he grew a beard so bushy it covered half his mouth. Even so, his grin was poorly hidden behind the hair.

"An easy week here and you're still jittery," said Bremer. "What's your story, Collin?"

Collin made a show of acting calm, casually leaning up against the crenelated wall beside the old warrior. "Jittery? Who's jittery?"

Bremer's laugh sounded like a pig rooting in the mud. "Why your village selected you for service here I'll never understand."

"It's the duty of each clan, which I took very seriously. I spent my life training for the privilege to serve."

"Of course you did," said Bremer. "Look, I've patrolled this pass for twenty-three years and the only people to come across the plains have been disgruntled fortune hunters who can't find their own toes, let alone a tomb full of gold. Each one returns empty-handed. Relax, Collin. We're safe."

"I am relaxed."

"You look like a scared deer listening to a hunter's footstep."

Collin tried to look more relaxed, but he feared that his stance had become more exaggerated than before. "If it's so safe, why do the clans patrol this pass day after day?"

"I don't know every story your elders spoonfed you," replied Bremer, "but whatever threat was chased into the Canopy Mountains has long since died off. I'm sure of it. It was seven generations ago."

"We're not wasting our time here."

"Who said we were wasting our time? Certainly not me. I get two hot meals a day and a warm bed every night."

The strange sense of unease gripped Collin again and he almost said something about it to his companion. Bremer's eyes were on him, watching his every move, measuring him.

The old warrior chuckled. "You're a homesick boy, that's all."

As Collin searched for a clever comeback, a familiar sound answered his unease. "Did you hear that?"

Bremer lifted his head, listening. "A lone rider. Heavy-laden, I'd say, and coming fast. You have good ears, Collin. I'll give you that much."

As the galloping grew louder, other sentries stopped to listen. Because the gorge carried sounds from the far end of the pass, Collin had been instructed on his first day to listen to anything out of the ordinary, as the first sign of trouble.

A horse bearing two riders burst out of the fog below, their mount covered in foamy sweat, breathing heavily.

"Speaking of disgruntled adventurers," said Bremer.

Both riders were clothed like traveling pilgrims, with cloaks, wide-brimmed hats, and leather riding chaps. One of them had a sword.

They halted before the closed gate and the front rider hollered, "Let us through!"

"I remember those two," said Bremer. "Travelers from the far south. They claimed last month's eclipse would show them the way to fantastic riches."

Again the rider called out. "I beg you . . . open the gate!"

All along the rampart, warriors looked over the wall to catch a better glimpse of the riders. None were in a hurry to comply.

"We can't die out here! You must open the gate."

"Aren't we going to let them through?" asked Collin.

Bremer, too, appeared amused by the show of panic coming from the men below. Yet, as he continued to watch the pair, he slowly lost his humor and squinted into the fog, as if seeing through it.

"Something's wrong here," he said. "Very wrong. Do you feel it?"

Collin could barely contain himself as he called down to the riders. "What are you running from?"

Before the men could answer, Bremer seized Collin by the shoulders and spoke straight into his face. "Go to the stables and take the first gelding you can find. Ride south. Warn the lowlands."

The foremost rider's voice was stricken with terror, "You can't leave us out here!"

Collin tried to pull back. "Bremer, I thought you said . . ."

"Go, boy. Don't argue with me." Without another word, the old warrior took Collin firmly by the arm and ushered him to the stairs. Collin reacted slowly. Despite Bremer's casual talk moments ago, he seemed to have changed his mind. It didn't make sense. Did he know something he'd dared not discuss earlier?

Halfway down the steps, Collin stopped and turned back to look up at Bremer's worried face. Above the old warrior, thick clouds slid across the moon.

"What warning should I give the lowlands?" he asked.

Bremer opened his mouth, but shut it quickly as a terrified cry echoed through the gorge. In the same instant, a fiery orange light drew his attention.

Fireballs streaked across the night sky, flying in from the north. Bremer held up his arms in a vain attempt to shield himself from a blazing sphere. It enveloped him, burned him to ashes in seconds. Hot air blew across Collin, instantly drying sweat from his forehead and singeing his eyebrows. Soon the whole top of the wall was engulfed in flames.

Collin leaped down the stairs, taking two and three steps at a time. The stables were not far off.

THREE

Young Jarin Langheart lay in the thick weeds along the banks of Willow Stump Creek, trying to keep from being seen, trying to move as stealthily as a cat on the prowl. Unfortunately, all the plants growing near the water obscured his sight. His hair was too long and ratty, he realized, and had collected so much dead grass and—what were they called?—*stickery* things that he was having a hard time seeing more than a foot in front of him.

He took a moment to focus on every sound, like a hunter would do. Birds warbled in the trees on either side and a faint rustle of something in the grass told him that an animal was not far behind—probably one of the many hedgehogs living along the bank. The wheels of a wagon rolled along the road not far away.

The sound of splashing water told him he was close, very close. He carefully pushed away a clump of grass in front of him. His sight remained blocked in places, especially where a view of the swimming hole would have been best, and at first he could not see his quarry. Then a flash of brown skin came into view.

Was that a shoulder? An arm? A neck? It was hard to tell.

As quickly as it appeared it was gone.

He would have to move closer to see her.

Inching forward, he held his breath and . . .

Suddenly his black pet retriever, Razor, discovered him, sniffing his feet and legs, panting loudly. The dog walked over Jarin's back and licked his face.

It was difficult to scold the dog with a whisper. "Get down, boy. Down!"

Razor whined, tail wagging.

"You dumb dog. We're supposed to be expert hunters."

Jarin tried to grab Razor by the neck, but something distracted the pet and it ran off to investigate.

A gruff voice called to him from behind. "Get out of the weeds, Jarin."

The boy poked his head above the grass and saw his father, Shem Langheart, big-shouldered and surly, sitting in a wagon on the road ten yards away. His father wore a wide-brimmed hat, which shaded every part of his face except a huge jaw, which at the moment looked like a blacksmith's iron mallet ready to strike. Razor bounded around the wagon, briefly disturbing the team of horses, and retrieved a freshly tossed treat from the road.

"There's stinging nettle growing right next to you," said his father.

Jarin stood, pulled a dead twig from his hair, and looked at the water. The girl had swum farther away and, save for a quick glimpse of dark hair, was now completely hidden by the weeping willows.

"I know what stinging nettle looks like," Jarin said, dragging his feet as he made his way to the wagon.

"Good, because you used the last of the soothing cream last week."

Jarin hopped onto the back of the wagon and began rummaging through the supplies. "Did you get me anything in town?"

"I bought seasoning for the pork, like I said I would, and other goods for winter. And a book for Mira."

"I thought you were going to buy me a Hawkie knife when I turned eleven."

The wagon lurched forward as his father urged the team down the road. Jarin held onto the buckboard to keep from falling off.

"That's what you get for doing your own thinking," said his father.

FOUR

Mira Kaul, age eighteen, swam in the water underneath the branches of an overhanging willow, enjoying the cool water against her skin. She paid little attention to the wagon trundling down the road once she'd spotted her foster father, Shem, fetch that spying son of his from the bushes.

For the most part she liked Jarin, who was cheerful and willing to help, but the boy could be snoopy, if not annoying, and it was obvious he had a childish crush on her. More than once she had told him that she thought of him as a younger brother—placing special emphasis on the word *younger*.

Shem, on the other hand, acted like a stern father, having adopted Mira seven years ago when her real father and mother had been killed in a freakish roadside encounter with a mountain troll. On most days, Shem treated her with a measure of fairness, but he was rarely kind, sheltering her only out of an unexplained sense of duty. She ought to be thankful, because no one else had volunteered to take her in, all those years ago.

Enough of such gloomy thoughts, she decided. Today was a good day. The first few notes of an old song she'd heard her mother sing to her father had come to her, and she was trying to work out the tune by humming notes as she swam. It helped her forget the night her father had turned to her, just before the troll's attack, shouting at her to run for town and never look back. That was the last time she'd seen her parents alive.

Mira didn't have her mother's singing voice, and she eventually gave up trying to hum the song. She dove deep, coming up for air near the opposite bank, where something had caught her eye.

There, in the reeds! A green creature with a long neck and webbed feet—tiny as a tree frog—stepped into the open. It glowed with a rhythmic pulse of green light.

Mira cupped her hands and scooped up the tiny animal. "A yeni! What luck."

The creature hopped onto her wrist and raised its head to study her. Its skin glowed with a peculiar green light, which grew steadily brighter. Dark eyes turned orange.

Mira could hardly contain her excitement. "Shall your magic color my dreams tonight?"

The yeni jumped off her arm and vanished beneath the ripples. Mira frowned but just as quickly spotted another treasure in the grass where the yeni had been hiding. Digging into the muddy bank, she pulled out an iridescent stone the size of an acorn. She rinsed it off in the water and held it up to the light of the sky. The colors of the stone shimmered as she moved it between her fingers.

She laughed and recited a childhood rhyme:

> *The gift of a yeni is more than just spite,*
> *For love will soon come as true as your sight.*

Giggling, she swam back to the opposite bank, where she slipped on shorts and a shirt over wet skin. A stiff breeze had picked up and she would be dry before she reached the mill.

She walked down the road with a lazy stride, remembering more of the rhyme as she polished the stone against her cotton shirt.

> *Refuse not a yeni and his gift of mad fate,*
> *For demons once did and their love became hate.*

Mira glanced once behind her, where far to the north the sky had turned dark with billowing storm clouds. There would be extra work when she arrived at the house, work securing the animals from the wind and the rain, and Shem would be anxious for her return. But she hardly cared about that now, for she had obtained a yeni's gift today.

FIVE

The gusts were already strong by the time Mira arrived. The wooden windmill near the house creaked and its sails flapped in the wind, threatening to rip free. Shem held the end of a sailbar, trying to furl its sails, but the thin rope used to slide the canvas up and down the armature had snapped halfway up and was swinging out of reach. A ladder had been set against the mill house, next to the sailbar, and Jarin stepped upon it, hastening to follow his father's sharp commands.

"Hurry! Up the ladder now! This wind will tear those sweeps apart."

Jarin scrambled up the ladder and, grabbing the frayed end of the rope, tied it to the end of a fresh coil he had tucked in his belt. He handed the rope to Shem, who resumed his task of furling the sail.

Mira paused long enough to see that the two were all right, then went into the barn. Inside, she secured the stalls of two workhorses, a milk cow, and a family of hogs. Her favorite horse, Moby, followed her with wide eyes; he was jumpy when the winds first began to howl, and now he looked ready to kick the walls down to escape. She went over to a box near the entrance and brought out her stash of sugar cubes.

"I won't tell Shem if you won't," she said as she fed the treat to the horse and rubbed his neck. He calmed visibly.

The wind sighed heavily through the planks of the barn. The roof rattled.

"Don't worry. It'll be over in the morning."

She gave Moby a final pat and then hurried outside.

Fighting against the force of the wind, she pushed with all her strength to lock both doors. The storm was going to be a fierce one, no doubt about it. Strange that it blew in from the north so late in the summer, which typically saw gentle rains from the southwest.

She turned toward the windmill as Jarin stepped down the ladder. He spotted her and sent her a teasing kiss.

Such flirting from a prepubescent boy might have disgusted a lesser girl, but Mira shrugged it off with a laugh. The boy had risked receiving a whipping from his father by sending her that kiss. And even though he'd gotten away with it, he glanced warily at Shem, who was busily tying off the rope. Jarin smirked, then abruptly slipped on a rung, catching himself in the nick of time.

Below him, Razor watched it all with a wag of his tail.

Along with the wind came the scent of rain . . . and something else, like the smell of a dead animal. If she hadn't known any better, she'd have thought a rotting carcass lay nearby. The stink turned her nose and sickened her stomach. Then as quickly as it came it was gone, replaced by air too cold for comfort. Her summer clothes, though dry now, suddenly felt too thin.

Mira went to the far end of the yard and into the house, but here it was hardly warmer than outside. A lighted lantern sat on the fireplace mantle, presumably left there when Shem had first heard the wind. The fireplace was cold, containing nothing but a single charred log half buried in a pile of ashes. She walked past it and up the steep steps to the loft.

From under her bed, she retrieved her lockbox and opened it. Her newly found yeni stone would have to be stored here until she could fashion a necklace. She wondered about the luck it would bring, the love she might find. Reluctantly, she set the treasure carefully inside and tucked the box back under her bed.

Jarin and Razor entered, followed closely by Shem, who stomped dirt from his feet, walked over to his big chair in front of the dark fireplace, and promptly sat down.

Lines in the man's face sometimes made him look old, but he was neither weak of strength nor dull of mind. His bright blue eyes could pierce a lie when it suited him, and his tongue brooked few arguments. Mira sometimes dared confront his bullying with her own cutting comments, but such defiance usually earned her a harsh scolding.

She hurried down into the main room to help Shem remove his boots. Jarin and Razor wandered into the kitchen.

The miller watched Mira remove the right boot, and before she could pull off the left one, he leaned forward and seized her jaw. He moved her head from side to side none too gently, examining her face with his big, calloused hands.

"You look more like your mother every day."

"So you've told me before."

He let go and rested against the back of the chair, never taking his eyes off her as Mira fought to remove his other boot. He seemed to make this task more difficult than it ought to be.

"She was very beautiful, you know," he said.

"Yes, I remember her."

"Prettier even than Jarin's mother."

"By the looks of that boy, his mother must have been a cow."

"*Hrmph*," said Shem. "Both women were more polite than you."

Mira yanked off the boot, somewhat roughly. As ornery as Shem acted, he was typically in a better mood after returning from town. Tonight he showed little desire to berate his adopted daughter. She noticed a hint of rum on his breath.

"I bought you a gift," he said.

"A book!"

"Aye, a rare find."

"We have so few books. Was it expensive?"

"Very."

"Where is it? Can I—"

"You can read it after you've fixed supper. I'm so hungry I could eat raw trout."

Mira dumped the boots next to the woodbin and stormed off. She had long ago concluded that the only reason Shem had taken her in was to have a servant. A slave. If his own wife hadn't died giving birth to Jarin, making Mira feel sorry for the boy, she would have run away long ago. Just once she wished Shem was kind enough to expect nothing in return for his rare attempts at charity.

Frustrated, Mira marched into the kitchen and began throwing kindling into the stove. Jarin was sitting at the table gnawing on a sliver of jerked pork. Razor sat at his feet, eagerly awaiting scraps.

"Mira, I wish you weren't my stepsister."

"Shut up."

Jarin tore off a huge bite and then spoke with a full mouth. "Did he promise to give you something?"

"A bribe."

"Good. What are we having to eat?"

SIX

Jarin stole glances at Mira as he finished the last of his meal, watched how the dark curls of her hair fell down the sides of her face and along her neck. She seemed to be getting prettier every day, and it was hard not to stare. He understood now why people said Mira had an exotic beauty uncommon in these parts. Her mama was known to have been pretty too, a foreign woman rumored to have come from one of those unlucky clans that suddenly found itself in a world full of strangers. Had the Creators dropped Mira's family into the wrong part of the world by mistake?

It didn't matter. Jarin was simply thankful it had happened.

He couldn't take his eyes off her face, her dark eyes, her full lips parted to reveal stunning white teeth. Mira caught him staring and made an obvious attempt to ignore him by turning her head. She wasn't in a good mood tonight and had barely said two words to him during supper. She and Papa were in a silent contest of wills.

Mira got out of her chair and began to clear away the

dishes, tossing them carelessly into a wooden tub near the stove. Jarin handed his plate to Razor and waited as the dog licked it clean.

His father pushed away from the table and belched loudly. "Jarin, help your sister."

The boy hesitated but made no attempts to defy his father. His shoulder was really starting to itch and burn—the all-too-familiar pain of having brushed up against stinging nettle. He dared not say anything, or scratch too much, for fear of admitting it to his father.

Papa picked up a satchel lying at his feet and pulled out a thick, leather-bound book. He tossed it unceremoniously on the table. "Supper was delicious."

Jarin seized the prize first, but Mira stepped up and tore it from his hands. She thumbed through the pages.

"Whoa, pictures too," said Jarin, craning his head to see.

Dishes now forgotten, Mira plopped down at the table in the light of the lamp and began to read. Jarin barely knew his letters, despite Mira's efforts to teach him, so he tried to make sense of the drawings. Even this was difficult, because the itch on his shoulder was getting too bad to ignore.

"Quit squirming," said Mira. "You're making it hard for me to read."

Then came another gift: a knife. Papa was more careful with this one, setting it gently onto the table and sliding it over to his son.

"A Hawkie knife!" His itching shoulder momentarily forgotten, Jarin pulled the knife from its leather sheath and waved it around like a sword. The blade was fat and slightly curved, making it appear shorter than it really was. He tested the tip gently with his finger and found it sharp. No doubt about it: this was the finest gift he'd ever received.

"A man can't go without his hunting knife," said his father.

"Nope."

"If you ever threaten Mira with it, I'll tan your hide and rub a salt lick on it to remind you."

"Yes, sir." Jarin was about to carve a hole into the table, but thought better of it. "I'll bet it's just like the one Silo Prophet used to kill all those pirates and protect Princess Hannah." He turned to Mira. "Does that book have any stories about Silo Prophet?"

"It's a history book," said Mira.

"It's more than that," explained his father. "It's a copy of the Encoda—and it cost me a week's worth of milling to convince that crooked shopkeeper to part with it."

"Does it have any adventure stories?"

"It does," said Mira, "but they're all true and happened a long time ago, even before humans arrived in the world. This book is special to the people on the other side of the Trestammer Mountains."

"It's their holy book." Papa pulled himself up from the table and walked out of the kitchen.

"Is it boring?" Jarin was glad to see Mira's mood change. He liked it when she was nice to him.

"You'll enjoy some of it, I think," she said. "It talks about evil things. But you'll have to let me read it first."

"Will you tell me one of its adventure stories?"

"Of course. Now let me be."

Jarin turned back to admiring his knife. Out of the corner of his eye, he spotted Razor waiting for some attention.

Feeling tough and invincible now, he poked the point toward the dog's face.

"Wanna die?"

Razor barked, hopelessly unafraid of him.

SEVEN

The storm raged on outside; lightning flashed and thunder boomed. Thick raindrops pelted the walls, but the sturdy house had seen worse, and not a drop of water leaked through.

Jarin listened to the rain from his bed in the loft. It would be muddy outside, making his work of feeding the chickens and pigs a slippery and wet chore in the morning. By the fierce sound of the wind, the chicken coop might even need to be repaired.

Below, Shem slept in his chair, his low, rumbling snores carrying up into the loft, almost as loud as the thunder. Razor lay quietly at his feet, no doubt enjoying the warmth of the coals in the hearth.

"You can turn around now," said Mira.

Jarin winced against the pain as he sat up and saw that Mira had pulled a nightshirt over her underclothes. His skin was on fire, running from his shoulder down the left side of his back.

Mira picked up a bottle and went to his side. "Hold still."

Her hands were wonderfully cool on his skin as she spread salve onto his back and shoulder. For a moment, he thought of nothing but the sensation of her touch, savoring every movement of her soft hands upon his skin.

"Papa said there was no more left," he said.

"Lucky for you he was only teasing."

"He's grumpy and he hates me."

"He wouldn't have given you that knife if he hated you."

"But *you* hate me."

Mira's laugh made him grin. "Don't be silly," she said.

"Will you tell me one of the stories in that book tonight?"

"It might give you nightmares."

"Really! I can't wait."

"They might even give *me* nightmares."

"I wouldn't let anything happen to you, Mira. I have my Hawkie knife now."

Mira lifted her hands from his back and set the bottle aside. "There you go."

"It still itches."

"You'll only make it worse by scratching."

"You need to spread more."

"Uh-uh. I think you enjoyed it too much already." Mira went to her side of the loft and climbed into bed.

Jarin lay on his side and pulled the blanket up to his waist, careful not to let it touch his back and thus wipe off the salve. As the medicine numbed his skin, the burning died to a dull warmth. He rested his head on his arm.

Mira was on her stomach, turning the pages of her new, thick book, the light of a candle next to her.

"I've only read a dozen pages," she said. "It explains the time of creation and the place where life began."

"Papa said it all started with a tiny seed planted by the Creators."

"I guess so. Your papa tells you a lot of things to keep you wondering, but I don't think he cares much for these old tales. The Encoda talks about a great tree so big and ancient it's the size of a mountain. The first people, the woodtrolls, made it their home, and tunneled through it like termites. All magic is sustained by the Tree. It's hidden by a heavy mist that shrouds the valley where it grows."

"I bet me and Razor could find it."

"You have to be able to feel magic, and few humans can do that. Only one person has ever found the Great World Tree, and that was the wizard, Nolath—a long time ago. He went there on a quest to obtain the power to fight the spirit demon of Maran."

"Oooh, tell me about the demon."

"I had to skip ahead to read that, but I got confused because the wizard did something I didn't understand, something about branding a girl with an acorn. So I'm reading the book all the way through, from the front."

Thunder rolled on outside as Mira flipped through the pages.

"They called the spirit demon a skinwalker," she continued. "It could take over a sleeping body and wear it like clothes."

"Scary . . ."

"And it liked to possess human bodies the most, because we usually don't have magic protecting us."

"I have a yeni's head for good luck."

"Yes, but that's not the kind of powerful magic the wizard was searching for. Our gift lies in crafting tools and weapons. Not in controlling magic."

"Like my Hawkie knife."

"When humans first arrived, the archers of King Aidan wiped out a whole army of forest imps that attacked them. The imps had never come across people with weapons."

"I wish I could have been there."

"If it weren't for the arrows of Aidan's knights—"

Razor growled and Mira stopped. Jarin looked over the railing to see the retriever stand up and bark at the door.

Below, Papa awoke at once. "Huh? What is it, boy?"

Razor went to the threshold, growling, his tail down and ears held back.

Shem got out of his chair. "Mira! Curse you, girl. Did you forget to lock up the barn? The hogs have gotten out again."

"No, sir, I did not forget!"

Mira kicked off her covers and jumped out of bed, quickly putting on a pair of overalls and slipping on boots. Jarin hastened after her as she stomped down the stairs. Papa was already heading out the door.

Jarin collided into Mira's back as she halted on the first step out of the house. The hard rain stung his face, chilled his skin, the gusts as cold as a late-autumn wind.

Standing in the middle of the yard was a frightened horse, saddled for riding. A lantern hung from its saddle, still burning. Razor barked and the horse stepped back.

"Quiet, Razor," said Papa as he approached the skittish horse. "What have we here?"

Lightning flashed and the animal shied back, but Papa

snatched up the reins before it could get out of reach. "Easy now. Nothing to be afraid of."

Razor barked.

"Jarin, take that pet of yours inside. Mira, open the barn."

Jarin sloshed through the mud and grabbed the dog's collar. He couldn't take his eyes off the strange, riderless horse. The brand was not one he recognized. "Where'd it come from?"

"Don't know," said Papa. "Now do as you're told."

Jarin tugged on the collar, but only halfheartedly, because he wanted to stay near the mysterious horse. Razor squirmed as he clasped his hands over the dog's mouth.

Papa managed to coax the horse into the barn, where Mira held the door open. Jarin allowed Razor to pull him close enough to the barn doors to hear the two talk. They seemed to be having an argument.

"The rider is still out there and might be hurt," said Mira.

"He was a fool to be riding in this weather and deserves what he got," said Papa.

"How can you say that?"

"Well, he probably stopped to relieve himself and the animal wandered off. Happened to me once, before I learned my lesson."

Jarin dared catch a peek inside the barn.

Papa led the wet horse to an empty stall and unsaddled it. Mira remained near the door, facing Shem with hands on hips, clearly angry. Jarin crouched low to the ground, keeping Razor calm by scratching the dog's belly.

"What lesson?" said Mira. "That he shouldn't relieve—"

"What do you expect me to do, girl? Go out in this weather

and get lost? That would be stupid, plain and simple." Papa began to wipe down the horse's coat with a wide brush.

"Take Razor," said Mira. "The dog can find a wounded bird in the highest treetop if he wants to and he never gets lost."

"A wounded bird isn't what I'd be looking for."

"Exactly. You'd be looking for another human being who might need our help."

Papa shook his head in frustration. "I swear, Mira, you have a tongue like your mother."

"Well, what's it going to be, Shem? It's either you or me."

Papa pointed the brush at her. "Now don't threaten me or you'll find that pretty face of yours scowling from hard labor. Besides, where would I look?"

"How about the north road? That saddle has the markings of Trollgate Pass. Or hadn't you bothered to notice?"

Apparently out of excuses, Papa examined the saddle markings and then gave Mira an irritated yet resigned glare.

"So it does," he said.

EIGHT

Shem was grateful the storm had let up, the wind dropping to a light breeze, but he wasn't happy that it was still raining.

He wasn't happy about much of anything right now. That fool of a girl had cajoled him—no, *tricked* him—into risking his life in the middle of the worst storm of the year. What was he doing out here anyway, two miles from the comfort of his house? It was *his* house, not hers! *He* should be making the decisions about when to leave and when not to leave.

"Stupid, plain and simple," he repeated to Razor, who padded at his heals, sniffing the road.

Rain pelted his hat and water ran across the brim, falling in streamlets onto his long leather coat. He carried a quarterstaff and a bullseye lantern that could focus its light into a narrow beam.

Shem adjusted the lantern and shone it down the road, where it pierced the pitch-black night. He scanned the trees and bushes on either side of him, but he couldn't see past the puddles in the empty road.

He walked around a bend and stopped. Not three paces away, and in full view, stood a forest animal unlike any he had ever witnessed. It had long, sleek legs, a tangle of silver antlers, and a pelt that was white as newly fallen snow. The animal froze, golden eyes shining in the light of his lantern.

Shem was spellbound. Legends spoke of such animals wandering the forests at night. His own brother once claimed to have tracked one up into the mountains.

"A *kend*," he breathed in wonder.

Razor barked and the animal bounded into the trees. The dog gave chase.

"Razor, come back here!"

But the dog was gone. Shem hastened after.

"Follow a kend and be led into a trap every time," he said. *Isn't that what the storytellers say?*

The trees at the side of the road were thick, the undergrowth dense. Shem could hear the dog barking close by, but Razor was nowhere in sight. He stumbled through wet branches and leaves, trying to follow the sound; the light of his lantern danced wildly about the trees.

"Razor! You deserve a thrashing, you good-for-nothing..."

Without warning, Shem barged into a clearing and immediately found himself staring at two bear-sized trolls a dozen paces away. Their dark scales were slick with rain, the tusks of their long, boar-like snouts dripping with strands of saliva. Arms as thick as human thighs ended in sharp claws capable of ripping a man open in a single slash. The trolls made angry swipes as Razor badgered them, but the dog was too quick, darting in and out of their reach.

What were mountain trolls doing in the lowlands?

At the far edge of the clearing, the kend halted for a final glance at the skirmish. Then it disappeared into the night.

The miller wasted no time widening the door of his lantern and flooding the clearing with light. Both trolls shaded their eyes with their arms and howled in fury. Mountain trolls despised bright light and were known to slip into a frenzy just to stamp it out; soft firelight was all they could tolerate. Ignoring Razor, they snarled at Shem and dropped onto all fours. Then they charged.

Shem set the lantern on the ground, keeping its glare pointed squarely into the trolls' eyes. He carried a long, straight dagger, sharp and ready for just this kind of encounter. Unlike Mira's father, Shem wouldn't be caught without a weapon during a troll attack.

The first one charged the lantern. Shem stepped aside and drove his dagger between the eyes, killing it instantly. The troll's momentum plowed its carcass into the wet grass and mud, knocking the lantern over. The clearing was plunged into darkness.

Shem was blind now, but that didn't stop the loud charge of the troll as it turned toward him. He knew the beast could see in the dark and would be upon him in seconds. He had one chance.

Taking his quarterstaff in both hands, he faced the sound head-on and struck with all his might. Two strikes, one with each end of the staff. The first punched soft flesh, as though hitting a bag of flour. The second crunched against something hard as stone, snapping his staff in half. There was a low, final snort as the troll's body thudded upon the ground and slid into Shem's legs.

The miller jumped back, fully expecting sharp claws to sink into his calf muscle, but the troll didn't move. He waited a few seconds, listening. Razor began barking at something off to his left.

The staff was ruined, so he tossed the pieces away. Then he went over to where he had last seen his lantern. A few steps was all it took before his foot kicked the iron-framed cage. The flame had gone out and several of the mirrors inside were cracked. But the wick was still dry, and within moments he had light again.

"Razor, would you stop your yapping?"

At the opposite side of the clearing, the retriever was barking at a huge oak tree.

Shem yanked his dagger out of the troll's head, wiped the blade clean on wet grass, and then went over to investigate Razor's find. He had never heard of trolls cowering in a tree before, but he wasn't going to take any chances.

"What is it, boy? Have you found more trouble for me?"

At the base of the tree he spotted a third troll, this one lying dead, its gray tongue hanging out of its mouth. The broken blade of a sword poked out of its neck.

Leaves rustled and a shower of water fell out of the tree. Shem readied his dagger. Moments later, a body dropped out of the branches, landing awkwardly before falling over.

It was a young man, hardly older than Mira—disheveled, with a leather jerkin worn underneath a torn and water-soaked surcoat. One eye was swollen shut.

The man shaded his good eye against the light. "Thank the Creators," he breathed. "I'm saved." Then he passed out.

The miller examined him from head to foot, unimpressed. "Mira was right," he said. "Razor found a wounded bird."

NINE

Mira sat by the hearth, chewing on a fingernail, watching Jarin sleep in Shem's big chair. The boy was in a crooked position, one arm behind his back, his face and shoulder pressed against the seat; drool ran out of his mouth, pooling on the chair. She had tried to straighten him twice, but the boy was determined to return to the same awkward pose.

Where was Shem? The rain had let up an hour ago and still no sign of the man.

The waiting was unbearable. She got up and paced the floor, idly fingering her yeni stone, which she had fastened in a tight net to a leather necklace. Its mild warmth did little to settle her nerves.

Impatient, she seized her coat and headed for the door.

Before she had taken two steps, Shem burst through, bringing a gust of cool air with him. The miller supported a man who was half-conscious and clearly having a hard time walking.

Jolted awake, Jarin sat up, bleary-eyed and obviously coming out of a dream, mumbling, "I didn't see anything, I swear."

Mira rushed over to help Shem. "I knew it!" she said. "Is he hurt? Who is he?"

"Step aside, girl," said the miller. "Move out of my way."

The man moaned, his head drooping to his chest. "I can't make my legs move . . ."

Shem dragged him over by the fireplace and unloaded him onto the floor.

He wore the remains of a soldier's uniform: padded armor, torn woolen surcoat, and an empty sheath meant for a short sword. The insignia of Trollgate Pass—a simple white shield on a field of black—was sewn onto the left breast of his surcoat.

Mira hurried to comfort him by rolling her coat into a ball and gently putting it under his head.

Shem rubbed his neck and shoulders. "I'm going to be sore for days. Jarin, get out of my chair and shut the door."

His son was slow to move, apparently mesmerized by the sight of the unknown man.

Shem urged the boy with a shove. "He's one of those clan warriors based at Trollgate Pass. Been riding hard for days, I'll wager." The miller sank into his chair. "Spent the last hour or so cowering in a tree while mountain trolls tried to shake him down."

"Trolls?" cried Jarin.

Fear caught Mira's breath. Nightmares of trolls troubled her sometimes, ever since she'd seen one tear out of the darkness of the trees and charge her father's wagon. "This far down from the mountains?"

"Not the first time it's happened," said Shem, a not-so-subtle reminder of how her parents had died.

"How many?"

"Three, but I saw signs of more."

Jarin made for the stairs of the loft. "I'll get my knife."

His father stopped him with a command. "Fetch me a bottle of ale. We have a long night ahead of us and I need a drink."

Jarin halted on the first step, looked earnestly at the loft, then turned around and scuttled into the kitchen.

The warrior stirred and sluggishly opened his good eye. "I must warn the lowlands . . ."

Mira moved wet hair from the face of a man barely older than she. His eye was swollen so badly that she might have to slice it open to release the pressure.

Jarin returned and handed his father a bottle. Shem drank noisily.

The warrior responded to Mira's touch. "An angel," he whispered.

Mira shook her head. The man was clearly delirious.

Shem stood and shoved the bottle into her hands. "Give him some of this. It will clear his addled mind." Then the miller went to his hunting supplies hanging on the wall by the door and gathered items for traveling, which included, among other essentials, a hunting bow and a quiver of arrows.

"Shem, what's going on?" asked Mira.

"Far as I can tell, the mountain trolls have united and overrun the north pass. He was either a coward who fled the fight or he was sent to warn the lowland villages. I suspect he's a deserter, but I'm not taking any chances."

"Come sunup, trolls scatter and hide, right?"

"Not while under the cover of dark storm clouds, they don't."

Jarin, who had been listening quietly to their conversation, seemed to remember something and scrambled up the steps to the loft.

One look at the warrior told Mira he had fallen asleep. "Then we must do as he says and spread warning."

"First things first," said Shem. "You and Jarin head for the safety of Uncle Sedric's hut, in the foothills of the western mountains. And take that sorry excuse of a soldier with you."

From the loft, Jarin said, "We're going to see Sedric the Hermit?"

"The man's crazy," said Mira.

Shem slung the bow over his shoulder and opened the door. "It's only a day's journey, and my brother knows the ways of survival. He'll keep you safe."

"But—"

Shem went outside before Mira could protest.

With her anger rising, she chased him outside, where he was heading for the barn. From the front steps she said, "But the town is only a few hours away."

"That's the first place a band of trolls will go," Shem answered over his shoulder. "They'll be a hungry bunch ready for plunder."

Mira didn't know what to say. Events were moving so fast she barely had time to think. She went back inside and started barking orders of her own. "Jarin! Pack up what you can and meet us outside. And hurry. We're leaving."

She walked up to the warrior and poured the rest of the ale onto his sleeping face. With a sudden intake of breath, he sat up and coughed.

"I really wanted to be kind to you, warrior," Mira said, "I really did, but we don't have time for that anymore. You'll have to make yourself walk. I can't carry you."

TEN

A quarter-hour later, Mira was tightening the last of their traveling supplies onto Moby. She named off each item, one by one, to make sure she hadn't forgotten anything.

Beside her, she caught sight of Jarin double-checking and triple-checking the Hawkie knife strapped to his belt. The boy seemed blind to the real danger, choosing to view their departure as a thrilling episode in one of those adventure stories she told him at bedtime. The boy had even called her Princess Hannah once, by mistake.

Maybe it's for the best, she thought. *Better than trying to coax a reluctant boy out into the cold night air.*

Everything was in order, save for one item she'd almost forgotten: her sling. Father had taught her how to use it, and her skill had improved over the years, despite Shem's grumbling that her hours of practice were a waste of time. It was the only weapon she truly knew how to use. Even Shem's determined efforts to teach her the bow had not given her the same deadly accuracy she had acquired with the sling. More than one field mouse or pesky magpie had fallen to her sling over the years.

She hurried into the barn and fetched the weapon hanging by a nail on a wooden post. Then, remembering Moby, she also grabbed her sack of sugar cubes. When she came back outside, she saw the warrior staggering out of the house. He took a few wobbly steps and fell into the mud. Shem was there at once, hauling the man over his shoulder like a sack of wheat. The miller went over to the gelding and draped him across the animal's back, and then bound him to the saddle with a length of rope.

As the warrior moaned, Shem tied a longer length of rope between the gelding and Moby. "Don't waste time," he said to Mira. "And watch this deserter, in case he slips loose and falls off. You have my permission to leave him at the side of the road if he slows you down."

"Aren't you coming with us?" Mira asked.

"No."

"What makes you think you can survive a raid by yourself?"

"This is no time to argue with me."

Mira had tried to mask the concern in her voice by acting stern, but she just couldn't do it as the big man turned his back on her.

"I'm worried about you, Shem."

"I'll not abandon the mill and let a gang of trolls destroy everything I've worked for. Besides, I want to give you a good head start by slowing them down—"

Razor started barking. To the north, the red light of a

flare soared into the dark sky, illuminating the road, its light reaching the mill brightly enough to cast a blood-red hue across the yard.

"Papa, what's that?" asked Jarin.

"Signal flares," said Shem. "Enemy scouts have found the mill."

Mira watched the flare hover beneath dark clouds, mesmerized by its eerie light. "What if it's the town militia?"

"It's not. Only magic flares burn for so long in wet weather." Shem went up to Mira and, moving with sudden purpose, seized her by the waist and threw her into the saddle with Jarin.

Mira barely had time to react. "What are you doing? Let me go!"

Shem slapped the horse's rump, and Moby went into a determined trot; the other horse followed. Mira grabbed the reins.

The miller called out to them as they left the yard. "Go south to Cottonwood Creek and then follow it west. Don't stop till daylight!"

Jarin twisted in his saddle and shouted, "Bye, Papa! Hurry back to us when you can."

Mira was about to turn Moby around and return to the mill so she could give Shem a tongue-lashing, but her resolve withered as fear took hold of her. She had never seen Shem so worried.

Razor came trotting up beside them, barking once at Jarin. Moby reacted to the sound by picking up the pace.

"That's a good boy," said Jarin. "Take us to Uncle Sedric. We're going on an adventure."

ELEVEN

Shem watched the retriever dash off, waited long enough to make sure that fool of a girl didn't try to turn around. Then, when he was satisfied that she and Jarin were gone for good, he took up his lantern and slipped into the windmill.

The rich smell of ground wheat renewed his sense of purpose, steeled his resolve for what he was about to do. His anger mounted as he stacked heavy sacks of grain against the front of the door in an effort to secure it against potential intruders—anger at trolls that dared threaten his mill and his way of life.

He'd built this place from practically nothing, buying it from a lazy old miller who had let his entire operation go to ruin. It had cost Shem every penny he'd earned as a fighter in Lord Abbot's small company of mercenaries hired to repel an incursion of mud jiks from the southern marshes. But it had been worth it.

Those had been uncertain times, but his life had been full of purpose and the promise of good things ahead. He could still remember the smile on sweet Constance's face when he told her he was ready to settle down and marry. With no clue about how to mill grain, he had handed his entire loot over to the lazy old miller.

Despite his wife's sudden death a few years later, he was now so proud of his holdings he had no intention of letting a bunch of adventurous trolls destroy it all.

He piled the sacks of grain as high as he could and then made his way up the steep ladder to the top. This level of the windmill was a cramped space occupied by the brake wheel and a wooden wind shaft that went outside to the great sail arms. A big man, Shem had to stoop as he moved around to avoid bumping his head against the pitched roof. Years ago, he had installed a hatch in the roof, thus providing an area where he could stand up straight and look out upon the lands beyond his farm.

He pushed the hatch open and scanned the north road.

As one flare faded and dropped out of sight, another launched into the air, providing some visibility through the darkness. But it wasn't enough for his human eyes, for he could barely see past the old sycamore tree that grew outside the northern corral fence. The trees beyond were visible only as a screen of darkness blacker than the red-tinged sky.

Behind him to the east, the tall trees growing along Willow Stump Creek provided another dark barrier, hiding evidence that Jacob Hobson's wheat fields lay on that side of the water. The old codger was probably sound asleep, unaware of Shem's plight. No help would be coming from that direction tonight.

Shem covered the lantern and waited for his eyes to adjust

to the poor light, as he had learned to do while traipsing about the marshes as a young mercenary searching for the elusive mud jiks: creatures that appeared only after sundown.

Funny how most of the world's magical creatures sought the darkness of the night, he thought, whereas humans and their domesticated animals favored sunlight and all it revealed. If that didn't tell a man which creatures were on the right side of things, nothing would.

It wouldn't be a long wait, he knew; trolls would come rampaging out of the trees in no time.

He took up his bow and quiver. Twenty-three arrows should make do. Trolls didn't hunt in packs larger than that, did they? Perhaps not. He wished he knew more about them.

What worried him was the flare. That meant a tribal mage was traveling with the band and had probably convinced the stupid trolls to leave the mountains on a quest for human riches.

The mage might prove to be a shrewd adversary, but Shem had a few tricks up his sleeve. Three special arrows rested in his quiver, one of which had been enchanted by the queen of the mud jiks herself in exchange for her life. Shem had always felt a bit ashamed about that moment in his past, for he had defied Lord Abbot's express charge to bring him the queen's head on a platter. But what was a man to do when granted a wish? When he and three comrades had captured the frightened creature and she offered them each a magical boon if they spared her life, their greed got the better of them. As a young soldier in the middle of a deadly campaign, Shem had wished for a weapon that would slay his enemies. In answer, the queen had taken the arrow that had wounded her and cast a spell upon it, turning it hard as iron, light as ash, and black as pitch. Testing its point, he had nearly severed his thumb clean off.

The other two arrows were expensive shafts fletched by his brother, a curious man who possessed an uncanny talent for creating expert tools. Sedric had even boasted about a few magic spells he had learned—enough magic to enchant these two arrows to be as deadly as the queen's arrow.

There! He saw movement.

Five trolls loped out of the trees, ran past the sycamore, and halted in front of the fence, sniffing the air with their big snouts like bloodhounds. Shem took up his arrows, one by one, and counted them as he fired at the trolls.

One. A troll fell back as the arrow hit the beast squarely in the chest.

Two. Through the neck.

Three. A miss.

Four. A graze upon the snout. This troll turned and ran back into the trees.

Five . . . Six. Both in the hindquarters.

Three trolls were dead and a fourth lay squirming in the mud, crying out like a skewered pig. Shem chuckled softly. They had chosen the wrong homestead if they'd been after easy plunder. Maybe the one that had escaped would warn the others to stay away. That would give Mira and Jarin plenty of time to get away.

Wait . . . What was that?

Something huge stepped out of the line of trees, lurking right at the edge of light.

Could it be?

His brother once claimed to have stumbled upon a hulking brute in the mountains called a bergris. Twice the size of a man and three times as strong as a bear, a bergris's inborn magic gave it unbelievable strength. As proof that he spoke the truth, Sedric pointed to legends of underground dwellers that tunneled through mountains by crushing rocks in their bare hands.

This huge figure hiding in the shadows might be a bergris, Shem thought. It was certainly big enough. So why did it wait?

He chose an arrow fletched for distance, nocked it in his longbow, and pulled back on the string as hard as he could.

"You are called Bergris Slayer," he whispered to the arrow, aiming it high.

The arrow flew into the sky, but quickly vanished into the dark of night. Seconds later the shape standing at the tree line fell to the side, and a mighty roar echoed across the yard.

Shem was congratulating himself when the figure drew itself up and launched out of the shadows, howling with rage. It had long, thick arms, which it used to propel itself forward by planting its knuckles on the ground and swinging forward.

It charged up to the sycamore tree and without noticeable effort ripped a fat limb right out of the trunk. Then with a great heave, it threw the branch across the entire length of the yard, where it became embedded in the north wall of the house.

"By the Creators," Shem said in astonishment.

The bergris pounded the ground, splashing water and mud across its hairy chest. Then it moved up to the fence and destroyed it, tossing logs aside, two by two, and ripping posts out of the ground.

Shem could hear the workhorse, Nando, neighing in fear in the barn. Now it was time to use one of Sedric's special arrows, for the bergris was heading straight for the barn.

The arrow had strange markings scratched along the shaft, and Shem worried that it would fly wildly through the air. But when he launched the arrow, it flew true and appeared to gain speed just as it drove into one side of the bergris's neck and out the other side.

The huge beast stopped suddenly, put a big hand to its neck, and then collapsed into a heap in the pig's wallow.

A horde of trolls stormed out of the trees yowling, their clawed fists raised into the air. Shem stopped counting after twenty. All around the trolls were smaller creatures, much like the spindly mud jiks, carpeting the ground in droves. Forest imps.

It was worse than he had feared. This wasn't a small band of greedy trolls out for a quick raid; this was a full-scale invasion.

Hundreds of trolls, thousands of imps, and a handful of bergrisi came into view. Some of them approached the barn, discovered their slain comrade lying on the ground, and launched into a frenzy. The chicken coop was smashed to bits, its inhabitants chased down and eaten. The pigs, too, barely lasted two minutes before they were snatched up and devoured.

Nando emerged from the barn, kicking and screaming, attempting to make a run for it. But a mob of trolls surrounded the horse, preventing its escape, giving the imps a chance to scurry up her legs and gnaw at her hide. Nando fought desperately, bucking and spinning wildly, stomping a few imps into the mud, but soon she went down.

The army swarmed into the barn. The cow would be next.

Shem was in shock. He could do nothing but watch his farm be destroyed, piece by piece. Everything he had worked for was being torn up before his eyes, all of it demolished or eaten. His remaining arrows would hardly save his mill now.

Then a new figure came into the reddish light of the flare, different from the rest of the creatures. He was tall and surprisingly human in appearance, wrapped tightly in strips of cloth that covered his entire body and concealed his head. He rode a fat slug-like creature that looked like the colossal white maggot of a fly; it had beady eyes and a snout wreathed with needle-like teeth.

No enemy upon the field looked so menacing. Here was the mage Shem had thought was an enterprising troll-shaman from the mountains. Here was the mighty commander responsible for destroying his farm.

This was his true foe.

Dragged along by a long chain tied to the maggot were three human men, each of them shirtless and barefoot, clad only in frayed pants. Shackled to the chain by an iron collar, the men trudged behind the maggot with shoulders drooping, their skin wet with rain, their feet and legs covered in mud. They might have been mighty men once, soldiers even, but now they were beaten into submission and enslaved. They didn't defy their captor, but merely followed without resistance.

Shem wasn't about to be the fourth man bound to that

length of chain. He wasted no time choosing the arrow enchanted by the queen of the mud jiks and fitted it in his bow. Aiming carefully, he fired it at the head of the maggot rider.

The queen's arrow flew straight and fast, exactly like Sedric's arrow, except a flash of bright light burst forth from its shaft, a lightning strike that bathed the yard momentarily in blinding light. The commander raised a warding hand, but he was too late. The arrow went through his hand and pierced his forehead. Strips of cloth burst into flames and the rider toppled off the maggot, falling into the mud, where he lay motionless. Flames guttered in the breeze.

"Ha! That'll show 'em."

For an instant, the nearby trolls stopped in their tracks and turned toward the giant maggot, which inched away from the flames. Many of the trolls let out wails of grief when they saw their fallen commander lying on the ground, while others appeared ready to bolt back into the trees. A bergris standing next to the maggot stooped to touch the burning corpse, but recoiled when it neared the fire.

They'll scatter, Shem thought, a glimmer of hope returning. *They'll scatter and run off now, and none too soon. A few things might yet be salvaged from the barn.*

Two strange newcomers hurried out of the woods, riding two-legged reptilian beasts with stubby necks and no arms. The ranks of trolls and imps parted hastily, permitting them to pass; those that might have fled stopped and waited, watching.

These riders had snakelike skin and wore almost nothing save leather belts carrying all manner of trinkets and old bones. Their bodies were covered from neck to foot in scars, many of which glowed like thin rivulets of molten gold. In their hands they held gnarled quarterstaves.

Weerlords.

Fourteen arrows remained in Shem's quiver, but only one was enchanted—his brother's second arrow. The newcomers were far more powerful than any mage serving a tribe of trolls, he knew, and might be able to survive an ordinary arrow, no matter how good his shot.

Shem hesitated, unsure of what to do next.

One of the weerlords dismounted and examined the dead body next to the maggot. It barked at the other, who then reached over to one of the slaves and, with a touch, released the shackle from the man's neck.

As if knocked unconscious, the man crumpled to the ground and lay still. Tensions grew as the army waited. Shem held his breath in fear.

The giant maggot inched forward as a single imp tried to move around its fat body and get a better look at the weerlords. With sudden speed, it narrowed its mouth and slurped up the unsuspecting imp—head, body, and legs. Hardly a whimper escaped the imp's lungs before it was devoured.

A cluster of imps loitering nearby saw their comrade disappear into the grub's mouth and backed away with cries of panic.

Shem's gaze fell back to the slaves. The unshackled human who had fallen to the ground stood, stretched his neck, looked at his hands, and tested each finger. Apparently satisfied, he turned and shouted at the nearest trolls in a tongue that sounded more like barks and growls than any human words Shem had ever heard. The trolls retreated, giving the man ample space.

One of the weerlords approached the human and handed him a dingy robe so full of holes that it might have sat for years in a wardrobe full of starving moths. The man put it on, his head held high, wearing the disgusting garment as if it were a nobleman's expensive robe.

At first Shem didn't want to believe what he was seeing. But as the man climbed onto the maggot—the army watching in anticipation—he couldn't deny his fears.

The slave had been possessed by a skinwalker, one of those ancient spirit demons said to have been vanquished ages ago when King Aidan's men invaded its dominion, forcing it to flee to the remote mountains to the north. Legend said skinwalkers could never truly be killed, unless their fabled spawning grounds were found and their source of power destroyed.

One magical arrow remained in his quiver. But he wouldn't shoot the maggotrider this time; killing it would only force the demon into the body of another slave.

So Shem did the next best thing and shot the maggot.

His brother's magical arrow went through the center of the maggot's beady red eye, sinking deep enough to bury the entire shaft. With a low cry, it reared up, stretching for the sky, and tossed the rider to the earth. Squirming, it fell backward and crashed heavily onto the two remaining slaves. It writhed in pain, rolling from side to side, crushing the new rider, as well as a few nearby trolls. The weerlords hurriedly danced out of its path.

Finally the giant maggot went limp. A gush of yellow

slime poured out of its slack mouth, revealing several dead imps in the muck.

Shem grunted. "That turned out better than I expected."

One of the weerlords pointed at the windmill. At him.

Intense heat spread from the top of his head, down his neck and over his shoulders, across his chest, and then down his legs. It was like hot oil was being poured over him.

He ducked inside and the pain immediately stopped.

And just in the nick of time. The roof exploded in flames, showering him in hot embers, exposing the entire top level to the sky.

Shem nearly broke his neck as he raced down the ladder to the next level. Here he took hold of the rope used to hoist sacks of wheat up to the grain hopper and slid down it to ground level, barely noticing the rope burns on the palms of his hands.

As the enemy crashed against the door, half the sacks of grain piled against it tumbled down. The powerful bergrisi would be on him in seconds.

At the back of the windmill, a trapdoor in the floor led to a short underground tunnel. The previous miller had tried to dig a passageway from the mill to the house but had given up on the job before going half the distance. Shem had found little use for the tunnel, save as a cool cellar in which to store a few barrels of beer.

When he opened the trapdoor and stared down into the dark place, he realized he had no light.

Another crash against the door. Big hands grabbed ahold of the wooden planks, ripping the door from its hinges.

Shem jumped down into the dark tunnel and closed the

trapdoor. All he had was his dagger for protection, but if luck held, he wouldn't need to use it. Here was the only place he could hide.

He could hear the sound of heavy feet stomping around the windmill and of objects crashing to the floor. A bergris was probably tearing the place apart in an effort to find him. So much for saving the mill.

Then silence. Shem crouched low, hardly daring to make a sound, not even to breathe. He held his dagger ready.

The trapdoor flew open. One of the weerlords was staring at him. It raised a snakelike hand and pointed a clawed finger at his head.

"*Sleep*," it said in a hollow-sounding voice.

Shem lunged, tried to stab the creature's leg, but his arms and legs suddenly became too weak and he lost consciousness.

TWELVE

Being a hero was hard work. Seated behind his stepsister, Jarin had tried to keep his eyes open as the hours went by, had tried to search for trolls in the darkness beyond the road, had tried to keep his hand on the hilt of his Hawkie knife, ready to draw it at the first sign of danger, but at some point he dozed off.

When he awoke, he was slumped against Mira's back, his neck bent and hurting, his face soaked from the cold rain. It was a wonder he hadn't tumbled to the muddy road. Then he felt the rope wrapped around him, a rope Mira must have used to strap both of them together after he'd fallen asleep.

"Where are we?" he asked, rubbing his neck and shoulders.

Behind him, a man replied, "A long way from home." The warrior, mounted upon his horse, nodded to Jarin when they locked eyes. "You had a good long nap, kid, which is more than I can say."

It was true; the warrior looked dead tired, and his bruised eye had swelled to the size of a biscuit. He slumped in his saddle, holding the reins in one hand while the other hung limply in his lap. His surcoat dripped water.

Mira said, "We're almost to Cottonwood Creek." She paused as she gave each of them long looks, then she added, "Where you can both get some rest."

"Why are we stopping?" Jarin asked. Even though he wanted to stretch his legs and take a moment to play with Razor, he didn't like the idea of waiting for trolls to show up while they were out in the open.

"I want to warn some of the homesteads farther south," said Mira.

"Papa said—"

"I know what your father said, but we need to spread the word. There are good people not far away, and they won't have any warning of troll raids unless we tell them. Isn't that right, Collin?"

"And my horse is about to collapse," said the warrior. "We need to take a break."

Jarin took a deep breath. Collin was about to topple off his mount.

They came to tall cottonwood trees that lined a creek flowing from the west, where melting snows of the great Trestammer Mountains fed the creek throughout the year. The narrow banks were overflowing from the recent storm, and the top of the water came up to the small stone bridge.

Mira stopped, untied the rope around them, and dismounted. As Razor came up to her, tail wagging, she tossed him a sugar cube from her saddlebags.

"Hop down, Jarin," Mira said.

"I'm going with you."

"You're exhausted. The Samson farm is about an hour away, and I'll travel much faster alone."

"I'm not *that* tired."

"Don't argue with me."

Jarin slid off the horse. "Now you sound like Papa," he said.

Collin dismounted too, but he was clearly unsteady on his feet and took a moment to brace himself against his mount. He rested his head on the saddle and moaned.

Mira untied the rope between Moby and the gelding. "Stay here," she told Jarin, "and make sure Collin keeps breathing."

"Don't leave me here," said Jarin.

"I'll be back in no time."

"But I think something's following us."

Mira lightened Moby's load by removing their bags and setting them on the grass at the side of the road, away from the mud. "Razor would have heard it already," she said as she remounted. "Move aside, Jarin. I don't want to run you down."

Jarin stepped back as Mira whipped Moby into a gallop and crossed the bridge. She was gone before he could so much as call out her name.

The rain was not heavy, but the air was cold. He was wet and sleepy. For the first time since beginning this adventure, he wished for the comfort of his own bed.

Jarin turned to say something to Collin, but the warrior had made his way to a thick patch of grass beneath the limbs of a cottonwood tree, where he lay without a pillow, asleep. The gelding was nearby, feeding hungrily on tufts of wild wheat and barley that grew along the banks of the creek.

It was quiet all around, save for the gentle patter of raindrops on Jarin's hat and cloak.

He wondered whether Papa was safe.

THIRTEEN

Time passed slowly as the rain soaked the vegetation and drenched the ground. Jarin's leather cloak leaked from every seam and fold in the cloth, making him wet and miserable. He wondered when the morning sun would finally come to chase away the dark.

After what seemed like a hundred years, he retrieved the warrior's horse, afraid it would run off, and led it back under the relative shelter of the cottonwood tree, where he tied the animal to the branches of a big bush. Collin had not moved an inch from his spot in the grass, though sometimes he let out a groan that sounded like the start of a growl. Jarin put a hat over his face to keep some of the big drops of water falling off the branches from hitting him.

Even though this place hid them from the road, Jarin had to admit it wasn't a good spot to hide if Razor were looking for him. And that worried him when he thought about it too much; he had heard trolls could sniff out their prey as well as any dog.

Jarin sat halfway in the bushes, hunched against the rain, his freshly oiled knife ready in his lap. Razor rested a head on his leg, enjoying a scratch behind the ears.

"She's probably dead by now," he said.

Razor lifted his head, perking his ears and staring at the bushes.

Frightened, Jarin crawled out into the open, his weapon at the ready. He heard rustling in the undergrowth.

Razor jumped up and barked once, twice.

The rustling grew louder. For an instant, the rat-like eyes of a creature half the height of Razor peeked out of the bushes. It had a flat face, with two tiny slits for a nose, and a body covered in black mud.

As quickly as it came it retreated back into the leaves.

Razor barked again, plunging headfirst into the bushes. Jarin stood and backed away. The creature burst out the other side and scurried past the gelding, which raised a hind leg and kicked, missing it by a hair. Making a beeline for the creek, the creature dived into the water and with amazing strength swam to the other side. Razor gave chase, jumping in after it and paddling in pursuit.

Papa had often told stories about these elusive creatures he had fought as a soldier. Mud jiks.

"Razor!" called Jarin. "Come back here!"

But the dog was gone. Both Razor and the mud jik disappeared into the darkness at the south side of the creek. The dog barked a few times, but the sounds quickly grew softer and more distant. Soon he couldn't hear them at all.

"Don't leave me," Jarin said in a quiet voice.

What was he going to do now? He couldn't chase Razor

in the dark. The dog was supposed to protect him, warn him of danger, but now he too was gone. Where was Mira?

Thus far, Jarin had been careful not to light a fire, but it was so dark in the rain that he felt the night pressing in on him, choking him . . .

He made up his mind. A lighted lantern would allow him to see evil trolls marching down the road. Weren't they scared of bright lights?

As he moved toward the supplies, he saw a dark figure standing in the middle of the north road. It seemed to be watching him, appraising him. At first he thought it was a man over ten feet tall, but then he saw that the figure sat atop a two-legged riding beast with a thick neck and a large head. Jarin had never seen a horse quite like it, if it was indeed a horse.

The skin of the rider's chest and arms were tattooed with strange designs that actually glowed orange and red, their soft light casting shadows across a chin and mouth that didn't look normal. The man's face appeared disfigured, like a mold of clay that hadn't yet seen the sculpture's finishing touches.

Jarin held up his knife. "Who are you?"

The strange man did not move and, for a long moment, said nothing. His riding beast shifted slightly and snorted, revealing a mouth full of sharp teeth. When the man finally spoke, his voice sounded hoarse.

"Do you travel alone, boy?"

"No, I . . ."

"Where are your companions?"

"Th-they will be right back. Any minute now."

"Left you alone, did they?"

"I can handle myself."

"Tell me, was a Trollgate clansman traveling in your company?"

Jarin glanced at Collin sleeping in the tall grass, then wished he hadn't. "No."

"What are you hiding?"

"Nothing."

Silence.

With a kick, the man urged his steed closer. The muddy road sounded like pig's slop beneath the weird riding beast's massive birdlike feet and mud oozed out between its huge clawed toes with each step. Jarin crossed to the other side of the road, hoping to divert the man's attention away from Collin, but it did no good. The man halted near the cottonwood tree and studied the warrior lying beneath it. Not far away, the gelding started pulling upon its rope in an effort to escape.

Jarin was close enough to see that the man's tattooed skin was not skin at all—at least not as far as he could tell. Below the sculptured head, tiny scales covered his body, and the tattoos looked more like shallow wounds that flowed with glowing blood.

That meant magic.

This was no ordinary man. Here was a native of Kalor, one of the many warlike creatures said to have been abandoned by the Creators long before humans arrived to set things right. Jarin had been taught that most natives were enemies, though a few daytime animals, such as the yeni, were known to aid humans in times of need.

"Did you see trolls on the road?" Jarin asked.

The rider swung one leg around and dismounted, landing deftly onto the grass. He appeared to be looking for something as he studied Collin and the horse and the supplies. He replied in a distracted tone. "They have gone to ransack a human settlement."

"What? You mean they're destroying the town? My home . . . the mill . . . and Papa . . . is he . . . ?"

The manlike creature wheeled around. "Your *father?*"

Terror struck Jarin. "Did he survive?"

For a split second, they faced each other in the rain, neither one flinching. The two-legged beast's muscles twitched, shaking rainwater to the ground. Then the man pointed a finger at Jarin. The boy had a second or two to run, but he hesitated, unsure of where to go or what to do.

In a voice full of menace, the man said, "*Die!*"

Jarin fell backward and landed on his back, his Hawkie spilling out of his hand. Roots burst out of the ground and wrapped around his arms and legs. They tightened, dug into his skin, dragged him down. Muddy earth flowed over him, burying his chest. He sank deeper, the mud coming up to his chin and sliding into his ears. He tried to twist free, but he wasn't strong enough.

He panicked and tried to scream, but mud went into his mouth.

As his enemy turned his attention away, the roots relaxed just enough that Jarin was able to raise his head and spit out some mud.

Collin was on his feet, threatening the creature with the point of a long stick. "Release him, weerlord."

"Where is the mask?" asked the manlike creature.

"You'll never find it." The warrior wobbled on his legs and let his meager weapon droop.

The roots around Jarin loosened their hold even more as the enemy focused his attention on Collin. With a slap of his hands, the creature said, "*Crush!*"

One sinewy branch of the cottonwood tree slammed down on Collin's shoulders, forcing him to his knees. He tried to push it away, but the force of the blow was too much and he dropped face-first onto the ground.

Collin let out a cry of pain.

Both the warrior and Jarin were going to die.

Then Mira appeared, galloping across the bridge, swinging her sling. Her stone soared through the air and smacked the head of the two-legged beast. With a throaty wail, the beast stepped onto the weerlord's leg, snapping bone and pinning him in place. The beast toppled over, crushing its trapped master beneath its huge body and burying him in the thick mud of the road.

The roots went slack. Jarin hastened to untangle himself. He was crying, he realized, bawling like a baby. When Mira came up and dismounted, he tried to shore up his courage.

"Jarin, are you all right?"

He hacked up mud from his throat and plucked it out of his ears. "Is he dead?"

"I think so," said Mira. "C'mon, I'm afraid it was only a scout." She helped him mount the horse.

His knife!

Jarin hopped off Moby and began searching the mass of exposed roots and mounds of mud. For an instant, he thought it was lost, but he found the hilt poking out of a tuft of grass.

Mira went over to Collin. "What about you?"

The warrior staggered to his feet, rubbing his shoulder. "That was not good for my health."

"Quit moping and hurry up. We have a hard night of riding ahead." Mira threw a bag onto Moby and lashed it down. In her haste, she abandoned the rest of their supplies to the rain.

Collin approached his spooked mount and, with surprising speed, managed to calm it down with soft words and a gentle touch. He checked his own supplies, then led the animal to the road and mounted.

Knife in hand, Jarin started for the dead riding beast . . . and the strange rider crushed beneath it . . . intent on stabbing both creatures with his knife, to make sure they were dead, but Mira promptly grabbed him and spun him around, forced him back atop Moby.

Before long, they were galloping west along a narrow path beside the creek.

FOURTEEN

Mira was scared and that made her angry. Not only had Jarin and Collin almost died at the hand of a monster, but she had also learned from the boy that trolls were ransacking one of the nearby towns, likely Moristad. That meant the surrounding farms had been attacked as well—or would be soon.

Why hadn't that oaf of a miller come with them? Stubborn man!

As the two horses trotted beside Cottonwood Creek, Mira tried to hold back a surge of guilt. It was now obvious that her attempts to warn the Samson farm had nearly caused the deaths of Jarin and Collin. The image of the boy half buried in mud, screaming for his life, was fresh in her mind. If he had died, it would have broken her.

She was angry with herself.

"What happened to Razor?" she asked testily. "Where was that stupid dog when the scout attacked you?"

Even though it had been a full hour since the encounter

at the bridge, Jarin had not relaxed his tight hold around her waist. "Gone," he said. "Chased a mud jik."

A mud jik? This far from the marshes? If the jiks and their new queen were in league with the trolls, this side of the Trestammer Mountains was in more danger than she realized. The nighttime creatures of Kalor rarely united under a common cause, but when they did, it was bad for all humans. That's what the Encoda seemed to say. Maybe Razor had actually done the group a favor by chasing the sneaky thing away.

Collin rode up beside her. "That was no scout back there," he said.

"What was it then?" asked Mira.

"Can't be certain, but I think it's what my clan calls a weerlord."

Mira's breath caught in her throat. Weerlords were said to be mighty sorcerers able to command armies. "What was it doing on the road alone?"

"It was hunting."

"Hunting for what?"

"Me, I think."

Mira turned in her saddle to get a good look at him. The warrior was so beaten and worn she wondered how he managed to carry on a conversation. "Why you?"

He shrugged, but it was clear he was holding something back.

Mira pulled Moby to a stop. "I almost forgot," she said. "Goodwoman Samson prepared this for you." From her saddlebags, she handed Collin a poultice wrapped in cheesecloth. "The Samsons are the best healers in these parts, outside of Lord Abbot's own doctors."

Collin examined the bundle suspiciously. "For my eye?"

"Yes. And this will give you strength." She gave him a small brown bottle sealed with wax. "I'll bet it's mostly strong whiskey, but Goodman Samson says he uses it for aches and pains."

"Whiskey, eh?" Collin wasted no time ripping off the wax with his teeth and downing the entire bottle in two swallows. He coughed once and nodded to her.

As they were about to set off again, Jarin pointed to something between the trees by the water and called out excitedly. "Razor!"

Climbing onto the bank was the boy's pet, a dead rabbit between his mouth.

"That's not quite the mud jik you said he was chasing," said Mira.

The boy hopped off Moby and rushed to tackle the dog. "You're alive! I missed you, Razor. I needed you."

Razor nipped at him, as excited about the reunion as Jarin was. The two wrestled.

"That's enough," said Mira. "We need to keep moving."

Mira stayed in the lead, but rode at a slower pace than before. She had noticed that the gelding's breathing had become heavy and ragged, which meant it was fighting to keep up with Moby's steady pace. Collin's mount was a warrior's steed, conditioned to bear an armored soldier and supplies for long journeys, but a hard ride from Trollgate Pass meant that this one had already covered a lot of rough terrain. It would need to be tended to soon. Shem had been wise to saddle her favorite horse for this journey, leaving the wagon behind, for Moby had been bred to plow fields all day and could easily carry two riders for long distances.

Collin kept the poultice pressed against his eye, and whenever Mira checked on him he was no longer hanging his head. As Goodman Samson had promised, the alcoholic elixir appeared to have revived him.

Jarin continued to hold her about her waist, his cheek resting against her back, hugging her it seemed. The boy had quit talking about going on exciting adventures, and Mira suspected he was holding her because he was afraid she would leave again.

Ahead, it was too dark to see anything more than the nearest trees alongside the road. She had been to Sedric's hovel only once, years ago, and the turnoff was easy to miss in the dark.

"Jarin," she said, "keep an eye out for a huge oak tree on your right and a large boulder on the left. We need to follow the path from there."

The boy didn't say anything for a while. Then he said, "I don't feel so good."

"How are the bruises on your arms and legs?"

"They sting, but now my stomach hurts."

"You've felt your first dose of powerful magic," said Mira. "It can make humans sick."

"Why?"

"Because it tried to kill you."

"Does magic make all people sick?"

Behind them, Collin answered, "No, but too much of it can make your head spin, and that makes a person queasy. Don't worry. Now that you've felt it once, it will be easier for you the next time. You were a brave kid back there, Jarin. Not many people who face the death curse of a weerlord live to tell the tale."

Jarin relaxed his grip. "Do you feel sick too?"

Collin chuckled. "I hurt all over, and not just because a tree limb tried to crush me."

"I mean, was that your first dose of strong magic?"

Collin's silence spoke volumes. When he replied, his voice was subdued. "No, not the first."

"When—"

"Jarin," said Mira, "leave him be."

"No, it's all right," said Collin. "Can't blame your kid brother for being curious."

Jarin stiffened in the saddle. "I am *not* her kid brother!"

"Sure. How old are you? Eleven? Twelve?"

"What Jarin means," explained Mira, "is that we are not brother and sister."

"Ah, that explains things."

"What do you mean?"

"Such an ugly boy can't possibly be related to such a good-looking woman, not in a thousand years."

Mira sputtered for a quick rebuttal, but all she managed to say was, "You lie."

Jarin, who might have chosen to be offended by the insult, seemed to understand it was all in fun. "I'm not as ugly as *you*."

"I beg to differ with the both of you," said Collin. "I am not the ugly liar you think I am."

Much of Mira's anger faded as they bantered back and forth. "Then you are a handsome liar."

Collin laughed. "I'll take that as a compliment."

"Don't get your hopes up."

"Yeah," said Jarin. "Don't get your hopes up. She doesn't talk to handsome men."

"Well said, kid. I guess you would know."

"Yup. She ignores me all the time."

They laughed, and for a time Mira forgot about murderous weerlords on the hunt.

FIFTEEN

Collin was grateful for the arrival of dawn, because Mira had promised they would stop and rest the horses when it was light. "Must keep moving till we see the sun," she had said. And Collin had grunted in agreement.

But the last hour had been brutal—so much so, he wasn't sure he and his horse were going to make it. He dared not complain, though, not to a simple miller's daughter—or whatever she was—but when the rain had ceased and a ray of sunlight poked briefly through the clouds, he was the first to point out how pretty the sunrise looked.

The horses drank from the stream and cropped the grass along its banks. The big farm horse, Moby, nipped once at the gelding, then seemed to realize how weary the other horse was and left it alone.

Collin too was dead tired and wasted no time finding a comfortable spot beneath the limbs of one of the many cottonwood trees. Mira handed him two biscuits from her bag.

What he really needed was a long rest.

As for resting, Jarin was curled up next to him, sound asleep. The boy had an uneaten biscuit clutched in his hand.

Collin propped himself up on his elbow, eating his cold breakfast, watching Mira stroll to the edge of the creek, where she stooped and began rinsing her face and hands. The swelling in his bad eye had gone down enough that his view of her was better than it had been during their frantic escape from the mill—not that he remembered much from those hours.

Mira was stunningly attractive, with big brown eyes nearly as dark as her pupils, and long eyelashes. Whenever she flashed her eyes in his direction—usually when she was about to order him around but sometimes to ask how he was doing—he found himself thanking his good luck. And then there were her curls of black hair, now bound into a thick ponytail . . .

He stopped chewing, fixing his eyes upon her.

As though sensing his gaze, Mira turned to look at him. Collin swallowed his mouthful of food, but did not shy away. Instead he grinned.

She playfully tossed a wet rag into his face, but a slight grin was on her lips.

"Keep your eyes on your biscuit, Collin of . . . of whatever clan you're from."

"Lothgar. I'm from clan Lothgar."

"Do all men of Lothgar stare so openly at homely girls from the lowlands?"

"No, only me."

"Just as I thought."

"You needn't worry," said Collin. "My people are known for their sense of decency and honor."

Mira choked on a giggle. "Oh, really? I hadn't noticed."

"What I don't quite understand is why such a hardy woman of your age hasn't been chosen by a strong man yet."

Mira went rigid and her grin vanished. "*Hardy?*"

The sudden edge in her voice told Collin he'd made a mistake. He tried to cover his blunder by thinking of a clever comment, but the only words that came out were, "I . . . I . . . It's just that . . . Maybe *hardy* isn't the right word . . ."

Mira glared at him for several long seconds. Then she marched over to the horses and pulled Moby away from the creek. "What I don't understand is how the men of Lothgar have ever found women to kiss!"

Collin cringed and muttered in the direction of the sleeping boy, "That's what you get for trying to flatter a woman."

"Jarin!" Mira called. "Wake up. It's time to leave."

"Wait a minute," said Collin. "We've barely had time to rest, and my horse . . ."

"You'll have to lead it on foot. Or maybe you would prefer to stay and terrorize all the troll women who happen by."

Collin stood and walked over to the gelding. Under his breath, he said. "Didn't realize I already had."

Jarin grumbled and complained as Mira jostled him awake, but when she promised him a soft bed at Sedric's place, the boy got up and, with head sagging, climbed back on top of Moby.

Without another word to Collin, Mira set off.

They progressed in silence, guiding their horses along the narrow pathway, through hills covered with thick bushes and ferns growing under the shade of tall trees. Jarin's head bobbed up and down with sleepiness. Razor followed, though he left the trail from time to time to investigate other animals or to mark a bush.

Collin kept his distance for most of the morning, unwilling to confront Mira's force of will. She reminded him of a trapper's daughter he'd met once in his home village, when he was fifteen. That girl had arrived carrying a heavy load of furs from the badlands, where she and her father trapped beaver and muskrat along the headwaters of the Valin River.

Keena, he remembered. *That was the girl's name.*

Keena hadn't liked his comments, either. She had even knocked him flat on his back when he said something about her calloused hands and weathered—or was it dirty?—cheeks.

Mira might not try anything so rash, but she could be deadly with that sling of hers; he'd seen that with his own eyes. Collin thought it best to give her time to cool off.

As noon arrived, he decided Mira had calmed down enough that he could strike up another conversation.

"So," he began, "who is this Sedric?"

Mira's tone was direct. "Jarin's uncle. He possesses the Lothgar sense of decency. You'll like him."

"Ah, good," Collin let out his most charming laugh.

"Note that he lives *alone*," said Mira.

Jarin, fully awake now, said, "They call him Sedric the Hermit."

"A loner, eh?" said Collin. "Can he be trusted?"

"He keeps to himself," said Mira. "But he was kind to me when I met him years ago."

"After your mama and papa died," added Jarin.

"Yes, but we don't need to go into that, do we?"

"No, I guess not," said Jarin. "Your own papa—"

"Sedric will take us in," Mira said hastily. "And he'll feed us, but don't expect a king's feast."

"That's all right," said Collin. "As long as he has something better than biscuits, I'll eat it. I'm so hungry I could eat half a chicken right now."

"I could eat a *whole* chicken," said Jarin.

"You could?" said Collin. "Well, I could eat two chickens and a loaf of bread."

"I could eat a fat pig."

"I could eat a fat bull."

"I could eat a . . . a *dragon!*"

"There are no dragons," said Collin. "So I have you beat."

"Then why do some stories talk about dragons?"

"I don't know. Maybe they lived on Earth."

"Is that true, Mira?" asked Jarin.

Mira shrugged. "Collin might be right. I've only come across one story of a dragon in the Encoda, when it referred to the Creators' greatest enemy. I think all those other tales of dragons battling knights were handed down to us from the days of Earth."

"When I'm on Earth I'll eat a dragon."

"Good luck with that," said Collin. "In the meantime, let's hope Sedric has a chicken."

SIXTEEN

It's going to be fish," Collin said, his hopes dashed.

"I hate fish," said Jarin. "It tastes like an outhouse."

Both of them stared at a wooden rack lined with strips of fish drying in the sun. Next to the meat was the silver-white hide of some animal Collin didn't recognize—perhaps a deer, though he'd never seen a deer with such a pretty coat.

Collin sighed and took in his environs. A squat log cabin lay nestled against a hill, surrounded by huge pine trees. A woodcutter, likely nearby, had recently abandoned a chopping block and axe. A short distance from the cabin was the shore of a small lake, where a light breeze stirred the surface of the water, creating tiny waves. Half-buried boulders covered in moss and lichen seemed planted in strategic spots around the cabin, providing a feeling of security, like a walled fortress warding off intruders.

It hadn't stopped them, of course. They had waltzed right between the boulders and into the hollow by doing nothing more than following the thin column of smoke rising from the chimney.

Jarin turned his nose away from the fish and wandered with his dog down to the lake. The boy began to skip stones across the water.

Mira stepped out of the cabin. "He's gone."

"Yet a fire burns inside." Collin studied the strange silver hide. "He's not far away."

Mira walked up to the rack. "The skin of a kend. Very rare."

Collin nodded. "Haven't seen one in the wild, but now that you mention it, I recognize this color. On special occasions, the lord of our clan wore a coat made of this."

Mira appeared to lose interest in the hide and lifted her gaze upon him. "Why was a weerlord hunting you?"

"I killed one of them."

"So you're not the coward Shem thinks you are."

Collin chuckled. Was that what the crabby miller thought of him? "I got lucky."

"So it's revenge they're after?" said Mira. "Is it your fault the trolls and weerlords have attacked?"

Collin sobered up. He owed Mira an explanation, though it probably wouldn't satisfy her. "Not exactly. When Trollgate Pass was attacked, I was sent away to warn the lowlands. But leaving the battlefield felt wrong to me, like I'd shirked my duty as a defender of the pass. The next morning I headed back, thinking I was being clever by circling around using a different route. It was a dumb thing to do, because I almost got myself killed. In a dry ravine I came across a weerlord in its last moments of life. Dead clansmen lay everywhere. The thing bore a pack belonging to two travelers who had gone beyond the wall a month earlier."

Collin tried to push back the memory.

"And?" Mira prompted.

"The weerlord carried their heads in a sack." Collin watched Mira's face, but her only reaction was to blink. "Now they're hunting me for the contents of the pack."

"You have it now?"

Collin went to his saddlebags and pulled out an object wrapped in cloth, about the size of a dinner plate.

"The sight of it haunts me still, so I've only looked at it once." He began to unwrap it.

A man yelled, "Don't uncover it out in the open, you fool!"

Startled, Collin stepped back and reached for his sword, suddenly remembering he'd broken the weapon while fending off trolls. All he had was a knife.

A tall figure stood atop a boulder in the shadows of the trees. "Put that away, boy, unless you want another black eye."

The man hopped off the rock and came into the light, revealing that he had long frazzled hair and a beard. His cloak was dirty and rent in places, and in one hand he carried a walking stick. He had blue eyes, not unlike Shem's, but brighter and more intense. They examined Collin as the man approached.

"Sedric," said Mira. "Be nice."

Collin backed away, holding up his knife for protection, but before he knew what was happening, the man was upon him, bringing down his stick, disarming him, and shoving him back. Pain shot up Collin's arm where he'd been struck. The man stepped forward and snatched the wrapped object from his other hand, deftly replacing it with the carcass of a squirrel.

Without another word, Sedric went inside the cabin.

Collin was slow to recover; he threw the squirrel away and marched after Sedric. "Now, hold on a minute."

"Collin, wait," said Mira, but he ignored her.

The cabin was dark, save for the flickering light of the fire in the hearth. Hide-covered furniture and a cot adorned the room, seemingly tossed about without care. A shelf packed with books and scrolls lined the far wall. Animal traps, rope, and skins hung from low beams of the ceiling, forcing Collin to stoop as he entered.

He found Sedric kneeling near the light of the fire, slowly unwrapping the treasure.

"That almost cost me my life," Collin said in a stern voice. "You can't just . . ."

Mira entered as the object was revealed. Collin's first instinct was to look away, for he had already gazed upon it once and was filled with a sense of dread. Even so, the allure of gold—and something else, like the warning gaze of a predator—kept his eyes fixed on the gleaming treasure.

Sedric held the gold mask of a bearded man in tortured slumber.

"What is it?" asked Mira, her voice faltering a bit as she stepped past Collin and stooped beside Sedric.

The anguish . . . The pain . . . Put it away!

"Don't stare at it too long," said Collin. "It's an unnatural thing."

"Oh, but you're wrong about that," said Sedric, his voice full of wonder and awe. "It is imbued with the natural power of the Great Tree itself, which sustains our vibrant world of Kalor. Can't you feel it coursing through you?"

"Yeah, I feel it," Collin said. "And I don't like it."

"That's because you're a human who is frightened of death."

"What about you, then?"

"The magic of Kalor is of life and death. This is a death mask."

Collin tried to speak to Mira, "Look away or it will give you nightmares."

Mira seemed not to hear him as she reached out to touch the mask. Then at the last moment she withdrew her hand. "I saw a half-finished sketch of that in the Encoda. Who is it?"

Firelight cast bizarre shadows across the mask, and for an instant its golden eyes appeared to open and close.

"It's the wizard," said Sedric. "The face of the wizard, Nolath."

SEVENTEEN

Jarin found a perfectly flat stone the size of his palm, snatched it from the pebbly shore, and wiped it clean.

"All right!" he said to Razor. "I'll get twelve skips out of this one."

Twelve was as high as he could count, so it seemed a lot.

He drew back for a glorious throw, but a brisk breeze, cold and . . . and smelling like stinky fish made him pull up.

He pinched his nose and looked at Razor. "Ew, was that you?"

Razor looked up, sniffing the air.

The breeze blew through the leaves and stirred Jarin's hair. On the other side of the lake, a dense column of trees swayed back and forth in a strong wind. The air moved across the water, creating a few small white caps, before it hit Jarin full in the face.

Razor growled.

Jarin was about to run away, but as fast as it had come, the wind died down. The air calmed and the surface of the water became smooth as glass.

He remembered his perfectly flat stone.

"I think the mountains just burped," he told Razor. "Because they ate too much fish."

Jarin threw the stone, counting the skips across the water, one by one. When he had counted to twelve, he began mumbling imaginary numbers until the stone plopped into the middle of the lake.

"That must be twelve-eighty skips!" He turned and ran for the cabin, announcing his feat. "Twelve-eighty times! Mira!"

He burst through the front door and stopped. Why was it so dark in here? As his eyes adjusted to the dim firelight, he saw Mira, Collin, and Sedric the Hermit crouched by the hearth, conversing in hushed tones. They were staring at something on the floor wrapped in cloth.

"Guess what, Mira?" Jarin said. "Guess what?"

Nobody was listening to him. He caught Collin whispering to Mira, "How does this crazy man know anything, anyway?"

Sedric went to the bookshelf.

Jarin had never seen so many books in one place.

Mira replied, her own voice hushed, "Shem told me Sedric almost went mad from studying the magic arts. He knows things, secret things. He probably learned too much and that's why he's . . . *eccentric* now."

"Good reason for humans to stay away from magic," said Collin.

Jarin tapped the warrior's shoulder. "Collin, guess what? I skipped a stone twelve—"

Sedric returned from the shelves. "Quiet, Jarin," he said. In his hands, the hermit held a book. "Even though its power is from Kalor, it holds a link to Earth. The mask is a bad omen, and I will tell you why."

Jarin let his arms hang. Nobody cared about his achievement. Nobody was listening.

Sedric continued, "First I must tell you what the wizard was fighting against."

Ah, so this was going to be a time for storytelling. Jarin settled himself on the floor next to Mira, eager to listen to his uncle. He liked stories.

"When King Aidan and his people first awoke upon the land, they confronted a host of unfamiliar beasts they believed were demons. The worst were skinwalkers, of course, known then as spirit demons. But there were many others . . ."

EIGHTEEN

King Aidan's armor pinched the thick skin of his chest as he ducked out of the pavilion. Metal dug into a sore that was beginning to fester underneath his arm, oozing puss. He had always been a big man, tough as nails and strong as a bull, but age and too many berry pies had made him fat. The blacksmith had tried to make adjustments, but there was only so much that the crabby ironworker could do to make him feel comfortable in his old armor.

"Start marching alongside your men," the blacksmith had advised. "Work your muscles back into shape. Your armor will fit like a glove in no time."

Aidan should have punished the man for being rude in front of his warriors, but these were bad times and he had other things to worry about.

Outside, two guards nodded silently as he passed them. A third man, his captain, marched up and dropped the severed head of a monster at his feet. The beast's head looked like a bizarre hybrid of bear and boar, yet covered in scales.

Aidan nudged the head with his foot. "By the Gods, is this what harries us?"

His captain removed his helmet and wiped sweat from his brow. "A band of them charged us, made us run. And that's not the worst of it, my lord. The land is infested with mobs of unspeakable monsters roaming for no other purpose than to murder."

"No sign of my cousin and his men?"

"Ambiorix didn't follow us into the valley after crossing the river. Yet if he had, it wouldn't have helped him find us. The land seems to have twisted and folded to the point that nothing is familiar to anyone. Even the stars themselves have changed. We are lost."

"Then it's as the oracles foretold," said Aidan. "We have been sent here to cleanse a new land."

A horn sounded.

The captain drew his sword. "That came from the direction of the pens."

"From our livestock."

"Aye."

"Gather your men and protect the animals," said Aidan. "They might be all we have to eat before we can clear the land for planting."

"The attack may be a ruse."

"They carry no weapons, but they know warfare, my lord. They are a vicious foe that fights with a marked cunning."

"Then we must guard our northern flank while I secure the camp's perimeter and put up a defense in the south."

The captain saluted and departed.

If the attack from the north was indeed a ruse, Aidan mused,

then the demons have a leader coordinating their battle plans.
And if they have a leader, they can be forced to withdraw.

Aidan hiked through the sprawling campsite, which had
been hastily set up amid the tall trees of this unfamiliar forest. His warriors had managed to fell many of the smaller trees, using the timber to build a palisade, but the fence
wasn't finished yet. The southern end of camp remained wide
open to the wilds.

Aidan caught some of the soldiers hurrying toward the
sound of the horn, but he stopped them and ordered them
to remain at their posts along the fence. Then he stormed
into an area of camp that had become a refuge for the men
to gather with their women and families, a place where cook
fires burned and the smell of food was strong. A place to
relax.

Most families were from his own clan, but other groups of
strangers had gathered here as well. One group claimed to be
from Britannia, but they conversed easily with his own people
and appeared to be glad for his protection. Another group,
the noisiest of the lot, came from far-off Thule. Though few
in number, their holy men were quick to inform anyone who
would listen that their god, Odin, had sent everyone to this
forest by means of a great magical tree called Yggdrasil.

"To me!" Aidan shouted. "I need a company of brave men
and women to help me defend the southern breach."

Although Aidan had been named their king, some of his
own people regarded him merely as a loudmouth chieftain
of the largest clan. Ever since the disappearance of Aidan's
charismatic cousin, Ambiorix, the clans had begun to bicker,
some threatening to go off into the wilderness on their own.

It didn't help matters that Aidan was considered too old and soft to be a true king.

Things would be different now. On this day, they would witness a different kind of leader, one who remembered the days of his youth, when he had led a band of clansmen against an entire Roman cohort. Yes, those were days to remember!

His two guardsmen were hard soldiers accustomed to bullying their way through camp and enforcing their liege's commands with harsh orders of their own. Some of the men and women who watched them with bowls of steaming food in their hands tried to argue over the interruption. But the complaints were more out of habit than signs of true rebellion, for rumors of forest demons and the recent call to arms appeared to have had a sobering effect on most. Indeed, one of the rival clans' chieftains, Gitorix, came to Aidan's aid with barking orders of his own.

"Get up, you lazy grub-eaters!" yelled the chieftain. "You've been chosen by the Gods to prove your worth, and Fat Aidan has been assigned to be your judge."

Aidan wasn't sure how he felt about being labeled *Fat* Aidan, but the men and women around him quickly took up arms and went to the south end of camp. Gitorix would expect some kind of reward for his help when this was all over.

Thankfully, a ditch had been dug between the two completed ends of the palisade—a meager barrier, to be sure, but better than nothing. He ordered much of their precious stores of oil to be poured into the ditch, then he removed the logs that served as a bridge. Archers climbed the trees overlooking the area and waited for the enemy. Aidan himself would command from the center, but he wouldn't defend this place by himself; his two guardsmen were each given command of twenty warriors. Though most carried simple spears and shields, some of them were true soldiers wielding two-handed broadswords.

The enemy attacked exactly as his captain had predicted. The first creatures to burst out of the forest looked like tiny devils with red scales and pointy horns. They covered the ground like rats fleeing floodwaters, quickly scurrying into the ditch and up the other side. Aidan signaled the archers, who hurried to ignite the oil. Tall flames roasted a great host of the little imps. Yes, that's what he would call them. The smell of their cooked flesh was putrid and foul, sickening his stomach.

Then came the bearlike monsters he'd seen earlier—or at least the head of one. The men of Thule named these beasts trolls, and Aidan agreed, for the monsters reminded him of greedy creatures described in fairy tales his grandmother used to tell. The trolls halted before the fires and shaded their eyes, unwilling to go farther. Archers fired at them at will, killing many, while others died by thrown spears.

Then a monstrous giant twice the size of a man rushed forward and tossed a boulder across the ditch; its long, thick arms seemed to have the strength of a thousand men. Warriors scrambled out of the way, but one was crushed under the stone. The beast then leaped over the fire and began to swipe men and women aside as though they were ragdolls. His guardsmen, each flanked by several men with swords, confronted the giant and cut deeply into its flesh. It was slow to die, however, and managed to break the neck of a man who tried to step in to deliver a strike that would have slain a lesser beast. When it finally fell, its face looked surprised to have been defeated.

The chieftain, Gitorix, came up beside Aidan. "They fight like naked wild men who have never seen burning oil and sharpened iron."

Aidan nodded. "When they learn, they will be a formidable enemy."

Gitorix's grin faltered. "What will you do then?"

"We won't wait for them to adapt. We will pursue them and kill their leader, who must be hiding in the trees. Hurry, give the command. I'll need two hundred of our bravest to give chase."

Gitorix seemed to like the sound of that and wasted no time shouting orders.

Aidan watched his warriors finish off the few imps and trolls stupid enough to loiter near the ditch. He wondered what other kinds of monsters were lurking in the forest. Had they seen the worst of them? Or was this a minor skirmish from the vanguard of a great host? If he didn't do something now, fear of the unknown would undo his people. He had to take the fight to the enemy without delay.

Before long—though longer than he had hoped—he had an army of two hundred and thirty warriors, most of them from his and Gitorix's clans. Some came mounted atop trained steeds, but most went on foot. Gitorix's own clansmen were uncouth and wore little more than woolen kilts and painted skin, but he had seen their ferocity in battle and was glad to have them as allies.

Aidan decided that this was not the time to take his blacksmith's advice and march alongside the men and women; it wouldn't help the troops' moral to have their king collapse from exhaustion a mile from camp.

His own mount was strong because it had to be, and taller than every other horse in camp. It would give him a good vantage point from which to oversee the warriors.

Aidan's warriors soon overtook a band of trolls fleeing through the underbrush and dispatched them quickly before moving on. They stumbled upon another swarm of imps attempting to prepare an ambush. The little devils ran around in a panic, trying to escape the horses' hoofs.

Two giants accompanying the imps might have stopped Aidan had they turned and fought, but after feeling the sting of a few arrows, they turned and ran. Gitorix's own shirtless wild men summarily hunted the great monsters down, swarming them and cutting them down with curved blades.

Gitorix was all smiles. "This expedition is good for my men."

"We move too slowly," said Aidan. "Each skirmish keeps us farther from our real prize, which is their leader."

"You may be right about that. What do you suggest?"

"I'll take those of us on horseback and ride fast. You follow on foot and clean up whatever we scare out of the brush."

Gitorix shrugged. "I'll do as you say. But don't get caught in a trap, my friend. This is an untamed land which seeks to slay us at every turn."

Aidan spurred his steed. "And I aim to tame it!"

His cavalry, nearly fifty strong, thundered across the forest floor, chasing a creature they knew fled before them but couldn't quite see. Once, they glimpsed a two-legged beast dodging through the undergrowth in an obvious attempt to lure them into the tangle of the bushes. Aidan split his company in two and flanked the beast as it came out of a shallow defile.

Aidan, leading the pack above the defile, was the first to see that the beast had a rider—a scaly monstrosity with a snakelike head and long tentacles in place of arms and legs. It clung to the two-legged beast, its mouth clenched around its neck like a leech might latch onto a leg.

Aidan raised his sword and rushed the creature, but just as he came upon it, an unexpected blow, unlike anything he had ever felt before, threw him off his mount and into the bushes. When he landed, he couldn't breathe.

He rolled onto his back and unclasped his breastplate, fighting to inhale, to grasp a sip of air, so he wouldn't suffocate.

Somebody kicked him in the side and his lungs opened up.

On his hands and knees now, Aidan sucked in cool, clean air. Above him was—

His cousin.

Ambiorix grinned broadly, his thick, drooping mustache caked with dirt and probably something from his nose. "That's what you get for chasing a shapeshifter, cousin!"

His cousin clasped Aidan's hand and helped pull him to his feet. They embraced, slapping each other on the back. "How? Where?"

Ambiorix laughed. "All in good time," he said. "It seems your men have taken down one of the nasty ones."

Indeed, splayed out upon a stretch of trampled grass were two demons. The riding beast had nearly been cut in two yet twitched slightly, its tongue hanging out of a mouth raked with nasty-looking teeth; one of the warriors posed next to it, his chest puffed out, boasting about his miraculous kill. The bizarre snakelike rider lay nearby with three arrows buried in its back. The men and women avoided getting too close to this one, giving it a wide berth as they milled about the scene.

"Those are the smart demons," said Ambiorix of the rider. "They gather others around them like dogs attract fleas. They're lords of the forest, I tell you, and command a powerful sorcery that can toss even my fat cousin off his horse with a flick of its arm, as you know all too well."

"Is that how I ended up over here?" asked Aidan.

"It is. Saw that with my own eyes, I did. You flew through the air like a bird." Ambiorix's voice dropped to a whisper. "They have another power too, though I'm not happy to say it. If left alone, they will change shape—slowly, mind you, but in a clever way. My men and I captured one, kept it alive so we could study it, and that's what we learned. They can even take on the crude face of a man."

Aidan shook his head in disbelief. "What kind of land has the goddess Arduinna led us to?"

Ambiorix snorted and something yellow from his nose stuck to his mustache. "You know that I take little stock in the power of the gods and goddesses, but if I did, I'd tell you that they have abandoned this land. Whatever creators shaped our new home gave the demons free rein to do whatever evil they feel inclined to do."

Aidan nodded in agreement. "The oracles have told us we are here to cleanse the land."

His cousin agreed. "And there is one more thing I must tell you, Aidan, though you won't like it. Although the

shapeshifters be lords, they are not kings. No, that title is reserved for a mighty spirit that makes this forest its dominion."

"A spirit demon?"

"Aye, you heard me. A king among the demons. It possesses
an awesome sorcery. I caught glimpses of one hunting a great
bergris in the forest—you know, those giants that throw rocks
bigger than your belly. This demon could pass through the
densest brambles in utter silence and"—Ambiorix cleared
his throat—"take possession of another creature's body. In
such guises, it preys upon the unsuspecting."

"Can it take control of a man or a woman?" asked Aidan.

"That I do not know and I hope never to find out, for if it
could walk in your skin, I might be forced to slay you."

King Aidan brooded on his cousin's words, unable to find
comfort in them.

Ambiorix broke the tension with a hearty laugh. "Never
mind that now, cousin. The rest of my party is camped not
far from here, and we've caught a stag unlike any you have
ever seen. Its meat tastes better than most animals in these
forsaken woods, and its coat will make a cloak fit for an emperor."

NINETEEN

Sedric stopped his tale and went to a shelf beside the fire-place, where jars and bottles sat in rows upon rows, all placed neatly according to size. He fetched one of the big bottles at the back, uncorked it with his teeth, and drank noisily.

Suddenly thirsty, Jarin licked his lips and crossed over to the shelf, searching for something of his own to drink. Sedric might be crazy enough to let him take a swig or two of cider, if he could find some. But as he reached for a bottle, Mira cried out and Sedric seized his wrist.

"That bottle will make you deaf and dumb, boy, if it doesn't kill you first." His uncle turned him toward the door. "If you're thirsty, there's a barrel of fresh rainwater outside."

Jarin sighed. "Well, don't start talking again till I come back."

The water from the barrel was indeed sweet and had a subtle taste of pine needles. This only made him hungry, but as he surveyed the hollow, he saw nothing but dried fish.

Back inside, Sedric was already speaking: ". . . the king was wounded in the attack—"

"Wait!" said Jarin. "What attack?"

Sedric groaned in annoyance, but before he could say anything, Mira explained, "The spirit demon raided a hunting party and wounded King Aidan. Its sorcery almost killed him."

"That's when humans came face to face with the destructive power of magic," continued Sedric.

"The spirit demons are skinwalkers, right?" said Jarin. "Did it take over the king's body?"

"It hadn't employed that trick yet. But it wouldn't be long until it did."

"How long?"

"Now don't get ahead of me," said Sedric. "Spirit demons are territorial creatures, and this one was angry that men and women had suddenly shown up in its domain. It attacked, throwing sorcery around, killing a few and wounding King Aidan. The party managed to escape. But that night, the demon slipped into camp and took control of the chieftain, Gitorix, who was sleeping with the pigs. The possessed chieftain then began to sneak from tent to tent, stabbing people in their sleep."

Collin shook his head. "I thought Gitorix fought the demon and hurt it so that it ran off."

Sedric leveled his gaze. "It's a good thing I'm telling this story and not you. What did happen was that as the demon came close to the king, Ambiorix recognized the disguise and slew the possessed chieftain."

"Did it take over another person?" Jarin asked.

"I'm sure it would have, but as the camp woke up, people charged it with torches and chased the demon into the forest."

"Fire?" said Mira.

"Yes, the fire of an ordinary torch," said Sedric. "Of course, I know what you've been taught—that skinwalkers and weerlords wield fire—but back then it was a new threat to them, and they were frightened of it. Fire will hurt any living being, including spirit demons."

Collin's voice was strong. "I've felt the very heat of their fireballs as weerlords overran Trollgate Pass."

Sedric looked surprised. "Has the pass been retaken?"

"No," said Collin. "A few lucky ones escaped, I think, but the enemy was too numerous and swarmed through like a rushing river. I-I went back to help, and . . . and . . ." Collin trailed off.

Sedric took another swig from his bottle. "Can't be helped. I suspected things were bad, but not that bad. Now where was I? Oh, yes." He looked straight at Mira. "Your people are few now, forced to wander from one settlement to the next, but when they appeared in the shadow of the Canopy Mountains, they were numerous. Even before King Aidan's people had appeared, they fought a mighty demon, the greatest in the north and its minions. We know it as the spirit demon of Maran."

"*My* people?" said Mira.

Sedric nodded. "I'm afraid most were killed off, but they accomplished an important deed, and that was to expel the spirit demon from its own domain and into the forest, where Aidan's people battled their own skinwalker. As I said, spirit demons are territorial; the two of them fought and the forest demon was slain. Don't interrupt, Collin. It was slain by one of its own kind. They're not invincible, as you've been taught, just very hard to kill. The fight weakened the demon of Maran and it hobbled back to some faraway place to lick its wounds. For over five hundred years its whereabouts were unknown. Then it reappeared, stronger than ever. If not for the wizard, Nolath, the western kingdom would have perished."

"I wondered when you would get around to the mask," said Collin.

"If I hadn't been so often interrupted, I might have said all I wanted already." Sedric stretched his back. "Is anybody hungry?"

"Yes," said Jarin quickly. "I could eat a dragon."

His uncle stared at him a moment, as though debating what to say next. Then he went to the shelves by the fireplace and picked out a clay pot sealed with wax. "I can't help you there, but this will curb any boy's appetite." He handed the pot to Jarin. "Go on, open it up and share it with your friends."

Jarin scraped the wax away and lifted the lid, fully expecting honey. What he found inside turned his nose. "What is it?"

"A paste made from beans and other special ingredients, which are then left to ferment until it becomes truly nutritious."

Jarin set the pot next to Razor, who gave it a sniff but did not lick it.

Mira examined the paste. "It will cure your appetite because you'll throw it up."

"If you prefer," said Sedric, "I have smoked fish."

Collin sighed. "Go on. Finish your story."

"Suit yourselves." Sedric took a deep breath. "Seven generations ago, the spirit demon of Maran and a horde of monsters poured out of the north to regain lands on both sides of the Trestammer Mountains. The demon's goal was new. It aimed to rule rather than destroy humankind. The kingdom had its magicians by then, but their unpracticed skills were no match for the mastery of the weerlords. Those shapeshifters had become humanlike in appearance, but they were still deadly.

"Now back to Nolath. A court magician with a brooding mind, he knew the western kingdom could not stand against this new threat. So, in secret, he abandoned King Sandor and journeyed alone to find the lost birthplace of all magic, a valley where the fabled World Tree grew."

Sedric paused, staring into the fire of the hearth. "It was a desperate gamble, and I've often wondered how he had the courage to leave the castle at night and go searching for something that had only been whispered about."

Collin said, "The elders of my clan say the Tree is only a myth and can't possibly exist."

"Then your elders are simpletons," said Sedric. "It's true that Nolath had very little to go on but a sketchy account attributed to Ambiorix, whose adventures had made him a legend. But against all odds the wizard returned and claimed to have found the Tree and from it the power to defeat the demon. With that promise, he gathered a party of followers and went into the northern mountains to do battle.

"Two survivors returned—a man and a woman. The woman was silent, apparently in shock, but the man spoke of a duel between Nolath and the demon, a duel in which both had perished. Many doubted their story, but to their credit, the enemy retreated into the north."

Collin nodded slowly. "Two mountain passes, the only entrances into human lands, were sealed off in case the enemy returned."

"What about the mask?" asked Mira. "Why is it a bad omen?"

Sedric turned away from the fire, his face dour. "A third survivor returned much later. All we know of him was that his name was Orwin and that he looked like a beggar. King Sandor was old and proud by then and was known to dress too opulently for good taste, but he must have known the beggar, because he agreed to listen to his tale.

"Orwin told a bizarre story of how Nolath, beaten and maimed, had fled into the bowels of the Canopy Mountains, trying to escape the demon's wrath, or some such, and— there's little to go on here—awaken something not of this world. Deep beneath the mountains, the wizard came across a strange people who had never seen the sky, a people who worshiped a mysterious god they called the Wyrm.

"The survivor said Nolath lived there for a time, but he died after attempting to confront the god. To honor his bravery, the cave people prepared a golden burial shroud and a death mask. Orwin said the mask and the treasures in his tomb were worth a fortune."

"A whole mask made of gold?" Jarin said. "Is that true?"

"The king didn't think so and sent Orwin away before he could say more. I had always thought it a wild tale, invented by a clever opportunist who wanted to steal coin while organizing an expedition. Yet a seed of doubt remained. Only fragments of Orwin's story survive, but what we have suggests he let something slip, frightening the king. One witness later claimed Orwin confessed to wanting to rescue a friend who had been buried alive."

"Buried alive?" Jarin said. "That must hurt."

"It explains the mask's expression of pain," said Mira.

Collin's pinched his eyes shut. "I've felt it. Some sort of magic preserved the wizard's last moments. It's almost like a part of him still lives in there, suffering, holding on—"

Sedric cleared his throat. "We must consider a more important question. Did Nolath really defeat the spirit demon?" Sedric picked up the wrapped object on the floor and held it close to his chest. "We know now that he did not."

Mira stood and dusted off her pants. "So this recent attack from the north came not because the trolls have united. The weerlord, the trolls, the storm . . . it all means that . . . Oh, poor Shem!"

"My brother was a fool to stay and fight," said Sedric. "He always had the head of a mule. I fear the spirit demon of Maran lives on. A demon lord. What if it has been biding its time all these years, gathering strength, until the day when it will return to vanquish humanity?"

"I was there when the pass was overrun," said Collin. "The demon's power is beyond belief."

"What should we do?" asked Mira.

Sedric shook his head. "For you, there is no choice but to flee for the western kingdom and pray it can protect you."

"And you?" asked Mira.

Sedric went over to a large pack and stuffed the mask inside. "I've prepared a lifetime for my journey. I must find the World Tree."

TWENTY

Mira lay upon the hardwood floor, on top of a blanket that was too thin to provide comfort, and listened to Collin snore. Jarin, too, seemed to have fallen asleep, but that was no surprise; the boy could sleep through a raging thunderstorm, even after going to bed with a stomachache brought on by a dare to sample Sedric's bean paste.

The hermit's tale had unsettled her, not only because of what he'd said, but also because of what he'd left unsaid. Sedric had held back some knowledge about the mask's power. It was more than an omen of doom, portending the rise of an old demon lord; it held the key to the invasion itself. Why else would the weerlords be looking for it?

Were they trying to prevent the wizard from rising up again? Was Sedric intending to bring Nolath back to life?

As she pondered such thoughts, she must have dozed off, because when she rolled over, she saw that the coals of the fireplace had died down almost to nothing and the air had become cool on her face.

Over by the door, Razor whined softly. Sedric sat cross-legged next to the dog, scratching him behind the ears. Both faced the front door, which was open to the night air. No wonder it was cold.

"Soon," whispered Sedric. "Very soon."

Rain began to drum upon the roof, but as far as Mira could tell, the wind was not strong outside. Sedric and Razor seemed to be waiting for something.

What are they looking at?

Razor laid his ears back. Something was coming.

Lightning flashed, revealing for an instant a body standing in the yard. Razor stood up and barked.

Sedric was on his feet at once. "Come get me, you coward!"

Mira rolled onto her hands and knees, searching frantically for a weapon. The first thing she saw was Jarin's big knife strapped to the boy's hip. She tried to rip it free, but by the time she had it in her hand, she was already too late. The weerlord ran for the door and in two strides triggered a trap. A snare caught its legs and hoisted the monster feet first into the air.

"Ha-ha!" cried Sedric, racing out into the rain. "Gotcha."

Mira tried to follow, but in her panic she tripped over Collin's sleeping body. The knife went sprawling across the floor.

Outside, the weerlord thrashed against a rope snared around its leg, hissing violently. Razor jumped up and snagged an ear, ripping it free.

Sedric fetched the axe from the chopping block. "Can't cast spells with your head below your feet, now can you? Ha!"

Mira turned her head just as the sound of crunching bone abruptly became louder than the rain.

"Ah, curse it all!" Sedric complained. "I ruined its face. So much for a trophy."

*

When the morning light appeared and Mira had scraped together a measly breakfast for Jarin, Sedric was all business, giving orders and packing supplies, which included, among other things, a couple of old books and a bottle of apple brandy. Mira tried to stay out of his way as she strapped her things onto Moby, but the man was as ill tempered as his brother. When he insisted she take the pot of bean paste, she stood up to him.

"Carry it yourself," she said. "You're the only person within a hundred miles who will eat it."

Sedric grumbled quietly to himself, but in the end he left the nasty stuff inside.

The hermit had managed to bury the weerlord's body away from the cabin, though that didn't prevent Jarin from looking for it behind the big boulders.

"Come over here and help me," Mira ordered the boy, who had wandered too close to the mound of the dead beast.

"I wish I hadn't fallen asleep," Jarin said. "Why didn't you wake me up?"

"You don't need to see another weerlord."

"*Another* one?" The boy's voice cracked, his fear plain as the cloudy sky.

Sedric exited the cabin, carrying a loaded backpack and a walking staff. "It was probably the same one you met at the bridge," he said. "It was limping, as though from a broken leg, and was slow to see me—a sign it was hurt."

"Are you sure you killed it?" asked Jarin.

"I set a trap. It was coming for you, boy."

"Sedric, stop it!" said Mira. "He's scared enough without you teasing him."

The hermit shied away from the scolding, but he didn't apologize.

Jarin stared up at the rope hanging from the branch of a tree. "It didn't try to bury you in the dirt?"

Sedric harrumphed. "Magic takes a second to gather, even at the command of the oldest weerlord. You can catch most creatures of Kalor off guard, if you're quick enough and smart enough."

Collin came out of the cabin carrying his few possessions, which did not include the mask wrapped in cloth. The soldier was brooding silently, his stare fixed away from the others. After he strapped his things to his gelding, he waited a moment, closed his eyes as if to gather courage, then turned to face Sedric head-on.

"I'm going with you to find the Tree," he said.

Sedric walked past Collin and over to the rack, where he began to roll the kend skin into a bundle. "Why? So you can slow me down and make me late to save mankind? No, I'll take the three of you through the Trestammer Mountains, but after that we split up."

"And what am I supposed to do in the kingdom?"

"Join the castle guard," said Sedric. "What do I care?"

"The mask is mine, you know."

"Not anymore." Sedric made a shooing motion with his hand and told Mira, "Get this whining boyfriend of yours off my back."

"He is *not* my boyfriend!"

Collin and Mira glanced at each other quickly, as if she had prematurely declared their budding relationship at an end. On top of Collin's obvious frustration, he appeared confused and unwilling, or unable, to speak; he turned away and tightened the straps of his gelding.

The hermit chuckled. "C'mon, Jarin. Let these two lovebirds kiss and make up."

"Sedric, I swear . . ." Mira was fuming now. She swung up into her saddle and extended a hand to Jarin. Even before the boy had taken his place behind her, the hermit had begun to hike into the trees. Mira wanted to shout at the man, give him a piece of her mind, just as she had done to Shem a time or two, but it was clear Sedric didn't care what she thought, so she urged Moby after him.

Collin followed wordlessly.

*

At length they moved out of the cottonwoods and entered hillsides covered exclusively in pine and aspen. The clouds remained heavy in the sky and a light rain sprinkled over them. The path became rocky, slowing them down.

As she rode, Mira watched Sedric's back, thinking she might actually hate the man. "I feel like we're deserting Shem," she said.

"Trust me," said Sedric. "If he was stupid enough to defend the mill, he's dead."

"You don't know that," Jarin said defiantly.

"You're right," agreed Sedric. "I don't know. Go back and fight through a few weerlords to check on him, why don't you?"

Jarin went silent.

"How can you say that about your own brother?" Mira asked. "You act as though you don't care."

Sedric picked his way deftly between the many rocks in the path in front of him, never easing up as he spoke. "Shem and I rarely saw eye to eye and I long ago gave up caring what he did with his life."

"Did you know his wife well?"

"Ah, so you think you can get under my skin because we both loved the same woman?"

"I think that's why you hate him."

"I've never hated Shem. But he possesses a proud manner that could rankle any man."

"Saw yourself in the mirror, did you?"

Sedric halted and raised his head, but he did not turn around. "It may surprise you, Mira, that I made a great effort to convince him not to make the worst decision of his life."

"What, to not marry your true love, Constance?"

"I convinced him not to leave Constance for your own mother, before Jarin was born."

Mira felt Jarin go rigid.

"You lie," she said.

"It's the truth," Sedric said, resuming his hike. "But I shouldn't have said anything, and now you'll make me pay for it."

Mira didn't know what to say, though Sedric's news certainly explained a lot about Shem's willingness to take her in after her parents had died, and about why he had treated her like his own daughter. Then a terrible thought came to her. "Are you saying that Shem is my—"

"No, I am definitely not saying *that*." Sedric's amusement was maddening. "Jarin is the only child Shem ever fathered."

"But you led me to believe it."

"For one glorious moment I did."

"You're a despicable man!"

"That's what you get for trying to get under my skin, girl. Any more questions?"

Collin's voice conveyed pure exasperation. "Would you two stop it? My headache is bad enough without the sound of you both trying to cut into each other."

"At last," said Sedric. "The warrior makes sense at last."

The hermit guided them across the rough terrain to a narrow road that continued east into the foothills of the Trestammer Mountains. For a time the going was easier and the horses seemed to like the path, but as they entered the mountains proper, their way abruptly steepened as switchbacks took them up a rugged incline. Their mounts slowed, lowered their heads, and clopped along at a pace no faster than Mira could walk.

Here Sedric cut far ahead of them, going straight up the mountain for a long while, then waited as they caught up. The rains had washed away a bend in the road, leaving nothing but a thin stream trickling down rocks and gravel.

"Too bad for us," said Sedric, shaking his head. "We'll have to leave the horses behind."

"What about our supplies?" asked Jarin.

"Nothing to be done about it now. Take what you can and leave the rest."

They found they could carry much of the essentials on their backs, but Mira wasn't happy about abandoning the horses. Setting them loose on a mountain slope was a cruel thing to do, especially to Moby, a loyal workhorse that had never lived in the wilderness.

Sedric seemed to sense her doubt. "The horses know how to eat grass and drink water without your help."

"But Moby might try to return to the mill, and we don't know what dangers wait for him there," said Mira.

"Maybe he will, maybe he won't," said Sedric. "Worry about something else."

Mira looked to Collin for support, but the warrior was absorbed in his own thoughts, staring off in a different direction and gently touching his bruised eye. Turning back to Moby, she slapped the horse's rump and told him to find a nice mare to nuzzle.

"That's the spirit," Sedric chuckled. "A lively female will make any male happy."

"Not that you would know anything about that," Mira said.

To her surprise, the comment touched a nerve, and Sedric's face turned beet red. Realizing she may have crossed a line, she avoided him by climbing the rocky slope to the next switchback.

The four of them hiked farther up the mountainside for the rest of the day, stopping only when Jarin complained about his feet. They ate lunch and watched the clouds envelop them in a gray fog. The low visibility barely allowed them to see the road itself, and the air became ice-cold.

"These clouds aren't natural," said Sedric. "Can you feel it?"

Mira took a deep breath, but the damp air was all she felt. "No," she said.

"Feels like winter is on its way," said Jarin. "Is that what you mean?"

Sedric nodded. "We're at the end of summer and yet a winter storm has blown in from the north."

"I don't feel it," said Collin.

"I'm not surprised," Sedric grunted.

"Can't we go somewhere else?" said Jarin.

"Not much farther and we'll be out of this mess." Sedric picked food out of his teeth, urging them onward. "Watch your step."

After two turns in the road, the clouds abruptly thinned. A few more steps and the full light of the sun beat upon their faces. New energy poured into Mira's limbs and she hurried up the road to escape the last of the clouds.

Jarin followed her, grinning from ear to ear. He turned and looked east. "Wow!"

A blanket of puffy gray and white covered the land as far as the eye could see. In the distance, somewhat northward, flashes of light brightened dark clouds, presumably from lightning strikes. Behind them, snowcapped peaks reached out of the clouds, appearing to float on a bed of cotton.

"*Now* you feel it," said Sedric.

"The sun makes a difference," Mira agreed. "But something tells me that isn't what you meant."

Sedric closed his eyes and took in the sun's rays. "Unlike humans, many natives of Kalor prefer the dark; when they can't wait for the sun to go down, they use other methods of escaping daylight." He opened his eyes and swept his arm wide, indicating the cloud cover. "A skilled weerlord maintains this mess so creatures of the night can move about unhindered."

"Are they so powerful?" asked Mira. How could humanity defend itself against such magic?

"It's said that some of the old ones will hibernate for long periods, gathering their might, honing their skills as they sleep. If this storm isn't caused by a single weerlord, then several of them have joined forces."

"How can we fight such an alliance?" asked Collin.

"A good question," Sedric replied. "And one I'm not prepared to answer. But don't give up hope. The Creators wouldn't have put us on Kalor only to let us die. A way will be provided."

"And you intend to find it," said Mira. "Just like the wizard."

Sedric did not answer. Instead he resumed a quick pace up the road.

Collin came up to Mira. "His way is a long shot."

Mira agreed. "Desperation."

"Why don't we just stay in the mountains?" asked Jarin. "Seems safe up here."

"Because the sun will always set," said Mira.

This wiped the grin from Jarin's face. He stared after his uncle and then hurried to catch up.

*

By the time they reached the top of the climb, the sun had begun to dip behind the peaks. Two rugged mountains converged here, creating a box canyon with soft ground blanketed by fallen pine needles. Tall trees stood like dark sentinels keeping watch, their long shadows hiding the road.

Mira caught Jarin looking around as though he might discover eyes spying on them. He quickly helped set up camp and light a fire.

TWENTY-ONE

Mira shied away from a shower of embers stirred up by Sedric's careless tossing of another branch onto the fire. He was trying to agitate her, she knew, but she chose to remain silent by gnawing on a biscuit. The man could be as bad as his brother.

She took another bite and choked it down with cold water. Sedric had claimed that wild Earth grouse the size of turkeys lived up here, and the thought of roasting one over the fire made her mouth water, but nobody was in the mood to venture out beyond the campsite to snare a bird that might turn out to have a bad flavor. So dinner had been dry biscuits, a sliver of deer jerky from the hermit's own stash, and water.

Of course, their meager rations hadn't stopped Jarin from eating everything handed to him, even the crumbs. It hadn't been much, but it seemed to satisfy him for a time. He appeared to have made peace with the darkness all around, and sat quietly, eyelids drooping, ready for sleep.

Collin, on the other hand, had found the energy to strike

up a conversation with the hermit. "I've thought about what you said and I don't understand why the weerlord was more human than beast. Why the change?"

"Shapeshifters," said Sedric. "They seek to acquire human talents."

"Such as making tools?"

Sedric nodded. "But because they can't give up their magic, their tool-use remains primitive. Should they ever become human, they would lose their ability to cast spells. Humans and magic are like oil and water—they don't mix well."

"Then how did the wizard do it?"

"By going to the heart of Kalor's power."

"The Tree."

"I see you've been listening," said Sedric. "Humans can train hard to summon magic powers, with some people becoming better at it than others, but we're not born to it. Even the easiest spells slip through our fingers like dry sand. Only by going to the World Tree can a human be bound safely to magic in any permanent way."

"And if you're wrong?"

"Then I've wasted my time, haven't I?" Sedric took up his walking stick and began to draw lines in the dirt next to the fire. It appeared to be a picture of a tree, with a thick trunk and several short branches. As he spoke, however, it became apparent he had sketched out a crude map.

"Nolath was a cartographer in his younger days," said Sedric. "The first to make sense of the lands north of the Sidewinder Sea, and what he discovered was that our quarter of the world is laid out like a big tree, as seen from a high-flying bird. The mountain range we stand on—the

Trestammer Mountains—runs through the middle of the land like a great tree trunk, separating the eastern plains from the western valleys. Smaller ranges branch off in different directions, especially in the north, where granite peaks form most of the north wall bordering empty plains, and in the south, where twisting spurs vanish into the sea."

"Where's the magic tree?" asked Jarin, now wide awake and hanging onto his uncle's every word.

"Good question," said Sedric. "Nobody knows, but I think it lies somewhere here." He circled a large mountainous area in the south.

Collin opened his mouth, but the hermit cut him off.

"No, you won't tag along," said Sedric. "Tomorrow we split up."

Mira felt a queasy knot in her stomach. "What about us? Won't we get lost?"

"Not unless you're blind." Sedric pointed to the left side of his map. "When we reach the western side the Trestammers, go this way. The road was once well maintained, so you shouldn't have any trouble following it down into the valleys below."

Mira tried to burn into her mind the memory of the path, which followed the edge of the mountains, going north before swerving west.

"The first town you'll run into is Guldheim," continued Sedric. "The baron of that land is a greedy buttwart, but I know him and if you offer him the kend skin, he'll put you up in his castle." Sedric pointed at Collin. "Your mission is to tell him about the invasion."

Collin nodded, relaxing visibly, clearly relieved to have a solid purpose.

"What about me?" Jarin asked.

"What about you?" Sedric snapped.

"I want to help you find the Tree."

"Do you know the clues Nolath left behind?"

"No, but I bet Mira does," said Jarin. "She's always reading that big history book."

"Then tell me where the eye of the moon is, or how to survive the Perilous Road haunted by a guardian." Sedric looked at each of them in turn, receiving only blank stares. "I thought so." He smiled at Jarin. "Keep that knife handy, boy, in case you have the chance to protect your pretty stepsister."

The boy wrinkled his brow in a serious expression; ever since the crossroads at Cottonwood Creek, he had acted less sure of himself. *And no wonder,* Mira thought. *He was almost buried in the mud by a weerlord.*

Sedric clapped his hands and rubbed them together. "Does everybody understand? Good. I'm tired of talking and it's time for some shuteye." He went to his blankets and lay down. "Goodnight."

Jarin yawned as he went to his own bed. He and Razor curled up with their backs to the warm fire and quickly fell asleep.

Collin lingered a moment, as if to talk, but he didn't say anything and even avoided eye contact.

Finally Mira asked, "Should one of us remain awake, in case something comes near us?"

"I'll take first watch," said Collin. "Though I'll bet Razor will alert us of danger long before I hear anything."

Mira wasn't sure about that, but she didn't argue the point. She retired to her blankets and lay on her stomach while

Collin stared into the fire, idly poking at it with a stick. From her pack, she pulled out the Encoda and tilted it toward the fire, quickly discovering, to her dismay, that Collin's fiddling with the flames had diminished its light.

As she was about to close the book, the stone of her necklace began to glow, illuminating the pages. Startled, she touched the yeni's gift through the netting and found it warm. Out of the corner of her eye she noticed Collin look up.

"Does Sedric know you have that?" he asked in a whisper. "It must be magic."

Mira shrugged. "It was a gift."

"A gift from whom?"

"Does it matter?"

Collin seemed to think about it. "The light against your face makes you look mysterious."

"You know nothing about me, so you're right about that."

"I know enough. And . . . uh . . . I apologize for saying you were a hardy woman. I was acting stupid because . . ."

Mira rose up on her elbows. "Well?"

"Because I think you're pretty."

Mira buried a laugh and glanced at Sedric, who thankfully didn't stir. "Apology accepted. Now quit staring. I have some reading to do."

Collin nodded and went back to poking at the coals. He was holding back a grin, which made him look ridiculous.

She shook her head and began to read.

TWENTY-TWO

As the three companions broke camp, the morning sunlight crept down the rocky peaks, dropping low enough to warm the bottom of the box canyon and take away the chill. Ahead, the road passed between two great pine trees, then seemed to go straight into the west wall of the canyon.

Sedric stood between the trees. "Come witness one of the wonders of the world," he said.

Collin gave Mira a dubious shrug, hefted his pack onto his shoulders, and followed the old hermit into the pines.

The road disappeared into the round opening of a cave that had been hidden by the trees. It looked so dark inside that Collin wished he'd taken the time to light their only lantern or to prepare a torch. Would Mira's strange necklace be bright enough to guide them through the cave, he wondered?

"We're going in there?" he asked.

Sedric laughed. "If you prefer to climb up and over, be my

guest, but the way is treacherous—so deadly, in fact, that this tunnel was prepared centuries ago by King Aidan himself."

"You mean he actually dug a tunnel all the way through solid granite?"

"Of course not," said Sedric. "This is called the Wormgate, and it was discovered by the king's explorers ten years after he established his kingdom. It's three miles long and so straight you can see the other side when the sun sets on midsummer's eve."

Collin was in awe. "The walls are flawless. Did the Creators make it?"

"That's one theory. Some say it was prepared by the Creators so that King Aidan's people could settle the eastern lands."

"What's the second theory?"

"There's a reason it's called the Wormgate."

"Because a *worm* bored through the mountain?"

"An infantile dragon in larva stage."

Jarin edged closer to the opening. "What does that mean?"

"A huge grub," said Mira. "And it's only a story. Traders have traveled this tunnel for centuries."

"So it's safe in there?" asked Jarin. "It sure is dark."

"Lucky for you," said Sedric, "King Aidan made sure only humans and their animals could make the journey through the tunnel. Behold!" As he walked into the tunnel, wall sconces on either side burst into white flame. The once dark entrance became as bright as at midday.

Collin was taken aback. "How?"

"Follow me and I will tell you." Sedric started down the center of the tunnel. Every ten paces another pair of sconces ignited.

Jarin seemed hesitant to enter, but after a little prodding from Mira—and probably fearing to be left behind—he stepped over the threshold.

Sedric explained, "King Aidan's cousin, Ambiorix, was enthralled with the magical abilities wielded by natives of this world and he wanted the same power for himself. He captured many creatures, studying the ones most skilled with magic, eventually discovering that weerlords could accomplish things others could not. Fortunately for Ambiorix, weerlords were equally curious about humans. So they struck a bargain. He would teach three of them what he could about human skills and they, in turn, would instruct him in the art of magic.

"Things didn't go as smoothly as Ambiorix hoped, however. It turned out that weerlords, with their exceptional command of magic, had the advantage and learned more from him than he did from them. Magic was simply too difficult for Ambiorix and his kin to pick up with any degree of proficiency. They pieced together a few tricks, but little else.

"King Aidan was never comfortable while his cousin was carousing with sorcerers, but when the Wormgate was discovered he saw an opportunity to make use of these lords who would be men. Weerlords craved to be human and would do anything to prove that they were not so different from us. So he convinced the three to light this tunnel with a power only a human could trigger. And as you've seen, all you need do is cross the barriers at either end and there is light.

"The weerlords met the challenge all too well and humans became masters of the Wormgate. No creature of Kalor can comfortably step foot in here, save one. Even weerlords themselves are denied entrance."

Collin studied one of the stone wall scones and saw a reddish-orange design on the handle of each one that looked like an open human hand holding a flame. A sigil of power. "Why would the weerlords forbid themselves to enter?"

"It became a test to see if they had become human. As shapeshifters, they naively believed that taking on the shape of a human would allow them to adopt human talents. Yet after generations of shapeshifting, none are like us. None have been able to surrender their magic to become human."

Jarin's shaky voice revealed that he found no comfort in Sedric's tale. "You said one creature can come in here?"

"That would be a skinwalker, while it possesses a human body."

Jarin shivered visibly, though it was not terribly cold in the tunnel. The boy grew very quiet.

Traveling down the level passageway was much easier than anything they had done the previous day, allowing Collin to recover some of his strength. In fact, he felt so much better now, he wondered whether the magic of the tunnel held healing properties as well. With a new spring in his step and his head held high, he strode along.

They covered the three miles through the mountain in no time at all, and before Collin knew it, they were back among more pines, beneath a blue sky. With its view of majestic mountains, the high country reminded him of his homeland.

Sedric remained in the lead, walking with purpose. Mira, Collin, and Jarin lagged behind; the boy was especially slow, taking small steps, as though he needed another hour of sleep. Razor padded along happily, investigating every bug, animal, or bush beside their path.

The hermit walked energetically, suddenly announcing, "No time to waste when you're about a hero's business!"

Collin shook his head and muttered to Mira, "What a cock. Does he really think he can save the world?"

"This part of it, at least," said Mira. "Why? Do you envy him?"

"Hardly. Our mission will do more to save the kingdom and our own lands than his, hands down."

"Yet you wanted to go with him."

"I'll be glad to be rid of the geezer." Collin stopped and waited for Jarin to catch up. The boy was more than just sleepy; something was bothering him. "What's wrong, kid?"

Jarin shrugged but said nothing.

"The Wormgate wasn't too scary for you, was it?" Collin asked.

The boy shook his head. "I had a bad dream last night."

"About what?"

"Papa was in trouble."

Mira stepped up to the boy and put an arm around his shoulders. "What kind of trouble?"

"I don't want to talk about it."

"Telling us might help you feel better," said Mira.

"I doubt it."

Collin tousled Jarin's hair and tried to put on a smile. "Can't be that bad. It was only a dream, and dreams don't come true."

"Promise?"

Collin glanced at Mira and shrugged. "Sure."

The girl frowned.

Jarin took a deep breath. "There was mist all around me

and it was dark. I found Papa trapped under the roots of a tree . . . like he'd been sleeping for a long time and the roots grew around him. When I went to touch him, he opened his eyes and said he was going to enslave the consul."

"Who's the consul?" asked Collin.

"I don't know," said Jarin. "Papa had become bad—I could see it in his eyes and by the way he talked to me. I knew what he was thinking."

"Why would your papa be bad?"

"Because a skinwalker took control of him."

This bothered Collin, but he forced himself to laugh. "Your papa is too strong to be taken. That much I remember about him. Far too stubborn."

The boy thought on that and seemed to relax. "Yeah, he is, isn't he? All the people who came to the mill said he is stubborn as an old mule."

"That's the spirit," said Collin. "I told you dreams were nothing to worry about."

Mira, however, had worry written all over her face. After Jarin skipped ahead to catch up to his uncle, she leaned in close to Collin. "The word *consul* is mentioned in the Encoda," she said, "in reference to a powerful enemy who was chasing King Aidan and his cousin, Ambiorix, before they arrived on Kalor."

"So?" said Collin. "Can't be the same enemy. Not after so long."

"Maybe not, but don't you find it troubling that Jarin's dream spoke the same unfamiliar name?"

Collin didn't know what to say and for a long time he remained silent. What if the boy had been given a vision?

Collin had heard stories of special people sensitive to magic who had prophetic dreams, but he'd never believed them. Once, a man came to his village claiming to have seen a vision of a treasure hidden in the earth. People Collin had known his entire life, even wise folk who should have known better, became excited by the news and followed the man into the mountains, only to return three months later, starving and with a story to tell about being waylaid by trolls. The visionary man had run off at the first sign of trouble, never to be seen from again. No treasure was ever found.

"Best keep that to yourself," Collin said. "You never know what it might lead to."

"What if something *did* happen to Jarin's father?"

Collin almost repeated Sedric's words, *Then he deserved what he got*, but at the last second, he held his tongue. "Once we get the boy to safety and warn the baron, we can go back to the mill and see what happened." Collin chose not to say that it was probably too late to help the boy's father.

Mira gave him a resigned nod, but she was clearly troubled. Only when Sedric stopped and pointed west, beyond the end of the canyon, did she come out of her reverie.

Seeing what lay before them, they stopped in their tracks.

They had come to a precipice overlooking a magnificent vista of the western valleys. No cover of clouds obscured the view here; the air was clear, the sun bright and warm. Healthy trees and lush foliage colored the land marked by hills and streams and a patchwork of farmland far to the northwest.

"This is where we say goodbye, boys and girl," said Sedric. "Sorry . . . I know you're going to miss me, but you go that way"—he pointed to the right—"and I go this way." He pointed left. "Please no tears. I hate emotional farewells."

They had come to a crossroads, where the road split north and south, each path following the edge of the precipice. It was a comfortably wide road atop a natural jutting of the ground, as though the upper half of the north and south mountains had slid several paces to the east, exposing a natural highway.

"I want to go with you," Jarin told Sedric.

"We've already discussed it and there's no chance I'm babysitting you all the way to the Tree."

"But I didn't get a say in any of it."

"Even so . . ." Sedric looked curiously down the south road. "Huh? What's this?"

Razor stood alert, his ears perked up at a new noise. Distant, at first, a sound like the slow rumble of stones approaching. As it came closer, Collin recognized the rhythmic sound of marching feet. There must be thousands of . . .

"Soldiers," he said. "Coming this way."

"An army!" cried Jarin.

The marching sound crescendoed as colorful banners of the vanguard peaked over a rise.

"From the south?" said Sedric. "Impossible. The south road goes to a few mining towns only. There's no great civilization, no army that way." He took hold of Jarin and pulled him back. "Except perhaps . . . Can it be? Beyond the Sidewinder Sea?"

The banners were of varying colors, the tallest one red, attached to a wooden pole and topped with a gold eagle. Then the soldiers came into view. The front ranks were mounted on great horses with flowing manes, parading two abreast. Behind them marched foot soldiers clad in breastplates, helmets with grand plumes, and red capes, each man armed with short swords and long shields.

An entire legion! Not only was Collin amazed at how well equipped the soldiers were; he immediately recognized the discipline that years of training had given these men. They were no clan warriors pretending to be an army; these were professionals who made warfare a career.

"Come, Jarin," Mira prompted, standing beside a tree, as if it might hide her. At the sound of her command, the boy backed up, but he kept his wide-eyed gaze fixed on the approaching army.

At the front of the legion rode a middle-aged man whose helmet hung on the pommel of his saddle—the only man who dared sun his bald head in the mountain air. Unlike the others, who were strong and fit, he wasn't particularly imposing, but Collin knew a commander when he saw one. This man rode perfectly at ease, flanked by two captains sitting high in their saddles.

Directly behind the commander was a company of brutish-looking cavalrymen, each seemingly more sober than the next. They held spears aloft, almost as tall as lances, and kept a tight formation. If they rode to intimidate, they had succeeded.

Yet even these mounted soldiers were nothing compared to the three robed figures seated on donkeys, strange men who might have ridden from a land beyond all others. Their strangeness set them apart—men with tattooed faces and unnaturally yellow eyes, like those of wolves. Or of trolls. As they turned to look upon the four companions, their expressions were absent of emotion.

The rest of the legionaries, however, barely noticed them and might have vanished northward without a word had their bald commander not spotted Mira. Leaning over to one of his captains, he said something and pointed at her.

The captain and several guards pulled away from the column and drew near.

"You," he called to Mira. "What is your name?" The man's accent gave him a haughty air.

"Mira Kaul."

Collin saw Sedric tense up, but the hermit wasn't watching the captain. Instead, Sedric seemed to be having a staring contest with the three men on donkeys.

"General Krassus invites you to be his personal guest," said the captain.

Sedric leaned on his walking stick. Even though he was staring at the robed men, he spoke to the captain. "More likely to be his personal harlot. Who are you people? Why are you here?"

"A people more civilized apparently than *you*." The captain examined Sedric from head to foot with disdain, then turned back to Mira. "Your . . . *friends* . . . are invited as well."

Collin shook himself. "Yeah, who are you, anyway?"

"All your questions will be answered when we make camp," said the captain. "Come along. The general awaits."

The detachment of soldiers surrounded them.

Collin glanced left and right. "Do we have a choice?"

*

The name of the captain who had captured them—there was no other way to describe what the man had done—was Pontus. His title was prefect, and he was third-in-command of the legion. His comrade was named Lucian, a young cousin of Krassus and, as tribune, second-in-command. Collin hated both men, but if he'd been forced to choose a hunting partner, it would have been Lucian, who smiled as they traveled north, told jokes, and once offered Collin a swig of red wine from a skin he kept tied to the shaded side of his saddle.

Their niceties didn't fool Collin. Neither man was going to be his friend. Pontus leered at Mira when the general's gaze wandered elsewhere and Lucian's jokes turned off color.

Sedric seemed equally wary. After greeting the general, he took Jarin by the hand and drifted behind the commanders, where the legion quickly ignored them as "just an old man and a snotty little boy." That is, until Pontus spotted them and ordered one of the legionaries to keep an eye on the two. The hermit muttered something about staying clear of the robed men and then disappeared among the columns of heavy infantry.

Collin walked beside Lucian, struggling to keep up with the quick pace of the march, though he sometimes had to retreat to avoid being crushed between the tribune's warhorse and the side of the mountain.

Mira's situation worried him. Even though the general had given her a horse and a place to ride beside him at the front, she did not look pleased. Krassus talked with her about mundane things, such as the beautiful countryside and the cool mountain air, but her joyless expression told him she thought something sinister was behind the general's innocent small talk. What did he want with her?

As the day wore on, Collin gleaned details about the legion. Nearly six thousand strong—not including an almost-numberless herd of camp followers, servants, and slaves—the legion had come from the Republic of Jihenna, far to the south. General Krassus said more legionaries were on the way, but this expeditionary force, which included some of the finest soldiers in the republic, had arrived to establish a foothold in lands north of the Sidewinder Sea.

Collin had mixed feelings about the presence of the legion. It seemed incredibly fortunate that such an experienced military force had arrived at the precise hour weerlords and trolls were invading from the north. But the Jihenans appeared to pose their own threat. Would the general side with his fellow humans against the creatures of Kalor, thus defending them, or would he stand by and wait to see how things played out?

By late afternoon, the legion had descended the mountain road and began to enter the rugged foothills east of Guldheim Valley. A scout galloped up the road to report that a level area above the valley, deep within the hills, with good grass and abundant water, was a suitable campsite.

"An abandoned building, perhaps an old trading post, is the only sign of human habitation," said the scout. "The area is protected on three sides by steep hills and can be easily defended. A long, narrow canyon is the only path into the lower valley."

The general listened silently to the scout's report, never ordering the march to slow down. When the scout had finished, he asked, "Is the building sturdy enough for my bed?"

"I'm afraid not," said the scout. "Its roof is missing and its walls might collapse in a stiff breeze."

"A pity." Krassus turned and gave Mira a smile. "It seems I'll spend another restless night in my tent." He waved the scout off and then went back to conversing with her about the kinds of clothes she preferred to wear.

TWENTY-THREE

Jarin sat on a stool outside one of the many fine tents the commanders used to bathe in private. His hair was damp and combed, and he smelled like pretty flowers. New woolen clothes fit him well, but they itched around the collar and the sandals were stiff. He wondered if Razor would even recognize him now.

It was evening and he was hungry. Jarin watched people go busily about their tasks, wondering when he would get something to eat. The campsite was huge, yet orderly and clean. Always clean. Plainly dressed slaves, many of them women, bustled from tent to tent, serving the soldiers according to their various needs.

Two women carrying perfumes, oils, towels, and fresh clothes made their way to the tent where he sat. They were pretty, Jarin thought, though perhaps a bit too top-heavy for his tastes.

Inside the tent, he could hear Sedric complaining to one of the servants about having to undress. Candlelight from within revealed the silhouette of his uncle standing beside a tub. It was the same tub Jarin had complained about too, but it hadn't done any good.

"I don't want to take a bath!" Sedric bawled.

The women smiled at Jarin as they entered the tent. Upon their arrival, Sedric's voice caught for a moment and in a sweeter tone he said, "Well, maybe a quick scrubbing won't hurt."

The scent of food wafted over Jarin, and he stood and went to find its source. A short distance from the bathing tents, servants carrying huge steaming pots were setting up a chow line; other servants with wooden bowls hurried to queue up at the serving tables.

Jarin rushed over and got in line. A slave girl, no older than he, handed him a bowl and then pointed to one of the tables, where a big woman hovered over the pots with a ladle in her hand.

The woman eyed him as she dumped a pile of greasy mush into his bowl. It looked like something meant for the pigs at home.

"Where's the good stuff?" Jarin asked.

"Soldiers get the best food," said the woman. "Slaves eat this."

"I'm not a slave."

The woman chuckled. "Not yet."

Jarin wandered over to a spot where a group of boys sat eating with their hands. The boys devoured their mush as though dining on the finest meal in the world. Jarin sat next to them and stared at his bowl. He wanted to run away.

A boy with freckled cheeks bulging with food said, "It's

not so bad here when they trust you." He swallowed and sneered. "If you're lucky you'll get bought by Master Onwi himself. He likes to whip scrawny boys like you."

The other boys laughed at the comment but quickly grew quiet as a fat man holding a whip came close to them. The man wore what appeared to be a long linen shirt embroidered with gold designs, tied about the waist. Two toughs, carrying clubs banded with iron, followed him.

When the slavemaster's eyes drifted over to the boys, Jarin quickly averted his gaze and pretended to be interested in the ruins of an old building nearby.

The slavemaster grunted and seemed about to speak, but then a commotion over by the chow lines distracted him.

By the building, a figure stepped into the deep shadows of one of the walls. The man had big shoulders, thick arms, and a wide-brimmed hat commonly donned by farmers on the other side of the mountains.

"Papa?" Jarin jumped up, dropping his bowl and running to the building.

The man was gone. Jarin scanned the area desperately, made a loop around the building, walked inside, stumbled into two lovers kissing in a corner, and hurried back outside. Was he seeing things?

Next to the chow lines, Slavemaster Onwi spotted him. "You!" he shouted. "Come here!"

Jarin shook his head.

The slavemaster signaled the two toughs to retrieve the boy.

Jarin had no desire to be shackled as a slave made to serve a gross foreigner. So he ran.

Between tents, over cook fires, among sleeping soldiers, through a blacksmith's tent, knocking over a rack of armor.

"Why, you little . . . !" began the blacksmith, but Jarin was already gone.

He stumbled against another tent, tearing up a stake and ripping a hole in the canvas with his foot. A deep voice within cried out and tried to grab his ankle. Jarin darted back, found a different path, hurried as he raced haphazardly between the tents, deliberately trying to confuse his pursuers. At one point, he found himself ducking underneath soldiers in the midst of swordplay. Finally he spotted a team of horses and slipped in among them.

Tucked away beneath tall trees and between the animals' big bodies, Jarin found a good place to hide. The horses stirred a bit as a result of his intrusion, but they quickly went back to feeding.

Jarin was out of breath and could run no more. Peeking around the rump of a big roan, he saw that the slavemaster's toughs were nowhere in sight. But they could arrive at any moment. Trying to catch his breath, he stealthily made his way to the camp's southern border, where he'd seen Razor tied to a wagon. When he came up, the retriever yapped, his tail whipping back and forth ferociously.

With his knife, Jarin cut the rope. They wrestled playfully. "At least you're glad to see me."

But he'd come for more than just play. In the wagon he found his pack and a few other supplies. In another he found dried meats and fruit.

A guard nearby spotted him and shouted.

Jarin hopped off the wagon, scrambled over a berm surrounding the camp, and then ran for the trees, his hands full of pilfered supplies. "Come on, boy!" he called to Razor. "We're getting out of here!"

The dog ran at his side, tongue flapping in the air.

TWENTY-FOUR

Mira was a prisoner in all but name. Sure, General Krassus was all smiles, offering to give her anything she asked for, acting sweeter than a suitor at a town dance. But she knew what he wanted and it was only a matter of time before he would ask for it.

For now, he was content to lounge against big pillows at the head of a low table, swirling a goblet of wine, making light conversation with his other guests. Mira had been forced to sit next to him, so close their shoulders touched, but thus far he was behaving like a gentleman.

The same could not be said of Collin. The soldier had clearly drunk too much wine and his usually wary demeanor had vanished with the fourth goblet. Or was it his fifth? He laughed at Lucian's jokes, openly ogled one of the slave girls standing against the silk walls of the pavilion, and ate a mountain of food. At least he had the presence of mind to cover his mouth when he belched, but Mira was embarrassed for him. The captains, Tribune Lucian and Prefect Pontus, sometimes watched Collin with amused looks, though they were too occupied with their own entertainment—which included two women dressed in fine silks nibbling on the men's ears—to do more than observe.

Also at the table were the three tattooed men who had ridden silently all day on donkeys. They had traded their plain riding robes for fine, neck-high garments of muted colors, wrapping the tops of their heads in silks. Their presence worried Mira. Krassus had called them sangomas, naming them simply as the First, the Second, and the Third. All three sat crossed-legged at a table laden with fine dishes, but they ate very little. Their faces rarely betrayed emotion, save perhaps deference to General Krassus or disdain for everyone else.

The pavilion was huge and richly furnished, though much of it was partitioned with silk walls that provided only brief glimpses of elaborate furniture beyond, including a huge bed in one area and table and chairs in another. The Republic of Jihena must be a rich land indeed.

From the entrance, Sedric appeared, though Mira hardly recognized him. The hermit was clean now, with combed hair and a shaven face; he looked almost presentable.

"Sedric!" Mira was glad to see him.

The hermit winked, straightening his already perfect vest.

Krassus lifted his goblet. "Welcome, Sedric. Bathed and enlightened, I'm sure. Please join us."

Mira watched as Sedric caught the observant stares of the sangomas and purposefully sat away from them. A slave girl came forward and poured him some wine.

"Yes, well," mumbled Sedric. "I smell beautiful now, don't I?"

Collin was obviously excited to see the hermit and he spoke recklessly. "The general here has journeyed from across the southern sea—"

"From the Republic of Jihenna," explained Krassus.

"—to fight the weerlords' evil minions," Collin finished.

Sedric took a sip of wine, appeared to like the taste of it, and then downed the rest in two gulps. As he wiped his mouth with his sleeve, he said, "Is that so?"

The general chuckled. "Not exactly. I learned of these *weerlords* only two days ago, but I will fight them if they stand in my way."

Krassus nudged Mira for a response, but she gritted her teeth and concentrated on her grapes.

"Why come all this way?" asked Sedric.

Krassus grinned at the hermit. "Tame the land, expand the republic, gain fame, power—"

"Return and become emperor!" cried Lucian, slapping the tabletop.

The general gave his young cousin an appreciative nod. "The Senate has elected me as one of two consuls. And for most men that would be enough, but it's high time Jihena had an emperor."

Mira's pulse pounded in her neck as she remembered Jarin's nightmare. "Consul?"

"Doesn't have the same ring to it as *emperor*, does it?" Krassus said.

Sedric tore apart some flatbread and dipped it in a bowl of spiced olive oil. "The weerlords in these parts are rumored to be led by one who is very old and very powerful." As he ate, a little oil dripped down his chin. "A demon lord. He is said to be a mighty creature of magic. Are you sure you're powerful enough to face him?"

"Perhaps you should ask the sangomas that question," said Krassus.

"Sangomas?" asked Sedric.

Mira said hastily, "Sorcerers."

Sedric focused his gaze on the three men, who studied him quietly. "Ah," he said, reaching for a pomegranate and tearing it apart. "The kingdom here has its own magicians, but they're charlatans mostly. Humans. None have the power to withstand a high-order weerlord. Or a skinwalker . . . or whatever this demon lord is."

When Pontus spoke, his huge Adam's apple seemed to pop out of his neck. The prefect was more sober than the jovial Lucian and more apt to take offense. "I think you'll find the sangomas battle-hardened and tested," he said.

Collin was bobbing his head up and down in agreement. "They really do command a lot of power," he told Sedric. "You don't need to find the Tree now."

This appeared to irritate Sedric. "And how would you know?" Then he pointed at the sangomas. "Which rite of power is a lie?"

The First answered at once, "Every fourth one and the thirteenth. We know and are wary."

"What is the ichor of birth?"

"Water," said the Second.

"What's the best hour to summon the power for bloodshed?"

"Night," said the Third. "Before the rising moon."

Sedric lowered his finger and leaned against his cushions.

Krassus laughed. "The sangomas are not fakes. Their people paid the price of learning and nearly perished. But now they know."

Sedric shrugged. "So they've read the right books. Anybody can memorize, but can they hold the greatest rites in their minds when they scream madness?"

The Third steepled his fingers. "Have *you* gone mad?"

For several heartbeats nobody made a sound. Mira felt the hairs on the nape of her neck stand straight up. The Third's eyes changed color suddenly, from yellow to blue to green, and his pupils dilated before returning back to normal—if yellow could be called normal. Several of the tattoos visible on the side of his head transformed, changing shape. Mira couldn't breathe until she tore her gaze away from the man.

Sedric abruptly drank an entire goblet of wine. When he was done, he said, "You are three scary people and I wish you the best of luck." He stood. "But I must be off."

"You've hardly eaten a thing," said Collin, his mouth full of cake.

"I eat sparingly for the benefit of those who are starving."

The general's voice carried a hint of displeasure. "We have many questions to ask you, Sedric."

The hermit's smile lacked guile. "I apologize, but nature calls, as we say. I'll be right back."

"In that case, we will await your swift return," said Krassus.

Sedric left in a hurry, acting as if he could barely hold it in, but Mira knew he was pretending, knew she wouldn't see him again tonight. And perhaps not for many nights to come.

*

After Sedric's departure, Mira made an attempt to remain calm, pretending to enjoy the company of foreigners who found her to be nothing but eye candy. She was used to such attitudes, but between Lucian's teasing laughter and Pontus's lustful stares, she was becoming more uncomfortable by the minute. Collin seemed blind to her plight, all but ignoring her. In fact, he now appeared ill, sitting back and refusing all offers of food and drink.

Mira could not look directly at the general when he addressed her. She was afraid she might see something in his eyes she wouldn't like, afraid he might stare at her as Pontus did.

Out of nervousness, or perhaps to prevent his meaningless conversation from going down a dangerous path, she said to him, "General, your arrival could not have come at a better time for us. I can't help thinking of something written in the Encoda—"

Krassus raised a questioning eyebrow at the First Sangoma. "Encoda?"

"Codexes," the sorcerer explained. "Local book of prophecies."

"Ah," said Krassus, turning back to Mira. "Go on."

"I wonder about a prophecy concerning all the human tribes that awoke upon the four corners of the world. It says that when they meet, a terrible event would decide the fate of humanity. Most here in the north are of a group who followed King Aidan or those which make up Collin's clans. My people are a third group. And the Jihenans are of a fourth. Perhaps the fifth and sixth—"

"Such ideas are not new," said Krassus. "Another group belongs to the sangomas's people, and I've heard of wild people on the other side of the world who forsook the pleasures of a civilized life and became cannibals, or so say explorers. There are many groups.

"Yes," he went on, holding up his cup as a slave girl poured more wine. "We have similar prophecies, though we believe they foretell the might of Jihena gathering all of Kalor together under one rule. The event is only terrible in its mightiness and glory. The glory of Jihena." Krassus watched her over the top of his cup before taking a sip.

Mira allowed the challenge to rise in her. "Humans were put here to keep Kalor's tyrants in check, not seize the world from them. There must be balance. There must be harmony."

"There may have been harmony on Earth, but Kalor has always been against us." Krassus's tone was unwavering. "We must ensure our survival."

"I cannot believe that the world—or its creatures—will stand aside and let it happen," said Mira.

Her heart rose then sank as a messenger entered the pavilion and approached the general. She'd been hoping to see Sedric again. Lucian and Pontus looked up with interest.

Krassus added one more thought before turning his attention to the messenger. "We refuse to become like the people who went wild. There is no harmony in that, Mira. No survival."

The messenger spoke into the general's ear, but Mira was close enough to hear: "Our scouts have returned."

Krassus rose from the pillows. "It seems I will soon have more news of Guldheim." He took Mira's hand and kissed it gently. "Please excuse me. Indulge yourself as long as you like. I look forward to your visit later on."

Pontus and Lucian began to rise, but the general shook his head and departed with no one but the First Sangoma and a single guardsman.

Mira caught Collin staring at her. His mouth was agape . . . and covered in a sheen of grease; wine stains adorned his shirt.

She barely noticed. The general's final words to her—said so casually and decisively, from a man accustomed to being obeyed without question—were like a hot brand waved across her cheek, threatening to burn. Collin had clearly heard it too.

Mira was the general's plaything.

Pontus, buried in the pillows with his mistress, poked his head up for a breather.

"Say, Lucian, what happened to that grumpy old troglodyte?"

"*Nature* must be calling him to the grave by now!"

Their laughter served only to unsettle her more.

TWENTY-FIVE

Sedric hiked south beside a shallow stream, fast and sure. With a sky devoid of clouds, a gibbous moon illuminated the hills around him, making his path easy to follow. He was sure an alarm had sounded at camp, but he hoped the general was too preoccupied to order a concerted chase though an unknown country at night.

These hills directly east of Guldheim were familiar to Sedric, so often had he crossed the mountains in his younger days to explore new lands of adventure. In fact, this gully gave rise to memories of a pretty baroness who had flirted with him until her husband had become suspicious and chased Sedric all the way to the headwaters of the Vonspryer River.

He rounded a bend, climbed out of the streambed, took three steps, and stopped. There were fresh tracks in the dirt.

"I don't believe it," he said under his breath.

Following the tracks, he marched up to a bush near the bank of the stream.

"Come out, you little weasel."

Not a sound, not even of breathing. Sedric was actually impressed. But the silence didn't last long. He heard the whine of a muzzled dog.

"I know you're there," he said in a firm voice. "And if you don't show your face in two heartbeats, I'll—"

"Uncle Sedric? Is that you?"

Razor bounded out of the bushes and jumped excitedly against Sedric's chest.

"Jarin, come out before that prickle bush gets the better of you."

The boy emerged, his hair and face covered in dirt. Hadn't he taken a bath just two hours ago?

"I thought you were a weerlord," Jarin said, obviously relieved to see his uncle's face.

Sedric wasn't happy to see the boy. "What are you doing out here? If Mira found out that you'd run away—"

"I saw Papa."

"Nonsense."

"At least I thought I did."

"Is anybody else with you?"

"Only Razor." Jarin's face brightened. "We're going to be heroes like you."

"You're going to be dead."

Sedric took off, following an incline that went south, angling away from the stream. Jarin followed close behind.

"We're coming with you," said the boy.

"I know," said Sedric.

"You don't have a choice."

"I know."

Sedric made his way up a low hill and then back down the other side, where tall beech trees blocked most of the moonlight. Little had changed since he'd last walked beneath these limbs, save perhaps that the trees had grown taller. The pile of decaying leaves underfoot was soft and spongy, and the scent of fresh loam permeated the air. The ground was relatively flat as he followed an unseen path, which eventually went through a split between two boulders that looked as if a single great stone had been fractured by the stroke of a hammer.

As Sedric walked briskly through the grove, he heard Jarin struggling to keep up. To his credit, the boy didn't complain.

Rounding a corner, Sedric almost crashed into the trunk of a huge tree that had fallen in his way. This was a new obstacle and it stymied him for a second, made him stop to regain his bearings. Where was it?

Then he knew. It was right at his feet. The old tree itself had come crashing down, probably in a fierce thunderstorm.

Unable to see well enough in the dark, Sedric felt along the length of the fallen beech with his hands, searching.

"What are you looking for?" asked Jarin.

"Nothing you need worry about."

"Is this the big World Tree?"

"No."

"Razor can find anything if you ask him."

"He can't find this."

"Do you need a light?"

Sedric turned to the boy. "Do you have one?"

"Sure," said Jarin. "A lamp was with the supplies I stole."

"You shouldn't steal."

"Well, do you want it or not?"

"I'll take it."

Jarin dug out a small brass lamp with a single curved handle. The reservoir of oil inside was full. He then produced flint and steel, but Sedric grew impatient and snatched up the lamp. With a hushed word and a snap of his fingers, he lit it.

"Whoa!" Jarin's astonished face was bathed in the lamp's light. "Was that a magic spell?"

"A simple trick."

"Will you show me how to do it?"

"Not tonight." Sedric nudged the boy aside. "Now move out of my way."

Using the light of the lamp, he studied the bark carefully, searching for an ancient carving. He worried that it might be on the side lying on the ground, but this was a big tree, with an enormous trunk, and there was a lot of surface to examine.

Jarin crawled on his hands and knees. "Is this what you're looking for?"

Sedric crouched low and brought the lamplight close to the boy's pointed finger. A carving lay there in the smooth bark, of a symbol depicting two sets of lips engaged in a kiss. It brought back memories, a surge of emotions he thought were buried for good.

"No," he said. "That's not it. But now that you've found that one, I know where the other one is."

"It looks like two people kissing," Jarin said. "Who do you think put it there?"

"Two people in love."

Sedric walked around the fallen tree to the opposite side.

Sure enough, the intricate design of a man with an open mouth stared at him. Although the etching was much older than the lovers' mark on the other side, it had existed for as long as anyone could remember, never losing its intricate detail as the tree had grown tall and wide.

With his knife, he began to dig into the tree, beginning at the center of the open mouth. It didn't take long to ruin a carving that had stood there for centuries, but Sedric had a hunch it was only a marker to hide something grand.

Razor poked his nose into the hole he was making, snorted once, and then wandered off to investigate something else. Jarin, however, knelt beside the tree and watched him work.

"If you're going to sit so close," Sedric said, "at least hold the light up for me."

Jarin obediently took the lamp. "What are you doing?"

"Following my gut instinct."

"Huh?"

"Just wait and see."

"Do you need a better knife?"

"This one will do."

Jarin nevertheless produced a fat-bladed knife used by hunters to clean big game, though youngsters who liked to fight with knives sometimes also wore it. Sedric's own worn blade looked puny in comparison.

"Give it to me," Sedric said.

Jarin eagerly handed him the big knife and Sedric began to dig into the trunk with ease.

"Do you know why it's called a Hawkie?" Sedric said.

Jarin nodded vigorously. "It's like the one used by Hawkie Trollhunter to kill a hundred trolls at the same time!"

"More likely it was only two or three sleepers stranded out in the daylight. Trolls are easier to kill after baking in the sun's heat."

"Papa killed two when he rescued Collin, and it was raining then."

"Your papa is a tough ol' bird. He owned one of these knives as a kid."

Jarin was silent for a time. "I miss him."

"Of course you do. That's why you thought he was at camp."

"It sure looked like him."

Coaxed by Sedric's strength and Jarin's big knife, a large splinter of wood popped out, revealing a metallic object buried beneath it. With a little more chopping and digging, the object came free—a cylinder twice the size and length of his thumb. It looked like a very fat nail or a stake.

Held in the lamplight, the cylinder showed a thin line around the middle. Sedric gave it a twist and managed to unscrew it. A roundish bead, slightly larger than a pea yet shaped like an acorn, rolled into his hand. Squiggly green lines ran around the top of its circumference, and it was warm to the touch.

"What's that?" Jarin asked.

Sedric had been expecting something like a map or a magic spell that would provide additional clues to his journey. He hadn't expected something so . . . wondrous.

"It's a seed," he said.

"What kind of seed?"

"A seed from the World Tree."

TWENTY-SIX

Mira could hardly wait for the feast to end, but afterwards she wasn't free to go as she pleased. Instead, she was ushered to a smaller tent, where slave girls brushed her hair and decorated her face. The girls seemed overjoyed as they went about their tasks, singing songs or giggling quietly. Yet a sadness lay beneath it all. Their interaction gave Mira the impression that she had been offered a special opportunity they would never want for themselves. And, as if to confirm her suspicion, they insisted she sip on sweet wine, to sooth her nerves.

Collin was waiting outside when she emerged from the tent, and he fell in step with her as she made her way back to the pavilion. A tall soldier strode behind them, supposedly as her guard, but she knew he was also her minder.

"You're not actually thinking of entertaining him tonight, are you?" said Collin.

"Where's Jarin?" said Mira. "I haven't seen him all night."

Collin put on a brave smile, as if to tease. "You're scared."

"You're jealous."

The soldier chuckled.

"Would you quit saying that," Collin said. "I don't walk around feeling jealous."

"Could have fooled me."

When they reached the general's pavilion, Collin gently took her arm and forced her to face him. "Why are you doing this?"

Mira kept her voice low. "Krassus is the one with the power to make decisions right now—to save our people." She placed a hand on Collin's cheek. "Don't worry. I'll be careful."

She didn't wait for his rebuttal, choosing instead to break his hold and enter the pavilion.

Behind her, she heard the soldier say, "Smart girl."

Collin's sigh came next. "I'm not so sure."

Mira looked around the lavishly decorated tent, but only a lone slave girl was here to greet her, and unlike the girls who had dressed her earlier, this one timidly avoided her gaze.

"I'm afraid the general will not be able to meet with you tonight," said the girl.

Mira felt a wave of relief, which quickly turned into concern. Had she offended him?

"Why?" she asked the girl. "Am I now in disfavor?"

"He is discussing important matters with his commanders."

Mira heard voices coming from a cordoned-off area of the back and, despite the girl's protests, went to the divider and entered a large partition. Krassus did not immediately see her. He stood with his two captains, the sangomas, and several centurions around a table, upon which rested a canvas map.

Two of the men were dressed in camouflage, and by the

appearance of their soiled boots and clothing, they had recently returned from a scouting trip. Only the sorcerers turned to Mira as she entered.

Krassus was speaking to the scouts, "The valley below us?"

The shortest of the two scouts replied, "A fertile land full of overtaxed farmers. It can be defended easily from the narrow north passage, but this Baron of Guldheim must be a fool, because he keeps the bulk of his forces inside the castle walls, where they must do nothing but pick their noses."

"Can the few soldiers he sent north hold the passage?" Krassus asked.

"Only if this demon lord sends old women against them. Even at that, the baron cannot defend against sorcery. He has one scrawny magician who knows a few card tricks, nothing more."

Lucian chuckled while the others grinned. "I take it you didn't see old women marching with the demon lord."

"Hardly," said the scout. "Implings and northern satyrs, which the barbarians call trolls, make up the bulk of the army marching toward the passage. But giants march as well. It's surprisingly well organized. They're led by human-like creatures that punish with sorcery."

"Weerlords," Mira said without thinking. The men looked at her.

Upon seeing her, Krassus's face softened. "I'm sorry, Mira, but our visit must wait for another night. Get some rest for an early morning's march."

Mira turned to leave, but the First Sangoma stopped her with a question. "These *weerlords*," he said sonorously. "Are they indeed human?"

"Sedric said they are natives of Kalor," Mira replied. "Shapeshifters. Their faces are more human than their bodies, which are covered in glowing spells."

The Second exchanged a knowing look with the Third Sangoma. "Intulo."

"Though perhaps more advanced than the Intulo tribe," said the Third. "Transformed to appear more humanlike."

Krassus looked to the scouts for an explanation. The short one, who had done all the talking, shook his head. The other scout shrugged. "I couldn't get close enough to tell. The whole army travels under the cover of clouds, which darkens the land."

The general then asked the First Sangoma, "Do you think they pose a serious threat?"

The First was a proud man, usually speaking with his head held high, as though everyone were beneath him. But when the general addressed him, he lowered his gaze out of respect. "In Jihena, our people exterminated the Intulo two hundred years ago," he said.

"Yet we look forward to battle," added the Second, a hint of fierceness in his tone.

"Excellent," said Krassus.

Mira watched them conduct their war council for a while longer. They were hardened professionals itching for a fight. Most had turned back to the map, ignoring her, but after a moment Lucian looked up and winked.

Pontus saw the wink and scowled.

"It will be a hard march," Krassus said to the men. "If luck prevails, the baron's knights will hold the north passage long enough for our arrival. If not, I have a secondary plan to rid ourselves of this demon lord . . ."

As Mira left, the general's voice faded away behind her.

TWENTY-SEVEN

Collin's belly had never been so full, but as he strolled through the camp, he couldn't stop eating.

He'd managed to secure a delicious orange fruit, sweeter and juicier than anything he'd ever tasted. Much of the food the legion had brought was strange, or too spicy, and required care when eaten, but this fruit was a true delight.

As he ate the orange, trying not to get too much of the sticky juice on his face, he passed a handful of shirtless legionaries sparring with wooden swords and shields. Collin hardly paid attention to them until one of them called out.

"Barbarian!"

Collin turned in time to catch a wooden sword thrown at him. To his dismay, he dropped his remaining wedge of fruit in the dirt.

Several of the men laughed, but the apparent ringleader, a muscular soldier with dark eyes and a grin marred by a chipped tooth, taunted him.

"I hear you boys know how to play with a blade, barbarian."

"We do more than play," said Collin, testing the weight of the wooden sword. "What's this? A child's toy?"

A legionary standing behind the ringleader raised his brow in surprise. "This barbarian fool would duel an ally with cold steel," he said. "What say you, Sergius? Will you answer the challenge?"

The ringleader's face clouded over. "This isn't a challenge," he said to Collin. "Only a show of skill for sport."

"Fine, then," said Collin. "I'll slap you around with a wooden stick."

Sergius narrowed his eyes, but his companions enjoyed the jab, laughing and making halfhearted bets with each other. One soldier tossed Collin a round, wooden shield. It was lightweight and intended for practice only.

He and Sergius faced off, circling each other in the torchlight.

His opponent was quick to strike, using both his sword and the edge of his shield as a weapon, but Collin fended off the attack. He'd trained with the best warrior of his clan, an old man nicknamed Crackskull Knut, who had never been bested in battle, even in advanced age.

They sparred for a moment longer, until an opening presented itself and Collin managed to slap Sergius on each cheek.

"My grandmother taught me that move," Collin taunted.

Sergius's cheek turned red from the sting. "It appears sticks are the weapon of choice among barbarians," he said.

Collin made a mock bow. "I think I enjoy this sport."

Sergius growled, tossed his wooden sword away, and then fetched a fine short sword called a gladius. Frowning, he took another gladius from a comrade and threw it at Collin's feet.

"Sergius, what are you doing?" asked one of the legionaries.

"We test your true skill now," Sergius told Collin.

"Careful," warned another. "The barbarian is a scrappy opponent."

Sergius brushed off the warning and rushed Collin at once, pressing the attack with three fast strikes, chopping hard and cracking his shield.

Their fight was serious now. As a trained professional, Sergius was clearly a better fighter, but Collin had always been fast on his feet, dodging several deadly blows and even parrying a swing that would have split his belly wide open. Sweat began to collect on his forehead, stinging the wound above his eye.

He had two options: yield or try something desperate.

Crackskull Knut, a traveler in his youth, had taught Collin how to forego all weaponry and fight with nothing but his hands and feet. It was a style of combat few could master, because it involved long hours of practice. More like dancing than fighting, Collin had mastered it because he enjoyed showing off in front of the village girls.

He dropped both his sword and shield and crouched low, ready for Sergius's next attack.

"Do you yield?" Sergius asked. In that moment, Collin knew that the centurion was not familiar with this style of hand-to-hand combat.

"Of course not," said Collin. "My sword was getting in the way."

The onlookers appeared confused, and one even called the

fight unfair. Sergius ignored the outcry and charged so reck-lessly he left himself wide open.

Collin ducked low as Sergius's gladius whooshed above his head. He was now in a squatting position. As his opponent took a step closer, he spun, sweeping with an outstretched leg and tripping the centurion.

Sergius rolled upon the ground, quickly coming back to his feet, but Collin was upon him, kicking and jabbing. In no time at all, he managed to seize the centurion's sword arm, twist him around, and punch him in the head.

Sergius dropped into a heap, disarmed now and shaking his head in a daze. He looked at Collin, fury in his eyes, seeming ready to do something stupid, such as lunging for Collin's legs.

One of the onlookers said, "The barbarian has beaten you, Sergius. He deserves the honor of winning a fair fight."

Sergius gave Collin a long look of appraisal. Then he relaxed.

The centurion grinned broadly, his chipped tooth now colored with a bit of fresh blood. "I hope you're with us in battle."

Collin was all smiles as his new comrades congratulated him. Several of them demanded that he teach them his winning move.

It was all fun and games until Mira called out for him. "Collin!"

He feared the worst. "Are you all right?"

She was on the verge of tears. Her single guard followed her at a brisk pace.

"Jarin's gone." Mira was gasping. "I can't find him anywhere."

"I know," said Collin. "A slavemaster told me the boy ran off."

"A slavemaster? Is that who Sedric handed him to?" Mira ran her painted fingernails through newly curled hair. "No wonder he ran. He probably thinks we abandoned him."

Mira had never looked so beautiful, though the thick designs around her eyes seemed a bit much. He stepped close and tried to comfort her by taking her by the waist, but she stepped back.

"Help me look for him," she said.

"I don't think they'll allow that."

Mira's face became angry and she turned to confront her guard. Collin grabbed her by the shoulders.

"Mira, don't worry," he said. "Razor's rope was cut. The dog's gone too."

"So?"

"And Sedric escaped. He must have taken the boy with him."

A single tear ran down her cheek. "Are you sure?"

"I heard some of the guards talking about two slaves, an old man and a boy, who escaped across the perimeter. It must be them."

"If you're wrong, so help me . . ."

Collin hugged her as she buried her head in his chest.

Her guard tried to step between them, to split them up. But Sergius called out to the man.

"The barbarian's all right," he told the guard. "Say, Brutus, why don't you show us a few of those fancy moves I heard about?"

Brutus puffed out his chest and strode over to Sergius, leaving Mira and Collin standing alone together.

TWENTY-EIGHT

"What's so special about the seed?" asked Jarin.

"All seeds are special," said Sedric. "Magnificent trees grow from them."

Sedric turned away from him and spread blankets across the ground. The dying coals from a campfire showed little of their makeshift camp, but Jarin felt safe beneath the boughs of the beech trees.

"Can I hold the seed again?"

"You've manhandled it enough already," said Sedric. "Now get your bed ready and go to sleep."

"It felt warm in my hands."

"I know."

"Is it magic?"

"All seeds are magic."

"And special," said Jarin. "You said that already."

"I get what you mean and the answer is yes. The World Tree is itself a growth of magic, and so are its seeds."

"I wonder who put that seed in there." Jarin hoped his

question didn't sound like a question, because his uncle had said he asked too many.

"The wizard, Nolath, put it there," said Sedric. "It's the only explanation that makes sense. He probably brought it back after finding the Tree."

"Yeah," Jarin mused. "He probably wanted to hide it for a rainy day, kind of like Papa hiding his rum."

Sedric lay down and pulled the blankets over him. "That's not a bad guess, but it still doesn't explain everything. Why go to the trouble of carving out the face of a screaming man, or whatever it was?"

"He looked like he was singing."

"Perhaps."

"That seed might give you powerful spells." Jarin was guessing, but maybe it would draw out his uncle's storytelling.

"Hmm," said Sedric. "At best, its magic will guide me to the Tree. I think that's why Nolath left it there. As a sign-post."

"Will we find other seeds along the way?"

"I doubt it. Such seeds are too valuable to toss around like breadcrumbs. You don't go to the trouble of gathering a bag-ful of rare seeds just so you can bury them in trees around the countryside. Only one will do."

"I wish I had one."

"It's said there are others, called Earth Seeds," said Sedric. "They were carried by chosen people from our home world, in remembrance of the weak magic of Earth."

"But humans don't have magic."

"Not in a powerful way. There were isolated pockets on Earth that held special seeds, and thus magic." Sedric clasped his hands behind his head, gazing though the branches. "One story passed down from the days of Earth tells of the Tree of Life, which had a delicious fruit that bestowed great rewards upon those who ate it."

"Do you think one of those Earth Seeds came here?"

"I've often wondered about that, but I really don't know. You could say that Kalor is just like Earth, except that one of its seeds grew into a tree so divine it was able to cast its vast power over the whole face of the world. Some say that Kalor was a garden, shaped and tended by the Creators until something bad happened and they had to leave. The magical creatures here didn't know how to control their newfound freedom and almost destroyed each other. The lifeless Plains of Maran are thought to be an ancient battleground from that era. The Creators may have departed for a time, only to come back to find their garden in ruins. So before they abandoned Kalor for good, they brought humans here to provide a balance."

Jarin liked the idea of humans being special. "So smart people held onto a few magical seeds from Earth, to remind them of home?"

"Now you're paying attention. That's a good boy."

Jarin unrolled his blankets and lay quietly between them for a time, feeling the warmth of Razor's body against his, listening to Sedric breathe. His uncle hadn't closed his eyes yet.

"Uncle Sedric?"

"Hmm?"

"Will General Krassus kill Mira?"

"Yes."

"You're teasing again. Right?"

"Then don't ask dumb questions. Go to sleep."

"Have you ever been in love?"

Sedric turned his head and gave Jarin a direct stare. "What?"

"I think you once liked a girl."

"Of course I did."

"What happened to her?"

"You ask too many questions."

"Well?"

Sedric sighed. "There was more than one. But the one that hurts the most married your father. Constance chose Shem because he had money and all I had were books and promises. At least that's what I told myself at the time, but your mother made the right choice. I was a young fool chasing after magical shortcuts."

"I didn't know that."

"Well, now you do."

Jarin had another question, but he waited for Sedric to cool down before asking it. "Why do creatures like weerlords and skinwalkers hate us so much?"

"Because we don't belong here."

"Yenis don't hate us."

"Aren't you sleepy yet?"

"Too much has happened."

"I don't know about yenis, but skinwalkers fear we might learn magic and eventually grow to be more powerful than they. Weerlords envy us and want to become human. As I told you, some were even accepted into King Aidan's court for a season, where they taught curious men the roots of magic."

"Then why do they hate us now?"

"Their shapeshifting ability made them humanlike, but not human. They are ugly and putrid. Aidan's dying command was to banish them from the kingdom."

"Ugly and putrid? I think the king would banish you, then." Jarin snickered into his blankets.

"Oh, great," said Sedric. "I'm traveling with a comedian."

TWENTY-NINE

Mira stirred as hands shook her. It was all she could do to peel her face from the soft pile of skins and open her eyes to the light of day. Why was she so weak?

"I've never seen a woman sleep through such a racket," said Collin, standing over her. "Wake up, Mira. The cavalry left hours ago."

"Huh?"

"They must have put something in your wine. I hardly slept a wink."

As Mira sat up, a wave of dizziness kept her from rising. She put her head in her hands and waited for the spinning world to right itself.

Collin began stuffing things into her pack. "Our hosts will be here any minute," he said. "You might want to make yourself presentable."

He threw her a puffy white shirt provided by the general's slave girls. It was supposed to be plain garment meant for a noblewoman going out for a ride, but it was finer than any-thing Shem had bought her.

"You mean our captors," said Mira.

"Hardly." Collin sounded cheerful. Did he actually like the Jihenans now? Only yesterday he was warning her about Krassus's overtures. "They're going to let me fight with them!" He showed her the shiny gladius hanging at his hip.

Mira was none too excited as she said, "I'm happy for you."

The racket turned out to be servants packing up, wagons rolling away, and the march of the foot soldiers. She barely had time to get dressed before a group of men ushered her out and took down her tent.

At least she hadn't slept in the general's pavilion.

The legion of Jihena moved fast. A long column of soldiers snaked its way into a cleft in the western hills, which, accord-ing to the map she'd seen in the general's pavilion, would eventually take them to Guldheim Valley. At its current pace, the legion might enter the valley before nightfall. Mira and Collin joined the column on foot, hurrying to keep up, but Lucian spotted them and ordered them to mount up.

"Can't have you slowing us down," he said. Lucian was a dashing man when attired for war, a captain quick to smile and give compliments. No doubt he had charmed more than one woman's heart.

As she stared at the tribune, she caught Collin watching her out of the corner of his eye. Thankfully, he remained quiet.

Mira was glad for the mount, grabbing the reins and wait-ing for Collin to take a seat behind her. The clansman seemed a bit put out about the arrangement, but he didn't complain.

They rode up behind the sangomas's donkeys, which were positioned near the front of the legion.

"Mira," Collin said after a stretch of silence. "What does Shem look like?"

"Don't you know? He saved you?"

"I was a little . . . out of it at the time. I mostly recall how he acted towards me, how he insulted me, not the shape of his nose or the color of his hair."

"Shem looks a lot like Sedric, except that his hair isn't gray. He's also bigger and grumpier than his older brother, which means he never smiles. Why do you ask?"

"I could have sworn I saw a man this morning who could have been his twin."

"Don't be silly. Shem would never allow himself to become a slave."

Collin went quiet for a minute. "I guess that makes sense."

The cleft through the hills turned out to be the entrance of a narrow canyon winding out of the foothills, deep enough to shade them for most of the morning. A tight footpath running along a stream forced the legion to march single file, but after a mile the canyon opened up and permitted them to go three or four abreast.

They passed wooden dugouts cut into the side of the canyon walls, but the locals appeared to have fled, for none were seen peeping out of the narrow doorways. Mira spotted legionaries stationed at various waypoints along the way, posted as lookouts among the cliffs and trees. How many of the locals had managed to escape Krassus's men before being snatched up as slaves?

By midafternoon, the sloping trail leveled off and turned

south for about two miles, slowing their progress. Mira heard Pontus say to the general, "We won't make it to the valley before nightfall."

Krassus merely nodded and glanced back at the sorcerers with a smirk.

"Perfect," said the Third Sangoma.

"Aye," said the Second. "It will be a fine battle."

Mira was left wondering what kind of scheme Krassus had concocted with the sorcerers that would give them joy in nighttime combat.

As the day waned, their path turned westward again. The canyon was rapidly engulfed in a dark cover of clouds similar to the storm in the west, with chilled air and a sprinkling of rain. The sangomas stared at the sky for a long time, as if sniffing an odd scent, then nodded at each other.

Krassus called a halt so the legion could rest. Collin and Mira dismounted, glad to stretch their legs. Servants carrying huge bags walked down the column, handing out sweetbread and wine. The soldiers ate in silence, their faces lacking concern. Mira had no appetite, but Collin devoured the small meal with big bites.

"You ate enough last night to feed this whole army," she told him. "How could you possibly be hungry now?"

Collin shrugged. "It's a new day and I'll need my strength when I fight." Then he lowered his eyes sheepishly. "Besides, I threw most of it up before going to bed."

Several of the legionaries heard him and laughed.

Before long, Mira was back on her mount. When Collin moved to join her, Pontus ordered him to march at the front of the legionaries, directly behind the standard of the eagle.

"It's almost time," said the prefect.

Collin began stretching his arms and legs and neck, breathing in and out dramatically. Mira thought he was either making a poor attempt at showing off in front of his fellow legionaries or he was trying to drum up the courage to face a deadly foe.

Pontus looked on critically, shaking his head. When the legion set off again, marching in double time, he warned the warrior to keep up or be punished.

The canyon widened to a width of about fifty paces, but the soldiers stayed in two columns, each one following a captain. A mere ten minutes later, the legion encountered two torch-bearing scouts who quickly fell in with the legion, jogging beside General Krassus.

"The baron's men are braver than I thought," reported one scout. "But they have lost the pass. Now they battle for their lives in the center of the valley, across from where this canyon opens up."

The second scout added, "We've found high places overlooking the valley for you and the sangomas."

"Excellent news," said Krassus. He then addressed his captains. "You two know what to do."

Pontus and Lucian took the legion and two sangomas farther down the canyon, following one of the scouts. Krassus and the First Sangoma veered left with a handful of guards, chasing the other scout.

"Come with me, Mira," said Krassus.

Collin had been doing a good job keeping up with the legionaries, but when Mira moved away from him, he asked, "What's going on?"

Mira called to him, "Be careful, Collin! Don't get yourself killed!"

Collin moved quickly away from her, hurrying after the flame of the other scout's torch. Above the sound of stomping feet, she heard Lucian laugh. "I'm sure he was planning on it."

Krassus's scout took them up a narrow footpath cut into the southern side of the canyon. It was barely more than a game trail, but many such paths existed in these hills and were used by local prospectors panning for gold—a treasure found in abundance by those persistent enough to look. Their small party soon left the canyon and entered the easier slopes of the surrounding hills, heading west.

After a short distance they halted.

What Mira saw almost took her breath away. They had come to the top of a flat ridge overlooking Guldheim, a narrow valley that ran north to south. Colorful lights and orange flames illuminated pockets of the valley where a huge battle waged. Despite her high vantage point, the roar of battle reverberated up to them—of men shouting, monsters screaming, people dying.

Difficult as it was to discern the movement of troops, Mira knew the battle was not going well for the people of Guldheim. Humanlike weerlords cast great fireballs or discharged entangling webs of silver at the clusters of warriors arrayed against them. Each flash of light revealed more of the carnage.

Krassus dismounted and stalked up to the edge of the overlook, which dropped off steeply into the valley. "Talk to me," he said.

The scout pointed at a hill across from them. "The baron's men are making a stand on that rise. They are led by a minor lord named Sir Garon and a company of loyal knights. The court magician is with them, but his paltry spells are useless. They seem to be hoping for rescue from the castle."

To the south, the castle's torches showed numerous soldiers on the walls, watching a battle that had not yet reached them.

"Will rescue come?" asked Krassus.

"Unlikely. The baron has shown little stomach for battle thus far."

The First Sangoma looked searchingly at the hill. "He abandons brave men who refuse to retreat so that the last of his serfs can escape into the castle."

"You can see them?" asked Krassus.

"I see." The sorcerer's eyes brightened with an eerie blue light. "The Intulo—these *weerlords*—crave to be human, yet they mock Earth's true essence. They must be slain!" He faced the general. "My brothers are ready."

"Show this demon lord the power of Jihena."

"I will light the way."

Extending his arms and crying out, the sorcerer sent a chain of magical flares above the battlefield, one after the other, in rapid succession. In the north, the other sangomas, each standing on bluffs overlooking the valley, about a half-mile apart, answered with spells of their own—of white or yellow fire, which descended upon the enemy. Weerlords that had been punishing the knights on the hillside were suddenly engulfed in flames, and the ground around them exploded. Their molten wounds brightened with an intense light, as if a furnace within their bodies had been stoked with oil, and they became searing rods of fire. Some trolls fled the blinding flames, while others went into a frenzy and attacked their comrades.

Weerlords that had not been struck turned and responded with fires of their own, but the sangomas deflected these counterattack with waves of energy that turned the spells in midair, causing them to dissipate into cascades of harmless sparks.

Below, to Mira's right, the stream flowed west from the mouth of the canyon until it came to the base of the hill. There it curved south beside an orchard butted against the southern slopes of the hill, winding its way through farmland east of the castle. Much of the orchard was in flames.

Mira was horror-struck. Despite the sangoma's efforts to stop them, the enemy surged against the men on the hill. Sir Garon's knights were trapped on an island in the middle of a vicious swarm that sought to drive them into the raging fires of the orchard.

Krassus watched on with unblinking calm.

THIRTY

Collin was convinced he had run straight into an inferno. Fire rained down from above, scorching unsuspecting imps and trolls, while nearby explosions torched a weerlord and a pair of giant bergrisi. And as if that wasn't enough, a huge fire promised more ruin from the southwest. It was all he could do to keep his eyes focused on Prefect Pontus.

Behind him, two columns of legionaries funneled out of the canyon, one column splitting left across the stream to follow Lucian, the other with Pontus.

There was movement on a hill to the west, but despite the fires, Collin saw the enemy only when brighter flames passed overhead or when a nearby explosion revealed a swath of destruction. The sea of monsters seemed endless.

A bright light flared, revealing a knot of heavily armored soldiers on top of the hill, each man fighting heroically for his life. The baron's knights.

Collin swallowed nervously and wiped his damp forehead. "Merciful Creators," he said, "help me survive this night."

Suddenly he realized that he'd lost track of Pontus and the standard of the eagle. He searched frantically to locate one or the other. Behind, he heard the prefect's voice shout an order for the troops to form up into phalanxes.

Pontus's command drew out a rare complaint from one of the legionaries, a centurion who wanted to fight with greater freedom than the tight formation allowed. But the legion did not hesitate to form a phalanx, a line of soldiers pressed side by side in tight rows, three deep, which allowed the front line to stab with their swords or spears while sheltering behind a wall of shields. Collin had no such shield, and he quickly became confused, unsure of where he should go. Where was the standard of the eagle?

He was standing out in front of the phalanx, exposed to the madness ahead. To his dismay, he discovered Pontus had moved to command from the rear of the phalanx.

The legion's line was formidable, thousands strong, but it hadn't advanced after forming up. Collin stood out in the open.

"What are we waiting for?" he shouted at the legion. "They're getting killed up there." Although he pointed toward the hillside, he hoped the legion would step in to protect him.

The legionaries stared at him with blank faces. Somebody yelled a warning.

Out of the dark, a band of imps—small, devilish creatures with scaly red hides—swarmed Collin, their needle-like teeth sinking into his skin, their tiny claws drawing blood. The intense pain surprised him almost as much as the sudden attack.

Collin swung his sword, slashing at some, stabbing at others. His blade caused one imp to back off, but then two others replaced it. Three jumped onto his back. Then a fourth. And a fifth. Their high-pitched squeals were calls of victory.

He was going down.

This is how I die, Collin realized. *By the greedy mouths of the weakest kind of demon.*

The weight of them forced him to his knees. He cried out.

The Jihenan phalanx pushed forward, one step at a time, butchering everything in its path. The imps responded by jumping off Collin and attacking the legionaries, whereupon they were impaled by spears.

The soldiers stepped over him and he quickly found himself safe behind the lines. He couldn't believe his luck.

Pontus reigned in his mount, nearly trampling Collin in the process. "Only an idiot rushes into battle," he said. "Stay back and watch how soldiers of the new empire engage the enemy."

Despite being saved, Collin was seething. He stood in defiance. "The baron's men are getting slaughtered on the hill. We can't waste time with a slow march."

Pontus shot him a look of scorn. "We'll save the baron's men when it suits us."

The prefect galloped off, followed closely by a regiment of reserve troops. Collin tried to catch a glimpse of the hill, where the battle raged fiercest, but he couldn't see the knights well enough to know if they had survived.

I need a horse, Collin thought. *Where is the cavalry?*

A long line of archers trailed behind the slow march of foot soldiers. A salvo of arrows flew into the air, vanishing beyond the Jihenans. Such blind efforts seemed pointless against an enemy hidden by the poor light and the chaos of battle, but the archers kept up the barrage without fail. He discovered, however, that thin streamers of light pointing westward were guiding their aim—streamers of purple cast by the sangoma sorcerers perched high in the bluffs behind him.

A wagon train loaded with bundles of arrows kept the archers well supplied, and for a second Collin was tempted to unhitch one of the horses from a wagon and make a daring, bareback charge into the fray. He thought better of it, though, when he saw that grizzled veterans itching to dispatch any threat to their supplies guarded the teams.

Collin jogged crossways behind the legion's phalanx for about a quarter-mile, until he reached the northernmost flank. Soldiers here were locked in a spirited battle with bands of trolls slamming into the shield wall in an effort to break the line. The scaly, bear-sized brutes died by the scores, but still they came. Pontus was here with his reserve troops, shouting to shore up the right flank.

Before the reserves could get into position, however, a dozen trolls lowered their heads and rammed a weak point in the line, pushing and shoving, slashing and biting. Legionaries stumbled and fell, crashing to the ground. A narrow breach opened up.

Several of the trolls managed to scamper on top of the fallen soldiers, pausing barely long enough to see that they had broken through. They saw Pontus and attacked.

Lightly armored and able to move fast, Collin ran ahead of the reserve units and met the trolls as they confronted the commander.

One went down as his sword pierced its snout. A second

took a deep wound in its thigh and reeled back with a cry of outrage. A third blocked two of Collin's blows with its hands, snorted in triumph, and right away fell dead, Pontus's sharp gladius pierced through its skull.

They had no time to celebrate their successes. The prefect's warhorse reared up suddenly and kicked an aggressive troll in the face, throwing Pontus to the ground. Without thinking, Collin stepped over the commander as the troll pounced. A claw raked across Collin's chest, slicing through layers of leather and wool, cutting into his skin. With a scream, he jabbed his sword into an eye and delivered a kick into the troll's boar-like jaw. The monster cried in anguish as reserve troops cut it down.

Pontus rolled onto his feet, shouted orders to seal the breach, then gave Collin a curt nod of thanks.

As the prefect remounted, Collin grinned. He couldn't have felt better if Pontus had tossed him a medal of honor.

If only Mira had seen it all.

THIRTY-ONE

Krassus and the First Sangoma surveyed the battle as they conversed loudly enough to be heard above the roar. Mira stood off to the side, holding the horse's reins, feeling useless once again. She tried to catch a glimpse of Collin amid the chaos below, but the movements in the valley were too hard to follow from this far away. At times, when a particularly bright flash appeared, she caught glimpses of the legion arrayed north to south, pushing as one body toward the baron's knights fighting on the hill. She had not seen the warrior.

The First explained what he saw upon the hill. "The baron's captain, Sir Garon, is a big man, a mighty warrior, arrayed in full battle armor and wielding a barbarian's broadsword."

Krassus nodded. "Is it Aidan's fabled claymore?"

"Likely just a replica of that mysterious blade."

"Of course."

"Garon fights alongside another knight, who answers to the name of Sir Rydel. This one wades recklessly into the enemy's ranks with a double-bladed axe more suited for the storybooks than for efficient fighting. Nevertheless, the two of them have inspired the others defending the hill, and they have kept the enemy at bay."

"And their magician?" asked Krassus.

"His skills are nothing against the Intulo weerlords, and I've seen only one of his spells cause damage. Yet it was enough to keep the enemy cautious."

"What of the demon lord? Have you spotted that pretender yet?"

"I detected the awesome power of a very old weerlord commanding the invasion," said the sangoma. "He might be the enemy we seek."

"Can you take him?"

"He hangs back near the north pass, as if sensing peril. I cannot reach him from here."

"Bah!" Krassus spat over the ledge. "I want him. Signal the cavalry to attack. If his offense collapses, perhaps we can force him to move in closer to Pontus."

The First Sangoma cupped his hands over his mouth, and Mira thought he meant to holler like a bullhorn across the battlefield. But before the sorcerer could say a thing, a stone the size of his head struck his right arm. For an instant, the sound of snapping bone was louder than the screams of battle.

A numerous host of monsters climbed over the lip of the ridge. Krassus seized Mira's arm and pulled her back. The horses bolted down the trail. Guards sprang forward to engage trolls and imps alike, but they were horribly outnumbered and their fighting rapidly became desperate. The sorcerer lay in a heap, unmoving, his body trampled underneath the enemy's feet.

Mira drew a knife and stabbed at an imp that got too close. With few means of defending herself, she felt exposed and vulnerable. Krassus drew his gladius and singlehandedly slew a snarling troll.

Trolls and imps died in droves, but still the enemy came, soon gaining a foothold on the overlook. And with that foothold, a monstrous, long-armed beast scaled the cliff and planted itself upon the ledge. It was covered in short hair except upon its face, which was flat, with widely spaced eyes; as it snarled, it revealed huge canines.

With powerful hands, this giant beast seized two of the guards and tossed them over the edge. Other guards, numbering less than a dozen now, confronted the beast, hacking and slashing desperately, but its hide seemed warded against their blades.

Mira recalled accounts of these terrible giants in the Encoda. Named bergrisi, many were said to have become impervious to all but the sharpest weapons.

"This way!" cried the scout.

The path down into the canyon was now blocked, but the scout urged them up the hill behind them. Another legionary went down as the guards formed a half-circle around Krassus and Mira. This gave them just enough time to turn and begin scrambling up the hillside.

Mira, the most agile, climbed quickly, outpacing the general in three strides. Now out in front, she halted and looked back the way she'd come.

The bergris had decimated the last of the guards and was

examining the body of the First Sangoma lying at its feet. The beast reached down and picked him up, lifting the sorcerer's limp body over its head in victory.

"No!" cried Mira. "Not here . . . Not now!"

Mira ripped the yeni stone from her necklace and fitted it in her sling. With three rapid turns over her head, she let it fly.

For one instant, the bergris looked up at her, grinning wildly, daring her to hurt it.

The stone shattered its teeth and went into its mouth.

The bergris's head burst into flames, fire pouring out of its mouth and ears and eye sockets. As the sorcerer's body dropped, the beast collapsed like a fallen statue. Trolls and imps took one startled look at their dead champion and turned in fright, fleeing for the canyon or leaping off the edge of the overlook.

By the time Mira climbed down to investigate, the bergris's head was an empty, charred skull. The yeni stone lay inside, too hot to touch.

The First Sangoma sat up slowly, cradling a broken arm. "A blaze stone," he said, gazing at the empty skull. "How fortunate."

Krassus helped the sangoma to his feet. "Indeed," he said. "Mira, you are full of surprises."

THIRTY-TWO

Collin yanked his sword out of the scaly belly of yet another troll that had managed to slip behind the legion's phalanx. This one had come soaring through the air, high above the front lines, as if thrown by a catapult. There was no such war machine out there, only a giant bergris that had tossed the troll from a distance in the hopes of getting it behind the Jihenan's impenetrable line.

A few paces away, Pontus gave him a nod. "Good work."

Collin's weapon was now beginning to feel heavy in his hand, but he dared not hang back and rest while the prefect needed him. Pontus continued to be a harsh commander with an acid tongue, but Collin sensed things had changed between them. He no longer dismissed him outright or scorned his fighting sense.

The prefect twisted in his saddle and looked toward the hills where the general commanded. "Signal the cavalry, Krassus," he said, as if to himself. "The time has passed."

No spells had come from the First Sangoma's hand for a while, and the ridge was obscured in darkness.

"Maybe he was attacked," Collin said. Then in a quieter voice, he added, "And Mira too."

"Concerned for your pretty little wench?" said Pontus. "It's the general you must worry about. Should he die, the legion could fall into anarchy. We've been away from Jihena too long."

Collin had no reason to doubt that, but he continued to worry more for Mira's safety than for the general's. "Should I go check on her—I mean, on the general?"

Pontus allowed the hint of a smile, the only sign of amusement he had ever received from the man. "It won't do us any good if he's dead. We're better off learning of such bad news after the battle is over."

Collin's heart sank. He'd hoped for the excuse to see Mira.

Then a new noise rose above the battle cries. It first began as a high-pitched whistle, growing louder and deeper until it sounded like the wail of a battle horn. Three violet flares left the bluff and exploded, their light coloring the bottom of the clouds.

"He's done it!" Pontus held up his fist in victory. "You worry too much, barbarian."

"What does it mean?" asked Collin.

"Listen and learn."

The phalanx halted and legionaries dug in, bracing themselves against their shields. Collin waited in anticipation.

A desperate cry moved through the enemy's ranks as a wave of monsters crushed up against the phalanx's shield wall. The enemy packed in close together, trying one massive shove to break through.

Collin watched the legionaries struggle against the on-slaught, grunting and cursing, and for one terrible moment it seemed the phalanx might break. The front line slid into the second line, the second into the third, which pushed against both of them. They were trained for this kind of combat, but even this assault tested their limits.

Many of the enemy died against the legion's spears. Some trolls attempted to turn back, but found they had nowhere to go. Eventually they quit fighting the soldiers and turned to wrestle their own numbers—numbers crowding in behind them. Some tripped and fell, even as others climbed atop each other in an attempt to escape. Any that came within range of the spears were stabbed and maimed or killed.

What were they running from?

As the ground shook, a rumbling sound declared the truth. From the west. The cavalry!

"Caught between a rock and a hard place!" cried Pontus. "If a cavalry charge doesn't break the enemy, nothing will." His eyes were fierce and proud. He shouted at the men to hold the line.

"How?" asked Collin. "I mean . . ."

"The cavalry made their way across the valley and moved into the western forest before the baron's men lost the north passage."

"You mean the general had rested soldiers in the valley while the baron's men were getting slaughtered? Were they hiding in the trees the whole time?"

"Brilliant, don't you think? The baron's retreat drew the demon lord straight down the center of the valley so we could crush them in a vise."

"But how many of the baron's men have died?"

"Better his men than ours." Pontus spurred his steed down the line, shouting commands, threatening harsh punishment to any soldier who gave up his position.

THIRTY-THREE

Bursts of white light illuminated the battlefield in flares brighter than any that had come before it. With the foot soldiers lined up on the east side of the valley and the cavalry charging in from the west, the enemy's numbers became compressed. Mira watched in horror as the baron's knights struggled to defend the north face of the hill, which saw a surge of trolls driving against them. The bright lights had enraged the enemy, now stampeding in the only direction that might provide an escape: the hilltop.

Scattered here and there, bergrisi, like the one that had attacked them on the overlook, stood above the horde, each one pushing and shoving trolls around them. Their allies had panicked and the trolls' hatred of bright lights had caused them to attack anything that got in their way, including the giants. The big hairy beasts fought the trolls, crushing many, but in the end they went down, howling in death, trampled underfoot or speared by the cavalry.

Few weerlords remained alive to offer resistance. Each one

had been a target of the sangomas long before the cavalry charge, and those still breathing tried to rally at the base of the hillside.

"Will the baron's men survive?" asked Mira.

The general shrugged. Despite the gash upon his head now wrapped in cloth, he gazed out upon the cavalry charge with an obvious show of pleasure. "Sacrifice is often the key to victory," he said.

Mira searched again for Collin among the infantry, but the warrior was hidden in the chaos. She hoped he'd been smart enough to stay away from frenzied trolls at the front.

Far to the north, beyond the reach of the legion, in an area that had previously been hidden in darkness, a series of explosions torched two trees. The fire revealed a circle of bergrisi protecting another creature mounted upon a great white horror that might have been a giant maggot.

In the hills east of this band, the Third Sangoma conjured a sphere of energy, his hands sizzling with pure red fire. With a sweeping motion and a thrust of his hands, he struck down the circle of bergrisi one by one. Crimson lightning crackled all around.

The rider on the maggot shied back, but seemed un-harmed. It answered the sangoma's attack with an upraised staff, raining gouts of liquid fire upon the hills.

Mira shouted a warning, but she was too far away, her voice drowned by the din of battle. She watched as flames poured over the Third Sangoma.

Krassus watched the duel impassively.

Beside Mira, the First Sangoma staggered and took hold of her shoulder for support. Beads of perspiration ran down his cheeks.

"My brother," he said in a punctured voice. "He has uncovered the Intulo chieftain."

"The demon lord?" asked Krassus.

"Perhaps. This weerlord wields a power greater than any known by our people."

"Can you help your brother?" asked Mira.

The sorcerer shook his head. "I am too weak, but the Second hurries to his aid."

In a rare display of concern, Krassus took in a deep breath and slowly let it out. Without the sorcerers, his advantage here would be gone.

The hills to the north burned fiercely, and Mira feared the Third might already be dead. She searched the fires. A charred figure stumbled out of the flames and launched a spell that shook the whole valley and rattled Mira's teeth.

Around the great maggot, the earth itself rose up in a wave of dirt and sod that crashed down with the force of a landslide. The maggot perished instantly, squashed by the sudden weight that sprayed white muck in every direction.

When the dust settled, the weerlord could be seen crawling out of loose dirt like an animated corpse pulling itself out of a fresh grave. It had lost its staff, but had managed to attack with an outstretched arm, casting a ball of fire at the Third.

The sorcerer's energy seemed spent, for as the flames took him he slumped to his knees and bowed his head.

The First gripped Mira's shoulder tightly and let out a cry of grief.

The Second Sangoma came into position, appearing on

rocks above the scorched body of his brother. Streamers of light flashed above the weerlord, wove into a ball of purple and silver flames like string that fell to the ground. As the ball ensnared the weerlord, it thrashed about, fighting against an unseen force. Then it went limp.

"Good," said Krassus. "We shall have answers soon." Though he sounded pleased, he was visibly shaken by the death of the Third.

"What's going on?" Mira asked. "Is the thing still alive?"

"The Second is talented at capturing his foes," Krassus said. "He knows I will want to question this demon lord."

The First's voice was subdued, but there was an edge to his words. "And my brother will want to hurt the Intulo for what it has done."

"Look!" cried the scout, pointing west. "The cavalry has broken the enemy's will."

Trolls and imps died in droves. Some few tried to set up a defensive ring, but their attempts were so uncoordinated that the cavalry ran them down before they could put up a fight. Others tried to flee, only to find themselves trapped inside their own ranks. The infantry's phalanx encircled the confused mob and, before long, only tiny imps skirting between their legs managed to escape.

Against all odds, the baron's knights had managed to hold the hilltop.

THIRTY-FOUR

Sedric's stride was long, but Jarin was determined to keep up. They hiked beside a stream, the terrain overgrown and wild. There was no obvious path through the trees, and every so often they had to hop down into the streambed to skirt an impassable tangle of briars or a jumble of boulders. Once, a close call with a beehive drove them into the water, where they made a fast getaway. His pants were still wet.

Razor seemed to enjoy the journey, splashing into the shallow stream more often than not, sometimes chasing bugs or birds, or the many squirrels that seemed to follow them. Jarin had given up ordering the dog to stay close.

Sedric never consulted a map, though he would sometimes halt with hands on hips, examine the sky, peer into the trees, sniff the air, and then continue hiking upstream. They never strayed too far from the water, however, and Jarin began to wonder if they were lost.

"Do you know where we're going?" he asked.

"Of course I do," said Sedric. "We're headed south."

"How long till we get there?"

"As long as it takes."

"I'm hungry."

"Then you shouldn't have come with me."

"I'll bet you don't even know where to go."

"You'd lose that bet." Sedric's voice wavered a bit.

"We have the seed," said Jarin. "Won't it tell us the way?"

"Seeds only talk in fairy tales."

"I've never heard a fairy tale with talking seeds."

"And neither have I, because such seeds don't exist."

"Then why did you bring it up?"

"To prove a point."

"You mean the seed isn't going to help us find the Tree?"

"I never said that."

"Then what are you saying?"

"That a mouth won't suddenly appear on the seed and speak to us."

"Why not?" said Jarin. "Maybe that carving of a man with an open mouth was meant to tell us the seed will start talking."

"That's absurd. There are other ways it can guide us."

"Like what?"

Sedric stopped and let out an enormous sigh. He reached into the pocket of his coat and brought out their prize, which he had carefully folded in a handkerchief. After unwrapping it, his brow puckered as he concentrated on the seed.

"I don't hear anything," said Jarin.

"Of course you don't!"

"Then what are you doing?"

"I'm trying to . . ." Sedric straightened and closed his fist around the seed. Jarin thought he looked embarrassed. "Never mind. To be honest, I don't know how this is going to guide us. We have entered an area I've never been."

Jarin caught sight of a tree twig floating down the stream, spinning this way and that, bobbing around rocks. "I have an idea."

"Hopefully not about talking seeds."

Jarin shook his head. "Some seeds float in the air until they find a place to grow, right?"

"Yes, but those seeds don't decide where they land." Sedric had been grouchy all morning, but now he seemed interested in what Jarin had to say. "You're thinking of a dandelion seed, which goes where the wind blows."

"And other seeds travel by water or are carried by animals."

"What are you driving at?" Sedric asked.

"What would carry a seed from a magic tree?"

His uncle raised his eyebrows. "You're not as dumb as you look." He opened his hand and examined the acorn. "Old texts refer to streams of power flowing from the World Tree in invisible currents that animals native to Kalor can feel. Some early magicians even tried to invent clever ways of detecting these currents, but their efforts yielded little fruit. Humans cannot see any streams of power, and I had thought the idea a bad one. And yet the wizard once claimed to have discovered a method of walking along the ribbons of spirit, as he called them, which might be the same things. Unfortunately, he didn't explain what he did."

"Maybe our seed can be carried by these invisible streams," said Jarin. "Because it's magic."

Sedric accepted the idea with a nod. Choosing a level spot

on the ground, he sat down and put the seed onto the dirt. Then he waited, his face hopeful. When nothing happened, he frowned.

"I don't even know how to begin," he admitted.

"Will it sprout into a tree if we leave it on the ground?" Jarin asked.

"It might, if the soil is fertile." Sedric picked up the acorn and looked around. Then he pointed toward the stream. "Hand me that rock over there . . . The large flat one the color of your dirty face. Can you carry it?"

The rock was about as big as Jarin's lap, but it was thin, bulging slightly on one side and weighing half as much as a sack of grain. He thought it looked like the perfect skipping stone. For a giant.

He dropped the rock next to Sedric, nearly banging his uncle's knee, which earned him a scolding.

"Don't cripple me," said Sedric, pulling his leg out of the way just in time.

"Sorry."

His uncle went to work pushing on the rock and leveling it out so the flat side lay toward the sky. Then he placed the acorn in the center of the stone and sat back.

"What are you doing?" Jarin asked.

"It can't grow on a rock, so maybe it will find a way to rich soil."

"By itself?"

Sedric shrugged. "It's magic, isn't it?"

As they waited, Jarin became restless. "Even if magic pushes it to the ground, we still won't know where the Tree is."

"You might be right." Sedric scratched the stubble of a

beard sprouting on his cheeks. "The wizard must have used it to reveal a path. When asked how he had found the Tree, he said, 'The open mouth speaks of hidden gateways unlocked by the seed of magic.' Everyone thought he was playing them for fools and dismissed the riddle. That is, until I stumbled upon the carving in the beech tree years ago. Then I knew."

"Why didn't you try to find the Tree after that?"

"You don't always see the answer to a puzzle on the first try. Besides, I was thinking of other things at the time."

Jarin wondered if those other things had something to do with the carving of two people embraced in a kiss.

"In any case," Sedric continued, "this isn't working." He reclined upon the ground with his hands behind his head and stretched out his legs, almost kicking one of the three squirrels that had wandered close to his feet. "That's how it is with us and magic. There's a lot of guesswork and luck involved before we get it right. *If* we get it right."

"Are you going to take a nap?" Jarin asked, worried that his uncle had given up too soon. There *had* to be a way the seed would guide them to the Tree.

"I need to think," said Sedric, and shut his eyes.

Jarin was thinking too. And as he was thinking, the acorn moved. At first it did little more than jerk sideways. Then it rolled in a half circle and stopped.

"Did you see that?"

"Huh?" Sedric sat up.

"The seed. It moved."

"It's not moving now."

"I saw it roll around. Watch this." Jarin turned the seed and then waited.

It didn't take long for the acorn to repeat the movement he'd seen before and end up in the same position.

Sedric grinned from ear to ear. "It's trying to align itself with a ribbon of spirit."

"Will it roll all the way to the Tree?"

"That might ruin it." Sedric looked toward the sky. "If it's like a dandelion seed, the wind will carry it." He stood and held up a wetted finger to find the direction of the breeze.

"But it's not a dandelion seed," said Jarin. "How is the wind going to grab it?"

"The stem of the acorn is pointing southwest," Sedric mused, looking off into the trees.

At that moment, one of the squirrels darted onto the flat stone, snatched up the seed, and scurried off. Jarin shouted, diving for the squirrel's tail, but he was too slow to catch it. Three squirrels bounded into the trees, chittering excitedly.

Sedric scanned the empty stone in confusion, then cursed Jarin for letting thieves steal their greatest treasure. "Where is that infernal dog of yours when we need him!"

He and Jarin ran into a grove of tall pine trees, where the squirrels had gone.

"There!" said Jarin, spying the black-tailed thief high in the limbs.

Sedric picked up a stone and threw it at the animal, but his aim went low and smacked into the trunk. The squirrel climbed higher.

"Hurry, boy," said Sedric. "Go up there and get it back!"

Pines were not the easiest trees to climb, but Jarin was too upset by the turn of events to care. He went up, ignoring the needles poking his head and the sticky sap on his hands.

Above him, the squirrels became agitated, running around the trunk and climbing higher. Near the top, the squirrel with the black tail skipped along a skinny branch until it reached the far end. It turned and screamed at him, the branch bobbing up and down from the added weight.

Jarin had climbed as far as he dared. Higher up, the branches were too thin and he knew that to go any farther would cause one of them to snap under his weight. Maybe if he threw pinecones at the squirrel it would drop the seed into his uncle's hands below?

That's when Razor showed up and started barking at him.

He knew that bark. Razor was trying to warn him of some new danger.

Suddenly afraid, Jarin stepped down onto a larger limb and hugged the trunk of the tree, caring little for the rough trunk against his cheek.

It came out of the sky, swooping down in a sudden red blur—a huge bird resembling a raven the color of blood. It was much bigger than any raven Jarin had seen, however, with talons the size of meat hooks.

The bird took the squirrel—and the seed—and quickly soared out of sight.

THIRTY-FIVE

Jarin expected his uncle to shout at him in anger, but when he returned to the ground, Sedric was staring into the sky, dumbfounded.

"That was not a coincidence," he said softly. "A blood raven doesn't show up out of the blue and swipe your magic seed without reason."

Jarin felt sick to his stomach. One minute he was showing his uncle a hidden path to the Tree; the next minute they had nothing.

"Is that how the currents of magic work?" he asked.

"I think we know now how seeds of the Tree find the right soil. They're carried by animals that can sense the currents."

"How do we follow it?"

Sedric was barely listening. "Maybe humans weren't meant to know the way. Maybe we'll never harness the powers of Kalor."

"The wizard did it."

"I'm beginning to doubt that."

"What about those sorcerers from Jihena?" Jarin asked. "They seem to know a lot about magic."

Sedric's eyes came into focus and he finally looked at Jarin. "True, they know a lot, and they do indeed command great power. But at what cost? They've sacrificed so much of what makes them human that they're barely recognizable as men. I should know. I started down a similar path long ago, a dangerous path that almost killed me."

"Why aren't they dead then?"

"The sangomas are the last of their kind—the survivors— of a people that perished as they experimented upon weerlords. I suspect the consul has established a link with those three in some way that provides a lifeline, but I can't say exactly what that link is, or how it happened. For myself, I came to realize that the only safe way humans would command great magic was by finding the Tree."

"So what do we do now?"

"Well, first off, let me make this clear. I am not abandoning my quest to find the Tree, you hear?"

Jarin nodded with relief.

"I'll have to find it the old-fashioned way," said Sedric. "Through gut instinct."

"By guessing?"

"It's more than that . . . And don't give me that look . . . I've come across enough clues here and there that I have a pretty good idea where to look. I just need a pointer in the right direction. Southwest is where we'll start."

"There must be a better way." Jarin was in no mood to watch his uncle pretend to know where to go. He'd done enough of that already. "Your way could take forever."

"Do you have a better idea?"

"What about the seed?"

"I'm sorry, Jarin, but unless you know how to sprout wings and fly, the seed is gone for good. Forget about it."

"Isn't the raven taking it back to the Tree?"

"And why would it do that?"

"Because it's a magic seed. Maybe the best soil for that kind of seed is in the valley where the Tree grows. Why would the wizard even leave it behind in the first place?"

Sedric threw up his hands. "He probably didn't want to lose it! How should I know?"

"But—"

"Look. You make a good point, Jarin, but there's nothing to be done about it now. We can't follow the raven, and because we can't follow the raven we've lost the seed. It's that simple."

In the distance, Razor let out two distinct barks, the kind meant to get everyone's attention. In the past, whenever Jarin followed such barks, he was often led to some treasure the dog had uncovered. Most finds were rabbit holes, but sometimes he came across interesting things, such as a troll's skull or even a dead yeni.

His uncle shouted at him to stop as Jarin took off between the towering pines, chasing Razor's calls. He went slantwise to the upslope. The dog was waiting for him, with head up and tail whipping from side to side. He took off into the trees, stopping only as Jarin caught up. It wasn't long until they came to a ridge that overlooked wooded hills descending into a valley. Far below, a river snaked southward.

"What is it, boy?" Jarin asked, petting Razor.

Sedric came up, huffing and puffing. "That pet of yours is trouble, no doubt about it. If he hasn't found the seed, I'm going to beat him senseless."

Jarin pointed southwest. "Look!"

"That's the Vonspryer River, and I already knew it was in this direction," said Sedric.

"No, not that. Look higher, in the sky. The raven!"

Sedric removed his hat and squinted. "It's flying south and a bit west, roughly following the course of the river."

Jarin was so excited he congratulated Razor with a big hug. The retriever licked his cheek. "Does that help us, Uncle Sedric?"

"It confirms what I should have realized long ago, that the river is key to finding the valley of the Tree. But it's only half the puzzle. The river enters a deep gorge, hard to navigate, before it eventually empties into the Sidewinder Sea. We'll need to find the correct path before then."

"It's a start, don't you think?"

Sedric seemed to be holding back a smile. "If it were any other bird than a blood raven, I'd have scolded you for a fool. But the wizard beheld great flocks of them flying around the Tree, protecting the seeds. I think we have our best clue yet."

"Why would they be protecting the seeds?"

"To keep them from leaving the valley of the Tree, I suppose, and the proper soil there, just like you said. Who knows what kind of magic tree they might sprout in the wrong soil outside the valley?"

"Does that mean you're not going to hurt Razor?"

Sedric put his hat back on and began to work his way down the hill. "Not today."

THIRTY-SIX

After the legion decimated the forces of the demon lord, another kind of invasion began. Supply wagons, servants, slaves, and an army of camp followers poured out of the east canyon and began setting up tents and pavilions beneath the shadow of Castle Guldheim. Mira was amazed by the efficient and orderly work of the Jihenans and by how quickly a city of tents arose.

The first order of business was to care for the legion's troops, a task that was more important than burning the corpses littering the field, which was covered mostly with imps and trolls.

That's not to say that the dead were left to bake in the sun for long. While the servants treated the wounded, slaves were immediately tasked with cleaning up the battlefield. Legionaries who had died were buried at the crest of the central hill, where the general said noble words about the men's sacrifice. Then he ordered a monument to be erected in honor of the fallen.

The mass of enemy corpses was stacked in wagons and carted off to the north, beyond the pass, where they were set ablaze upon the Rusted Plains. The billows of black smoke rising in the sky were grim warnings to all of Kalor to stay away from the valley.

All this happened under the nose of the Baron of Guldheim, who finally made an appearance atop the wall of his castle, where he waved his fat, ring-covered fingers at all the people on the field. Only a few local peasants bothered to wave back. Krassus ignored the baron, choosing instead to position his camp around the castle in what was effectively a siege. Legionaries patrolled an inner circle near the walls, in case the castle's knights were thickheaded enough to test the Jihenans' resolve. Krassus, however, seemed certain the baron was in no mood to fight. If he knew what was good for him, said the general, he'd open his gates and swear fealty.

After a morning of worried searching, Mira found Collin alive and conscious. Upon spotting him, she tried not to show her excitement, but in the end, she couldn't help herself. She rushed over to him, smiling all the while, and almost gave him a hug, stopping short only when she saw he was wounded. She took up the bandages from a slave girl trying to wrap Collin's scabby chest and ordered him to lie still while she treated him.

He was clearly happy to see her too, and that made their reunion sweet.

Collin bragged a little about his battles, but Mira could see that the fighting had changed him. He was more reserved, more sober, and took the time to listen attentively to Mira's account of the skirmish on the ridge.

"Sounds like you had your own bit of excitement," he said.

Mira took a damp rag from the girl—age eleven or twelve, by the looks of her—and began to wipe dirt and dried blood from Collin's shoulder.

"The general trusts me completely now," she said. "And the First Sangoma says he owes me a life-debt for what I've done."

"What does that mean?" Collin lay in the shade of an apple tree, propped up by their meager supplies from home, which consisted of blankets and a single bag of clothes.

"I'm not sure," Mira said, ignoring Collin's poor attempts to hold back a wince of pain. "Notice we don't have a guard hovering over us anymore."

Collin glanced up at the slave girl and grinned. "Are you our guard?"

The girl kept her eyes lowered as she shook her head, but Mira caught a smile escaping her lips. Despite the girl's good humor, it was impossible to dismiss the injustice of owning slaves, and Mira intended to say something about it to Krassus when things had settled down. At least this girl seemed well fed and unabused.

"What's your name?" Mira asked her.

"I am slave to Master Avidicus of New Ithaka."

"You have no other name?"

The girl shook her head.

"You may look at me," Mira said gently. "I'm not from Jihena."

The girl lifted her gaze. Her eyes were a striking green and contrasted perfectly with her straight dark hair, which she tucked carefully behind her ears. Even dressed in a plain frock, she was very pretty—too pretty to go unnoticed in a camp filled to the brim with proud citizens of the republic who felt entitled to every pretty person or fine thing around them.

Mira instantly wanted to rescue the girl, take her away and show her the joys of freedom, but she knew there was little she could do right now.

She lowered her voice so that only the three of them could hear. "Is there a name you wish you had?"

The girl hesitated, studying Mira, no doubt wondering if she was being tricked into confessing a forbidden desire. "I," she whispered, "I like the name Saffron."

"That's a pretty name," said Mira. "Does it have special meaning for you?"

"On Earth, saffron was a flower used to make a delicious spice."

Mira nodded. There were many such stories of Earth, so many, in fact, that she didn't believe them all.

"It's perfect," Collin said. "From now on we will think of you as Saffron, our kind friend from New Ithaka."

Saffron began to tear up and for a moment appeared ready to embrace both of them. Then, with a sudden change of heart, she slapped her hand over her mouth and ran off. Mira watched her vanish into the crowd.

"I must talk to Krassus when I see him," she said, half to herself, half to Collin. "This way of life hurts innocent people."

Collin reached over and ran a finger lightly across her skin. "I'm glad you weren't hurt on the ridge."

Mira shook her head to clear her thoughts and almost pulled her arm away. "If you're trying to flirt again with a *hardy* lowland girl, you'd better stop now before you embarrass yourself."

"I can't stop."

"Embarrassing yourself?"

"Flirting with you." A ridiculous smirk appeared on Collin's face.

She laughed. "Oh, you're a bold one."

"When I saw you go into the general's tent that night, I was jealous."

"Tell me something I don't know."

"I think I love you."

A surge of emotion overcame Mira and she almost got up and ran after Saffron. Collin took hold of her arm and slowly pulled her close to him.

He kissed her.

She didn't withdraw, but instead endured the gentle touch of his lips, first to satisfy her curiosity, then because she enjoyed it. When Collin tried to align his position and take her in his arms, he let out a yelp of agony and released his hold.

Collin sat back. "Now I've done it." The bandage wrapped around his chest was spotted with fresh blood.

"You should be more careful," Mira said.

"I told you I can't help it."

Mira took another strip of cloth and pressed it against the wound to slow the flow of blood. It was the best she could do under the circumstances, but it frustrated her that nobody but a girl had been assigned to help him.

"You need a skilled healer," she said, scanning the campsite. She'd seen pairs of older women roaming among the wounded, carrying sacks of poultices and skins full of potions. One had even attended the First Sangoma, doing more to heal his shattered arm in an hour than a week of resting would have accomplished. Perhaps she could entice a healer over here to treat Collin.

What she saw, however, was Krassus's own guard escorting a strange prisoner to a wooden coop erected a short distance away from the tents.

The prisoner was clearly a weerlord, but this one was different from the hunter Sedric had slain outside the hermit's cabin. Although it possessed the skin of a snake and the rough, unfinished head of a human man, its arms were thin and unnaturally long, ending not in hands, but in a kind of stump split in two, like small mouths able to grasp objects.

With arms wrapped tightly with cord and legs hobbled by chains, the weerlord scooted beside the guard in a hunched-over manner, as if cowering from the sun. Into the coop it went, a cage barely large enough for the creature's gaunt frame. Two big legionaries, both high-ranking centurions, and the Second Sangoma—a man intently studying his prize—stood guard.

"Do you think the demon lord can be held prisoner for long?" Mira asked.

"They're not even sure it's him," said Collin.

"That's what I mean. Maybe they have the wrong commander."

Collin shrugged. "Whoever he is, he caused a lot of suffering for us and the people of Guldheim last night. Just look at what happened to *me*."

Mira couldn't help laughing. "Oh, poor boy. Does it hurt

here? And here?" She touched his shoulder, his chest. "Now you're faking it."

"Am not."

"Need more sympathy, do you?"

"No, just another kiss."

"Why?"

"Do I need a reason?"

Mira didn't say anything as she kissed him again. Then she rechecked his bandages and went to find a healer.

THIRTY-SEVEN

Something was up with Sedric and it wasn't good. For the last hour he'd hardly said two words to Jarin, and what he had said was brusk and rude. His uncle was brooding.

What had happened?

Only yesterday Sedric had congratulated him on spotting the blood raven flying southward. Jarin had even kept an eye on the bird for a long time after that, to make sure it didn't turn in another direction, and his uncle had praised his sharp eyes.

But when the next morning arrived and they had come upon a weed-choked wagon trail, Sedric's mood went from good to bad, from that of a friend to that of a parent.

No one else was on the road, and when Jarin asked where it led, Sedric would only say, "To the river."

By midafternoon, the sound of children's voices announced the sight of a wooden house built upon the banks of the Vonspryer. Five barefooted girls, all younger than Jarin, held hands and danced in a circle, singing a rhyme about summoning a spirit that would deliver them from the stomach of a troll. Their dresses were barely more than sacks with holes cut out for arms and legs and a head, and except for grass stains and homemade belts of flowers, they displayed no other color than dull yellow.

Their worn clothes didn't seem to bother the girls. They smiled as they sang, skipping in a circle. Unable to keep in step with the other girls, the youngest one, probably no older than two, tripped, planting her head into the trampled grass. On either side of her, the two oldest girls picked up the toddler and resumed their play. One of the girls moved in a way that gave Jarin the urge to stand a little taller and flex his muscles.

Upon the porch sat a man smoking a pipe. Two women—one old and wrinkled, the other tired and pregnant—sat with the man on a long bench. Neither woman wore shoes, and the boots the man had on were so thin and worn they might as well have been painted on his feet.

Sedric inclined his head and gave Jarin an order. "Don't be a farting little boy now, you hear? Let me do the talking."

Jarin nodded.

"And keep that pet of yours out of mischief."

Unfortunately, before Jarin could so much as blink, Razor bounded ahead and began to sniff the girls from head to toe, his tail whipping back and forth. One of the girls screamed, another ran to the steps of the porch, while the remaining three squealed with delight and mauled the dog. The toddler seized Razor by the ears and tried to give him a slobbering kiss, but the retriever simply licked the girl's face clean, snot and all.

All three adults sprang to their feet, and the man with the pipe hurried down the steps to console the girl who was screaming. "Easy now, Violet," he said. "It's just an agreeable puppy."

The girl quieted almost at once and exposed a near-toothless smile at Razor.

The man took a long draught from his pipe and sauntered up to Sedric. "You're not from the mines."

"Hello, my friend," Sedric said in an unusually kind voice. "No, I'm not. Yet I need your help all the same."

The other man blew out a perfect smoke ring. "The river's too dangerous right now. When the level drops, I'll ferry you across."

"Don't want to cross the river," said Sedric. "I want to go down it in your boat there."

The ferryman turned and regarded an overturned, weather-beaten rowboat on the riverbank. Then he gave Sedric a doubting look.

The old woman on the porch shambled over to the railing. "Who are you?"

Sedric removed his hat and gave the woman a nod. "Just a traveler, my fine lady."

"Your *lady*?" said the woman. "How charming."

"No more charming than the two of you and your family."

The women hooted. One of the younger girls kicked Sedric in the shin. The pretty one noticed Jarin staring at her and abruptly closed her eyes and puckered her lips.

"No sane man wants to go down a swollen river in a leaky boat," said the ferryman. "What are you after?"

Jarin said, "We're on a quest—"

"The boy is not going with me," Sedric interrupted.

"Where's he going?"

"I was hoping that maybe you'd take him under your wing, as your apprentice."

"Don't need an apprentice," said the ferryman. "Besides, it don't take much to operate a ferry."

"Even so, the extra hand would serve you well."

"Are you blind? I have enough children of my own."

"What's one more?" asked Sedric. "He's a good boy with a keen sense of humor."

The old woman heard this and cackled, then went into the house.

Jarin suddenly heard what his uncle was telling the man and all but forgot about the girl. A sense of panic came over him. "Uncle Sedric? No."

"Keep him till I return," Sedric told the ferryman. "That's all I ask."

"You can't . . . ," Jarin began, realizing his uncle had been planning this all morning.

The ferryman shook his head. "It's true, I've always wanted a son, but you can't possibly possess enough to entice me to take on another hungry mouth."

Sedric opened his pack, took out the shimmering kend skin, and unrolled it before the ferryman's feet. On the porch, a gasp of surprise came from the pregnant woman.

The ferryman took his pipe out of his mouth. "By the Creators. How?"

"A cloak made with this will keep you warm on the coldest night, and when worn during the light of day, you will be all but invisible to most animals, should you wish to go hunting." Sedric stepped back and waited as the ferryman stooped to examine the animal skin. He added, "I'll be back before the seasons change."

The ferryman shoved his pipe back into his mouth and puffed on it with relish. Then he straightened and nodded once.

*

With a mighty grunt, Sedric pushed the rowboat halfway into the river and held it steady as he examined the bottom for leaks. The ferryman watched from the sidelines, shaking his head in disbelief, sucking on his pipe, the kend hide draped over him like a king's robe. The sweet scent of pipe smoke filled the air.

Jarin sulked nearby, arms crossed, trying to put on his most bitter frown. This was the only way he could keep from shedding tears of anger and frustration.

"You might die on the water the first hour," said the ferryman.

"Your boat is in better condition than I thought," Sedric replied.

"I'm talking about a stretch of rapids not far downstream."

"I went down this river once, years ago, on my way to Moss. I'll be fine."

"Well, remember when you come to a split in Aidan's Gorge called the Wedge, stay right. The river is running very high, because of the rains in the north, and the east branch of the gorge will be flooded."

"Of course."

"If you go left, you'll be torn to pieces and your bones will wind up at the bottom of the Sidewinder Sea."

"Thanks for the reminder," said Sedric.

"This is a bad hour to start your river run," said the ferryman. "By my calculations, you'll come to the Wedge in the dead of night. The gorge will be as dark as a witch's mouth by then."

"It's the only way to see the clue I need," said Sedric. "I know what I'm doing."

The ferryman bit on his pipe, furrowing his brow.

Sedric tossed his backpack in the boat, as well as a lunch made by the grandmother, who had taken a liking to him. She currently slept on the porch bench, snoring, her mouth hanging wide open.

"I thought we were both going to be heroes," Jarin said.

Sedric didn't look at him. "That's what you get for doing your own thinking."

"Go left and you'll surely die," warned the ferryman.

Sedric climbed into the boat and pushed off. "Jarin, work hard for the man. Do what he says, you hear me?"

"Yes," said the ferryman with a smile. "I have plenty of work for you."

Sedric paddled out into the river until the current took him.

Jarin felt betrayed. Not even his papa would have abandoned him to a family of strangers, no matter how bad things had gotten. He was sure of that. In fact, Shem had sent him to be with the hermit precisely because he trusted his brother to take care of him.

It wasn't fair.

Jarin ran along the bank, following Sedric's boat the best he could, hopping over rocks, skirting bushes and trees, trying to keep up. The ferryman didn't make a move to stop him; he didn't even shout a warning.

At a bend in the river, Jarin saw his chance and dove into the water. It was colder than he expected—colder than Willow Stump Creek, that was for sure—but he was committed now and nothing short of drowning was going to stop him.

When he came up for air, Razor was swimming behind him, paddling as hard as he could. Ahead, Sedric shouted insults and complaints. Jarin put his head down and swam with all his might, finally reaching the current's strong pull, at which time he raised his head and saw that he was still too far away from the boat. He couldn't swim any faster.

His pack was slowing him down, so he removed it. This made his strokes easier.

"Jarin, you halfwit!" yelled Sedric. "We'll be entering rapids soon."

His uncle spun the boat about and paddled hard against the current, which allowed Jarin to catch up and grab the gunwale. With a little help from Sedric, he managed to drag himself into the boat.

Upstream, Razor had snatched up Jarin's pack in his mouth and was struggling to catch up, his black snout bobbing up and down in the waves.

"Come on, Razor!" said Jarin. "You can make it."

Sedric's complaints never ceased. "I swear, Jarin, this is the dumbest thing you've ever done. What's got into you?"

"My own thinking," said Jarin.

Razor came close. Jarin reached out over the water and grabbed the pack and threw his waterlogged things—mostly a blanket, a cloak, and a bit of food—into the boat. Then he took hold of Razor's front paws and gave a great upward heave, but the dog was too heavy for him. Sedric came up, wrapped a strong arm around Razor's belly, and lifted him into the boat.

Glaring at the boy, his uncle returned to the oars.

Jarin slumped against the inside of the boat. They were going to be heroes at last.

Razor stepped back and shook his wet coat from head to tail, spraying water everywhere.

Jarin ignored Sedric's new round of curses.

THIRTY-EIGHT

"Jarin, wake up."

Sedric's voice pierced his mind and melted a dream. What had he been dreaming about? Oh, yes. Mira was spreading ointment on his shoulders again. Or was it the ferryman's cute daughter this time?

It was dark when he opened his eyes; the only useful light came from the flame of his lamp fastened upon the bow, barely illuminating two feet beyond the boat. Above, a narrow band of stars cast a dim, silver light upon the high cliffs on either side of them.

"Where are we?"

"Aidan's Gorge," Sedric said. He guided the boat with an oar held in the crook of his arm. "We'll be coming to the Wedge soon. Keep those sharp eyes peeled. I'll need help navigating the river."

Jarin was shivering. The afternoon sun had dried his hair earlier, but a cold breeze blew through the gorge, chilling his damp trousers and freezing his feet. The boat was moving fast, dipping down and going up ever-increasing swells, water spraying against his face.

"I hope Mira's all right," he said.

"Would you stop it," said Sedric. "You have a senseless crush on a girl almost twice your age."

"Do not."

"Oh, I forgot. You're worried about the safety of your *stepsister*, or whatever you call her."

"Now I know why you never got married."

Sedric gave him a hard stare, then looked away. He worked the single oar with an expertise and strength that maintained the boat in the center of the river.

"Nothing to be ashamed about, really," Sedric said. "She's a fine-looking young woman—the spitting image of her mother. Can't blame you for liking her."

The cliffs on either side quickly became narrower and taller, the current fast and strong. A heavy splash of water doused the light, plunging them into darkness. The noise of the river increased to such a loud roar that Jarin could barely hear Razor whining in his lap.

"We're near the chute now!" yelled Sedric. "What do you see?"

As Jarin scanned the dark cliffs on either side, his eyes were barely able to perceive the rocks in the dim starlight. The way downriver was at first too black to see anything, but soon a gray outline revealed whitecaps in the water and the straight course of the river.

"What am I looking for?" Jarin shouted over the noise.

"It's called the Wedge," said Sedric. "A narrow mountain of granite, shaped like an axe's blade, that divides the river in two. It will be directly in front of us."

The boat dipped low and then began to climb again. Waves drenched Jarin so completely that it felt like a hundred barrels of water had been dumped over him at once. The rank smell of fish assaulted his nose. He held onto the gunwale until his fingers cramped, and still he would not let go.

"No more rapids!" he shouted. "The river gets skinny . . . Now I see it! Straight ahead."

Jutting out into the middle of the river was a massive pillar of stone, darker than the night sky, higher than any tree, shaped like a long axe blade poking out from the cliffs. It forked the river down two pathways.

As they neared the Wedge, a sliver of moonlight peeked through a cluster of dark clouds and touched the top of the granite column, briefly creating the illusion of a colossal candle dripping with wax along the left side.

"That's it!" yelled Sedric. "The moonlight is the key!"

Sedric leaned hard on his oar, trying desperately to steer the boat, but the powerful current took hold of the wood and snapped it like a twig.

Razor yelped. Jarin screamed, "He said *right!* Go right!"

Sedric took up the remaining oar and paddled wildly on the starboard side in an effort to guide the boat to port. Why was he trying to go the wrong way?

"We're going to die," Jarin wailed. "Go right . . ."

"Look for the eye of the moon!" Sedric shouted. Then his oar was wrenched from his hands, disappearing beneath the waves. His eyes went wide. "Now is your chance to be a hero . . . Hang on!"

Suddenly the boat turned to the side and went belly-up, spilling Jarin and Razor and everything into the water. Seconds later it crashed into the Wedge with a horrific *crunch* and broke apart.

Jarin went under. When he came up, he was sputtering and coughing and trying to breathe. All he could see was that he was speeding down the wrong branch of the river. The current spun him around and around amid a pile of debris. He managed to seize a length of the broken boat and hang on for dear life, but it did little to ease his panic.

He collided with the rough cliff and succeeded in grabbing hold of a knob of rock, stopping himself. The current was so strong here it pushed him against the side of the Wedge, crushing him, pulling him down. An undercurrent ripped his sandals from his feet.

Something dark caught his eye.

Razor!

The retriever sped past with his snout in the air. The glimpse was brief, however, and Jarin could do nothing to help.

His grip on the knob of rock began to weaken, forcing him to abandon the piece of wood. He felt along the stone wall with his free hand, searching for a better hold, but there was nothing else to hang onto.

It didn't take long for his grip to give out. The current took him. His cry for help was lost in the deafening roar of the river. He fought to stay close to the wall, to find another handhold, but he was tossed about so violently that he lost all sense of direction.

Suddenly he found himself pushed into a skinny crack in the cliff wall of the Wedge. Here a tiny branch of the river—nothing more than a fracture in the side of the cliff—

propelled him through a narrow slot that eventually took him into a circular space surrounded by rough stone. Moonlight shone down upon him.

It revealed where this tiny branch flowed.

Into a whirlpool.

He saw Razor go down into the vortex. Jarin tried to swim back to the entrance, back into the crack, but his strength was spent and he had no choice but to hold his breath.

Down he went.

THIRTY-NINE

He fully expected the air to be squeezed out of his body, but after going under, the pressure eased and he experienced the sensation of falling through an abyss. Going over a waterfall was probably something like this, he thought, where one floated weightless for an instant, unable to breathe, the water suspended all around, until . . .

He plunged into a deep pool of water.

When he came up for air, sputtering, his lungs burning, he found that the current was not strong. He managed to swim over to shore and climb upon firm ground.

He was in a cave. At one end, water gushed out of a hole in the ceiling in a howling torrent. He didn't need a bright light to make it out, to tell him how lucky he was to be alive, for the whole column of water glowed faintly from the moonlight above.

Razor came up suddenly and greeted him with enthusiasm, but it was clear the dog was on shaky legs; he stuck his nose into Jarin's neck, whimpering.

From the falls, the water flowed to the far wall of the cave, where it disappeared beneath a shelf of rock jutting out above the water. A tangle of branches and debris had piled up against the shelf with a hand gripping it.

Jarin got up and ran to the cave wall. "Uncle Sedric!"

His uncle was trapped among the mass of branches and pieces of the broken boat, struggling to keep his head above water. His backpack floated high upon the water, pushing against his head, but his legs and torso appeared to have gone under the shelf. Although he had managed to grab hold of it with a free arm, it was clear the current would eventually drag him under, if it didn't crush him first.

Jarin jumped onto the shelf, took his uncle by the arm, and tried to lift him out.

Sedric raised his head. "My other arm!" he said. "Free my other arm!"

The light from the waterfall showed Sedric's predicament: his other arm was pinned behind his back, underneath his backpack. A long board had somehow gone up between a strap of his pack and his shoulder, twisting the strap and then becoming wedged in the logjam. He couldn't move up or to the side, and the current was slowly pushing his chin into the shelf, water surging around his neck.

Jarin unsheathed his knife and lay on his stomach so he could reach the strap. His uncle gulped a mouthful of unwanted water and began to cough uncontrollably.

The wet strap was hard to cut, but Jarin was determined to get through it, even if his muscles hurt. When he finally sliced through, he nearly nicked Sedric's shoulder.

Now that his arm was free, Sedric reached up and grabbed

ahold of the rocky shelf with both hands. With a heave, he lifted himself halfway out and coughed water from his lungs. Then he crawled onto the shelf and over to the cave floor, where he lay a moment to catch his breath.

"Are you all right?" Jarin asked.

Sedric patted his knee. "I'll live, thanks to you."

Jarin flopped to the ground and wrapped his arms around Razor. "Where are we?" he asked.

"Where do you think?"

"Under a mountain?"

"Smart boy."

"I'm cold."

"You'll get used to it once you dry off."

"Can't you try—"

"No more questions," said Sedric. "Let me rest."

After a long time, the moon's light glowing through the falls dimmed and the cave grew dark. Sedric got up, found a broken piece of the boat, and with a snap of his fingers, lit one end. The torch's meager light flickered across the uneven ceiling of the cave to reveal icicles of stone reaching down like fangs. He strode a short distance from the stream and stopped long enough to say, "This way."

*

After a long walk, Jarin was no drier than an hour before, and his feet were freezing; the damp floor of this tunnel was ice-cold. When Sedric saw him suffering, he called a halt, retrieved leather gloves from his wet pack, and then knelt to lash them to his feet. The gloves weren't warm, but they were sized for Sedric's big hands and their thick leather managed to repel most of the biting cold.

"I wish you hadn't given the kend skin away," Jarin said, remembering what his uncle had told the ferryman. "I'll bet it would keep me warm."

"I'll bet you're right about that," said Sedric. "But it can't be helped. If you'd kept your pack strapped to your back, you'd at least have a blanket."

Jarin realized he would have been a wet blanket, but he didn't want to bring that up. "Do you have anything to eat?" he asked.

Instead of scolding him, Sedric chuckled. "You have a one-track mind, Jarin. Yes, I have a bite or two left."

"It's not more of that bean poop, is it?"

His uncle's sudden laughter eased the tension bottled up since being captured by the Jihenans. "I'm glad you made it out of the river, nephew, in more ways than one." Sedric put an arm around him. "I'd never be able to face your papa again had you drowned, and your company hasn't been as bad as I thought it would be."

"Thanks."

"Just keep your nose clean and do as I say."

Jarin nodded. "Are we going to find the Tree?"

"This is the correct path. The wizard wrote about diving through the eye of the moon during his quest, and that's exactly what we've done, don't you think? He didn't mention anything about a dangerous whirlpool, but the east branch of the Vonspryer fills with water only after heavy rains, and that alcove behind the Wedge was probably dry when he discovered the entrance. I suspect he jumped through a dry hole and fell into the same underground pool that we did."

"Then you knew where to steer the boat."

Sedric nodded. "When I saw the moonlight touch the top of the Wedge, I knew which branch of the river to aim for. The hard part was staying close to the wall, so the current would push us into the eye. And I might have done a better job of it had the water not been so high. A little luck saved us."

Jarin wasn't sure he'd call their present circumstances lucky, but at least they were alive.

His uncle handed him a strip of dried meat wrapped in waxy cloth. Jarin chewed on it as they resumed their trek through the tunnels.

*

Eventually the tunnel opened up into a large cavern riddled with tiny pools of water spaced between stalagmites no taller than Jarin's legs. Each pool glowed with a greenish light, making the dark floor appear to be covered in tinted stars. One particularly large pool in the center of the cavern swirled slowly with a mix of green and yellow light.

The torch went dark, leaving both of them in a verdant glow. "This is a good place to get some rest," Sedric said. "We will be able to see without my efforts to sustain a flame."

Jarin and Razor approached the large pool. "Is it safe to drink?"

Sedric pointed at Razor, who sniffed the water and shied away. "I think your pet has answered that question."

"I'm thirsty."

"The color of the water may be appealing, but a poisonous algae grows in the pools. Here, take a sip of this."

Sedric handed him a water pouch. Jarin took a hearty swig, complained that it tasted like the river, and then squirt some into Razor's face and mouth. His uncle paced back and forth, examining their surroundings, finally choosing a spot to sit against a stalagmite. A flat, whitish wall across from him seemed to occupy his attention.

"What are you looking at?" Jarin asked.

"See for yourself."

Jarin stood beside his uncle and stared at the cavern wall. A shadowy picture was there, as if drawn in charcoal—an image of a huge four-legged beast with horns.

Sedric explained, "The wizard said he defeated a guardian with a spell so intense an imprint of the battle was burned into the stone."

"Was this before or after he found the Tree?"

"Good question," said Sedric. "It must have been after he obtained greater magic or he might not have had the power to defeat the guardian."

Jarin looked around nervously. "Are there other monsters down here?"

"Perhaps."

"You don't sound too worried about it."

Sedric patted the ground beside him, urging Jarin to sit. "I want to show you something."

Jarin was glad to get off his aching feet and remove the sandal-like gloves. Razor came over, licked his hand, and settled down to be scratched.

Sedric handed him the hollow spike of metal that had held the special acorn from the World Tree, the acorn they had lost to the blood raven. The spike was no heavier than a block of wood, with one end filed to a sharp point. Jarin decided it would make a good weapon if he lost his knife.

"It feels warm," said Jarin.

"Indeed. Notice its coloring, which varies from top to bottom and around the sides."

"Like Papa's cherrywood chest."

"A fair comparison," said Sedric. "The spike is made of rockwood."

"How can it be both rock and wood?"

"It's just a word to describe how strong it is. This is a piece of the Tree itself."

"Is it magic too?"

"It's a key that allows passage through these caves."

"Even though we lost the seed inside it?"

"I'm hoping that doesn't make a difference. If anything still lives down here, we should pass unharmed, because we have rockwood."

The way in which Sedric glanced away made Jarin think his uncle had told a fib.

Jarin said, "If it doesn't work, you'll burn the monster to ashes, like the wizard, won't you?"

Sedric took the rockwood spike and put it back in his pack. "You give me too much credit. If I could wield such power, I wouldn't need to find the Tree."

Jarin pointed to the scrap of wood his uncle had been using as a torch. "You conjured fire out of thin air."

"That's not enough."

"What about the mask? Isn't it magic too?"

"I fear the mask is imbued with a dangerous power. I dare not tamper with it here."

"When we get to the Tree?"

"Yes."

At that moment, Jarin wished he hadn't forgotten to take his yeni's skull from home. Although it had never given him good luck, it might have been magical in another way. "Weren't you going to show me how to create magic fire?"

"No, I wasn't"

"Why not? Because I might *lose my soul* or something, like those evil sangomas?"

"Now you're sounding like a snotty little boy again. Learning magic is a lot of hard work for little gain."

Jarin crossed his arms and stewed. Sedric had used a parental voice again.

After a space of silence, his uncle said, "I made a bargain with the queen of the mud jiks so I could learn some spells, such as creating fire with a snap of my fingers, enchanting objects, and conjuring illusions. I'm not proud of what I did, for it endangered my friends and nearly cost me my mind. I once had a talent for making tools, but I gave that up for magic. And for a time, I didn't care. I wanted to be as powerful as Nolath, the great wizard from the stories. After my euphoria ended, however, I came to my senses and realized how close I'd come to harming those I loved. That's when I gave up such foolishness and began to research how the wizard found the Tree."

"What bargain did you make with the queen?"

"A simple thing, really. I taught her how to speak."

"That's not hard," said Jarin. "Everyone knows how to talk."

"For us it's an easy thing to do; children learn the trick in a few years and never forget it. But for all creatures of Kalor, speaking is harder than reading is for you, which means they can't do it without our help."

"I talked with the hunter who tried to kill me."

"Weerlords have expended great power and struck many bargains with humans of the past to gain the ability to speak. Skinwalkers, too, can communicate like us, but only when they take over a human body."

Hearing the word *skinwalkers* gave Jarin goose bumps. "So they can do magic spells and we can talk. That doesn't sound fair."

"Depends on how you look at it," said Sedric. "Weerlords have always envied our unique abilities, which is why they tried to become human. Now they're strange hybrids."

"Is that why they look so weird?"

Sedric nodded. "Despite all their magic, they will never become exactly like us. The power of speech is a magic gift from Earth. Did you know that on Earth, there were so many languages that one clan had to learn the language of another clan to communicate? What's interesting is that when humans arrived on Kalor, all clans spoke a common tongue. This fact has intrigued me, because it suggests that the magic of Kalor might be suppressing some of our own special talents."

As Sedric spoke, Jarin's eyelids grew heavy. He wasn't too interested in languages—whatever they were—and his body was tired. "Can we rest here a little longer?"

"Of course," said his uncle. "Get some sleep."

Jarin yawned, curled up with Razor, and quickly fell into a deep slumber.

FORTY

Sedric hated lying to his nephew, especially after the boy had saved his life, but Jarin was scared enough already and it wouldn't do any good to go over all the frights they might face. Dangers lurked in these cave, and despite his story about the rockwood spike protecting them, nothing but pure luck would let them pass without at least one life-threatening encounter.

The wizard himself had faced three life-threatening trials while on his journey to the Tree. The first was a titan's candle pointing to the eye of the moon, which Sedric now understood was the moon's light upon the Wedge. The second trial was a guardian roaming the dangerous way leading to the valley of mist. And the third had been wild children, who nearly ate him alive. This last threat had been avoided only when the children discovered Nolath's bottle of hard liquor and began to fight over it, giving the wizard time to escape.

Sedric's bottle of apple brandy had been lost when the boat capsized, but an encounter with wild children wasn't the trial he was worried about now. He feared a guardian still roamed these tunnels.

The huge imprint of a guardian loomed over the glowing pool like a dire warning. A trickle of water running down the wall had erased part of the imprint, replacing it with a crust of white limestone.

Curiosity got the better of him and he went in for a closer look. The outline of the bull-like beast was sloppy and misshapen. It couldn't possibly be real, could it?

He rubbed his hand across the outline and a dark substance smeared onto his palm, dark as soot but with a gummy texture. It smelled like oil . . . and something else.

Marsh mud.

Having lived for a time with the queen of the mud jiks, he knew this smell all too well. It came from the thickest swamps and gave off an odor of rotting plants mixed with the oily scent of tar. Bubbling up from remote bogs where strange plants grew, the mud held magical properties; the mud jiks disguised themselves with it, and their queen used it to set deadly traps. Few knew the mud's secrets, but Sedric's bargain with the queen had taught him some of its power.

It seemed Nolath had also known of the mud, a substance said to be decaying magic itself, which seeped into everything not of Earth. It might once have been the pure essence of the World Tree, but like juice turned to vinegar, it had become sour. The foul-smelling stuff soaked into the flesh of most native wildlife, making it nearly inedible.

Sedric stepped back in fear. This imprint wasn't the remains of a magic blast; it was a sigil of power.

And it was holding back a monster.

We can't stay here, he thought. *The water trickling down the wall has broken the magic seal.*

Of course, a trigger must first release a guardian. Such creatures were born of water and stone and activated only when humans crossed a forbidden boundary. Nobody knew how guardians had come to exist, but clues hinted that the Creators themselves had put them in a few deep places in Kalor to keep humans away.

Sedric took the rockwood spike from his pocket and, using the flat end, scraped off some of the mud from the seal where it looked thickest. The wizard must have been in a hurry when he drew the sigil, for the whole shape of it barely looked like the majestic bull it was supposed to be; globs of the sticky mud lay here and there, especially around the bull's nose.

After collecting a large sample, Sedric reached up to where the water had erased part of the bull's horn and redrew the line.

Then he stepped back to examine his work.

Because he wasn't the true author of the sigil, he doubted his efforts would renew the magic and keep the guardian at bay. But what else could he do?

He thought of the mask. It held a portion of the wizard's power, which might be used to renew the sigil's ward.

Did he dare unveil the mask?

Enwrapped in cloth, it was still damp with river water, but an inborn power kept it warm. As he took it from his pack, he realized the only way he might be able to unleash its power while away from the Tree was to put it over his face.

And that scared him. It was a death mask, after all. Who could say what horrors he might behold? Or whether he'd even survive the attempt?

"No," he said to himself. "I must wait until we find the Tree."

Without uncovering it, he moved to put the mask back into his pack. But a shocking pain suddenly went up his arm and he dropped it onto the floor.

The yellow-green pool stirred. Something was rising from the water. First came horns, followed by the head of a huge bull. When its nostrils emerged, the guardian snorted fire.

Sedric turned to wake Jarin, but the boy was already on his feet, his eyes wide with fright, knife drawn. Razor barked, but his tail was between his legs.

"Stay light on your feet," said Sedric. "We're going to make a run for it."

The bull's massive shoulders appeared, glistening with the glowing algae of the pool. Behind it, the sigil burst into flames and began dripping in fiery clumps from the wall.

Sedric took up the mask and shoved it into his pack. Then he pointed past the bull to the far end of the cave, where a dark exit lay. "Go!" he yelled.

The boy was indeed fast. He took off running, darting past the water, weaving between the stalagmites, and hopping over the smaller pools. In no time at all, he'd gone through the exit.

Sedric tried to follow, but the sudden effort made his legs pop and grind like rusted machinery. As he stumbled past the pool, the guardian lifted its front hoofs onto the floor and heaved its body out of the water.

The thing was enormous, easily twice the size of the largest bull he'd ever seen. Fluorescent water poured off its haunch-es. With its horns, it made a swipe at Sedric, missing his ear by inches and spraying him in the greenish liquid.

"Don't stop!" he shouted after Jarin, knowing the boy would be running blindly in the dark. "Follow your pet!"

In his hurry, Sedric lost his hat, and he tripped twice, bare-ly catching himself on stalagmites. He could hear the guard-ian smashing through the stone pillars behind him, felt the floor shake. The exit seemed far away and he wasn't sure he was going to make it, so it was a surprise when he reached the tunnel unharmed.

The darkness here was more than he had bargained for. As the light from the cave of pools faded, he felt sure he was going to run straight into a wall. All he could see were spots of glowing water on his hands and feet.

As the guardian came in the tunnel, its nostrils full of fire, periodic shots of red light were cast all around.

The tunnel was straight and wide, going beyond the bursts of light. Its ceiling was too high to see, creating a sense that he was at the bottom of a deep crevice. The level ground made running a bit easier, but there seemed to be nowhere to hide.

He felt the heat of the guardian's breath at his back. It wouldn't be long now. The bull would soon run him down.

Jarin's voice echoed, "Up here!"

Sedric looked left and right and then left again. Razor's barks guided him. Jarin and his pet had found a way up to a ledge high above the road.

A blast of intense heat enveloped him, burning his ex-posed neck and ears. Terrible pain covered his head.

With nothing to lose, he turned sharply. The bull bellowed

and, in its effort to give chase, toppled over. The sound of the crash was like a building falling.

The guardian's fire revealed the narrow path Jarin had taken to reach the ledge. It wasn't much more than a jutting crack in the wall. It would be tough to climb, but Sedric kept going anyway. Panic gave him strength, fear gave him speed; his old bones strained to keep up as he scrambled up to the boy.

A mighty tremor spoke of the guardian's attempt to knock them down; horns ripped into the wall beneath them, tearing away dirt and rock. The bull's wet body glowed faintly; its nostrils snorted red fire.

For some unknown reason, Jarin removed his wool shirt and threw it recklessly over Sedric's head. All went dark. *That fool boy is going to make me stumble back to the bottom!*

"Your hair is on fire!" Jarin yelled.

Sedric grabbed the shirt and patted his head. No wonder he'd been able to see the path up here so well.

The ground shook again and he fell hard to one knee. First a burned head and now a bruised knee!

The front of the shirt had a few fresh holes in it when he handed it back, but the boy hardly noticed as he urged him to get up.

"This ledge keeps going!" said Jarin. "This way."

The boy could obviously see in the faint light of the bull's fire, and Sedric had no choice but to chase his dark shadow, hoping Jarin knew where he was going. The crack became a wider pathway, where Sedric stumbled less. Thirty feet below, the guardian followed, ramming its head into the wall and shaking the earth.

Suddenly Jarin and Razor disappeared. Had they fallen?

He stopped to peer over the edge. The guardian was grinding its head into the wall below him, bellowing in frustration. A whole section of the path in front had crumbled. He hollered for the boy.

Something grabbed his sleeve, yanking him into a narrow alcove. "What were you looking at?" Jarin asked.

"I thought you had gone over the side."

"There is a tunnel back here. Do you think you can squeeze through?"

It was too dark to see what the boy had seen. "It's better than staying on the main road with the guardian." Sedric took out the rockwood spike and snapped his fingers. The end of the spike was still covered with a residue of mud and flared with an intense light.

Jarin shielded his eyes, voiced his amazement, and then went down a narrow tunnel barely wide enough for Sedric to wriggle through. Behind him, the guardian hammered against the rock.

Raw pain on his head and ears was torturous, and the closeness of the torch's flame made it feel as if his head had reignited. Most of his hair had burned away, and he could feel blisters beginning to bubble upon his skin.

"Here, take the light," he told Jarin, who was more than happy to comply.

When the tunnel widened, he stopped and poured some of their drinking water over his head. It did little to ease the pain, which meant he had no choice but to endure it. He told the boy to keep going.

Their way turned in a direction that roughly paralleled the main road. On their left, the light revealed hints of broken columns embedded in the earthen wall and stairways leading to enormous doorways, all collapsed and clogged with stone. Could this have once been a fabled palace of the Creators?

Despite his suffering, Sedric breathed a sigh of relief and managed to grin. "I'll bet the wizard never discovered this passageway beside the Perilous Road."

Jarin seemed to sense his mood and looked back happily. "I told you Razor and I could find the Tree."

"If not the Tree, at least a wonder."

FORTY-ONE

When the drawbridge lowered on the morning of the second day after the battle, it was too late for the baron to make a dignified exit. He'd waited too long to thank the legion properly for saving his lands, and his panicked attempts at negotiation during the night—all delivered by an exhausted pageboy dressed in pauper's clothes—did little to endear him to the general.

A single trumpet sounded from the castle walls as the baron, garbed in a purple robe trimmed with ermine, black leather riding chaps, and high riding boots jammed around his fat calves, spurred a white stallion between two columns of legionaries standing at attention. Mira waited at the end of the columns, ordered at the last minute by Krassus to greet the baron as a guest of honor.

She knew what it meant to be the consul's guest.

This was a thinly veiled surrender, which the baron insisted was a truce. He surveyed the columns of soldiers with his nose in the air, forcing his mount to prance sideways between them at an unnatural angle.

Yet, despite the worst rumors Mira had heard about the man—some involving his selfishness and greed—a sense of pity came over her. Here was a nobleman clearly out of his league. And the fact that the general was not here to welcome him seemed like an unjust snub to show Jihenan strength.

Standing alongside Mira were two of the baron's mightiest knights. Both were enormous men clad in full battle armor—one as tall as a draft horse, the other so wide he looked fat. Sir Garon and Sir Rydel.

Cowering next to the knights was a smaller man named simply Kreyd—a mousey conjurer with a purple goose egg on his forehead and a few missing teeth. He claimed to have been struck in the face while fending off a weerlord's potent spell, but as he had related the encounter to Mira, the quiet looks Sir Garon and Sir Rydel had given each other said that Kreyd might be lying.

As the baron passed between the columns, the Jihenan legionaries turned their backs on him and walked away, leaving the nobleman alone in an open field. Sir Garon stepped up quickly, took the stallion's reins, and helped the heavy man to the ground.

Sir Rydel dropped to one knee, and Mira decided she should do the same. Kreyd, however, merely bowed at the waist. The baron picked his way daintily through the mud and grass like a child afraid he might crush a flower. He told the two of them to rise.

"These foreigners are rich," he said as he scanned the campsite.

Sir Rydel's voice was hoarse, presumably from shouting orders two nights ago. "Don't let their opulence fool you into thinking they're soft, my lord. The battle revealed their true nature."

"Their tactics killed many of my men."

Sir Rydel hesitated, then said, "None of us would have survived without them."

"Hmm . . . ," said the baron.

The conjurer, Kreyd, was quick to add his own opinion. "They'll use us, then cast us away like table scraps when they're done. Be wary, my lord."

"Of course." The baron's eyes fell upon Mira. "Who are you?"

"Mira Kaul."

"You're one of the barbarians from the east who claimed your lands were overrun by trolls."

"Yes, milord."

"Have you forgotten how to curtsey?"

"I chose to kneel."

The baron squinted at her. "I like a girl who curtseys. It reminds me of her proper place among men. Why are you here?"

Kreyd cleared his throat. "She is a local peasant acting as spokeswoman. Meant to ease General Krassus's takeover of your land."

"A clever ploy," said the baron. "But it won't work. If he'd sent somebody other than a *girl*, I might have listened."

Mira instantly regretted the pity she'd felt for the man, and her rising temper almost made her lash out with a rude comment of her own. With great effort she said nothing.

Abrasive men were no strangers to her, and besides, she was here to keep the peace, not inform a pompous nobleman he would likely be made a slave soon.

She curtsied. "General Krassus is anxious to meet you. Unfortunately, he is tied up with urgent business and asks that you wait in his pavilion."

The baron frowned. "I consented to meet him outside the comfort of my castle and then he makes me wait? Perhaps he doesn't want to trade for my valuable goods after all?"

Sir Rydel scrutinized Mira at a height even with hers. "What could be so urgent that he ignores the baron? He is a busy man."

"You must be patient," Mira said. "These Jihenans are a touchy people, and they do things on their own terms or not at all."

"They are in *my* lands, where *my* word is law," the baron said, his voice rising. "And you have the nerve to tell me that—"

"The general is interrogating the prisoner," Mira blurted out.

Kreyd inhaled in surprise. "The demon lord?"

Mira nodded.

"If that's the case," said the baron, "then I have a right to meet the monster. His armies invaded my lands, after all."

"That may not be wise," said Mira.

"Why not?"

Sir Garon, who had been quietly holding the baron's stallion, asked, "Where are they keeping the demon?"

The ominous tone in Sir Garon's words caused Mira to step back in fear. The tall knight sounded like a man ready to draw the sword at his side and slay everyone who stood in his way here and now.

Seeing the hard stares of all four men, Mira decided it was useless to argue. With a shrug, she pointed to an area of the field surrounded by a tall canvas fence.

The baron's party immediately marched over. Mira followed as quietly as she dared.

Two legionaries standing guard drew their swords and tried to stop the baron from entering the enclosure, but Sir Garon and Sir Rydel positioned the stallion as a shield and forced the guards to step aside to avoid being trampled. One of the guards managed to come back around as the baron and Kreyd were entering, but Sir Garon unsheathed his longsword and turned the other's shorter gladius with a loud clang. The big knight then kicked the guard in the chest, knocking him down.

Mira slipped inside after the baron.

"By the Creators," breathed Kreyd, stopping short at what he saw before him.

Chained to two metal poles hung the captured weerlord, stripped of garment. Its half-beast, half-manlike body was thin, with the scale-like skin of a snake, which now flaked and shed in the heat of the sun. Upon its forehead, two red scars shaped like upside-down crosses marred the otherwise unblemished skin of its head. Deep etchings adorned its body, each one the color of mud.

With its ribbed chest heaving from weariness and pain, the creature raised its head.

Mira was shocked to see humanlike eyes.

The baron, too, was taken aback. "What . . . *is* it?"

General Krassus and the Second Sangoma turned to face the intruders. As the guards came rushing in to confront the baron and his men, he waved the two away and told them to stand down.

The knights murmured quietly, obviously disappointed that they were not going to be fighting after all.

Krassus looked the baron up and down. "You must be the Baron of Guldheim."

The fat man straightened, grasping the lapels of his ermine robe. "Indeed I am. You must be—"

"I gave instructions for you to wait in my pavilion."

"I thought it prudent to meet the monster responsible for terrorizing my lands and murdering my subjects."

"And threatening your wealth," said Krassus. "Yes, I know about you, baron. Your money-grubbing hands probably hoped your king would pay handsomely for this creature."

The weerlord, his arms stretched out to the side with shackles clasped tightly around his bizarre hands, made a gurgling noise that might have been an attempt at laughter. "Humans spy wealth in everything," it said. "I am but the first in a new uprising against your kind."

Krassus turned to face the creature. "What do you mean you're the first?"

"The human scourge will end soon."

Kreyd regarded the weerlord from a distance. "Yes, that's it; I see it. You're merely a lieutenant sent to probe our strength."

"What?" said Krassus. "How do you know?"

Before Kreyd could open his mouth, the weerlord answered, "The conjurer sees the markings. He knows the truth."

Kreyd nodded. "I've read about you, Inokan of the White Hills. You and all of your kind were banished by King Aidan himself, long ago. The brand on your forehead was placed there to warn us that you are a demon of Kalor, that you cannot be trusted. You will never join the ranks of humanity, no matter how much your body changes."

"Now I do penance," said the creature.

"Who leads you?" asked Krassus.

The weerlord let out another gurgling laugh. The general looked at the Sangoma with concern.

"I maintain control," assured the Second. "We are safe."

The weerlord said, "The irony might buckle your knees, general. Just know that *our* lord has shown all of Kalor the path of redemption. And that path is your *death*."

"I say we kill the demon where it stands!" said Sir Garon.

Sweat ran down the baron's neck. "Yes, kill it," he said. "It shouldn't live another minute."

The weerlord's body went rigid, as if experiencing great pain. Then its eyes flashed red and it howled at the sky. The etchings in its skin suddenly became the color of hot coals.

The ground shook. Everyone took a step back.

Then silence.

The weerlord relaxed and turned its gaze upon the general.

"He knows you now, consul," it said. "He comes to slay you."

When the weerlord's gaze fell upon the baron, the fat man turned and fled for the castle gates.

FORTY-TWO

The hike through the tunnels under the mountain was taking so long Jarin began to wonder if they were lost again. After his uncle had aimlessly wandered through the forest a few days ago, he hadn't fully trusted the man's sense of direction.

So when they came into a huge cave and spied daylight at the far end, Jarin opened his mouth to let out a cheer. They'd made it!

Sedric clamped a strong hand around his mouth and pushed him to the cave floor. "Keep it down," he hissed. "Do you want to get eaten alive?"

A surge of fear rose in Jarin's throat and he shook his head. Had they stumbled upon the lair of another guardian?

Sedric let go. Crouched onto his belly, he edged forward to peek beyond a rocky rise in the floor.

Razor was staring ahead, a growl rising in his throat. Jarin hugged the dog and shushed him.

At the opening of the cave, a group of people squatted

around a fire, eating meat off bones. They were unlike any kind of people Jarin had seen. At first he thought they were children, but even though they were no taller than he, they had the thick muscles of adults. Their hair was long and messy, falling upon their shoulders in matted dreadlocks, and what little clothing they wore was filthy and torn. Their faces were flat, with noses almost too stubby to distinguish. The few sounds they made were the result of smacking lips.

"They look nice enough," whispered Jarin. "Maybe we can just walk past them."

"You're as blind as you are dense," said Sedric. "What do you think they're eating?"

"I don't know. Leg of lamb?"

Sedric grunted. "Ask them for a serving. I'm sure you'll enjoy the ribs."

"Then how do we sneak past?"

"I don't know."

"Why don't you cast a spell to scare them away?"

At first Sedric seemed ready to scold Jarin for being foolish, but then he rolled onto his back and grew thoughtful.

"You know, that's not a bad idea," he said. "An illusion is all I need. As simpleminded savages, they probably fear a mysterious beast lives at the back of this cave." Sedric rolled back onto his belly. "All right, stay out of sight until I tell you to run outside. And keep that pet of yours with you."

Jarin came to his hands and knees.

His uncle took a deep breath, then rose up slowly, favoring his good leg, and stretched his arms high into the air, as if to call attention to himself. After muttering the words, "*Divide the light,*" he then sang a clear note, "*Deceive!*"

Colors poured from his fingertips, twisting together, becoming a shape in the center of the cave. The image of a great four-legged bull with long horns appeared. The thing snorted smoke and fire from its nostrils, just like the guardian that had chased them yesterday. With a bellow, the illusion of the bull faced the cave entrance.

The savages jumped to their feet, grabbing clubs and crude-looking spears. All but one began to back out of the cave.

The brave one stood firm. He wore a cape of animal skins around his shoulders, finer than anything worn by the others, and in his hands he held a scepter fashioned of polished bone, topped with red feathers.

"Uh-oh," said Sedric.

"What's going on?" asked Jarin.

"Their shaman has a magic wand!"

The savage waved his bone scepter and the illusion of the beast immediately vanished, leaving Sedric standing out in the open with nothing to protect himself but his astonished face.

"Quick!" shouted Sedric. "Back into the tunnels!"

A stone flew past Jarin's ear, missing it by inches, and smashed against the cave wall behind him. Two more whizzed past.

Razor leaped up, barking fiercely.

Jarin started to run, but before he'd taken three steps, a net ensnared him and he went down in a heap. Savages swarmed in from all sides, jabbering incoherently. He spotted his uncle grappling with the shaman, fighting tooth and nail. Sedric might have won, but another savage came up and clubbed him unconscious.

The sounds of Razor's yelping grew distant.

A savage with a string of fresh meat hanging from his teeth approached and took Jarin by the arms. He was dragged from the net and quickly stuffed into a sack that smelled like cow dung.

He tried to scream, but his first dusty breath choked in his throat. Then everything seemed to swirl and his vision blurred.

He passed out.

*

When Jarin came to, his wrists and ankles hurt and his head felt ready to burst from a pressure behind his eyeballs. A loud thumping sound pounded rhythmically in his ears, to the beat of drums.

He tried to move his arms, but they were lashed to a tree at his back. The rope dug into his skin.

It was night. A huge bonfire raged in front of him, its heat so intense his clothes were hot to the touch. He tried to turn away, but he couldn't make his muscles budge. His Hawkie was still sheathed at his hip, but he couldn't grab it.

Shadows danced around the fire as the words of a chant echoed all around:

> *Spikes with poison, ball and chain;*
> *Trapped with horror—see their pain.*

Sedric's voice barely cut through the noise. "Jarin! Wake up!"

He could barely keep his head from hanging. He tried to say, "It's only a nightmare."

"You must clear your head before the spell begins."

"It'll go away when I wake up," Jarin muttered.

The chanting rose in strength, vibrating through his hurting head:

Ceaseless shivers, cold with fear;
Heroes falter, chilled to hear,
Screams of anguish, cries of woe.
Here comes red eyes from below.

"Lift your head," Sedric pleaded. "Focus on anything but their words."

With great effort, Jarin lifted his head and watched the dark shadows dance around the fire. One of the figures—a savage with thick, hairy arms—walked in front of him, swinging some kind of stick with a ball of spikes attached to a short chain. His father had spoken of such weapons, calling them flails.

"I thought only humans could speak." Jarin turned his head sideways and caught sight of his uncle. "Or use weapons."

"It doesn't make sense." Sedric was tied to a stubby tree, staring at him with eyes full of purpose. The blisters on his head had broken and a yellowish liquid ran down his cheeks. "I think they mean to frighten us."

"Well, it's working." Jarin's whole body shook.

"Look at me," Sedric commanded. "Yes, that's it! Don't think about anything else but my ugly face. And whatever happens, don't cry out."

"Can't you blast them with wizard's fire?"

"Now wouldn't that be something?" Sedric forced a smile. "Think on that."

"Can't you?" Jarin asked.

Sedric shook his head. "My hands are tied. All I can do is spit on them."

"Are they going to hurt us?"

"No . . . No, I don't think so. They want to harvest our emotions. *Human* emotions. They're trying to summon a great power."

The shaman appeared in front of them, creeping into the light of the bonfire like a mountain cat stalking its prey. He was covered with the red feathers of blood ravens, and he flapped his arms up and down slowly as he moved. Strapped to his chest was an object of gold.

The wizard's mask!

Lifting up a gourd-shaped flask, the birdman walked up to Sedric, took hold of his cheeks, and pinched his mouth open. Sedric struggled, trying to bite the other's fingers, but the birdman was too strong and managed to pour a thick amber liquid into his mouth.

Sedric sputtered and coughed.

And the chanting continued.

> *Might and power, ease the pain.*
> *Grant us solace from our bane!*

The drumbeats ceased.

The birdman raised his hands above his head in triumph, holding aloft the golden death mask. A wind picked up, stirring his red feathers. Lightning flashed across the dark sky, revealing something in the shape of a colossal snake hanging far above.

The eyes of the mask began to glow red.

Sedric tried to snicker. "That's it," he said. "Use the mask, you fool."

As if in answer, the birdman stepped forward and shoved the mask over Sedric's face.

Jarin cried out a warning, but there was nothing he could do, no words he could say to stop what was happening.

The force of the wind grew in strength and burning embers from the fire blew over him, blistering his skin.

His uncle shrieked. The red eyes of the mask brightened, their light too intense to stare at. The birdman hopped back as if stung, and yet the mask did not fall from Sedric's face.

His uncle seemed to lose consciousness and his body went limp.

Suddenly arrows flew through the clearing and two savages cried out. One fell into the bonfire; others fled into the trees. The birdman turned to confront the attack and instantly took an arrow into his chest, collapsing in a mound of bloody feathers.

The death mask dropped to the ground.

Sedric's head dangled from his neck like a ripe peach, his eyes clenched shut.

The wind died and the air grew still. For a long moment, an eerie silence settled across the clearing.

Then a company of squat creatures emerged from the trees carrying crossbows, going cautiously, examining every inch of their surroundings. They might have been cousins of the savages lying dead on the ground, but Jarin saw subtle differences. Their heads were shorn and their clothes were spun of a fine material colored with earth tones, neatly fitted around their legs and trunks. Boots seemingly made of leaves adorned their feet.

More of them arrived. Some carried wicker shields and wooden knives or fighting staves in their long arms.

One of them spotted Jarin. "Over here!"

Another loped up and his eyes widened. "Humans."

"How would you know?" asked the first. Like the savages, he had virtually no nose and his eyes were too far apart, but the hair of his head was shorn. In fact, the only hair on his face came in the form of an orange strip, neatly trimmed, extending underneath the slits of his nostrils and across his cheeks to his ears, looking like a bizarre attempt at a mustache.

"I dunno," said the other, whose face was completely free of hair, making him appear even more childlike. "They look like I pictured them."

"Only skinnier," nodded the first. "And frail."

Jarin's dry throat made speaking hard. "Uncle Sedric needs help."

"It talks," said the first. "Definitely human."

The hairless one nodded to his companion and both newcomers worked to untie them. Jarin collapsed, his strength all but spent, his arms and legs heavy. He managed to roll onto his back and look up into the sky, but the stars were blocked by something darker than clouds.

The face of the mustached one came into view, staring down at him. "You've been drugged by their sorcerer," he said.

Jarin wanted to nod, but the effort would have cost him too much, so he lay still. Out of the corner of his eye, he could see the one he knew as Hairless Face bend over a gleaming object in the dirt.

Jarin took a long breath. "Don't touch the mask. It's a bad thing."

"So I see." Hairless Face grimaced. "I'll just scoop it up in my bag for the council to look at later."

Jarin closed his eyes and waited for his head to stop pounding, but after many long minutes, the pain had not faded. So he used all his strength to sit up and crawl over to his uncle's side.

FORTY-THREE

Sedric had been stretched out upon the ground away from the intense heat of the fire, where he lay unconscious. Jarin tried to comfort him, though he was too weak to do more than wipe some of the sweat and yellow goo away. His uncle was breathing, but he was restless. Sometimes he moaned or absently clawed at the air.

"Something's not right," Jarin said. "I'm worried."

The two squat persons stood off to the side. "We'll do what we can," said Hairless Face. "Your uncle needs a healer."

The mustached one handed Jarin a metal flask. "Drink this."

After a long swig of water, Jarin realized the metal flask was not made of metal at all. It was rockwood.

"You're woodtrolls," Jarin said.

"Funny you should say that," said Mustache. "But no. We're not made of wood and we're not trolls."

"People of the Tree?"

"That's more like it. We call ourselves the treefolk."

"We call you woodtrolls."

"I'd prefer it if you'd call me Flaks."

"What kind of creature is a flaks?" Jarin asked.

"It's not a creature. Flaks is my name."

"Oh."

Flaks's companion chuckled. "I'm a creature called a Heldig."

Jarin realized they were making fun of him, but he was in no mood for jokes. All he could say was, "Thanks for your help, Flaks and Heldig."

The two woodtrolls frowned and walked away, whispering harshly to one another about how poorly they'd treated the first human they had ever encountered.

Jarin turned back to Sedric. "I think we're among friends," he whispered. "The woodtrolls will take care of us."

Nearby, the flail lay in the dirt, its wooden handle still grasped by the hand of the dead savage who had swung it about in a display of intimidation. Though the savage was not human, he had wielded a weapon like someone who knew how to use it.

Had the savages in this part of the world learned how to make and use tools? Jarin had been taught that native creatures were not born with that talent and could only manipulate tools after expending great power, such as the weerlords commanded.

The thought worried him.

As if to confirm his worry, the woodtrolls, Flaks and Heldig, returned carrying a freshly constructed stretcher made of tree limbs lashed together with vines.

"Ah, you're feeling better, I see," said Flaks, his silly mustache turned up in a grin. "Can you walk?"

Standing was difficult, but Jarin managed to get proudly onto his legs, a feat the woodtroll did not seem impressed with. Flaks handed him a roundish object that looked identical to the rare acorn his uncle had found, only larger.

"Don't just stand there gaping at it," Heldig said. "Many such nuts fall beneath the boughs of Yggdrasil and provide much nourishment. You must eat it."

The oversized acorn was hard and, despite a white-knuckled effort, would not crack open. The woodtrolls looked on with dismay until Jarin gave up, and only then did Flaks retrieve the nut. With hands larger than his father's, the woodtroll easily cracked the shell, revealing the acorn's white center. This he tossed to Jarin and bade him eat it.

The raw, inner flesh was nearly as hard as the outer shell and almost broke Jarin's teeth as he bit down on it. How was he supposed to regain his strength if he wasted his efforts chewing on food tough as hardtack candy?

The woodtrolls seemed puzzled by his efforts, but then Flaks's face brightened. "I remember! Councilman Laern once said that humans prefer to cook their food, to improve the flavor and make it easier to eat."

Heldig agreed with a vigorous nod and brought out another acorn, which he carried to the dying bonfire and dropped into the red-hot coals. This he stirred with an ordinary stick, until a loud *pop* rang out. Then he kicked the blackened acorn out of the coals, through the dirt, and over to Jarin's toes.

The roasted shell cracked under his foot, revealing the edible nut inside. This time, it was no harder than a walnut and tasted sweet.

He smiled as an unexpected sensation moved through

him. A surge of vigor spread across his body and into his limbs, fortifying his wobbly legs and aching wrists. When he swallowed, his headache vanished and his blistered skin smoothed over and healed.

The woodtrolls inhaled with surprise.

"So the legends are true," said Heldig. "The fruit of Ygg-drasil is like a healing balm to humans."

Flaks nodded. "They absorb its power like no other crea-ture on Kalor."

"Huh?" said Jarin. "What are you talking about?"

Heldig opened his mouth to answer, but one of the other woodtrolls in the trees whistled, signaling that it was time to leave. Without another word, Heldig and his companion moved swiftly to lift Sedric onto the stretcher.

"Come," said Flaks as both woodtrolls trotted into the dark forest, the stretcher held between them.

Fearing that he might get left behind, Jarin sped after them.

There was no path, but the woodtrolls traveled through the trees with a clear sense of purpose, tirelessly jogging up one slope and down another. At one point, they climbed out of a hollow and onto a rounded ridge, the top of which was covered in grass and mosses delightfully soft underfoot. Jarin trailed behind as the woodtrolls snaked their way along the ridge.

On either side of him, the tops of great oak and maple, tall pine and alder, passed by. It was not easy to see in the dark, but soon after leaving the light of the fire, Jarin's eyes began to adjust. He perceived his surroundings in an acute way he had never known before, not even when he was out hunting yenis at night with Razor. All his senses were enhanced.

After climbing the ridge, which provided a path more open than in the valleys on either side, he realized something truly massive was hanging in the black sky above him. When he tried to look at it, however, he wasn't sure what he saw. It didn't quite look like the snake he thought he had seen earlier. Were they beneath the limbs of the great World Tree itself?

He felt as though he could run forever—which ended up being a good thing, because the woodtrolls never let up as they worked their way along the ridge, climbing ever higher. His uncle did not wake through the whole ordeal, though he once cried out and blurted nonsense.

The upslope eventually ended in a massive wall made of deeply gnarled bark, and here the woodtrolls halted. Despite his heightened senses, Jarin could not discern the length of the wall on either side, for a heavy mist had enveloped them, obscuring all view from the left and right and from above.

Was this the trunk of the Tree itself?

Heldig whistled in three short bursts, and a ladder made of vines dropped through the mist.

The woodtrolls set Sedric upon the grass. "We're almost home," said Flaks. "Take a moment to rest."

Jarin shook his head. He hardly needed to catch his breath. He felt so alive! And his mood had improved too. "I'm a creature called a Jarin," he said, trying not to smile at the woodtrolls.

"O-ho!" laughed Heldig. "Indeed!"

Flaks seemed to like the jest as well. "Such folk as you are welcome among us." He pointed at the ladder. "If you need no rest, then climb."

The ladder felt warm to the touch, and when Jarin grabbed ahold it seemed to respond to his grip like a living thing. He snatched his hand away.

Heldig nodded in admiration. "Yggdrasil accepts you as a friend and seeks to help you climb."

"Yggdrasil?" asked Jarin.

"The Tree," said Heldig. "Thus named by the Father of Words. It is our home."

"Do you live in the branches?"

Heldig laughed. "Some branches are thick as a canyon is wide, so I guess we could build homes on top of them. We live inside, where it's safe and warm."

"Your people tunnel through the Tree like termites," Jarin said, remembering what Mira had told him. "Won't you kill it?"

"Termites!" said Flaks. "What a strange thought. Yggdrasil welcomes us. Besides, it's so big and grand we can't possibly damage it. A journey around it takes two days, when the weather is good."

Jarin braved the ladder again and this time he did not flinch when the vines shifted under his hands and feet. Once, when he missed a step, the lower rung seemed to reach out and catch his fall, ensuring that his assent was easy going.

Up, up, up he went, until he reached a large opening in the bark attended by a woodtroll with a rockwood spear in his hands. He was larger than the others, with a jaw nearly as chiseled as Papa's, and he scrutinized Jarin with a wary eye before inviting him to step into the World Tree.

Jarin braved a look out across the dark landscape beyond the wall and saw, in the misty predawn light, a great blood raven perched on a massive knotted branch directly above him. The bird watched him with a dark eye, then let out a mighty cry, like a weerlord crowing at him to die. Chills when up his spine and the vines of the ladder shook.

Then the bird launched away from the branch and flew out of sight.

Jarin wasted no time stepping inside the safety of the Tree.

FORTY-FOUR

Having said nothing for almost an hour, Mira sat dutifully silent on plush cushions in Krassus's pavilion as the general carried on with running the mundane affairs of the camp. Messengers came and went, delivering reports and receiving orders. The Second Sangoma remained close to the general during it all, though he rarely spoke.

Having been cleaned up and clothed in smooth silk garments, with her face painted once again, Mira felt more like a piece of artwork than a human being. At least she had been allowed to keep her homemade necklace with the blaze stone, a plain leather strap that didn't match the fine clothes given to her by the general. It was the only item she wore that linked to her past life—a simple life that seemed so far away now.

Krassus sat at a finely crafted desk, writing with a quill and ink. The Second Sangoma stood solemnly, reading a single sheet of parchment.

"Well?" Krassus asked the sangoma.

"I never believed such a creature could exist," said the Second. "Do you trust your scout's report?"

"He's the best I have, but he doesn't have your knowledge of such things. If the report is true, this new offensive is more aggressive than the last. Are you and your brother up to the challenge?"

The Second began pacing the fine rugs in an uncharacteristic display of what Mira believed was nervous fidgets. "A few legends speak of a dragon—one of the Creators—who remained on Kalor when the others departed, but nothing in our official canon mentions it."

Krassus looked up from his writing. "You're talking about Lotan the Deceiver, who was left behind by the other gods. Only barbarians believe in that devil."

The Second shrugged. "Nevertheless, secret texts circulate within Jihena warning of Lotan's return."

"Return to what purpose?"

"To keep humans in check, lest we overrun Kalor."

Prefect Pontus entered the pavilion and waited patiently while Krassus and the Second Sangoma stared at each other in silence. Were the two debating, mind to mind?

At length, Pontus cleared his throat.

Krassus turned his eyes upon the captain. "Are we in position?"

"Hours ago," said Pontus. "We could hold the pass against ten times our number. But that's not why I've come. The king of this land has finally decided to acknowledge your presence by sending a small party of observers to help the baron deal with you. Mostly petty magicians."

"Deal with me in what way?"

"They're here to provide the baron advice and to ensure that the riches of this valley don't get carted off to Jihena."

"Too late for that," said Krassus. "But their distrust is irritating." He sat back in his chair and addressed the sangoma. "These magicians will soon discover your mastery. Go to the pass and await my arrival."

The Second raised an eyebrow, but it was Pontus who voiced their concern. "Do you think it's wise to leave the protection of the sangomas?"

"It'll only be for a moment." Krassus glanced at Mira. "Besides, I have some business I wish to take care of alone."

Pontus gave the general a brisk nod, but he was obviously displeased with the orders. "So I see."

Both he and the Second Sangoma departed.

Krassus set his writing quill down and smiled at Mira. "I apologize for the wait, but as you can see I have much to do."

"Do you control the sorcerers?" she asked.

"The sangomas? Of course."

"How?"

The general's smile faltered. "Is this how a guest treats her host?"

"You mean, how a *slave* treats her master?"

"Mira, you are not a slave."

"Then what am I doing here?"

"I thought it was obvious."

"There's little difference between a concubine and a slave."

Krassus's smile returned. "There is a *huge* difference."

Mira was furious, and it was high time she said what was on her mind. "Have you even looked at all the people you've dragged out of Jihena? They don't want to be here. None of them. Most have dreams of their own, which they keep to themselves because there is no hope. Their wills have been crushed, general. Some don't even have names! They're miserable."

"Mira—"

"Slavery is wrong."

"Who do you want me to set free?" said Krassus. "Is it some man you find attractive? Or perhaps a serving girl who cried on your shoulder? Tell me and I will make it so."

"*All* of them."

"Don't be a fool. Half of them would die within a month if they had nothing to do and no master to feed them."

Mira's muscles tensed. "Your thinking is so backwards I can hardly speak."

"That's because you have no argument." Krassus's tone carried a new edge. "Come now. Enough of this talk."

"Are the sangomas your slaves too?"

Krassus gave her a hard look, but she was too angry to care. She stared right back, unflinching.

He said, "The bloodline of Jihena was actually bound into slavery once, to the sangomas's people."

Mira sat back, speechless. As a member of the bloodline of Jihena, it was clear that Krassus understood the horrors of slavery. Yet, for reasons unknown, he refused to abandon the terrible practice.

As she tried to order her jumbled thoughts for a new protest, a servant entered uninvited, carrying a platter of food. He was larger than any who had attended the general previously and his clothes were not clean; his face was veiled.

"I didn't ask to be served," Krassus told the man. "Get out."

The servant recklessly tossed the platter at Mira, spilling cake and fruit all over her lap. She saw his eyes above the veil and knew who it was.

Shem.

Krassus drew a knife, but Shem was too quick. Pulling out a length of rope from under his shirt, he swiftly closed the distance between them. Krassus called out to the guards standing outside, but none entered.

"Shem, what are you doing here?" Mira cried.

The big man's focus never left Krassus, who slashed with his knife, drawing blood from the miller's arms.

Shem answered by knocking the general back against the chair. He took the rope and wrapped it around Krassus's neck.

"The human neck is so fragile," Shem began. His voice sounded oddly flat and unemotional.

Mira came to her feet. Using the silver platter as a weapon, she struck Shem over the head.

The miller swung an elbow, catching her in the chest, and she went down to the floor, gasping for air.

In all the years of living under the miller's roof, Shem had never struck her, though he had threatened to beat her many times. Whatever had happened to him after they left the mill, it had affected him in ways she couldn't understand.

Knife in hand, Krassus desperately stabbed Shem in the belly, the thigh, the shoulder, but the miller barely winced.

"Harm this body all you like," said Shem. "I am finished with it. Yours, however, is valuable to me now. Relax, general. I only wish you to lose consciousness so I can possess your body. To walk in your skin, as humans put it."

The words were like a death knell to Mira's ears.

Shem was possessed by a skinwalker.

The general's eyes widened in fear as Shem twisted the rope tighter around his neck. Soon Krassus's struggles grew weak and his eyelids drooped.

Mira jumped on Shem's back and put him in a chokehold, but the miller's neck was so thick with muscle that it was like trying to throttle a marble statue. The skinwalker would finish strangling the general before she caused Shem to go unconscious.

Without warning, Krassus plunged the knife through his own heart.

Shem dropped the general's body and fell to his knees, a stunned reaction to the sudden death of his victim. Krassus had chosen to die rather than be taken alive by a skinwalker; his body lay twitching on the rug, the knife protruding from his chest.

Then the miller . . . no, the skinwalker . . . seized Mira's hair and pulled her over his head. She fell onto her back, landing beneath him. His big fingers grabbed her by the throat.

She struggled against his grip, tried to hang on as long as she could. Breathing was impossible. Her vision blurred.

Mira began to lose consciousness, but the wounded body of Shem grew weak and his strength gave way. As he collapsed on top of her, an unnatural cry tore from his mouth.

A shimmer of air, like a mirage, rose up from the body and swelled to fill half the pavilion. A touch of cold swept across Mira and the emotion of rage touched her mind—rage against humans and their might. Its vile nature overwhelmed her senses, forced her to turn her head and retch in disgust.

Shem's body went completely slack as the spirit demon departed in a gust of rotten-smelling wind that rent the canvas ceiling.

Mira heaved Shem off her and rolled the miller onto his side. His lungs labored for air.

"Shem!" Propping herself up onto her elbow, she pushed strands of hair away from his brow.

"Mira . . ." The miller looked at her through bloodshot eyes. "My beautiful girl . . . I couldn't protect the mill . . . I'm sorry."

"Don't worry about the mill."

"Jarin?"

"All of us escaped, thanks to you."

"He's . . . he's a tough kid." Shem closed his eyes and breathed his last.

Mira wept.

FORTY-FIVE

The hallway carried the scent of fresh sawdust, like Master Rowland's mill located far upstream from Papa's flourmill, at a place where Willow Stump Creek ran swiftly enough to spin a waterwheel and power the woodcutter's great metal saw. The walls here were smooth as polished marble, with tans and browns and even a little red and orange running in veins of color. Evenly spaced alcoves held glowing stones, providing a soft light.

As time and their passage through the tunnel wore on, Jarin's happiness faded, replaced by a deep concern for his uncle, who now slept on the stretcher like a dying man. Sedric had not stirred or called out in the last hour.

The woodtrolls said little as they jogged, save to ask how Jarin was holding up.

"I'm fine," he replied. "I feel like I could run forever in this place."

The woodtrolls ahead smiled.

Behind, Heldig explained, "Yggdrasil will sustain you, but

at a cost. You must eat a hearty meal before sleep, lest the wasting disease overtakes you."

Jarin didn't know what the wasting disease was, but he knew an empty stomach all too well and it always made him feel like he was going to shrivel up and die. In fact, he was starving now.

"Will you have more of those roasted nuts to eat?" he asked.

"Plenty of nuts," said Heldig. "All raw, I'm afraid. We do not use fire inside the Tree, so no roasting."

"How do you cook?"

"There are other ways to prepare food without using fire. Children eat a sundried mash and drink a milk made from the nuts that I think you will enjoy."

Flaks added, "And near the bark we capture grubs with a soft flesh and a delicious flavor."

Grubs were not Jarin's idea of good eating and he hoped the mash was tasty, but at least he wasn't going to starve.

"How much longer?" he asked.

"Very soon, my human friend," said Heldig. "Very soon."

At last the light ahead grew brighter and they entered an enormous cavern that looked more like the inside of a great alpine lodge than a dirty cave. Jarin tilted his head skyward, finding himself at the bottom of what appeared to be a wide, airy shaft that soared upward as far as he could see. If there was a ceiling, he couldn't find it. Hewn bridges spanned one side of the expanse to the other, and stairways led in myriad directions. Hundreds of woodtrolls bustled about their business, though many stopped what they were doing and peered over balcony railings to catch glimpses of him.

Jarin stopped mid-stride and gazed in wonder. This was a whole city of woodtrolls!

"No time for sightseeing," said Heldig. "This way."

Flaks and Heldig carried Sedric over to one end of the floor and up a narrow stairway that wound around the circular wall until they came to a bridge that crossed over to an archway leading into a wide concourse. Woodtrolls of all ages parted before them, gaping in open astonishment, curiosity, and even fear. Few were taller than Jarin, but they looked tough enough, even the young, whose longish arms and big hands suggested great strength. None carried weapons, except for the big soldier he'd met earlier who was now following closely behind him.

Flaks and Heldig turned down a narrow hallway, went up another stairway, crossed a short distance, and entered a small room. Here they placed Sedric on a squat bed too short for his long legs.

"No matter," said Flaks, stepping back to finger his mustache thoughtfully. "We'll have the artisans construct a human-sized bed."

A second bed lay against another wall, sized perfectly for Jarin.

Woodtrolls began to congregate outside the room, conversing in hushed tones. Jarin caught the word *human* many times, occasionally spoken in awe, though they were drowned out by countless warnings about Sedric's potential threat. They didn't seem to know how to judge the danger Jarin might pose, despite several comments about the fine craftsmanship of the Hawkie knife at his hip.

Flaks ordered everyone out except for two youngsters

holding platters of food, whom he ushered inside. Both hurriedly set the platters on the floor and then stepped back so they could stare at him with wide eyes.

"Eat," said Flaks. "Then sleep."

"That's it?" said Jarin. "You're just going to leave me here to eat and sleep?"

"I advise against sleeping and then eating, because the wasting disease might cause you to wake up dumb as a doorpost."

Heldig reached for a cookie-like wafer and began to munch loudly. "Are you sure about that, Flaks? Just because you woke up that way once doesn't mean our human friend will."

Flaks slowly took his own wafer and took a bite. "I hope that was said in fun."

Heldig laughed and turned to Jarin. "Eat up, young one. Someone will check on you soon."

"What about my uncle?"

Heldig pulled on an ear. "He's already asleep. When he wakes up, feed him something. The smaller flask there is fermented nutmilk, which I'm sure he'll enjoy."

"But . . . but . . . ," Jarin began.

"Relax. You're not our prisoners."

Flaks added quickly, "Gretten will stand outside the door to keep others from disturbing you. We're off to deliver our report to the council. When you've rested, feel free to take a look around."

Jarin wasn't too happy about being shoved into a room and expected to keep quiet like some farm animal put inside a barn, but he didn't dare leave Sedric.

"What about a healer?" he asked.

"The best thing to do is feed your uncle," said Flaks. "Remember when you ate a single nut? It appears that for humans its powers are more effective than our medicine."

That made sense. The healing magic of the nut had made him whole again.

The woodtrolls seemed satisfied by his reaction and promptly left with their goodbyes, dragging the two youngsters with them.

Jarin took a bowl of what looked like porridge—there was no spoon—sat on the bed, and gently shook his uncle. But no amount of nudging would wake him.

So Jarin turned to his own needs.

Eat then sleep, he thought.

Good thing he liked to do both.

FORTY-SIX

Staring at him with those eyes spaced too far apart was a young woodtroll girl no taller than his elbow. To Jarin's way of thinking, she was hardly tall enough to walk, and yet here she had stridden up to him, straight from the other side of the concourse. She had skin the color of walnuts and frizzy hair pulled back into a thick ponytail bound with vines. Her eyes glittered like polished riverstones.

"You're funny looking," she said.

"I'm a human," said Jarin.

"My mama says I should be nice."

"What else did she tell you?"

"That you spell trouble."

"What does that mean?"

"I don't know, but that's what she says."

"Is that why your people stare at me?"

"We stare because you're funning looking."

"Oh."

"And you smell like you haven't taken a bath all week."

"It's the fish," said Jarin. "I swam in a river a couple of days ago."

"Would you like me to show you the baths?"

"I really don't like to take baths."

"Then you're going to stink and we're going to think you spell trouble."

Jarin sighed. "What's your name?"

"Pratsom."

"What kind of a name is *Pratsom*?"

"My mama says I talk a lot."

"I don't understand."

"Me neither, but that's what she says."

"All right, Pratsom. Where are the baths?"

The girl led him into the main shaft, up a flight of stairs, around a spacious balcony where woodtrolls appeared to be bartering over goods and services, down to a—

"Hold up." Jarin spied a gathering of folk outside two tall doors fronting the balcony. One of the woodtrolls, an older man by the looks of him, with a long beard, stood in the center of the group, holding a white staff topped with a carving of an open-mouthed man.

The carving was identical to the one etched into the fallen beech tree Sedric had dug into to obtain the seed.

"That's Councilor Laern," said Pratsom.

"What's he doing?"

"Watch and learn."

One of the women cradled a baby in her arms and walked up to the councilor, begging him to bless it. Laern touched the infant's crown with the head of his staff and spoke in a bold tone, as in ritual.

"Receive the gift of speech," he said.

Three high notes of a woman singing issued forth from the mouth of the staff and the mother stepped away with joyous tears. Another woman came forward, held up her baby, who received the same blessing, and wept as the notes filled the air—these, the notes of a man.

"One for a girl and one for a boy," Pratsom explained. "When the babes speak their first words, their mothers will name them."

"What happens if they don't receive this blessing?"

"They will never speak a word."

"Never?"

"Isn't that what I said?"

"Where did he get the staff?"

"It was a gift from a wizard. A *human* wizard." Pratsom revealed a hint of envy in her answer.

"Is the gift of tool-making given later on?" Jarin asked.

The girl shook her head. "I think it comes with the gift of speech, but it only allows us to make things out of wood."

*

After bathing in a huge room full of oval pools surrounding a waterfall that smelled like clean rain, Jarin returned to his room. The chatty girl had not stayed to watch him bathe, and he was left to find his way back alone.

When he arrived in his room, he found that Sedric's bed had been replaced with one that was the full length of the wall. Considering the skill used to fashion it out of rock-wood, it was as good as anything Master Rowland had built.

Sedric was still asleep, so Jarin went to the tiny table sitting between the beds and touched one of the egg-shaped stones—probably rockwood too—and waited for its light to fill the room.

His uncle stirred wearily.

"Uncle Sedric?"

"Where are we, boy?"

"Inside the Tree, where the woodtrolls live." Jarin came closer, glad to see his uncle talking. "We made it here alive. We found it! Can you believe it? But . . . but Razor got lost and I don't know where to go looking for him."

"Would you forget about that stupid pet for once?" Sedric propped himself into sitting position, his back resting against the wall. He gingerly felt the broken blisters on his head, which had gone crusty as yellowish fluid had dried. "Are we prisoners?"

"No," said Jarin. "I think they want to help us."

"Where's the mask?"

Councilor Laern suddenly appeared in the doorway. Or had he been quietly watching all along? "Safe with us," he said. The old woodtroll was clothed in a fine robe the color of sage and carried his staff with an air of authority. "Good to see you awake, Sedric. I am Laern, High Councilor to the treefolk. We welcome you with friendship and hospitality."

Jarin offered his uncle the smaller flask, knowing he'd be thirsty. Sedric drank deeply, held the flask out in front of his face as if to admire it, then took several more swallows. When he addressed the councilor, his eyes were more piercing and focused than before.

"The mask is dangerous," he said.

Laern's face was unruffled. "As people of the Tree, we are well adapted to the dangers of powerful magic."

"See," said Jarin, holding up one of the glowing stones. "They have these rocks that glow by themselves. I'm taking a bunch home."

"I'm afraid their power will fade outside the valley, young one," said Laern. "Most magic we possess is given by the Tree itself, and cannot be taken beyond the mists. Not unless you are a great wizard."

Jarin sighed. "Mira would have been so impressed." Jarin put the stone back in place.

"The wizard, Nolath, obtained great magic here," said Sedric. "I have seen and know the truth. The mask is merely a modest remnant of his power."

"Nolath is a separate matter," said Laern. "When you are able, the council would like to meet with you."

"I am able now," said Sedric, climbing out of bed. "Let's go."

"Are you sure?" asked Jarin.

"What I have to say is too important to wait. Besides, the liquid in that flask has worked wonders for my tired limbs."

"You should try the roasted nuts," Jarin said. "They're even better."

His uncle gave him a long look and his eyebrows raised a bit, as though he'd stumbled on an idea.

"Very well," said Laern. "I will convene the council at once."

The councilor departed.

Jarin handed his uncle one of the delicious wafers. "Your face is still kind of green. Eat this."

Sedric leaned a hand upon the wall for balance and rubbed his bad knee. It seemed his renewed strength had been largely for show. "I'll be all right." Then he sat upon the bed and munched on one of the wafers. "We were such fools," he said. "The answer was obvious, but we were too dumb to see it."

"What do you mean?" asked Jarin.

"The seed . . . the open mouth . . . the Tree." Sedric sighed, shaking his head. "We were supposed to *eat* it!"

*

Despite the food and drink, Sedric had not recovered as well as when Jarin had eaten the roasted nut. Maybe it was because none of the food was cooked. Or maybe his uncle had experienced something so terrifying it would take days to flush it out of him. He looked old and worn and kept mumbling something about how he'd been such a fool to believe he could use the mask to bring back the wizard. As he limped though the hallways, he seemed to harden his resolve.

"This place is amazing!" Jarin said as he strode beside his uncle, trying to put on a cheery face. "The tunnels are like a huge maze where you could get lost but you don't. Every time I think I'm turned around, I suddenly find my way back to the central cavern. And, wow, it's *huge*, with winding stairs and bridges and balconies. Oh, here it comes!"

Sedric came into the open space and paused a moment to take in the sight, nodding appreciably as he did so. He said nothing, however, which spoke of his deep wounds, the kind that bruised the mind and scarred the spirit. They continued at a steady pace until they came to the doors fronting the wide balcony where Laern had blessed the babies. Their escort, Gretten, opened one door and waited as they went through, then he closed the door firmly behind them.

The walls of the council chamber were decorated with carved reliefs depicting scenes of woodtrolls and the Tree. One scene was unlike the others and portrayed a tall figure, unmistakably human, surrounded by the treefolk, who gazed up at him as if he were a teacher.

A single shelf on one wall had been fastened with two stands spaced far apart, as if to display a long narrow object, likely the staff. On a pedestal next to the shelf was a box with a lock. Jarin wondered what it might hold.

In the center of the chamber was an oval table seemingly hewn from the rockwood floor itself, expertly constructed and polished with a smooth surface. At the far side of the room was a door of masterful design, shaped like an ash tree.

Laern and two other council members made a motion for Sedric and Jarin to sit on a low bench at one end of the table. Two other councilors were seated in chairs, and they took a moment to introduce themselves.

The first was Viluk, a hairy craftsman who glared at Sedric in a cruel way Jarin had never beheld in a woodtroll before; his words were short and to the point, as though he was ready to explode with a long string of profanity.

The other was named Areen, a female philosopher, who was so slim she might have passed for a human from a distance. She was polite and even gave Jarin a pleasant smile.

"Am I early?" Sedric asked, gesturing to an empty chair.

Laern shook his head. "We are at war with the barbarous krek, so Captain Heldig could not join us. Nevertheless, Viluk, who heads up the artisan's guild, and Areen, our beautiful philosopher, are excellent councilors and more than capable of representing our people's interests."

"You are too kind, Laern," Areen said.

Viluk said nothing, focusing his hard eyes upon Jarin, who began to squirm with discomfort.

"Where is the mask?" Sedric demanded. "I must have it back."

Viluk released his gaze from Jarin and regarded Sedric. "So eager to destroy yourself?" he asked. "Haven't you learned that such power should be kept out of human hands?"

"What I've learned is that Nolath obtained his power from here years ago, in a place he called the heart of the Tree."

Areen raised an eyebrow. "Have you come to gain such power for yourself?"

Sedric addressed her without flinching. "My people are under attack. Our very existence is in danger."

"My papa needs help," Jarin added.

Viluk ignored the comment, apparently deciding to direct all his words at Sedric. "Humans have threatened the existence of every rightful heir of Kalor since their arrival. Did you expect the spirit demons of the north to sit back and watch idly as you eliminated their hunting grounds?"

Sedric pointed at the guild master. "Your ancestors helped Nolath defeat a high-order skinwalker ages ago, so what's your problem?" He sighed and shook his head. "That's beside the point. After what I've learned, we must—"

"I'm afraid Nolath's full story is unknown to you, Sedric," Laern interrupted, his voice remaining calm.

"I doubt it. I . . ."

Laern raised a hand. Then the high councilor nodded to Areen.

The woodtroll philosopher took a moment to gather her thoughts, and when she spoke, her voice was full of reverence. "After Kalor emerged from the void, this home was given to us by the Creators as a reward for serving as their loyal servants. It must have been a long and faithful service, to be given such an honor, though we have no memory of that time. When Nolath arrived, he found a simple people living without language. Our ancestors lived much as the krek do now, wild and uncouth."

Jarin glanced at the carved relief of Nolath teaching peaceful woodtrolls and wondered how the savage krek had become so mean.

Areen continued, "Nolath bestowed the gift of speech and taught us our words. He even chose the name of the Tree, Yggdrasil, which comes from a great Earth legend. In return, we showed him the heart of the Tree so that he might combat the spirit demon of Maran."

Viluk's nostrils flared. "Our ancestors made a terrible error."

"Yes," said Areen. "They were too naïve to know that humans were not meant to control the power that flows naturally through the blood of every heir of Kalor. You might think of magic as a tool of war, but to us it is a means of survival."

"Humans wish to use the power to destroy," said Viluk. "We use it to live, as the Creators intended."

Sedric had been grinding his teeth throughout Areen's story and when he spoke he sounded cross. "Not only did Nolath give you language, he apparently dumped a hokey religion on you as well. Have you forgotten that humans are here because some natives almost ruined this world?"

Areen sat back with a sad expression, while Viluk appeared ready to explode, his eyes popping out.

Sedric waved a dismissive hand. "Regardless of what magic means to you people, power was given to Nolath by your ancestors. I don't doubt that. He used it to enslave the skinwalker of Maran, and he is using it now to invade our lands. Yes, you heard me correctly. *Invade.*"

"We thought Nolath was killed by the spirit demon," said Laern.

Jarin felt this was a good time to pipe in. "That's what you get for doing your own think—"

"If you're brave enough to wear his mask," Sedric interrupted, "you'll learn his secrets. He never died. Our lands stand helpless against his power."

Viluk laughed in a way that made Jarin think the guild master was evil. "Human against human! What a refreshing turn of events."

"If that's the case," said Laern gravely, "then the dark creatures of Kalor have chosen to fight for a human master. I find that hard to believe."

"I can't fathom how it all came about, either," said Sedric. "But the mask gave me a vision of the past, through the eyes of Nolath himself. I know the truth."

The three councilors looked at each other in confusion. Then Areen said to Sedric, "Tell us."

Sedric nodded and took a deep breath. When he spoke, he seemed to take on a new voice.

"Sit up straight and listen!" he said. "The wizard chose an evil path when he journeyed into the Canopy Mountains . . ."

FORTY-SEVEN

Nolath had captured a demon and he intended to keep her.

The foothills of the Canopy Mountains were a hard and unforgiving land, worse than the dying plains that lay a backbreaking journey to the south. A stiff wind sighed through the rocky hills, making every decision to stop and rest a bitter choice. It never let up. The frigid air seemed to penetrate every open fold in his clothing, freezing the skin no matter how diligently he tightened the clasps and cinched his belt.

The others were suffering too, but only proud Ivan had the energy to complain about it. As for Orwin, the murder of Reena had caused him to turn inward. Perhaps the simple man blamed himself for his sister's death? Ivan, who had loved her too, certainly did, finding fault with everyone who had failed to see that one of their number had been possessed by a skinwalker.

Nolath stepped over a corpse similar in appearance to the

reptilian trolls, but with a barbed tail. Other slain beasts littered the barren hollow, their blood staining the gray shale red.

The woman, Naomi, lay on her side beside a boulder, bound hand and foot with rope, her long black hair spilling out upon the shale. The fresh brand of an acorn blistered her forehead. Only luck and a surprise attack had allowed Nolath to put it there, thus binding the spirit demon inside the woman's body. She had quit struggling against her cords, but her glower spoke volumes of hatred.

Ivan saw him approaching and eagerly came up beside him. "I say we kill it," he said.

Naomi's dark eyes were slits of defiance, watching the soldier's hands finger his blade.

"Easy, Ivan," said Nolath. "We need her to guide us to the Wyrm."

"This demon slaughtered Reena!" Ivan shouted. "It should be executed."

"Kill the body and you kill Naomi."

"Release the demon first, then execute it."

"It's not that simple," said Nolath. "I need her to keep the demon trapped inside her body so I can control it. Reena would still be alive if I'd been smarter when the demon took possession of Orwin's sister." He rechecked Naomi's ropes and then searched the ridges surrounding them. "Where's Orwin?"

As if in answer, the hunter appeared upon the hillside and waved his arms. He had straight blond hair, cut like an upside-down bowl, stained on one side with troll's blood. "I found it!" he called to them. "Up here!"

*

The cave opening was nothing more than a stack of crushed shale holding up a huge slab of slate that created a dark space underneath no wider than his shoulders. Nolath studied the entrance, then turned to Naomi. Ivan held her firmly by a length of leather salvaged from the reins of his slain horse.

"The Wyrm is in there?" Nolath asked her.

Naomi smirked behind the long strands of her hair flapping sideways in the breeze.

"Have you seen it?" Nolath prompted.

The possessed woman hesitated before shaking her head.

"Must be deep down or hidden," he said. "You know where it lives, don't you?"

Naomi nodded.

"This isn't why we came," said Ivan. "We have the skinwalker right here. Let's kill it and go home."

Nolath watched his friend's grip tighten on the leash and wondered how the thin soldier mustered the fortitude to argue day in and day out.

"Haven't you ever wanted to meet one of the Creators?" he asked the man. "A being that tampered with magic and imprisoned us on Kalor? Its power must be awesome."

"What are you talking about?"

"It's true, Ivan. One of the Creators never left this world with the others, and now it slumbers deep under this mountain."

"Where it should stay put."

"I think not. But if you wish to wait here in the cold wind, I won't stop you."

As Ivan's eyes fell upon the woman, he touched the hilt of the sword at his hip.

Nolath added, "I'll be taking Naomi with me."

"Do as you please," Ivan said with a huff. "But if you ask me, the demon is helping you because it thinks we'll die in there."

"Perhaps. Orwin, are you with me?"

The hunter's flushed cheeks were likely frozen, causing his normally placid face to appear less emotional than usual. "Always."

"Three days then," said Nolath. "If we don't find what I'm looking for in three days, we kill the demon and go home."

"Fair enough," said Ivan.

*

The possessed woman directed the party into the caves beneath the shale, guiding them downward, always downward, even when the way was so steep they had to tie a rope around their waists and descend with their hands. The only time she veered away from the steepest path was when they came to the top of a chasm. A torrent of water plunged into the pit on the far side, barely visible in the light of their torches. Water vapor filled the air, condensing onto their faces and dampening their clothes.

Even though Ivan was loath to relax his grip on the woman's leash, Nolath positioned himself between the skinwalker and the edge of the drop-off. He feared the demon might try to dive over the edge and shatter Naomi's body at the bottom of the unseen depths, thus freeing itself.

The spirit demon studied him through Naomi's eyes, as

if reading his mind, and then pointed her chin to the right, where a circular fissure led into a tunnel carpeted with gravel. The demon knew Nolath could inject pain into the brand of the acorn, and with any luck, it believed he could keep it trapped inside a dead body.

Ivan pulled on the leash, as if sensing that Naomi might try to push the wizard into the abyss.

The spirit demon aroused Nolath's curiosity. He could see why its kind had once dominated this world, for it was more intelligent than any other native creature, and far more gifted. If spirit demons hadn't been solitary creatures by nature, with fierce territorial instincts, they might have banded together and easily defeated humans years ago. Nolath could accomplish much by keeping one enslaved to his will.

"It's warmer in here," said Orwin, stepping carefully into the fissure. "And a mossy plant grows on the walls."

The warmth was a welcome change, but it told Nolath that they were nearing the lair of the Wyrm. Didn't the devil breathe the hottest fire?

As they wound their way down an old lava tube, the possessed woman began to sing. It wasn't the kind of tune one remembered fondly or wanted to repeat around a campfire, but its high pitch reverberated so effectively in the round tube that it began to hurt his ears.

Was she singing a song or starting a spell?

Too late, Nolath realized she was calling for help.

A huge white maggot with beady eyes came into the cast of Orwin's torchlight and sucked the hunter into its pulpy mouth. Then with a great heave that shook the floor, is slid forward.

Nolath was next, but as he raised his arms to cast a spell, Ivan's outcry made him turn around. The possessed woman was scratching the soldier's face, digging in with all her might. She had forced him to the ground, her mouth wide open, an ardent light pouring out of her throat. Boils sprouted across Ivan's skin.

Uttering the word "*Pain!*" and snapping his fingers, Nolath made the woman suffer, made her reel back, made her writhe in agony. Ivan backpedaled away from her, clutching his face.

Then the mouth of the maggot took Nolath in its heinous grip, sucking him into its narrow gorge and coating him in an acidic slime. Not daring to open his mouth, he wrenched his legs and arms and shoulders this way and that, twisting, punching, kicking—fighting to keep from disappearing deeper inside. The maggot's powerful muscles propelled him down.

One arm was pinned to his side, useless; the other was extended above his head . . . and it was this arm that touched Orwin's boot. His friend was squirming, still fighting to stay alive.

Nolath knew of the knife in Orwin's boot, had seen him use it to gut a boar with its razor-sharp blade.

A chance!

His lungs burned for air, but Nolath stopped resisting and allowed the maggot to swallow him closer to Orwin. He felt the hilt of the knife, pulled it free. Gripping it in his fist, he stabbed with all his strength, tore into the maggot's fibrous tissue.

The effect was immediate. In a gushing wave of goop, he and Orwin were disgorged back onto the ground. A single torch lay among the gravel next to a moaning Ivan, providing just enough light to see that the maggot had backed off.

The hunter recovered faster than Nolath and drew the long dagger at his hip. With sweeping arcs, Orwin slashed at the retreating monster, never saying a word as he advanced, never complaining.

At last, when the thing finally died, Orwin turned and asked, "Did you forget to practice your magic today?"

Nolath grinned. "The bargain I made compels me to speak when unleashing the power of the Tree. I had no chance of that while being swallowed."

Ivan had pulled himself to his feet. Not only was the left side of his face scratched and bleeding, but it was also covered in leaking blisters that extended to an ear burned down to a blackened nub. He had the wide-eyed look of someone surprised by how much he hurt.

Next to him sprawled the possessed woman, unmoving. Nolath feared that Ivan had killed her out of revenge, but the soldier prodded her with his foot. "Get up, demon," he said. "See what you've done to me."

Slowly, the woman rose to her knees, but she didn't look at him.

"Here," said Nolath, handing Ivan his last roasted acorn. "It may not regrow your ear, but before the hour is up, you will be healed."

Ivan didn't hesitate to take the nut and pop it in his mouth.

And thus ended their first day in the caves.

*

When the last of their torches burned to stubs and sizzled out, Nolath brought out the light-stones. In the heart of the Tree, he had infused them with a power that would maintain a spark even far away from their home, but making them had been time-consuming and he had grown impatient. As a result, he had only two stones to light their way.

Creatures stranger even than giant maggots dwelled in the maze of tunnels and caves, and many times the group was forced to avoid them by hiding in an alcove or choosing a different path. Some creatures were oversized versions of ordinary surface dwellers, such as spiders and centipedes, but a host of unworldly beings roamed these depths as well. Blob-like rollers caked in hard coats of gravel tried to pin them against a cave wall. Swarms of bat-sized flyers armed with dozens of sharp needles poured suddenly out of a hole in the cave floor and siphoned Orwin's blood so fast he passed out in seconds before being dragged to safety. Tall snapper plants leaned down and almost caught Nolath by the head as he wandered too close. And, worst of all, shadow-hunters, seemingly made of the darkness itself, stalked the group for a long time. These last horrors ambushed them as they sat sleeping beside an underground stream. Nolath slew the hunters with a sonic bang that almost brought the ceiling down on them.

Naomi guided them wordlessly, never offering assistance or providing a warning when they were attacked, though the encounters fell off dramatically when Nolath, fed up with her singing antics, gave her an hour of pain.

Orwin touched his shoulder gently. "I think she's paid the price. Remember, the real Naomi is still in there somewhere."

Nolath released his hold and watched as the woman lay face down on the stone floor, panting from exhaustion. In his anger, he'd forgotten about the pretty serving wench from the king's court who had volunteered to accompany his party into the north. In these tunnels full of perils, her face had become synonymous with the spirit demon.

"I'm sorry," he said, hoping the real Naomi could hear him.

Naomi raised her head and gave him a faint smirk.

"Bah!" said Ivan. "Did you see that? It mocks us. The girl's spirit is too far buried beneath the demon to hear you apologize."

"We don't know that," said Orwin.

"I wonder . . ." said Nolath. He squatted next to the woman and laid his hand upon her forehead, covering up the brand of the acorn. She flinched . . . but he wanted something more from her than pain this time and so kept his touch light. He had placed the brand here to anchor the spirit demon inside Naomi's body, but maybe he could use it as a window into the serving woman's soul.

"*View!*" he commanded, invoking the power of the Tree.

A vision sprang forth in his mind of a girl slumbering in a forest, underneath the boughs of a moss-laden tree. She was a younger-looking version of Naomi and appeared unharmed, resting peacefully.

Following Nolath's will, the vision focused on the tree. It was old, with gnarled limbs and a trunk of thick, wrinkled bark. Two exposed roots cradled the girl in an elbow-like crook, as if shielding her from the elements. But something wasn't right. Despite the idyllic scene, a sliver of smoke rose from the bark and the smell of burned flesh upset the moist, earthy scents of the forest. The shape of the burn was the same as the brand he had put on Naomi's forehead.

He understood the spirit demon now. It was the soul of a tree growing in an unknown forest—a uniquely magical tree that might once have been a seedling from the World Tree itself.

Much more of the skinwalker's true nature was unveiled to him as he maintained the vision—most importantly, the way in which the demon enslaved another creature's body to its will.

He removed his hand from Naomi's forehead, ending the vision. The possessed woman looked at him with naked fear now, because she knew what he had learned.

"Naomi sleeps," he told the two men. "She is unaware of the skinwalker's pain."

Orwin appeared relieved, but Ivan grinned broadly. "Good! A little vengeance would help me sleep at night." The soldier unsheathed his knife.

The wizard forbade harm to come to her. "Leave her alone," he said. "Though Naomi sleeps, we must care for her until I decide to release the spirit demon trapped inside."

"*Release* it?"

"There will come a time when I will be able to control the skinwalker without binding it to Naomi."

"You promised to destroy it."

Nolath shrugged. "We shall see."

*

"What is it?" Orwin asked as he stood below an archway fashioned of stone blocks. The carving of a long, lizard-like dragon adorned the keystone of an entryway into a dark, sloping tunnel. Unfamiliar characters were etched above and below the dragon.

"A warning," said Ivan. "That's what it is. We would do well to heed it."

"Writing," mused Nolath. "Which means humans have been here."

"So we're not the first to go this deep."

Nolath turned on Naomi. "Where have you led us?"

The possessed woman's eyes were bright as she stared upon the arch, but she said nothing.

Nolath continued, "Perhaps I should kill you now and be done with this maze."

"Now you're talking," said Ivan. "It's our third day here, anyway." He scratched his chin in thought. "I think."

"Did you hear that?" asked Orwin, looking back the way they had come.

As everyone went quiet, listening, the distinct sound of scurrying feet was unmistakable.

"Another trap!" cried Ivan.

"We survived the last ambush," Nolath reminded him. "Now step aside so I can get a clear shot."

Ivan drew his sword as he pulled the woman out of the way. Nolath slipped past her, decided it was too dark to see what had been following them, and concluded that there was no time to investigate. He thrust his hand forward, palm toward darkness, and with the word "*Fire!*" cast a ball of fire up the tunnel. Superheated air swept over him as the flames rolled forward.

The fireball was fast and deadly, swiftly vanishing in the

cave beyond the tunnel. A chorus of screams echoed from ahead, then died.

"Come!" said Nolath, rushing up the scorched passageway. At the entrance to the cave, he stumbled upon a company of burned corpses.

"Human," Orwin said.

"What have you done?" said Ivan.

More scurrying feet came from the hidden recesses of the cave.

Nolath held up his stone, pushing its light against the darkness, whereupon it brightened tenfold and cast a beam of light into the cave.

A metal disk came soaring into view, fast as an arrow, humming as it sliced through the air and lopped off Nolath's hand. The light-stone fell to the ground and went dark.

Falling to his knees and crying out in pain, the wizard thrust his maimed arm under his armpit to stanch the flow of blood.

"Nolath!" Orwin held up his light-stone and stooped beside him.

Another metal disk hummed past, missing Ivan's neck by a hair. "Fall back!" yelled the soldier. "Toward the arch!"

They retreated down the tunnel until they passed underneath the archway. Naomi let out a cry as a disk grazed her thigh.

Excruciating pain traveled up Nolath's arm and his vision blurred, but before it overcame his senses, he turned his eyes upon the keystone.

"*Crumble,*" he said.

The archway crashed down in a cloud of dust, blocking their exit.

*

He must have blacked out for no more than an hour, because when he came to, his clothes were still covered in dust and he sat beside the pile of rubble that had been the archway. His throbbing arm had been cauterized.

Orwin raised a gourd of water to Nolath's lips and he drank.

Nearby, Ivan pressed a knife against the woman's neck. "If Naomi weren't sleeping in there, you'd be choking on your own blood right now."

Orwin's tone was matter-of-fact. "Killing her will only free the demon so it could possess one of us while we slept. Nolath is about to go unconscious again, so who do you think would be its next victim?"

Ivan pulled the knife away and sat back on his heels. "Curse this place!" he said. "What do we do now?"

"Release me or we will all perish," Naomi said softly, her voice flat and emotionless. These words, her first since taking hold of the serving woman, came as such a surprise that even Ivan backed away.

"What are you talking about, demon?" said Ivan.

"The wizard has trapped us on the wrong side of the archway," she said. "Servants of a powerful being dwell below us and they must offer sacrifice."

"To the Wyrm?"

"To a god."

Ivan squirmed and looked to Nolath, who mustered enough strength to say, "Let them come."

"We'll be captured," said Ivan.

"If we're lucky."

"You *want* to be captured?"

"It's better than being killed, don't you think?"

The possessed woman hissed, "Release me! I can protect us all."

Ivan stared at her with hatred. "You're afraid of this Wyrm, aren't you?"

"You should fear it too," she said.

The soldier shook his head. "I'd rather take my chances with human captors. Maybe when they discover your true nature, they'll take you as their only sacrifice." He turned to the hunter. "What about you, Orwin?"

"I'm with Nolath."

"Of course," said Ivan. "Why bother asking."

*

The four didn't wait long before the orange flicker of torch-light appeared down the tunnel, soon followed by the sounds of human feet. Warriors approached wielding metal spears. They were a tall people who wore little clothing, save skins wrapped about their loins and golden torcs bent around their necks. They bound Ivan, Orwin, and Naomi with brass collars fastened to a single long chain. Nolath faded in and out of consciousness as the strongest-looking warrior carried him over his shoulders.

A warm breeze grew humid as they descended. Eventually, they entered a cavern full of light and sound. On the far wall, a huge waterfall spilled down to a ledge, then cascaded into a pool on the main level, where people worked and children frolicked. Gigantic ferns grew alongside a stream and thick mosses carpeted the floor. Three of the adults rode beasts of burden that walked on two powerful legs. Nolath couldn't spot the source of all the light, but he suspected the variety of colors near the waterfall indicated a growth of luminescent plants there, similar to the underground algae he'd seen during his journey to the Tree.

The people uttered words he'd never heard, and they did not understand Ivan, who began shouting at them in frustration. Here was a place where the people spoke a language different from anyone, where the magic of Kalor had not been able to touch their tongues after they arrived from Earth.

It soon became clear that the people were not interested in communicating with anyone other than themselves. Nolath and the others were tossed into a cell.

And there they remained for a length of time that might have been weeks.

*

Nolath healed poorly in captivity. Painful streaks of red began to snake up from the stump to his armpit, where his skin became so tender even a light touch caused stabs of pain. The infection was serious and he'd be dead soon if nothing was done.

He devised a plan, an enormous risk that might kill them all. Tapping into the skinwalker's mind had revealed a secret that might save his life. And, should he succeed, his power might be as the gods themselves.

At some point, all four of them were shackled to a chain and escorted back through the main cavern and into a deeper cave so hot it sapped much of his reserves.

"You were right about one thing, Nolath," Ivan said, walking in front of him.

"The Wyrm exists?" said Orwin from behind.

"Aye, and we're the yearly sacrifice," said Ivan. "I guess surrendering to a tribe of baby-talking humans wasn't the smartest choice we could have made."

"Have faith," said Nolath.

"Faith in what? Our deaths? Now is not the time to be holding back on your powers, my friend."

"When we see the beast, I will act. Not until then."

"You mean to fight it?" Ivan sounded hopeful.

"If I must."

"You look like death. How do you feel?"

Nolath remained quiet. The possessed woman, shuffling forward at the front of the chain, managed to turn her head and catch his eye. She appeared to be afraid of his silence. She knew what he meant to do when he saw the Wyrm.

"Nolath?" Orwin prompted.

"If I reveal my full might now, the Wyrm will flee from me."

They came to a wide fissure in the floor separating them from a dark alcove in the wall on the far side. An altar extended over the edge, where far below, hot magma flowed, bubbling in spots with fire.

Standing next to the altar, a tribal priest, robed in a strange vestment made of big scales fastened with wire, held an obsidian knife. He waited as guards unshackled Naomi from the chain and dragged her forward.

The possessed woman scanned the craggy walls and ceiling as though expecting to see a terror emerge, but there was no sign of the Wyrm. A priest and a few guards stood before her, and a crowd of onlookers hung back. Naomi's look of fear slid away and she quit fighting against the guards; it seemed the skinwalker had realized that slaying the woman's body would free the demon.

As she came close to the altar, the priest leaned forward to examine her forehead. His eyes widened; he'd seen the brand. As he reached up to touch it, Nolath delivered pain upon the demon.

The skinwalker screamed and fell to the ground. Astonished, the priest turned his attention immediately upon Nolath.

Guards dragged the woman back into line and Nolath took her place at the altar.

"Don't worry, demon," Ivan said to the skinwalker. "You'll get yours soon enough."

The wizard hardly had the strength to put up a fight, but he made a show of it by pretending to be unwilling to go to the stone block overlooking the fissure. The guards treated him harshly as they shackled him to the stone block.

Nolath turned his head to look into the dark alcove on the other side. "Show yourself, dragon!" he yelled. "Behold the true purpose of Kalor's magic."

The priest raised his knife, mumbling incoherently.

"Come forth, abandoned God," said Nolath.

From the darkness of the cave, the massive head of a dragon came into the magma's golden light. It was bigger than Nolath had expected, with a long, scaly neck and a body extending far into the dark alcove, where its full length could not be seen. As it raised its head, webbed claws gripped the sides of its lair. It possessed no wings.

Humans gasped. Naomi screamed. The priest mumbled fervently.

Nolath peered into the Wyrm's catlike pupil and, for an instant, caught sight of a power beholden to no creature of Kalor. The dragon lived in the depths of a world he had helped create, an outcast driven from his watery realm by brothers and sisters who had abandoned him, forced him to live far from the sea, away from the Tree. Now only a tribe of humans worshiped him in isolation.

Nolath called upon the magic of the Tree, even its very heart, and effortlessly broke the bonds around his good hand. He pointed at the Wyrm with two fingers.

"You are mine," he said. "*Bind!*"

The skinwalker let out a wail of despair, for as wearer of the brand, she was key to the binding.

The priest plunged his obsidian knife into Nolath's chest.

FORTY-EIGHT

Sedric the hermit held his blistered head in both hands. "I lost consciousness and saw no more from the mask. But this much I do know: The wizard enslaved the dragon to his will."

Councilor Viluk leaned forward, his face red with utter disbelief. Jarin thought the veins around his eyes might pop. "You said he was stabbed!"

"That was part of the spell," Sedric said. "A powerful spell of sacrifice so that he could leave his body and take control of the dragon. His spirit lives on somehow, because of a link he established to the Tree."

Councilor Areen was thoughtful, her reply calm. "Nolath is like a skinwalker now."

"Yes."

"But why has he turned against humans?" she asked.

"I don't know," said Sedric. "It has something to do with what he learned since visiting Yggdrasil."

Viluk snorted with strained laughter. "I find it the greatest joke of all. A human wizard goes on a quest to defeat a great enemy and ends up becoming a devil seeking to destroy his own kind. Ha!"

Old Councilor Laern turned to the guild master. "This is nothing to laugh about, Viluk. Our ancestors unwittingly contributed to this war by giving Nolath the power to tear down the people he once loved. His own people."

Viluk looked away. "Turnabout is fair play, I say."

"A human expression," said Areen.

"*All* of our expressions are human," murmured Viluk.

Laern sounded like an old man who was used to lecturing others. "Humans live on Kalor to prevent us from using magic to destroy ourselves. We can't allow them to use that same power to commit suicide. Sedric, what do you need from us?"

"I must take the mask to the heart of the Tree."

Viluk snapped his gaze back to Sedric. "Why?"

"The heart will show me the full extent of Nolath's power. It will show me how to defeat the wizard."

Councilors Laern and Areen nodded.

Viluk stood from the table and his chair toppled back. "This is madness!"

"Councilor . . ." warned Laern.

Viluk kept going. "Listen to yourselves! Our ancestors turned Nolath into a monster by taking him to the heart, and now you want to do the same to *another* human? Have you all lost your minds?"

"The wizard was corrupted by his contact with the dragon, Lotan the Deceiver," said Areen. "Not by the heart of the Tree."

"*Pretty, pretty* Areen," said Viluk, with a leering smile. "Nolath was no angel while he lived among us. You seem to have forgotten that the warring krek learned their twisted spells from him."

"That was a mistake," said Areen. "While he lived here a faction of our own people tricked him into doing evil."

"Nolath caused a civil war!" said Viluk.

"A mistake," Areen repeated.

Jarin needed answers and all he was getting was mixed-up talk. "Are the krek the savages with the ball and chain?" he asked. "They tried to scare me and my uncle."

Laern regarded him with sad eyes. "Yes, I'm afraid so, Jarin. The krek were once numbered among us. When the wizard arrived, many of the treefolk became so charmed by his tricks that they convinced him to teach them how to speak and to make tools."

"Are you talking about your staff of speaking?"

Laern shook his head. "Before the wizard entered the heart of the Tree and made the staff, he taught some of our people a different way—a hard way—of acquiring human talents. By this method, the krek were the first treefolk to obtain language. It gave them power, which quickly turned to a desire to lord over those who could not yet talk."

Areen seemed to sense Jarin's confusion. "I'm sure you know people in your village who think they're smarter than everyone else and want to be chiefs."

It didn't take long for Jarin to think of somebody. "My papa hates a man in town called Horace the Quick, who is always stirring up trouble. Papa says he has a silver tongue, which means he can win friends with a funny word or with a lie. Papa once punched him in the nose for saying that our mill was infested with bugs called weevils."

"Then you understand what the krek did to all of our people who couldn't talk. They wanted to be overlords." Areen looked toward Viluk to emphasize her next point. "Nolath saw the danger the krek posed and made amends by creating the staff of speech, which makes a hard task easy for us."

Viluk pressed the palms of his hands onto the table. "That's one way of seeing things. He didn't exactly rid us of danger, Areen. Remember, the krek still flourish in the valley and seek to retake this home of ours. They even tried to kill you, boy."

Jarin looked at his uncle. "You said they just wanted to scare us."

Sedric shrugged. "I thought that was all they needed to suck out our human talents, but maybe not. What do I know about powerful magic? That's why I need to get to the heart of the Tree."

"I vote against it," said Viluk.

"And you, Areen?" asked Laern. "Should we take this human to the very center of our home?"

The woodtroll philosopher sat back, studying Sedric, as though she didn't quite trust him. Then her gaze fell upon Jarin. "Only if the boy goes with him."

"What!" cried Viluk. "Why him?"

"His heart is pure and I suspect his uncle won't do anything foolish in front of him."

"A hostage then," said Viluk, nodding. "I like that."

"That's not what I said or what I meant, councilor," said Areen.

"Well, that's what I heard. And it's the only way I'll permit it."

Laern cleared his throat. "Then it's decided." He climbed to his feet and went to the lockbox on the pedestal next to the display shelf. Producing a huge key from the folds of his robes, he then worked the lock. From inside, he retrieved the mask wrapped in cloth.

He ushered everyone toward the tree-shaped doorway. "This way."

FORTY-NINE

Chaos reigned throughout the camp. As word spread of the murder of General Krassus, a yell rose up among the slaves like a battle cry. Joy and celebration quickly turned to defiance and rebellion. Bondsmen at every office and duty left their posts and shouted through the camp, the rebellion gaining in strength as slaves beheld their brothers and sisters rise up against their overseers. Slavemasters and their puny contingent of guards soon found themselves battling gangs of angry slaves.

The legion's soldiers remained disciplined, but the shock of losing their beloved general slowed their attempts to quell the uprising. Brutality became their first choice, and as individual centurions managed to marshal bands of troops, scores of slaves died in isolated skirmishes.

The most grievously affected by Krassus's death were the two sangomas. The First was seen collapsing headfirst into the mud, while the Second let out a cry heard across the valley. Both men wandered off then and were not seen again for much of the day.

Atop the castle walls, the baron saw the bedlam erupting outside and ordered the gates locked.

Prefect Pontus was on his way to the pass when the grieving cry of his sorcerous companion put an abrupt end to his journey. As he and his guards hurried back to camp, the slaves were in full-scale revolt and had overrun the few legionaries guarding the captured weerlord.

The First Sangoma was there as well, but he lay motionless beside the cage, seemingly lifeless. A mob of slaves had assembled, vowing to free the fake demon lord in the hopes the Kaloran native would help them against the legion's heavily armed infantry.

Collin was one of the first to realize that the slaves running past his tent were heading toward the makeshift prison, so he hustled to the aid of the First Sangoma, whom he knew had been stationed there to ward against the weerlord's attempts to use magic. He was still too fatigued to outpace the slaves, but he went all the same. Later, he explained to Mira what had happened after Pontus arrived.

The prefect set out to disperse the crowd at the point of the sword, his commands permitting no mercy. Many slaves perished, but some who wielded stolen weapons fought desperately, holding back the guards long enough for their fellow slaves to unshackle the weerlord.

Inokan of the White Hills was a withered creature, wasted by the sun and by the harsh treatment of its Jihenan captors. Long strips of scaly skin had shed away, and its face was sunburned and blistered. One might have wondered how the ancient weerlord held the strength to cast a spell while frightened slaves propped up its body and begged for his protection.

The weerlord looked at Pontus with hatred, pointed a snakelike hand at him, and uttered the word, *submerge*. Underneath the prefect's feet the earth vibrated so rapidly that the mud became as fluid as water. Pontus sank like a rock and the vibrating stopped, leaving nothing behind but thick muck to dig away.

Then the weerlord collapsed and its skin sloughed off, flesh and bone smoking in the heat of the afternoon sun.

*

It fell upon Lucian, tribune and second-in-command, to assume control of the legion. Unfortunately, Mira found him lying unconscious on his cot, his guards holding back a mass of terrified noblemen and loyal Jihenans begging for protection. When Pilus Julian, a grizzled centurion who had nonetheless been kind to Mira, saw her approach the tent, he allowed her to pass uncontested.

And it soon became apparent why he had done so. Julian hoped Mira's presence would stir Lucian into action.

Upon seeing the young commander, her first thought was that the skinwalker had taken him. She stood frozen with fear as she recalled the attack in the general's pavilion and the bruise around her throat. Her hand went instinctively to her blaze stone necklace.

"Tribune?" she said cautiously.

His body did not move.

She went to his side and gently shook his shoulder. He lay on his stomach, his face turned away from her, but he didn't stir. She touched the skin of his neck and found it warm.

Not dead, she thought. *Asleep then?*

"Lucian." Mira shook him gently, but he made no sign that he had noticed. Even his breathing was shallow.

She straightened and examined the inside of the tent.

His armor rested nearby, seemingly tossed to the floor without care, and his gladius lay upon a footstool, halfway out of its sheath. No servants were present, and Julian had not followed her inside. She and Lucian were alone.

Next to the washbasin sat a full pitcher of water and a folded towel. She considered wetting the towel and placing it on Lucian's neck, but when the noises outside grew very loud, she realized she had no time. So she took up the pitcher and dumped its contents over his head.

Then, grabbing the sword, she stepped back, ready to confront a roused enemy.

Lucian coughed weakly, but didn't rise straightaway. When he finally pushed himself up, he seemed disoriented, perplexed. Then he saw Mira and the start of a smile appeared. "It's about time you stopped by for a kiss."

Mira knew right away he wasn't possessed by a skinwalker. She threw the towel at him. "The general is dead."

As Lucian patted his face dry, his expression turned serious. "I think I knew that. Yes, it makes sense now. I wanted to lie down, right here on this bed, get a little rest. I . . . I fell into a stupor. A songbird tried to lead me into a forest, where all was safe from the evils of the world. It was like a vivid dream. But . . ." He suddenly focused his gaze. "The sangomas!"

Mira shook her head. "One of them went with Pontus to fortify the north pass. The other was watching the weerlord's pen."

"They protected me."

"From the skinwalker? How?"

"Who can understand the full breadth of their talents? When the general died, they sought to join forces against the spirit demon in revenge . . ." Lucian frowned and pressed a fist to his forehead. "No, that's not it. They joined forces to protect *me!* I felt their aid."

"Because you command the legion now," said Mira.

Lucian stood and went for his armor, but seeing his sword in her hands, he stopped long enough to take it from her. "You'll have to help me with the straps, Mira. I think my servants ran off."

"The slaves are in revolt."

"Ah, so that explains the blare of violence I hear outside."

"It's ugly," said Mira. "Many have died."

"We can't lose the sangomas," said Lucian, apparently unconcerned about the deaths of lowly slaves. As Mira helped him don his armor, he explained, "The sangomas require a living member of House Jihena to act as proxy for their lost humanity. Though they look like us, they have abandoned everything that made them human and will die without that last link to Earth."

"Are they dying now?"

"No, but only because I live."

"You're a member of House Jihena?"

Lucian nodded. "A distant cousin of Krassus, but apparently my blood is rich enough to maintain the sangoma's human link. By protecting me they ensure their own survival."

Mira remembered Krassus's news about a dragon at the head of a new army in the north. The legion would need the magical defenses of the sangomas to survive. If only Lucian didn't look weak and unsteady on his feet. "Is there no other way they can live, except through you?" she asked.

Lucian shrugged. "Not unless there is another member of Jihenan blood in this valley. The circumstances that bound the sangomas to House Jihena all those years ago are not fully known, though I've heard rumors that it had something to do with repaying a life-debt."

Mira's heart beat faster. The First Sangoma had said he owed her a debt for saving his life.

Bedecked now in his armor and looking dashing as ever, the tribune grinned at her, thanked her with a peck on the forehead, and then strode out of his tent. Once outside, he ordered Pilus Julian to fetch him a horse.

FIFTY

Redgate Pass north of the valley was not as deep or as narrow as Trollgate Pass, which Collin had patrolled on the other side of the Trestammer Mountains, but the fortress here was more formidable. The gatehouse was chiseled from a single mass of rust-colored stone that butted against the eastern cliffs and stood like a plug against the wild north. Days earlier, the gate itself had been wrenched asunder by Inokan's magic blasts, and char blackened the gatehouse tunnel.

A manmade wall extended from the gatehouse, sealing off a gap less than a hundred yards to the western cliffs. A company of the baron's soldiers commanded by Sir Garon manned the wall, each one observing with long faces as a column of legionaries filed out of the gatehouse.

Collin stood aside as the Jihenans marched south. They were leaving the valley and he wanted to go with them, but he dared not abandon Mira, who had vowed to remain in Guldheim until either she was dead or the battle had been won.

Mira sat on the rocks of an old landslide on the east, just

south of the gatehouse. It was a fine vantage point from which to view Guldheim Valley to the south, but the girl wasn't even looking up. She had her nose in her book, the Encoda.

If I stay here I'm a dead man, Collin thought. *Mira must see reason.*

He decided to make one final attempt at persuading her to go with the legion.

Climbing the rocks shouldn't have been difficult, but Collin was still hurting from wounds not yet healed. When he reached her, Mira didn't even acknowledge his presence.

"We should leave," he said.

Mira turned a page and gave no sign she had heard him.

Collin chose a spot to sit next to her. "The legion is going back to the republic. They won't be here to protect us."

"And the sangomas?" said Mira.

Collin had seen a strange bond form between her and the sorcerers, especially the one whose life she had saved. It had changed her, made her distant.

"The First still claims he owes you a favor," he said, "so he'll stay if you do. The Second swore allegiance to Lucian, though I think he's losing his mind. For reasons unknown, he has climbed a dead tree at the mouth of the east canyon, where the legion gathers to depart. We should go with them."

Mira closed the book and hugged it to her chest in thought. She looked at Collin. "Remember the slave girl, Saffron?"

"Of course."

"The legion has abandoned most of the slaves it hasn't killed, including the girl. I saw her collecting fallen apples. She has almost nothing of value, but she is *happy*. And she's living in the valley with friends who are now free to act for themselves."

"We can't save everyone," said Collin. "We can only save ourselves."

"I won't leave her to die."

Collin had suspected Mira would say this. "Take her to the Wormgate," he said. "It's a safe place for humans."

"I had the same idea, which is why I was reading just now." Mira looked at him. "I wanted to find out how Sedric knew that skinkwalkers could enter the tunnel. The Encoda describes what happened during the last invasion, generations ago. While Nolath was searching for the Tree, this valley was overrun and many people fled into the Wormgate for safety. But they had nowhere to go after that. On their first night in the tunnel, a skinwalker took hold of a man sleeping just outside the entrance and began killing people in the tunnel as they slept. He was eventually discovered and slain, but the next night the skinwalker took another man, and more people died. This went on for days. Nobody dared go to sleep. The tunnel became a deathtrap. I can't take Saffron and her friends there."

"Then the only safe place is with the legion."

Mira sighed. "Where's the First?"

Collin pointed his chin northward. "He's with Lucian, who is overseeing the legion's retreat."

Mira stood and hopped down the rocks to the road. Collin tried to call out to her to wait, but she was too fast. He groaned and picked his way back down.

He hurried after her as she made her way into the dark corridor of the gatehouse and out the other side, where the

Rusted Plains stretched all the way to the White Hills, too far to be seen from there. Mira approached Lucian and the First Sangoma as they conversed side by side, but she did not interrupt them. They seemed to be talking about her.

Collin hobbled up to Mira in time to overhear Lucian tell the sorcerer, "You're a fool to stay, you know that?"

"I must protect her," said the First.

"If I didn't know any better, I'd think you were fond of the girl."

When Mira came up, the tribune acknowledged her with a nod, and then focused his attention on the soldiers climbing out of a half-dug trench. The wind picked up and in the distance a dust devil moved across the plains.

Mira turned to the sorcerer. "You don't need to stay and protect me."

"Yes, I do."

"Go home with your brother. I'll be all right."

"Unlikely," said the First. "The baron's men are too few to hold back what is coming."

"Can you defeat the dragon?"

"It's not just the dragon we should fear, but its master."

"The *real* demon lord?" she asked. "Who is he?"

"A human."

Collin heard this and stepped closer. "You're sure of this?"

The sangoma nodded. "Only a human can exist on Kalor without being bound by magic's power. If this dragon is, indeed, one of the Creators, then only a human could resist becoming a slave to it."

"I don't understand," said Collin.

"My people learned long ago that magic was originally a

tool of enslavement. It's like a drug that every native of Kalor cannot live without, a means to command others. The nature of magic means that a higher power used it to keep all creatures under its control."

"A higher power?" said Collin. "Do you mean—"

"The Creators," said Mira.

The First bent his head toward the plains. "I believe the dragon is Lotan the Deceiver, one of the Creators who sought to enslave all creatures of Kalor. Many here in the north name him Jormungand the Eater, a powerful serpent that seeks to destroy all."

From behind the thin whirlwind of dust, a line of Jihenan cavalry appeared, stirring up their own column of the burnt orange, powdery dirt. They passed next to a black mound where thousands of corpses—mostly trolls and imps—had been piled high and burned. Wisps of dark smoke still rose from the mound, dissipating in the breeze.

"Yet humans survive without magic," said Mira, trying to come to grips with what the sorcerer had told her. "We can choose to resist its allure. If Lotan is somehow taking orders, it must be from a human, as you said, because humans are the only beings on Kalor that can resist being enslaved by the dragon's own control of magic."

The Sangoma nodded. "This human wizard may have found a way to turn magic's power against one of the Creators—to enslave the dragon."

"Why would the wizard attack human lands?" asked Collin.

"How can anyone know the motives of one who believes he is above the gods?"

Lucian snorted, shaking his head; he'd been listening. "Another good reason to forsake this land."

The cavalry crossed a makeshift bridge over the ditch, the horses' shod hoofs clattering upon the wooden planks, and then pulled up before Lucian. Mounted on the lead horse was Sergius, the centurion Collin had defeated in a contest that might have turned deadly but had instead earned him a friend.

Sergius dismounted, touched his fist to his chest in salute, and then handed the reins to Lucian. "Tribune, the enemy forces have left the White Hills, but it's difficult to know their true numbers. They travel beneath a cover of darkness."

Lucian mounted the horse. "It doesn't matter. We'll be gone before they get here."

"Then godspeed, tribune," said Sergius.

Lucian gave the centurion a long look. "Your name will be honored among the greatest in the republic."

"We will do all we can to slow the enemy."

Lucian nodded and spurred his horse, but he was forced to pull up as Sir Garon's huge body blocked his path. Hiding behind the knight was a girl perhaps eight to nine years old.

"I must speak to you, tribune," said Sir Garon, his mammoth voice cutting through the wind like a horn.

Lucian frowned. "We're not staying, Sir Garon, no matter how often you beg me. I can barely keep the legion together as it is."

"I never beg for anything."

"Good. Then we'll be on our way."

"I urge you to reconsider," said the knight. "Our families, our homes, our children . . ."

"If it makes you feel any better, a company of volunteers will stay and do what they can to slow the advance of this dragon." Lucian glanced at Centurion Sergius. "It's a suicidal mission and they know this, but I need time to get back across the mountains, and their sacrifice will give me that time. When I reach Jihena, I will inform the Senate of your plight."

"That could take months!" roared Sir Garon.

"More likely years," said Lucian. "I'm sorry, but that's the only hope I can offer you."

The knight was visibly upset, and for a moment Collin feared he might attack the tribune. Sir Garon urged the girl into plain view. "In that case, I ask that you take my daughter with you. Protect her, keep her safe. Her mother is dead."

"Now you beg," said Lucian with a hint of disgust. "Come to Jihena yourself. The republic would welcome a barbarian of the north. You would be treated like a king."

Sir Garon wagged his head from side to side. "Impossible. I've sworn to protect the baron."

"Then you are a fool." Lucian gave Mira a parting glance and then spurred his horse around the knight.

Sir Garon kept himself planted defiantly in the middle of the road, forcing the cavalry to go around him. Mira ran forward and pulled the girl out of the way.

When the last cavalryman had gone through the gatehouse, the knight fell to his knees and hung his head. Sergius went to him and placed a hand onto the man's big shoulder. "We'll die together, my friend. Protecting your girl."

Sir Garon's stare was full of hatred. "Protecting your *legion*."

FIFTY-ONE

The long descent from the tree-carved doorway ended in an immense, domed chamber with walls intricately sculpted into the forms of unfamiliar plants and animals. Some of the forms were so foreign they might have come from another world.

A soft glow illuminated a large ring within the center of the chamber, about the size of the swimming hole back at Willow Stump Creek. And within this glowing ring, different shades and colors swirled about, like slowly moving paint beneath a sheet of ice.

Jarin trailed behind the three council members, feeling tiny and useless. Sedric's limp had gotten worse, and he seemed relieved to step upon a level floor.

Laern crossed to the ring and clapped the butt of his staff upon its edge, as if to announce his presence. "It is said the Creators often held council in this chamber to view the far corners of the world."

Sedric stared intently at the colors. "The wizard learned of

Lotan's lair while standing in this place."

For an instant, Jarin thought he saw inside the ring the form of a bird flying from one branch to another. Nobody else seemed to notice. "Will it show me where Razor is?"

Sedric grunted. "We are not here to find your dog."

Areen came to Jarin's side. The colors within the ring appeared to gravitate toward his feet, then move outward like ripples in a pond. "Not everyone has the talent to see," she said. "But if you try hard enough, you might catch a glimpse."

"I just want to know if he's all right."

Areen touched his arm, which Jarin interpreted to be permission to look for Razor. He concentrated on the floor, but when nothing happened he squinted so that he could see nothing but the swirling colors. "Razor," he whispered.

Suddenly the colors splashed outward and became a spiral that converged in the center of the ring. Then they pulled away, like the pupil of an eye, revealing the retriever sniffing the huge trunk of the World Tree. Razor lifted a hind leg and urinated on the bark.

Viluk let out a wry chuckle. "He looks fine to me."

"Razor!" Jarin said.

Areen looked at Laern in astonishment. "Not even Nolath could call up a vision so quickly."

Laern agreed with a slow nod.

"Come here, boy," Jarin called out, patting his knees. "Come to me."

"He can't hear you," said Viluk. "Not unless you know powerful magic, and you don't look like the type. At best, this place acts like a silent window to the outside world."

"Where is he?" asked Jarin. "I want to go to him."

Sedric took hold of his hand. "Razor could be on the other side of the Tree by now. Step aside, Jarin. We don't have time for this."

Jarin backed away and the vision of Razor vanished.

From the folds of his robe, Laern pulled out the mask wrapped in cloth and, after a contemplative moment, handed it to Sedric. The hermit tore off the cloth and held the mask out in front of him. The golden face of the wizard was unmoving, but its presence seemed to entrance the hermit.

"Uncle Sedric?" Jarin said.

Sedric shook his head, then immediately threw the mask out toward the center of the ring. "*Speak,* wizard!"

The mask froze in midair, remaining suspended above the surface of colors. The eyes of gold began to glow red.

Everyone in the room seemed spellbound.

The mask righted itself and hovered at eye level. Then, as if it had become the visible face of an unseen man, it directed its gaze around the room. The swirling colors moved in time with the rotating mask.

A haunting, ethereal voice echoed throughout the chamber. "Who are you?"

Viluk and Areen gasped.

"It's the wizard," said the guild master.

"Giver of speech," said Areen. "Father of Words."

"Nolath?" said Laern, with reverence. "It is *us*: the treefolk."

The mask turned toward the old councilor. "I can hear you, but my sight is faint. How did you come to possess my burial mask?"

"It was given to us."

"By whom?"

"By one of your own kind," said Sedric.

The mask turned upon the hermit. "I beheld a human in my nightmares. I even tried to destroy him by releasing a guardian several night's ago. Are you the thief who stole my mask?"

"Your evil was shown to me, wizard," said Sedric. "You betray all of humanity."

A black smoke lifted from the ring and slowly enshrouded the mask, blocking all color but the red eyes. From the center of the ring the vivid colors were replaced with an oily blackness, like a taint spreading outward.

"He corrupts the Tree!" cried Viluk.

The mask remained fixed on Sedric. "Who are you, human?"

"Your unlikely nemesis. *Expose!*" Sedric flicked his wrist and pointed a finger; a ray of white light struck the mask. The blackened mist fell away and disappeared into the floor, swiftly replaced by the normal colors of the ring.

"I see," said Nolath. "A magician who learned a thing or two from a pixie queen."

A blast of crimson energy burst from the mask's eyes and smote Sedric's chest. The hermit flew back toward the entrance, sliding upon the floor, where he rested, motionless. Jarin ran to him.

"Surely your learning has taught you the truth," said the ethereal voice. "The Creators sent humans to this world as prisoners, not as saviors. They meant to enslave us, as they had enslaved all other creatures. Lotan the Great defied them and so they left him on Kalor. Humans should never have been taken from their true home on Earth."

The mask turned to Laern. "Cherish your gift, my small

friends, or lose it through poor judgment."

The mask abruptly dropped to the floor with a clang and its eyes returned to the dull, closed eyes of one who is either asleep or dead. Viluk and Areen gave each other meaningful frowns. Laern appeared lost in worried thoughts.

"Sedric." Jarin slapped his uncle's cheeks. "Uncle Sedric?"

The old hermit stirred, catching Jarin's hand and preventing another slap. He sat up. "A little stunned and bruised, nothing more. I'll be all right. Nolath expended a lot effort to strike me." He chuckled. "He must really dislike me."

"Were you trying to kill the wizard?" Jarin asked.

Sedric shook his head. "I wanted to learn how he is able to draw upon the heart of the Tree's power from so far away. What I discovered was that the staff is his anchor."

The council members approached in unison. "I'm sorry, Sedric," said Laern.

"Sorry for what?"

Laern was too quick for Jarin to intervene, tossing a fine powder into Sedric's face. The hermit turned his head, obviously attempting to hold his breath, but Viluk punched him in the gut and he inhaled.

"Sleep," commanded Laern.

FIFTY-TWO

The crossbow Collin held was so cumbersome the effort to load it was a strain on his bandaged chest. It was all he could do to pretend he was going to be useful, to show the volunteers he wasn't a coward. Every soldier faced the real chance of dying here by day's end, and nobody wanted to hear the whines of a barbarian.

The wide area atop the gatehouse was crowded with soldiers and equipment. A wooden contraption unlike anything he had ever seen occupied most of the open space, attended by a company of grim-faced engineers from Jihena. They had fastened a long beam cut from a straight tree trunk onto a frame that allowed the beam to pivot up and down like a giant teeter- totter. Attached to one end of the beam, a wagon-sized bucket of rocks became a counterweight that, when dropped, slung the other end, which held a boulder cupped in a net. It was supposed to throw these boulders far out across the plains.

"It's called a trebuchet," said Sergius. "We'll be able to toss rocks at the enemy as they march toward us. With any luck, we'll smash the dragon's head to pieces in time for supper."

The centurion sounded upbeat, providing some relief for Collin's worry, but Mira held onto her serious expression, as if she remembered the true risk of staying here. The wind whipped her hair, brushing it across the chest of her ever-present sorcerer, who stood behind her. The First Sangoma had hooded his bald head against the cold, and together they gazed out across the plains.

The northern horizon had turned dark, a clear sign that an army of monsters was marching with the dragon. A lone scout galloped across the rust-colored plains and passed into the gatehouse.

"This wind will throw off our aim with the trebuchet," said Sergius, turning to the sangoma. "Can you do something about the storm?"

"Perhaps."

Collin liked the sound of that. "A little sunlight over the army might disrupt them."

"Controlling the weather is most difficult, and I can't yet measure this demon lord's strength with it."

"Regardless," said Sergius, "my legionaries are ready."

The scout who had entered the gatehouse came up the stairs and saluted the centurion. Behind him was Sir Garon, followed by Kreyd, the baron's weaselly magician.

"They're a chaotic bunch out there," said the scout to Sergius. "Less organized than the first invasion but ten times the size."

"And the dragon?" asked Sergius.

"Scarier than I had imagined."

"Have we got a chance to defeat the devil?" asked Sir Garon.

"No."

Sergius addressed the knight. "Our purpose is not to win an impossible battle, but to hold back their numbers long enough for the legion to get away."

Sir Garon's chest expanded as he took a breath, stoking his anger with fresh air. Kreyd fidgeted.

"With all due respect, commander," said the knight, "my people are more important than your retreating legion."

"We're going to fight to the death, sir. What else would you have me do?"

"Suppose the legion sets another trap in the valley?"

Sergius let out an exasperated sigh. "Lucian already went over this with you and that option is unavailable. Forget about the entire legion. Maybe you should beg your own king to give you more men. Oh, wait! He's a coward like the baron and sent nothing but a bunch of petty magicians too scared to help. Jihena cannot save you this time."

Kreyd said, "You're using us to save your legion."

Sir Garon heard this and his face turned red. "Just like the last battle!"

"Which you survived," said Sergius.

The knight snapped his mouth shut, then turned on his heels and hurried down the steps. Kreyd trailed behind like a puppy on a leash.

"Do you trust them?" the scout asked Sergius.

The centurion shrugged. "What else can they do but help us fight?"

"Retreat," said Collin.

"What do you mean?"

"Look up on the wall."

Sergius stepped up next to him to gain a better view of the lower wall extending from the gatehouse. Sir Garon had arrived, bellowing a command to his men to leave their posts. The baron's soldiers hardly needed to be told twice, speeding down the stairs to the valley road.

"The fools!" said Sergius.

"A desperate ploy," said the First Sangoma. "They hope to force the legion to engage the enemy before it has time to escape."

Sergius turned to the scout. "Go now. Tell Lucian of our predicament."

The scout saluted and departed quickly.

"What now?" asked Collin.

"The knight's plan won't work," said Sergius. "Lucian will order a hard march through the mountains. The old and the weak and the few slaves still with him will be left behind to die."

"And us?" asked Collin.

"A hundred men cannot hold off a hundred thousand, no matter how you look at it."

So much for the centurion's earlier show of confidence. Collin's chest began to ache worse than ever, and not just because of his wounds; he and Mira were going to die if they stayed here.

Perhaps thinking the same thing, Mira said, "Slay the dragon."

"Huh?" asked Collin.

"All creatures of Kalor believe the dragon is a god. Slay it and the army might stop."

"Demoralize them," said Collin. "Sergius, didn't you say the trebuchet could crush its head?"

"Only with a lucky shot," said the centurion. "But what have we got to lose? Even if we simply knock it out, it will buy us some time."

"Or force the dragon's master to rethink his invasion altogether," said Mira. She turned to the sorcerer. "Can you help guide the trebuchet?"

"I will do what I can."

*

The first launch of the contraption fell short, landing in a rust-colored plume of dust well ahead of the storm. The engineers hurried to make adjustments to the machine, adding more rocks to the counterweight and lengthening the rope tied to the net holding the boulder. When it launched again, the stone flew beyond Collin's sight.

"Well?" Sergius asked the sangoma.

"A miss. Too far to the right."

"Adjust for their advance," Sergius told the engineers.

The engineers shifted the trebuchet and launched again.

"One of the Intulo weerlords and many satyrs are wounded," said the First. "It landed far behind the dragon."

"Like trying to hit a fly with a piece of gravel," complained Sergius. "Aren't you guiding it at all?"

"I can nudge it only so much against the momentum fixed by the machine. Launch again."

Sergius ordered changes to be made, though the engineers were already making the necessary adjustments.

This time, when the boulder went soaring overhead, the

sangoma followed its flight with a pointed finger.

Impatient to hear the results, Collin blurted out, "Did you hit it?"

"Look out!" shouted the sangoma, diving to protect Mira as a ball of flame suddenly appeared out of the north, flew overhead, and exploded against the trebuchet. As Collin ducked for cover, his crossbow fell over the side.

The contraption was in ruins and several engineers lay dead.

Sergius brushed hot sparks from his cape, cursing a god named Mars that the Jihenan soldiers worshiped. "Apparently we scored a direct hit. What damage did we do?"

The First peered across the Rusted Plains. "The dragon appears unharmed."

Sergius put on a grim face and stared long at the sorcerer, as though urging him to accept the path of last resort.

Mira saw the look between the men and asked the First, "Are you going out there to fight it?"

"If you leave, Mira, I will go with you instead."

"You know I can't do that."

"You take advantage of my life-debt."

The hurt in Mira's expression revealed a faltering resolve. "Am I now even as Krassus was? A slavemaster?"

Collin attempted to comfort her. "What possible help are we, anyway?"

Mira acted deaf to him as she spoke quietly to the sangoma. "Don't fight to the death. If you cannot defeat the dragon, come back and . . . and then I will go with you to Jihena."

The First Sangoma nodded and gazed out across the plains. He scanned the sky, searching, squinting. He spoke two spells: "*Find* the currents of power" and "*Ride* them like a bird." A gust of wind blew his hood back, revealing a tattoo of the sun's rays on the back of his head; it glowed so brightly that Collin stepped back in wonder. Then the tattoo vanished, leaving a blister on the skin. The First disappeared in a rushing wind and a cloud of smoke, his last words lingering in the air.

From the far north, Collin beheld a magically charged battle erupt like a distant storm. Bright flashes of yellows and greens and reds disturbed the dark horizon. Sounds like thunder rolled across the plains, stirring up dirt and shaking the gatehouse's foundation.

Sergius took a deep breath. "This might take a while."

FIFTY-THREE

Once again, Jarin thought about how hard it was to be a hero. And this time the reminder came from his uncle, who had become as grumpy as an angry goose.

"Just climb inside," he said, holding Jarin's ankles as the boy stood on his shoulders.

They were in big trouble and Jarin knew it. The woodtrolls didn't trust them anymore, especially the mean councilor, Viluk. They had even taken away his Hawkie knife.

The woodtrolls hated Sedric more than ever. He and Jarin might be locked up forever.

He tried to see into the dark confines of a round air duct high in the wall of their new room, which Sedric called a prison cell. "There's freezing air coming out of here," Jarin said.

"It's fresh air so we can breathe," said his uncle. "Now hurry, will you? My bad knee can't support you for much longer."

"It's dark in there."

"You big baby. I thought you wanted to be a hero."

Jarin took a light-stone out of his pocket and tried to shine it down the narrow shaft. A single stone provided only as much light as a candle, but it was better than nothing.

Sedric's support seemed to falter then recover. "Just go out across the hallway so you can drop down and unlatch the lock of our door. I'll take it from there."

Mustering his courage, Jarin crawled into the narrow hole, scooted on his stomach until he turned a corner where the duct opened up and allowed him to inch forward on his hands and knees. The rockwood surface here was rough to the touch, unlike the smoothly worked areas where the woodtrolls lived. Was this the right way? Maybe he'd gotten twisted around.

He came to a crossroads and chose the easiest path.

Shouldn't he be above the hallway by now?

He kept going until he saw light ahead. The sudden sound of voices made him go cautiously.

Crawling farther, he came to a long narrow slit in the side of the tunnel, which showed the council chamber below. He was at a vantage point near the room's ceiling.

He'd gone too far.

"We cannot trust humans," said Viluk's voice. "They're unpredictable and power hungry."

Viluk came and went from Jarin's sight as the guild master paced back and forth beside the council table.

"So you've told me a hundred times," said Laern. "We've discussed this enough tonight and I'm tired."

"What do you intend to do?" asked Areen.

Viluk stopped and turned. "We need Captain Heldig's soldiers at a time like this."

"First off, Areen," said Laern, "I will not surrender the Staff of Speech."

"Which is what the humans would want," Viluk said.

"But I'll not kill them, either. I'm appalled you even suggested it, Viluk."

Some of the tension in Areen's voice relaxed. "I am relieved to hear you say that."

Viluk said, "There's one more thing—"

"We'll make our final decision in the morning," Laern interrupted.

Jarin could see part of the narrow shelf with the two raised stands, and across these stands Laern laid the staff. Then the councilor turned and went away. The light in the room dimmed and Jarin heard the main doors close.

Farther up the duct was a grated plug on a hinge like the one back in the cell. This one was not locked, and with the palm of his hand, Jarin popped it out. Then he turned feet first, slid out of the air duct, and dropped to the floor. He landed flat on his backside, but it hurt no worse than jumping out of a tree.

First he tiptoed over to the box sitting on a pedestal. It was made of finely crafted rockwood and heavier than it looked. Jarin shook it and tried to open the lid, but it was firmly locked. If only he had his Hawkie knife he could break it open.

Next he turned his attention to the staff and reached to take it. The open mouth seemed to be shouting at him to be careful, and he hesitated. Up close he saw that the carved head had the same face as the wizard's mask.

It felt warm to the touch. This was far more special to the

treefolk than any other object, which meant that they would do anything to get it back, including let him and his uncle go free.

Sedric had once told him not to steal, but he hadn't sounded too serious at the time and, besides, they were in a fix. Once the treefolk released them, he would return the staff, if that's what Sedric decided. So in effect, he was only borrowing it.

Hefting the staff as a spear, he aimed for the air duct. His throw missed horribly and the staff hit the wall and then clattered upon the floor.

Jarin's heart raced. He ducked under the table and waited for the main doors to open. When nobody came through, he retrieved the staff, studied the opening high in the wall, and realized he was trapped in here. Even if he could score a direct hit into the air duct, he had no way to get back up there himself.

The latch on the main doors rattled. Somebody was working the lock.

Quick as a rabbit, he dashed for the intricately carved door to the heart of the Tree, slipping through in the nick of time. Slowly and quietly he shut the door, just as the main doors opened and light flooded the council chamber.

He turned and ran down the stairs as fast as he could.

FIFTY-FOUR

Sedric put his ear to the cell door and listened. "What's taking that boy?"

He had come to the conclusion that his brother's son had taken a wrong turn in the ventilation ducts and might now be hopelessly lost in a maze. There was no telling where he might wind up, but knowing Jarin's luck, he'd land in the bowels of a furnace, never to be heard from again.

Muffled voices approached the door. They didn't sound like the voices of a child.

He stepped back as Viluk and a party of rough-looking henchmen entered the cell. Each woodtroll carried a rock-wood club and a mark of the artisan's guild, interlocking triangles, sewn onto their tunics. The guild master himself maintained a crankier expression than usual, which Sedric didn't think was possible, and planted his legs apart, as if preparing for a showdown.

"Come to finish me off, eh?" asked Sedric.

Viluk hardly blinked. "In time, my people will thank

me for what I'm about to do. Our gift will not be taken from us."

"Your gift?"

"The wizard's gift." Viluk nodded to his ruffians and they advanced.

With nowhere to run, Sedric took up two light-stones and threw them at the head of the first woodtroll, who promptly dropped unconscious at Viluk's feet. The next ruffian approached cautiously, while another attempted to come at him from the side. Sedric retreated, but he was cornered.

"You might be able to kill an old man," he said, "but at least one of you is going down with me."

Both woodtrolls swung their clubs. Sedric tried to duck, but because their aim was low, he took two beatings to his shoulders. The pain was excruciating.

He kicked, pushing one ruffian over his unconscious comrade, and then tried to jab the other. He missed. His efforts earned him a blow to his forearm that might have broken bone.

"Wait!" cried Viluk.

The two ruffians halted.

"Where is the boy?"

"Search me," said Sedric, rubbing his arm.

The guild master spotted the hinged door to the ventilation duct, which had been wrenched open.

One of the ruffians followed his sight. "That leads to the council chamber."

Viluk's eyes went wide. "And the staff!"

FIFTY-FIVE

The cavern in the heart of the Tree was too big for Jarin's single stone to illuminate, so he couldn't see the carvings on the walls. Which was a good thing, because the strange forms on those walls gave him nightmares. Were they depictions of the Creators themselves, warning him to stay away? Or were they dangerous beasts of Earth?

Whatever they were, he didn't want to see them staring at him.

The ring, however, glowed with its own soft light, beckoning him closer, welcoming him.

As he approached the ring, he held up the staff so it wouldn't bang on the floor. This place felt holy, and he didn't want a loud noise to disturb the silence.

The colors swirled like candle smoke blown by a soft breeze. He stopped at the edge of the wide ring and focused on the floor.

"Mira," he whispered.

Inside the ring, a window opened to the outside world.

It was night. Mira sat on stone steps, reading by lantern light the big book Papa had given her.

"Mira! It's me, Jarin."

Mira raised her head as though she might have heard. Then she shrugged and went back to reading.

Jarin wanted to see where she was, and as he made the wish, the vision pulled back to reveal the opening of a tunnel.

He'd seen a drawing of this place in Mira's book. She was at the big gatehouse at the border of the Rusted Plains, sitting on cobblestone steps just outside the entrance, next to a ramp that led into the gatehouse.

Out of the shadows staggered a tall figure in a robe, his face obscured by the dark.

"Look out!" Jarin cried.

Mira got up, retreated in fear. But as the figure collapsed to the ground, she rushed over.

Sounds came through the vision, but at first they were barely louder than Jarin's beating heart, which meant he had to hold his breath to hear them.

"You must not stay," said a man's voice, from the figure who had fallen to the ground.

Mira removed the hood of the robe and Jarin recognized one of the sorcerers who had ridden on a donkey, one of three men Sedric didn't like.

"You're injured!" Mira sat and gently lifted the man's head into her lap.

"He is too quick with magic," said the sorcerer. "Like a human might be if he had all the power of the World Tree at his disposal."

"The dragon?"

"Mira, they are bound as one creature—human and dragon. I should have known. It's the only way to enslave a Creator."

"You need help." Mira looked up.

The sorcerer laid a hand softly on her arm and said, "I tried to sever their union, but a link to powerful magic sustains the bond. It's greater than any power I've experienced and must be anchored to the legendary Tree of Kalor itself." He winced as he took a breath, and his hand dropped weakly to his side. "Through this link, a human has managed to possess the dragon, Lotan."

"Mira," said Jarin. "Can you hear me?"

"Lotan is full of deceit," Mira told the sorcerer.

"And he has corrupted the wizard, turned him against his own kind."

Behind Jarin came a loud command, "Hand over the staff."

Viluk strode from the stairway with a crew of rough-looking woodtrolls in tow. They spread out as if to catch Jarin in a net.

The guild master pressed closer, the palm of his hand held out. "Give it to me, boy."

Jarin took a step back and realized he had crossed the ring of color. He didn't fall, as he had thought he might, but hovered atop the vision. The woodtrolls stopped in dismay, reluctant to follow him into the ring.

Viluk straightened in surprise and then turned his eyes upon the gatehouse of Redgate Pass. "I see you've been tampering with Yggdrasil's sacred powers," he said. "You'll pay a high price for that."

"Humans *can* feel magic," Jarin said. "At least in this place."

"As Nolath discovered." Viluk bared his teeth. "Now give me the staff!"

"Why can't you just make another one?"

"The treefolk have always been caretakers, not magicians."

Viluk took a deep, calming breath. "Are you going to stand there forever? Come out of the circle."

"You want to kill us."

"We need the staff to bless our children with the gift of speech."

"So?"

"Would you take that gift from us, boy?"

Jarin looked away and shook his head. The vision below his feet showed Mira cradling the sorcerer in her arms. He must be very hurt.

"I'm sorry," said the First to Mira. "The dragon comes. The wizard comes. I have failed."

Tears ran down Mira's cheeks. The tattoos on the sorcerer's head lost all color, turning gray and dull—save one, below the scar that had once been the rays of the sun. This one was in the form of a snake, which then twisted into the shape of an open flame suspended above a human hand, identical to the pattern imprinted on the wall sconces inside Wormgate.

The sorcerer's body went limp in her arms.

"Mira, don't worry," whispered Jarin. "I'm going to protect you."

Viluk laughed. "How can a boy like you protect her? You're a worthless nobody."

"I took the staff out from under your nose, didn't I?"

"That's because you're a sneak."

"And I opened this magical window to the outside world. Even *you* can't do that."

"You have no place to go, Jarin," said Viluk. "Step outside the ring and give me the staff."

"Let me talk to Uncle Sedric first."

Viluk gritted his teeth, but with a nod commanded one of his fellow woodtrolls to fetch the old hermit. Then he suddenly put on a big smile. "So, who is this pretty girl now mourning a dying man? She must be quite special for you to risk your life."

Out of the corner of his eye, Jarin caught one of the others scooting closer, ever so slowly, trying to avoid being spotted. In a fast move, this one made a grab for Jarin's sleeve, but missed it by inches as Jarin dodged out of the way. The woodtroll lost his balance and fell, with a loud *thump*, inside the ring.

Short even for one of his kind, the daring woodtroll had a tuft of unkempt hair, a dirty face, and soiled coveralls more suited for a groveling scraper in a grungy old mine than for a member of the guild of artisans. This ruffian was tougher looking than most in Viluk's crew, but the instant he fell inside the ring, his eyes went wide with childlike terror and he let out a whimper.

"Go away!" yelled Jarin.

Before the ruffian had time to scramble out of the ring, he sank suddenly through the floor and was gone.

Every woodtroll stepped back in alarm. "By the Creators!" said two of them at once.

Viluk's mouth hung halfway open. "I didn't think that was possible."

FIFTY-SIX

Go away...

There it was again: a faraway voice that sounded a lot like Jarin shouting from above. Mira looked at the top of the gatehouse, fully expecting to see the boy waving at her from the battlements.

What she saw, however, was something completely different. Against the black sky, a circular glow appeared, faint at first, appearing no more intense than an eyespot caused by a chance look at the sun. The spot swelled, grew brighter, seemed to be split in half by a flash of lightning. The sudden fresh scent of rain and trees descended upon her, made her think of a forest.

A body fell out of the sky and landed onto the cobblestone steps beside her.

Mira came to her feet, nearly dropping the head of the First Sangoma.

The body was a filthy man, short as a boy, but with unusually long arms, like a miniature bergris. He got up, tottered a bit, saw her staring at him. With a cry, he made a mad dash for the gatehouse entrance.

He didn't get far. The Jihenans had managed to repair the iron portcullis, a heavy grate meant to block passage into Guldheim Valley. Thwarted halfway down the tunnel, the man came running back toward Mira, screaming something about a devil on the loose.

"Must run, must hide!" he said. "The Wyrm devours all!"

Mira seized him by a strap on his coveralls. "Who are you?"

With surprising strength, the man twisted free. "Keep your skinny paws off me, human! First the boy and now you . . . You'll ruin everything!"

"Jarin?" Mira asked. "Have you seen him? Where is he?"

Before the man could answer, a Jihenan horn blared.

Collin hustled out of the gatehouse. "Mira, I don't care what you say. We are leaving!"

Sergius's loud commands came first, echoing across the battlements like a crazy man shouting. Then the sound of arrows flew from the wall, volley after volley. From the gatehouse, the *thwack* of ballistae pierced the air.

Out of the north, a thundering howl caused the ground to tremble, shaking pebbles loose from the cliffs on either side of the pass.

Dark shapes appeared in the tunnel of the gatehouse, silhouetted by a single torch still flickering there. Two massive bergrisi ran up to the portcullis and pushed against the thick iron bars.

Then came a bright flash of light and an explosion of fire. Burning oil poured from holes in the tunnel's ceiling, igniting the bergrisi's hair and skin. So intense was the heat that the pair barely had time to turn before they fell dead, drowned in the flames.

Mira cowered from the heat, retreated from the cobblestone steps to the dirt road. Collin shied away too. The little man ran into the darkness of the valley, heading for the lights of the castle.

"Wait!" Mira shouted at him, but he was gone.

Sergius shouted desperate commands at his fellow legionaries. Some of the men let out frightened yells and, despite years of discipline, backed away from something beyond the wall. None fled, however. The Jihenans regrouped, and arrows began flying again. Mira caught glimpses of engineers hastily assembling what looked like a large round shield on top of the gatehouse.

Oil streamed out of the tunnel and ran toward the stairs. When it reached the sangoma's body, his robe caught fire.

"No!" Mira tried to rush forward, but Collin grabbed her arm.

"Leave him," he said. "He'll be dead soon anyway."

But Mira would have none of it. She jerked herself free and raced to the sangoma's side, tried to drag his body away from the oil. He was still alive. But despite her best efforts, fire spread along his robe. When it ignited the cowl at the back of his neck, the flame tattoo seemed to answer with a flare of yellow and red.

The First stirred and climbed to his feet. He was on fire, but he hardly flinched. Dazzled, Mira stumbled backward.

Even as the sorcerer's body burned higher and brighter, the fire inside the gatehouse tunnel began to fade. On the far side, a few of the enemy had dared go tentatively inside, shading their eyes—trolls with tails armed with barbs. Some in the front went too deep, howled in pain as the heat scorched their legs and arms, and then backed out.

Jihenan arrows rained down from above. Many trolls went down, piling up in front of the north entrance to the gatehouse.

A few trolls seized imps scurrying between their legs and tossed them into the center of the tunnel, as if to test the danger. These little ones barely had time to shriek before being incinerated by the hot passageway.

"It won't be long," Collin said, tugging on Mira's sleeve. "We might still escape if we make a run for it."

Mira planted herself in her spot and shook off his hand. She thought of the girl, Saffron, picking apples in the valley behind her, the girl who now had a name of her own. This pass was the only obstacle keeping the enemy from overrunning her new home.

"There must be something we can do," she said, touching her necklace with the blaze stone wrapped in leather.

She carried her sling, but without a whole cartload of blaze stones it would be useless against so many trolls. She wondered whether the sorcerer carried magical objects, but she doubted he did, for she had never seen him use anything more than words and those ever-changing sigils tattooed onto his skin.

The sangoma climbed the steps, moving slowly and deliberately toward the gatehouse entrance.

Beyond the portcullis, trolls stepped aside as a dragon drew toward the tunnel. It was a truly massive creature, with a head nearly half the width of the opening itself and a long scaly neck that swayed from side to side as it trod on clawed feet. Horns as long as lances protruded from its temples, and when its mouth parted, rows of spiked teeth gave her a fright. Signs of a fresh wound went from jaw to horn, possibly caused by the First Sangoma's battle on the plains. Arrows and ballista bolts bounced harmlessly off its hide.

"It's too late," said Collin. "We're doomed."

FIFTY-SEVEN

The Wyrm, Lotan," said Viluk in awe. "So it is true he lives on Kalor."

Viluk and his fellow ruffians watched the vision at Jarin's feet with open astonishment. The serpent-like dragon appeared to be studying the portcullis inside the gatehouse.

"Mira," called Jarin, "I'm coming to help you."

Uncle Sedric came into the cavern, escorted by one of Viluk's ruffians, and told the boy to stop. "Don't try to go to her," he said.

"Sedric!"

Viluk turned to confront the hermit with a fat-bladed knife. Two of the ruffians kicked the back of Sedric's legs and he fell to his knees.

"That's my Hawkie knife," Jarin said.

"A fine example of human craftsmanship," said Viluk, pressing the knife against Sedric's throat. Then he looked back at Jarin. "The staff."

Sedric lifted his head as if daring the councilor to cut him.

"Jarin, listen to me. I heard what you did to the woodtroll you sent away."

"We need the staff," Jarin pleaded. "Mira was talking to—"

"I know," his uncle said. "Nolath left the staff here as his direct link to the Tree and its power. The dragon can't sever their bond while the object remains whole."

Viluk's eyes narrowed. "You've run out of time, boy. Surrender the staff and all will be well again."

Sedric chuckled. "Where better to keep it safe than with a bunch of pathetic woodtrolls?"

Viluk turned on him. "Language is greater than magic," he said. "Humans don't know the power they possess! Shall I cut out your tongue to prove my point?"

Sedric swallowed. "Jarin . . ."

"But Mira is going to die. I can't—"

"Jarin," Sedric repeated. "Listen to me."

Viluk nodded. "Yes, tell the boy to give up. This charade has gone on far too long."

A line of sweat ran down the side of Sedric's face. "Send the staff to Mira."

Viluk spun toward Jarin. "No!"

The councilor dove into the ring, heedless now of its sacred border. Jarin tried to dodge out of the way, but Viluk seized his ankle and they both crashed to the hard surface above the vision. The staff, knocked from his hands, slid out of the ring and over to the far side of the cavern.

The vision of Mira closed in a crashing wave of colors.

Jarin rolled onto his back. Viluk's gaze had followed the staff and his grip relaxed. A swift kick in the face made him let go.

Jarin got up, ran over to where the staff lay, and scooped it up in both hands.

He was trapped. Viluk and his ruffians closed in, encircling him in an arc that blocked his route back toward the ring. The guild master's mouth was bleeding.

Jarin had no time to think about what he was doing as he tried to smash the staff against the floor, tried to break it in half. But neither the staff nor the rockwood floor showed even a scratch of damage.

Viluk sneered. "It'll take more than your soft hands to break such a strong magical artifact."

Jarin suddenly remembered one of those tales of Silo Prophet, the one where the hero had rescued Princess Hannah by tossing her his rapier so she could fight off evil pirates.

He made a snap decision. With all his might, he threw the staff over the woodtrolls' heads. Viluk tried to reach for it, but he was too short.

The staff landed just inside the circle.

Jarin closed his eyes and called forth the vision of the gatehouse.

"Mira," he said.

FIFTY-EIGHT

Inside the gatehouse, the fire fizzled out.

With an enormous claw, the dragon reached inside the tunnel and ripped the portcullis free from its anchors. A few chunks of blackened stone fell into the passageway.

The First Sangoma halted at the entrance and raised both hands, as if to stop the enemy with a simple push. How long could he stay there before being consumed?

The dragon opened its cavernous mouth and belched a river of fire into the tunnel. It immersed the sorcerer, burning away the remnants of his robe. Mira and Collin dove to the side for safety.

The sorcerer then became a pillar of white fire, though he did not falter or step back. Leaning in against the dragon's breath, he seemed to absorb the flames, gather the heat into himself.

Then came a spell. With limbs nothing more than blackened bones now, the sorcerer spread his arms wide and brought them together, slapping skeletal palms against each other. "*Devour!*"

A scarlet ray shot out of his fingertips, parted the dragon's fire like water, and struck the monster's hideous eye.

With a deafening scream, Lotan reeled back and withdrew.

The First Sangoma disintegrated into a pile of smoldering ash.

Trolls barked in triumph and began pouring through the passageway.

In the same instant, the Jihenan engineers finished their work with the big curved shield, which turned out to be a huge mirror. They lit a bucket of something that burst into white flame and positioned it in front of the mirror. Suddenly a beam of reflected light shone out upon the plains, a blinding flare seen by a sea of trolls' eyes. Through the tunnel, Mira could see enemies climbing over each other in a stampede to go back into the Rusted Plains, where the darkness was deepest.

A company of trolls that had avoided the light by entering the tunnel came charging out of the gatehouse on all fours, scattering what was left of the sorcerer's body.

"Run, Mira!" said Collin, drawing his gladius. "I'll fight them while you get away."

The warrior rushed forward and skewered one troll that had leaped down the stairs in a single bound. Both crashed to the packed dirt of the road and lay unmoving. Once again she saw that Collin's tales of bravery were not the overstated boasts she'd once thought they were.

No time to run. Mira evaded the swipe of a claw, spun to the side, and found herself near the bottom steps, where the First Sangoma's body had first caught fire. Burning oil had pooled here and the flames reached high enough now that the trolls shunned the area, providing a momentary safe place for her to avoid being eaten.

Collin appeared to be alive, though he was pinned underneath the deadweight of the troll he had killed. Mira saw his legs squirming.

"Don't move!" cried Mira. "Pretend to be dead."

Either he didn't hear her or he chose to ignore the advice. With a mighty groan, he shoved the troll's heavy corpse off his chest. He paused to catch his breath.

One of the trolls scouring the ground for fresh meat saw Collin's efforts, bared its teeth, and bore down on him. More trolls closed in.

With nothing but a dagger, Collin tried to stab the troll's neck, but his awkward position on the ground made him clumsy, eliminating all advantage he might have had on his feet.

Mira fumbled for her blaze stone, but she knew she was too late.

Out of the shadows of the road galloped two knights on heavily armored mounts. Sir Garon bawled at the top of his lungs, catching the troll in the kidney with his lance. The force of the blow propelled it all the way up the steps.

Barely a pace behind the big knight, Sir Rydel plowed into the tightest cluster of trolls, wielding his axe like a storybook hero, first with an upward swing on his right-hand side and then with a downward strike on his left. Two trolls dropped dead.

"Get up, you miserable clansman!" yelled Sir Rydel. "This is no time to take a nap!"

Collin was already on the move. He rolled the dead troll

over and managed to wrench his sword from the beast's scaly chest. He came ponderously to his feet.

Sir Rydel laughed at him as he spurred his mount after the attacking trolls.

Sir Garon had abandoned his lance and was charging straight into the gatehouse tunnel. Without hesitation, he waded into the main host of trolls and the single bergris that were attempting to escape the Jihenans' fierce light.

Where is the dragon? Mira wondered. *Is it dead? Did the light scare it off too?*

She hurried over to Collin to make sure he didn't topple over.

The warrior smiled weakly at her. "I'm not dead yet," he said.

"Oh, Collin," said Mira. "That was a brave thing to do, and also stupid."

"Seems I had no choice." He looked around. "Why are we still alive?"

"The dragon . . . I think it's gone."

Even as Mira said the words, the colossal beast appeared on top of the gatehouse. It wasn't dead; it had simply climbed the four-story wall from the north side. An eye was missing, and one side of its head was a gaping wound where the sangoma's ray had ripped off an entire horn.

The Jihenans responded by throwing everything they had at the dragon, but the ancient Creator was unstoppable, sweeping legionaries aside with claws and tail. It had a long body, with massive legs and webbed claws. A forked tail acted as pincers able to seize foes and toss them over the side.

Sergius and a group of legionaries regrouped and attacked

the dragon with long pikes—and for an instant the thing flinched as if stung. Then it reared back, opened its mouth, and disgorged another river of fire upon the fearless soldiers. The awful sound was like a thunderclap.

Flames roiled along the battlements, consuming everything on top of the gatehouse that wasn't stone, both man and machine. The mirror was smashed to bits, extinguishing its bright light.

Sir Rydel quit laughing and turned his eyes upon the terrible sight. The blast spooked his mount, which reared up on hind legs, throwing the knight to the ground; he crashed with a grunt. One last troll took advantage of the fall and impaled Sir Rydel's thigh with a barbed tail.

The knight sat up abruptly, screamed something unintelligible, and punched the troll's snout. Bones shattered and the toothy jaw fell wide open. The troll dropped dead.

As the dragon chased the legionaries along the length of the wall, Mira ripped the blaze stone out of her leather necklace and tried to fit it into her sling. But the acorn-sized stone was hot as a red coal, singeing her fingers. Instinctively, she let go and dropped it.

Sir Garon strode out of the gatehouse, almost casually. He had lost his mount and his helmet. A line of blood ran down the side of his head and he walked with a limp. With both hands he clutched his claymore, its long blade reflecting the raging fire from above.

She looked upon his face. "He's just like Shem," she said. "Taken by a skinwalker."

"What?" said Collin. "Are you sure?"

"I've seen that blank look. And—"

"And he's got company." Collin took her by the hand, squeezed until it hurt.

Swarming out of the gatehouse was every kind of monster from the north: imps and trolls and bergrisi of every sort, including a few creatures spoken of only in legend, chief among them a horned dust fiend with six legs and a pair of eyeless shadow walkers. The host did not hasten to overtake the knight, but instead remained a step behind him, as if waiting for his command to attack. Mira heard their snarling threats and became more frightened than ever before.

Collin pushed her behind him, put himself in front of Sir Garon. With his gladius he looked woefully inadequate, like a boy threatening to stick a giant with a pin.

"Mira!" he hollered above the din.

"I'm so sorry, Collin. You were right to want to leave."

"If I kill the skinwalker, do you think it will scare the others away?"

His comment was meant as a ridiculous jest, but it gave her an idea.

She reached for the blaze stone at her feet, took it in her hand despite the scalding heat, and wrapped it in her sling. The dragon was on the western end of the wall now, chomping on the last of the Jihenan soldiers. It was a fair distance away, she realized, so a direct hit would be a miraculous feat.

Then something dropped out of the sky and landed next to her. At first she thought a bergris had thrown a tree branch at her, but the object was no ordinary stick. It was a finely crafted staff, topped with the carved head of a man with an open mouth.

Again the voice of Jarin reached her ears.

"Take the staff and break it!"

"Jarin, where are you?"

"Hurry, Mira!" said Jarin.

On the wall, the dragon whipped its head in her direction. Maybe it would come close enough now for her to score a direct hit.

"I can't see you!" she shouted.

Jarin's voice was fading. ". . . just break it . . . sister . . ." Then he cried out in pain.

The staff was warm to the touch, but pressed against the blisters of one hand, it felt almost cool, even soothing. Was it magic? How had Jarin sent it to her?

The dragon's thundering roar rattled her bones.

She swung her sling, eyed the dragon . . . and lowered her arm without releasing the stone.

Taking the blaze stone out of the sling's pouch—and receiving another burn—she stuffed it into the open mouth of the staff. Then, raising it over her head, she smashed it headfirst upon the ground.

The blaze stone cracked in an ear-splitting explosion, showering sparks everywhere and shattering the staff in two.

The dragon shrieked with obvious pain and started writhing atop the wall, clawing at its own hide, snapping at nothing. The wound on its head split down its neck and blood spilled out. Beneath the beast's body, the battlements crumbled.

Sir Garon halted and watched the dragon suffer. The army at his back went silent, each creature viewing a sight that seemed impossible moments ago.

Then Lotan the Deceiver, Creator and dragon, the forsaken god enslaved by a human, thrashed one way and the next, and then rolled off the wall. The ground shook as it struck the ground, and there it lay, unmoving.

Not far away, Sir Rydel was cheering.

The army turned tail and fled back through the gatehouse.

Sir Garon stayed at the top of the stairs, a mere four paces away from Collin. The knight lowered his big sword. "You have freed me," said the skinwalker, and for the first time, Mira heard something akin to emotion in its voice. "But take heed. None of us will truly escape the wizard while his mask remains unbroken."

FIFTY-NINE

The image inside the ring remained fixed upon the shattered staff. Viluk flung the Hawkie knife away in despair and fell to his knees. "Our newborns will never learn to speak."

"I'm sorry," said Sedric. "It was the only way to sever Nolath's link to the Tree."

"He was the giver of words," said Viluk. "Our most revered father. He warned us not to treat his gifts lightly or they would be taken from us. Now we are lost."

Jarin was barely listening. He rubbed his cheek where the guild master had slapped him moments ago to shut him up.

While everyone was lamenting the loss of the staff, the skinwalker's last words echoed in his ears.

The mask.

For the moment, the woodtrolls had lost interest in him as they tried to come to grips with what had just happened at the pass. He seized the opportunity to slip between Viluk and another woodtroll who was sniveling. Picking up his knife, he ran for the stairs.

"Jarin!" called his uncle.

It was a long hike back to the council chamber, but Jarin dared not slow down. He feared he might already be too late.

He was gasping for breath as he entered the room.

Smoke leeched out of the box on the pedestal.

Jarin kicked the box onto the floor, stood over it, jammed his Hawkie into the seam of the lid. A puff of smoke drifted into his face, smelling like the worst kind of stink. Then with all his strength, he twisted the blade and broke the latch. The lid popped open.

Inside, the cloth that had enwrapped the mask smoldered, flaking away from the golden face. Around the eye sockets it had burned all the way through, revealing two crimson orbs that flared so brightly it hurt to stare at them.

A sound like that of a man struggling to breathe came from the mask as the cloth around the nose and mouth moved in and out.

The haunting voice of Nolath said, "Take me to the heart of Yggdrasil."

With those words came an overwhelming need to obey. A power tried to clamp around Jarin's will and force him to question his desire to ruin the mask.

The wizard was enslaving him.

For a split second he knew the mind of Nolath. While upon the altar deep in the caverns beneath the Canopy Mountains, the wizard had tried to become like a skinwalker, capable of enslaving the bodies of others. His link to the Tree gave him the strength—greater even than the mighty Wyrm, who had become old and complacent, unprepared for the wizard's trespass. And his bond with the skinwalker, Naomi, gave him the key to possessing others.

But Nolath was human and therefore required a link, however small, to Earth.

His death mask, shaped into the human face he'd owned while whole, had become that link.

And now the wizard was struggling to stay alive.

A wave of nausea weakened Jarin's limbs, curbed his resolve. If he hadn't experienced a similar sensation after the weerlord's attack upon the road, he might not have found the will to resist.

Jarin pulled his gaze away from the crimson eyes, gripped his Hawkie, and stabbed the mask with all his might. The blade bent the cheek of the golden mask.

A cry erupted from the mouth and the red light flared. An invisible force hit him in the chest, shoving him away and pushing him to the ground. The box toppled onto its side and the mask tumbled out . . . no, the mask was scooting across the floor, face down. A ghostly body materialized, attached to the mask, no thicker than a shadow. It began to crawl toward his feet.

Jarin retreated.

The mask rose slightly and looked at him, one of the blazing eyes misshapen. "*Sleep!*" said Nolath.

Jarin's eyes became heavy as sledgehammers. Suddenly he wanted to find a place to dream about pleasant things. Maybe about a girl. This spot on the floor would be a good place to sleep.

Nothing would harm him here, not even the wind.

But something was hurting him. As he relaxed, a sharp pain jabbed his ribs. What was the matter? He had to find a better place to rest.

As he forced an eye open, he saw the mask's red eyes hovering over his face, glaring straight at him.

He instinctively struck it with his fist and rolled over. He'd lain upon his knife.

The body attached to the mask was on all fours. A hiss came out of its mouth, blowing the rest of the cloth away. With a misshapen eye, the golden face looked angry.

Taking up the Hawkie, Jarin attacked. He stabbed the good eye twice and the crooked eye once. Nolath screamed and the ghost-body vanished. The mask clattered to the floor.

Jarin kicked it toward the box. The mask tried to rise again, so he batted it inside.

Then he shut the lid.

The box was heavy, but weighed no more than a bucket of pig's slop. Waddling a bit, he carried it through the main doors and out into the hallways of the woodtrolls' city.

Although they lived hidden from the sun and the moon, the folk here maintained a humanlike schedule of day and night, probably taught to them by Nolath generations ago. The light was dim now, as though from a moonlit night, and few woodtrolls were about. Those who saw him made no attempt to confront him. After all, he was just the smelly human boy on his way to the baths.

The chamber of pools was dark, and Jarin was forced to set the box down so he could take his light-stone out of his pocket. The wound in his side was bleeding into his shirt, and he'd have to deal with it soon, but first things first.

In the bathing room, steaming water poured from the ceiling, collecting in a large central pool, which fed surrounding pools by means of connecting channels. As he'd learned earlier, the pool closest to the doors was far colder than the rest, and it was to this pool that Jarin took the box and dumped out its contents.

The instant the gold mask hit the water, steam erupted in a mighty cloud, forcing Jarin to pull back or be scalded. The pool boiled and frothed. Red light flashed beneath the surface. The bubbling cry of a drowning man spoke of such immense suffering that Jarin almost jumped in to save the mask. But acting on this desire would only enslave him to the will of the wizard, and so he waited as the cries died down.

He wondered what the woodtrolls would think if they learned he had just slain their revered Father of Words.

Nobody showed up as the boiling ceased and the red light winked out. Only then did he dare peek into the pool, his light-stone held above the surface of the water.

The mask lay at the bottom, cracked in half. Ruined.

Jarin slipped into the pool and retrieved both halves.

The mask was cool to the touch now, and empty holes were all that remained of the sinister red eyes. Jarin put the bent pieces back into the box, pressed the palm of his hand against his wound, and went to rescue Sedric.

SIXTY

Collin was convinced Sir Garon was going to come charging down the steps and cut him to pieces with his massive claymore. Yet he stood ready for the attack, knowing he would die if it came, hoping his sacrifice would give Mira enough time to run away.

Fires still raged on the wall and upon the gatehouse, crackling, tossing embers into the air.

Over to one side he could hear Sir Rydel's ragged breathing. The bleeding wound in the knight's leg had sapped his strength, and it wouldn't be long until he expired.

For reasons unknown, Mira began calling out for Jarin, telling the boy it was all right to come out. If the boy was truly hiding nearby, Collin thought he should stay out of sight and away from danger. A skinwalker in Sir Garon's body would be unstoppable if he started swinging in earnest.

After a few long moments, however, the big knight sat on the ground and let out a long sigh. He set the sword down and regarded Collin with flat, lusterless eyes.

"There is no need to slay this host," he said, speaking of the body of Sir Garon. "The grove where I was born centuries ago beckons, and I must return."

Collin tightened his grip on his sword. His aching body begged him to sit down and rest, but he didn't trust the skin-walker to stay put. "So you're going to sleep it off so you can fight another day?" he asked.

Sir Garon's head shook. "I am old and my hunting grounds much diminished. My final days will be dedicated to preserving my grove, enlarging it, protecting it against invaders."

"Against humans."

"Do not seek me out or you will perish."

"I don't like the sound of that."

"We are enemies forever, you and I, but this night's battle has shown me that this human intrusion cannot be stopped. The Wyrm stayed on Kalor in part to thwart total victory by your kind, should it come to that. But he is dead, killed by the choices of a human wizard. I will fight you no more."

Mira, who had stopped calling out for Jarin, said, "I don't believe you."

The skinwalker shrugged Sir Garon's wide shoulders. "It doesn't matter what you believe, but for me, the war is over. Others will take up the fight in my stead."

Sir Rydel started groaning and Mira ran over to help him.

"What are you waiting for?" Collin asked. "If you're going to leave, do it now."

"You must forgive me, warrior. I have possessed your kind for so long while in the forced service of Nolath that some human traits I hate to abandon. I am also waiting for . . . Ah, yes . . . Now I feel it. The wizard is finally dead."

What happened next was difficult for Collin to describe later on, when the king's scribes demanded an account for their history books. After the knight rested on his back, a ghostly figure rose from the spot and seemed to take a final look at Collin. Then it slipped through the gatehouse, visible only as it passed in front of the flames. It was a spindly thing, striding with many crooked limbs like a leafless tree.

Only after the spirit demon was gone did Collin lower his sword. Then he collapsed to the ground and passed out.

SIXTY-ONE

The currents and eddies moved inside the ring according to his will. Sometimes he would choose strands of blue and yellow, stretch them, twist them, and then crash them together to form a single ribbon of a green that split the ring in two. This barrier was hard to maintain, for green always wanted to curl into squiggly shapes.

So he experimented with each color. Green wasn't as bad as silver, which usually snapped into a glistening web, or orange, which was messy and unpredictable, like explosions. Brown made a good dam, but black was even better . . . until it began sopping up all the other colors nearby and he had to rip it apart.

Red was special. If there was too much of it in one spot, he would hurry to blend it with another color, because it reminded him too much of the wizard's eyes. He suspected it meant raw power.

His favorite color was purple. It was pliable, like blue, and would keep the shape he gave it for a long time, as if waiting for him to do something more.

Unlike the colors, the shapes didn't make sense. They seemed important, but with so many possibilities, he hadn't figured out how to make use of them yet. Remembering shapes was too much like reading, and he was never very good at that at home, even with Mira's help.

Jarin let go of the green ribbon and opened up a vision of the flourmill. The house had been gutted and the barn burned to nothing but a blackened spot of ground. None of the cows or chickens or pigs remained, though he spotted Moby cropping grass near Willow Stump Creek and was glad to see that the horse had survived. The windmill was open to the sky, its roof demolished, its gears warped and ruined by the rain. There wasn't much left of home to go back to.

Commanding visions like this made him feel like a bird. He could soar high as the clouds or swoop in to focus on a mouse's den. Razor sat on the rockwood floor next to him, observing the vision as it flew from the windmill to the house. The retriever whined in his throat and stood on all fours, obviously longing to go back to the place where times had been good—a place where Papa had made things safe.

A sinking feeling in his stomach made him turn the vision away from home.

Four days ago, while following Mira to a fresh gravesite, Jarin had discovered that his papa was dead. He'd seen Mira mouth the word *Shem* a few times as she shed tears over the mound. Jarin had wanted to speak to her then, but he hadn't been able to transmit sound since the desperate battle with the dragon. Maybe if he dared collect a lot of red he could pull it off.

He quit spying on Mira for a long time after that. It hurt too much to think about how Papa might have died.

With a whisper, he swung the vision east, across the open fields beyond the ruined mill, up the mountain side, where the opening of the Wormgate was dark—a place his vision could not enter—over snowcapped peaks, along the road to Guldheim, and down into the valley itself. It was difficult to focus on places he'd not been before, so he thought of the young warrior whom Papa had rescued from trolls. Collin was often with Mira, sometimes holding her hand, and once they were embraced in a kiss, which meant he had to be careful. Today's vision took him to a country road south of the castle, near verdant trees and bushes growing along the Vonspryer River.

The warrior traveled with Mira and the woodtroll who had tried to grab him in this very room on the night the staff was broken. It seemed like a pleasant day for a stroll, with a bright sun and few clouds, but Jarin saw that the three carried enough supplies to sustain them for a long journey.

Were they looking for him? The woodtroll had probably lied and told them he knew the way to the Tree.

"It's too dangerous," Jarin said. "Don't go." He tried to gather a lot of red in an area outside the vision, in the hopes it would allow him to speak to them, but an anxious feeling made his heart pound and then blue got in the way.

The three of them were a long way from the Tree, anyway, and as long as they didn't get in a boat for a nighttime ride to the Wedge, they would be fine. He watched them as they came to a bridge on the Vonspryer, paused a moment to talk among themselves, and then crossed to the other side.

A wave of relief came over him. They didn't know where to look. Mira might eventually learn some clues to his wherabouts in the Encoda, but she didn't have a seed from the Tree, and for now they were guessing. They were safe, but he would need to check on them regularly, to make sure they didn't do something dangerous.

In the meantime, he had more important things to do, such as fulfill a promise to the woodtrolls. They wanted a new way to bless their infants with the gift of speech, and only a human wizard could do that. Jarin felt he owed it to them, because he'd stolen their staff, and so he had asked Uncle Sedric to give him pointers. Unfortunately, the old hermit wasn't much help; he was easily frustrated and couldn't keep a vision open for more than a few seconds. "The mask has ruined me," his uncle had said in despair. "It's broken and I have no more magic."

So it was up to Jarin to figure out a way.

Feeling a bit lonely, he opened a vision of the pretty, green-eyed girl whom he'd seen hanging around Mira. She had a smile that never went away and a face that made him feel calm.

"Why are you so happy?" he asked out loud.

He heard somebody standing behind him. Councilor Areen.

"I didn't mean to startle you." Areen sat and handed him a roasted acorn. Without a regular supply of these nuts, Jarin's ability to control magic in this room seemed to fade. "Do you know that girl?"

He usually wiped such visions away before anybody could see what he was doing, but he liked the tiny philosopher, because she never pushed him to hurry up with his studies.

He shook his head as he took a bite. "I don't even know her name."

"Is that so important?"

"I guess not, but . . ."

"Names have always been important to humans, haven't they?"

"Aren't they important to you?"

Areen shrugged. "When Nolath gave our ancestors names, they became necessary; it's a part of language, after all. Before that time, we listened to the songs of magic as they resonated in our blood and bones. The world spoke to us in ways that carried meaning on a different level."

"Did it make you happy?"

"That's hard to say." Areen smiled at him. "Do you remember what it was like when you couldn't talk?"

"No. Of course not."

"Neither can I. In my grandfather's time, the old folk remembered how things were before the wizard came. Some of them would become angry and refuse to use their new gift of speech. They would wander into abandoned tunnels in search of silence. When they came back to their senses, they would talk about having gone deaf."

"Deaf to magic?"

"I think so. My great grandmother once imagined she heard a Creator's voice talk to her while she was hiding out in a tunnel."

Jarin glanced up at the carved reliefs crowding the walls of the chamber. Some of them were of ordinary animals, such as an eagle or a wolf, but others were strange creatures with the bodies of humans and the heads and tails of animals. One of two serpents had begun to go darker than the surrounding rockwood.

"What did the voice tell her?" he asked.

"She felt an overwhelming desire to prepare this place for the return of the Creators."

"You mean, she wanted to care for the Tree, Yggdrasil?"

Areen nodded. "She felt a strong impulse to obey. It made her feel good to comply, but I wouldn't call it a path to real happiness. After she recognized that she was being coerced, she wanted the voice gone forever. She left the tunnel and returned to studying human speech."

Jarin watched the girl as she gathered freshly cut wheat into neat bundles. He knew from experience that working in the fields was a hard chore, but the girl looked happier than ever. "I think the Creators might have been bad," he said.

"Why do you say that?"

"They gave a few creatures on Kalor an easy way to get the things they wanted. An evil way."

"Through magic?" Areen's look was intense and expectant. Had she been thinking the same thing?

"If that girl had a weerlord's magic, she could harvest all that wheat by forcing other people do the work for her," Jarin replied. "Then she would have as much as she wanted."

"Wouldn't that make her happy?" Areen asked, but Jarin thought she already knew the answer.

"It would turn her into a mean person," he said. "The Creators were bad like that."

Areen leaned back on her hands. "Not all of them were bad. I think most wanted to correct the evil they had done."

"That's why they put humans on Kalor."

"Indeed. You can't be swayed by the power of the Tree, because language makes you go deaf to the calling songs of magic."

"Then why can I feel it in this room? Why can I control it?"

"All good questions," said Areen. "This room is special. My people don't really know how it was used, but we think this is where the Creators governed the world. The treefolk may even have served those powerful beings as they came and went from the Tree, but because we had no language, a history of that time doesn't exist among us. So we must make guesses. And my guess is that the Creators wanted a place where they could project their power across Kalor without being bombarded by the Tree's power to enslave. They valued their own free will too much."

"Free will? I don't understand."

Areen straightened and pointed at the vision. "Outside this room, a weerlord has the power to command armies, to force the native inhabitants of Kalor to do what it wants, just as you said. In like manner, a skinwalker can take over a body and force it to do bad things. The Creators didn't want to be threatened by that power. In this room, they were free to do whatever they wished."

"So they came here to be safe?"

"That's one reason," said Areen. "Remember, the Creators made the Tree too, which meant they were using it to rule their world."

"Then something bad happened and they left?"

Areen shrugged. "We don't really know if it was a war among themselves or if they simply got bored after ruling for millennia."

Jarin thought hard on her words as he watched his strand of green at the edge of the vision form a shape that looked like a stalk of wheat. "The Creators had language," he said.

Areen raised an eyebrow. "That would make them like humans."

Jarin nodded. "And that's why I can hold onto magic in here when I eat the nuts. The shapes are letters or words that tell me what to do."

"What are they telling you now?"

"I'm not sure yet, but if I can find the right shape for language, I might be able to give it to woodtroll babies so they can learn to talk."

The councilor's face brightened. "What shape could that be?"

Jarin thought about Nolath's staff of speech. "It's probably an open mouth."

Areen went quiet and turned her head, but he caught tears in her eyes.

The girl in the vision appeared almost to be skipping as she went about her tasks beside the other children. All of them were opening their mouths at the same time, following a rhythm that told him that they were singing. None looked happier than the girl, and her presence seemed to cheer up the others as they worked and sang. Several of the adults cutting grain with sharp sickles looked back at the children and smiled.

Joy, thought Jarin. *That's what I'll call you until I know your name.*

Razor's tail wagged and he barked. Then he jumped into the ring, sniffing and licking the vision, his paws slipping on the slick surface.

Areen gasped in horror, but Jarin laughed so hard his stomach hurt.

THE END

GLOSSARY

Abbot: local lord of the Moristad township

Achilles: treasure hunter, younger brother of Hector

Aidan: clan chieftain from Earth, first king of the eastern kingdom on Kalor

Ambiorix: clan chieftain from Earth, cousin of King Aidan

Arduinna: forest goddess worshiped by Aidan's clan while on Earth

Areen: woodtroll councilor, philosopher

bergris: giant creature possessing incredible strength

blaze stone: magical stone containing fire

blood ravens: giant red birds that roosts in the World Tree

Bremer: old sentry stationed at Trollgate Pass

Britannia: region of Earth whose people settled in the fertile lands of the Valin River

Brutus: legionary from Jihena

Canopy Mountains: northernmost mountain range

centurion: officer in the Jihenan legion, commands a cohort of legionaries

cohort: unit of Jihenan infantry, numbering about five hundred legionaries

Collin: young sentry stationed at Trollgate Pass

Constance: Jarin's mother, deceased

Consul: governor of the Republic of Jihena, elected by the Senate

Creators: gods who abandoned the worlds of Kalor and Earth eons after creation

demon lord: the Kaloran commander seeking to destroy human lands. During King Sandor's reign, the spirit demon of Maran set off such a deadly invasion that he became known as the first demon lord. The identity of the current lord is unknown

Earth: mythical world where humans once lived

Encoda: holy book of history and prophecies

First, The: a sangoma sorcerer

Flaks: woodtroll soldier

giant: see *bergris*

Gitorix: clan chieftain from Earth

Goodman Samson: farmer

Goodwoman Samson: healer

Gretten: woodtroll guardsman

guardian: bull-like monsters that attack anything wandering through their underground warrens

Guldheim: rich valley ruled by a baron

Hector: treasure hunter, older brother of Achilles

Heldig: woodtroll captain

imp: small, vicious creatures related to mud jiks

Inokan: ancient weerlord from the White Hills, banished by King Aidan ages ago

Intulo: sangoma name for weerlords

Jacob Hobson: farmer

Jarin Langheart: an eleven-year-old boy

Jihena: republic located across the Sidewinder Sea, ruled by two consuls elected by the Senate

Jormungand the Eater: northern name for Lotan the Deceiver

Julian: high-ranking commander in the Jihenan legion

Kalor: world of magic

kend: magical stag with a highly prized coat

Krassus: general of the legion, consul of the Republic of Jihena

krek: savages living in the valley of the World Tree, cousins of the treefolk

Laern: high councilor of the woodtrolls

legion: a Jihenan military force, numbering about six thousand strong (infantry and cavalry)

legionary: soldier serving in a Jihenan legion

Lotan the Deceiver: the Wyrm, one of the Creators

Lothgar: highland clan descended from the men and women of ancient Thule

Lucian: tribune, second-in-command of the legion of Jihena

Mira Kaul: orphaned girl, age eighteen

Moristad: eastern town

Moss: western town

mud jiks: small creatures living in the marshes, ruled by a queen

Naomi: companion of Nolath, possessed by a skinwalker

Nolath: human wizard

Onwi: Jihenan slavemaster

Orwin: a hunter, companion of Nolath

Pilus: see *Julian*

Plains of Maran: desolate land of the north

Pontus: prefect, third-in-command of the Jihenan legion

Pratsom: young woodtroll girl

prefect: officer who is third-in-command of a Jihenan legion

Razor: Jarin's pet retriever

Reena: sister of Orwin, killed by a skinwalker

Rowland Mill: wood mill on Willow Stump Creek, north of the Langheart's flourmill

Redgate Pass: north pass to the Rusted Plain, on the western side of the Trestammer Mountains

Rusted Plain: lifeless land south and west of the White Hills

Saffron: slave girl

Sandor: king of the western kingdom during Nolath's lifetime

sangomas: human sorcerers from Jihena

satyr: Jihenan name for a troll

Second, the: a sangoma sorcerer

Sedric: a hermit, brother of Shem, uncle of Jarin

Sergius: a centurion

Shem Langheart: miller, Jarin's father, younger brother of Sedric

Sidewinder Sea: southern sea

Sir Garon: minor nobleman and knight, sworn to protect the Baron of Guldheim

Sir Rydel: knight of Guldheim

skinwalker: powerful spirit that can possess a sleeping body (a.k.a. *spirit demon*)

spirit demon: see *skinwalker*

Third, the: a sangoma

Thule: region of Earth inhabited by a people who told the first myths of Yggdrasil and Jormungand

treefolk: the woodtrolls' name for themselves

Trestammer Mountains: central mountain range

tribune: officer who is second-in-command of a Jihenan legion

troll: nighttime beast of Kalor; looks like mix of bear and boar, but with a scaly hide

Trollgate Pass: north pass on eastern side of the Trestammer Mountains

Valin River: eastern river

Viluk: woodtroll councilor, master of the artisan's guild

Vonspryer River: western river

Wedge, the: granite cliff that splits the Vonspryer River in two

weerlord: powerful sorcerers that seek to become human; shapeshifters

White Hills: hills and crags made of chalky white clay, north of the Rusted Plain

woodtroll: human name for the treefolk

Wormgate: ancient tunnel through the Trestammer Mountains

Wyrm: the dragon

yeni: small magical creature known to bestow charms to humans

Yggdrasil: name Nolath gave the Great World Tree of Kalor

ABOUT THE AUTHOR

After earning a BA in English, Vincent quickly realized that writing fiction would not put food on the table or a roof over his head, so he took the next logical step and got a job in IT. He currently works as a systems engineer by day and a writer by night. His family supports both endeavors, as long as there is food on the table and a roof overhead. He lives in Utah.